A Long Stretch of Blue

Denis Gray

A LONG STRETCH OF BLUE

iUniverse books may be ordered through booksellers or by contacting:

iUniverse
1663 Liberty Drive
Bloomington, IN 47403
www.iuniverse.com
1-800-Authors (1-800-288-4677)

ISBN: 978-1-4917-5730-7 (sc)
ISBN: 978-1-4917-5731-4 (hc)
ISBN: 978-1-4917-5729-1 (e)

Library of Congress Control Number: 2014922711

Printed in the United States of America.

iUniverse rev. date: 1/22/2015

"The blues is an autographical chronicle of personal catastrophe expressed lyrically."
                                                    —Ralph Ellison

Chapter 1

Arfel's body was on fire.

His eyes were closed, in a trance, tracing this tall, smooth-boned black woman as if she were some Saturday-night sin, black magic, a some-kind-of-blues in his soul. His slim fingers playing the blues—pushed up on Blue Fire. This woman's soft hips dipped to the B-flat chord. Her bottom sinking low like a too-full potato sack. Her hips singing slow on Blue Fire's guitar strings, quivering long like a low, sweet vibrato.

Sunny's Blues Shack's shadows hung like thick drapes swashed in a swamp heat, about as musty as twenty teamed mules. "Mmmm …" hummed out Arfel's mouth like a harmonica's hum. "Mmmm …" In this key almost too blue for Arfel's ears to hear. "Mmmm …"

Her black body moaned back to Arfel while she let her sweet backside dip down even more slowly, evenly into that B-flat chord's lazy, free-feeling twang. "Mmmm …"

Then "Gin-Water" Pete's bass guitar, Brown Georgia, belched the blues out of her belly as if she knew the best parts of a heartbreak night. And that black woman with her black magic, some kind of Saturday-night sin, couldn't stop from moving her backside back and forth, back and forth on the narrow, mule-musty piece of floor like this too was too good in her for her to stop.

"Oooo—baby, don't you run off now less you know where to (humpff!).
Don't let Gin-Water Pete's pistol—getta bead on you.
Ain't nothin' worse than a young girl—dyin' young.
Nothin' (huhn!) worse than Gin-Water drunk—wid 'is gun.

Oooo-baby ... rock crazy like you do ... (humpff!)
Yo'r sweet daddy comin' home tonight—jus' for you!"
"Aaaaaah!"

Gin-Water Pete's head then slumped over his guitar as if dead. But the music was still in the dark air dancing there. And Arfel still smelled the black woman's perfume, the sweet sweat in her skin like she smelled of flowers long ago picked out at Miss Ann's garden up at the Big House, but he knew this was Sunny's Blues Shack, where the blues was so to forget about such things.

"Woman—ain't gonna kill you,
Ain't gonna watcha when you go (humpff!).
Ain't need no remindin' how a perty gal look walkin' out my do'r.
Had to beat you.
Had to beat you.
See—what my blues doin' to me?"

Arfel and Gin-Water Pete kept playing in Sunny's Blues Shack, their strong black fingers spreading over Blue Fire and Brown Georgia like warmed baked blankets, playing those two pretty blues guitars of theirs.

Arfel's head lay back on the sack. "Don't see her when she leave. Don't hear a whisper." Gin-Water Pete was pulling down his pants. "Gotta keep a crease in them for tomorrow, Arfel. Tomorrow night—you know."

Arfel lifted his head off the sack. He nodded and then put his head back down on top of the sack.

"She a devil-woman. She gotta be a devil-woman."

Arfel's head rose back off the sack.

Gin-Water Pete was sitting in the hay, taking his boots off his feet—ponderously so. "Got me too much a this beef packed in the middle. I know it's so, Arfel. True. Hell ... nobody gotta tell me," Gin-Water Pete said, his hand slapping hard up against his rubbery belly.

"She's a devil-woman, Gin-Water Pete? You said that that woman's a devil?"

"Hell, gotta be, Arfel. One minute here, nex' minute gone. She like a devil. A devil's song," Gin-Water said, loosening the boot's shoelaces as deftly as his fingers played Brown Georgia.

"D-do you know her, Gin-Water Pete, her name?"

"Don't wanna, uh-uh, Arfel. Better not to," Gin-Water Pete said, biting off each word like it was bitter salt. "A woman like that? Who move like she do?" Gin-Water Pete's hand wiggled slowly in front of him, hypnotically. "Like a snake. Got that kinda blues in her."

Arfel's body was on fire.

"Yeah ..."

"Better not to know no woman like that. Let her come an' go. Go off to where she come from, Arfel." Gin-Water Pete's boots were off his feet. His hand reached for a cloth bag he'd put on top of the hay. "Warm. She warm—but fit to my hand fine. Real fine, Arfel." Gin-Water Pete's hand uncapped the bottle. "Make you forget 'bout things for the night." Pause.

"You know you welcome. More than." Gin-Water Pete was gesturing the gin bottle at Arfel. "Know you still thinkin' 'bout that devil-woman. Know I ain't upset the man in you so," Gin-Water Pete said, handing the gin bottle off to Arfel. "Know you got that much fire in you, man in you, juice in you. Know it don't die so fas'."

Arfel's hand wiped the top of the gin bottle. His swallow was as long and hard as Gin-Water Pete's had been.

"Don't worry none, Arfel. You know I got me 'nother bottle stashed 'way in the sack."

So Arfel took another swallow, only not as steady. "My eyes ain't playing tricks on me, are they, Gin-Water Pete?"

"Uh-uh. They seein' right. But she might as well come in from the swamp, from there. The swamp water 'round here."

"I-I just want to ..."

"She got the devil's tease 'tween them legs a hers, Arfel. The devil's tease." Then Gin-Water Pete reached for Brown Georgia, putting the gin bottle down for now. "Why I got me Brown Georgia," Gin-Water Pete said, his breath exploding. "The onlies' woman who know me, Arfel. Who I let get up wid me in the mornin'. Who don't wrong me when my back get turned 'way."

Blue Fire was out her case. She lay horizontally across the guitar case. "Blue Fire's the same. Same for me, Gin-Water Pete—"

"Perty—what I say, uh-huh, when first I seen 'er. Perty, like Brown Georgia."

Arfel grinned.

"Onlies' ain't got what a real woman got. What one a them she-devil womens got."

"Yeah ..."

"She comin' back, Arfel. That devil-woman. She know what she doin' to you. Ain't gotta be told, no explainin'. She feel what in your pants too. 'Tween your legs." Gin-Water Pete picked up the bottle of gin, taking it all in. Then he threw it across the barn, and it smashed against the side of the barn, shattering so much glass.

"Oooo—baby ... rock crazy like you do ... (humpff!) Your sweet daddy comin' home tonight—jus' for you!"

"Zzzzzz. Zzzzzzz ..."

It wasn't Gin-Water Pete's snoring that was keeping Arfel awake.

"Zzzzzzz. Zzzzzzzz ..."

It was that woman. That woman who danced like a black Jezebel in Sunny's Blues Shack tonight. Arfel's knuckles rubbed hard at his bloodshot eyes. "I ain't long for this town, me an' Blue Fire. We ain't long for this town ... uh-uh ..." But the thought of her, of not having her, was already haunting him.

"Zzzzzzz. Zzzzzzz ..."

Arfel's eyes caught the outline of Gin-Water Pete's body: big, stocky, bold, thick as rubber, black. Brown Georgia was right there to the right of Gin-Water Pete's large head opened out to the night air, to the stars if it wasn't for the barn's top. He and Gin-Water Pete had been sleeping in Sunny's uncle's barn for three straight nights going on five. Arfel chuckled. For he was going to stay in this town, he and Blue Fire, for another two days; and then it would be off to whatever new town he and Blue Fire pulled up to via train or however else they got there.

She loves the blues. The blues is all in that colored woman, like religion, Arfel thought.

It was like the first time he saw her he knew what she was going to do on the dance floor. It was like he and Blue Fire just had to play for it to happen, for she could slink her limbs out there slow like the music was spooning its song, as slow as the blues when it's thinking, pondering on things the day's brought on but can't finish. But when the blues stops thinking, then all it can do is feel the heartbeat of the day, snatch you up into it—whatever story it wants to tell: the truth, as hot as the sun heating the sky.

Arfel's eyes, as dark as they were, could see things. He wasn't making that colored woman any prettier in his dreams than what she was since he had no dreams at night to tell. He shut his eyes when she was on the dance floor tonight because he had to.

"Zzzzzz. Zzzzzz ..."

"I had to. I-I had to." She'd forced him to even if he hadn't wanted to. "Blue Fire. Blue Fire ..."

Blue Fire was in her guitar case.

"She come up on me like a shadow, that colored gal. A dark shadow. My body feel her like a spark, a hot flame. I ain't drunk, Blue Fire. T-talking silly. Gotta have her, Blue Fire—don't trust myself if I don't."

The left side of Arfel's head lay back on top of the sack. "Gotta—my body, Blue Fire ... it's on fire, Blue Fire. Burning like a hundred Sunday mornings. Days and nights." Pause.

"Let me see inside her. In there, Blue Fire. There."

Arfel looked down at one long leg and then the other. "But two more days we're staying here." Arfel looked over at Gin-Water Pete. "Don't know how long Gin-Water Pete and Brown Georgia staying.

Don't know their travel plans. Just ours. Yours and mine, Blue Fire." But Arfel knew he and that blueswoman, that they had a date for tomorrow night. He knew that she would be back in Sunny's Blues Shack: she told him that much.

"You're coming back, blueswoman, for one more night. Blue Fire and me be there for two nights more. You do something to me. Something good. I ain't gonna close my eyes and … you be gone this time. G-give Blue Fire and me the slip."

"Zzzzzz … Zzzzzzz …"

"Ain't gonna let it happen. Ain't."

Arfel shut his eyes, and then he eased them back open: No, he had no dreams to dream. Not tonight. Not on any night.

The morning had come and was bright as a glory day.

"Was thinkin', Arfel …"

"About what, Gin-Water Pete?"

"This life …" Pause. "It ain't so bad."

Both Arfel and Gin-Water Pete had washed up. Both felt clean and crisp.

"You hear me, Arfel?"

"Uh-huh sure, Gin-Water Pete."

"Hell, Arfel, you mighta washed up this mornin', but you still got that blueswoman on your mind. Don't you?" Pause. "Mind already thinkin' 'bout tonight, ain't it? Set on it.

"Don't blame you any," Gin-Water Pete said, grinding the cigarette he'd been smoking down into the dry hay. "You ain't the onlies' man she do that to. Put her sin in," Gin-Water Pete said, yawning, then shaking his head. Gin-Water Pete put his broad-brimmed hat on. "Gonna play hard tonight. Gotta a blues in me that's travelin' through me this mornin', Arfel. Makin' distance. Time. A long stretch of blue itchin' in me."

"It's what you call it, Gin-Water Pete?" Arfel asked, smiling.

"Yeah, Arfel: a long stretch of blue, man. Long stretch of blue," Gin-Water Pete said with a surge of wear and tear grinding down his voice.

There was a creak in the barn door when it opened. "Mornin', boys!"

A short flagpole-thin man stood at the barn door. He had a shiny belt buckle and a gray stubble on his face that made it seem like it would be somebody's crime if it were shaved clean (razor and soap). "How'd you boys sleep?"

"Fine. Jus' fine, Mr. Chester," Gin-Water Pete said to Sunny's uncle Chester.

"Sorry can't do better by you," Mr. Chester said, looking around the barn.

"It's fine by Arfel an' me."

"You boys still got you red in yo'r eyes," Mr. Lester teased. "Red-eyed."

"Uh …"

Arfel and Gin-Water Pete looked at each other and then laughed.

"Done me a morning's worth a work already."

"H-how many rows, Mr. Chester?"

"Oh … me an' Bessie, we don't count 'em. Might not wanna work if we do. No … can't do that. A man and his mule."

Arfel and Gin-Water Pete laughed along with Mr. Chester.

"Know them times, Mr. Chester."

"Seen 'em in yo'r hands, Gin-Water Pete. Feel 'em too," Mr. Chester said. "An' yo'rs too, Arfel. Know you know the mornin' gray, the land—what a man on a farm got to git up for. Turn in early." Pause. "Now y'all is bluesmen. Afford to sleep late."

"An' live poor," Gin-Water Pete said.

"Ain't how I see it, Gin-Water Pete. Not atall," Mr. Chester said, looking over at Brown Georgia who was exposed. "Love to play me one a them gui-tars jus' one time. Put a song in it. Right up in it. Say what's troublin' my mine. You an' Arfel—y'all boys lucky. Bluesmens," Mr. Chester said sweetly, his fingers treading softly over his gray stubble.

"Gotta song for every trouble. Every ache—what bones in you."

Arfel's hands went down inside his pockets, and he felt how warm it was down there. His body hadn't forgotten about that blueswoman. Mr. Chester hadn't caused him to forget about her. (No. No.)

"Now how 'bout some grit? Have Miss Henrietta cook it up special for you boys."

"Thanks, Mr. Chester."

"Yes, thank you, sir," Arfel said, knowing full well how Miss Henrietta cooked in her kitchen.

"An' when you through eatin', can clean up that mess in the barn somebody make."

Arfel and Gin-Water Pete looked at each other queer-eyed.

"Seen that broken bottle of glass at the barn door," Mr. Chester said, his eyes twinkling as he and Gin-Water Pete headed for the barn door. "What, some blueswoman at Sunny's Blues Shack get yo'r goat!"

"Ha."

The three laughed heading out the barn door and toward Miss Henrietta's heavenly kitchen.

# Chapter 2

His eyes were closed. She was there. He could feel her. He could smell her like an ocean breeze, like seawater.

Arfel opened his eyes: he wasn't going to miss her, uh-uh—not for one second of an hour.

The skirt's slit ran from her knee to her hip.

Arfel's breath left his lungs.

Gin-Water Pete's elbow nudged him. "She here, Arfel. That devil-woman. Come back."

Arfel nodded knowingly—sure about tonight, the stars. *I ain't closing my eyes*, Arfel said to himself. *Not for the night.* Her black skin already glistened, already singing a blues. Arfel struggled to keep his eyes open, playing Blue Fire just so, keeping her heart from racing just so fast.

But Gin-Water Pete put a wail in Sunny's Blues Shack, he and Brown Georgia, and the blueswoman dipped her bottom, her limbs moving to and fro, her legs strong and gritty, not letting go of the floor. Arfel's skin was tingly, and Gin-Water Pete kept wailing freely, feeling what Arfel and the blueswoman were feeling, not afraid to say the words welling in their black bodies, willing to speak them in the shapes of scultped language.

"Don't know where you been (humpff!).
Jus' know you fulla sin;
Gonna drink my gin—
Don't have to think no mo'e."

Gin-Water Pete went on—

"Don't know 'bout tomorrow,
Onlies' today;
Ain't let no cold winds,
Stan' in my way."

And on—

"Gonna luv you, ba-bee.
Gonna luv you, ba-bee.
Gonna make luv to you.
If it the las' thing I do."

And on—

"Drive me crazy, woman.
Drive me (huhn!) crazy …"

And Gin-Water Pete stood, and his body shook blue notes out of Brown Georgia's body and trembled like a red fever.

"Fever, ba-bee.
Fever, woman.
You know what you do.
Gin-Water Pete's (humpff!)—
Gonna make luv to you!"

And then Gin-Water Pete's body collapsed back down into the chair, all but spent, done for.

And this blueswoman danced on as Arfel's eyes shut, but stayed on her, followed her long legs like it was a long river leading him to some dark, secret bush sure to be found.

"*Ooooooo ba-bee!*" Gin-Water Pete said, putting his final blues wail in Sunny's Blues Shack.

No more music was in the air. Arfel stood before this blueswoman: she hadn't disappeared.

"I'm—"

Her fingers silenced Arfel. "You a bluesman."

"Yes … yes …" Arfel stammered.

"It all I got to know, bluesman. It all you gotta tell me."

"Yes … yes …" Arfel stammered again.

"Play the blues." Her voice was light, sweet, and delicate as moonlight. "All I need to know. All you gotta tell me." Her hand darted down inside the top of her dress where her breasts were, her cleavage running deep. She pulled out a handkerchief. Its white brightened the room. She wiped her soft skin, dabbing at it lazily, in no rush, no hurry.

"Play pretty."

"Thank you."

"Play pretty," she repeated. "Gui-tar you play—pretty."

"Blue Fire."

Blue Fire wasn't with Arfel. Blue Fire was in her guitar case next to Gin-Water Pete's foot.

"Blue Fire?" she said teasingly. "Onlies' name I gotta know. Onlies' one you gotta tell me."

Arfel stood taller than her even though this tall blueswoman wore high heels.

"You comin'?"

Arfel's gray shirt sweated more. "Uh … uh …"

"To my place, bluesman? To … to my place?"

"Uh …"

"Through playin' for the night—ain't you? Ain't you? You an' … an' Blue Fire?"

"Yeah, yeah, uh—yeah, me and Blue Fire."

"I through dancin' f-for here. For now."

"Wait, wait for me. I'll be back. Right back."

Arfel went over to Gin-Water Pete and whispered in his ear. Gin-Water Pete took a good swallow out the gin bottle and then looked over at the blueswoman, feeling her sin once again.

"Yeah …" Gin-Water Pete said, saying good night to Arfel. "See you at Mr. Chester's farm in the mornin'. For breakfast. Miss Henrietta's breakfast."

Arfel hardly heard Gin-Water Pete speak.

This tall blueswoman was out in the air, outside Sunny's Blues Shack, on the creaky porch smelling in the air—mixing in it. She looked at Arfel, and then at Blue Fire. "Gonna play for me, bluesman? Where I take you off to—gonna play for me?"

Arfel looked at that skirt's long slit, her legs flashing, pointing to the moon. "All night if you want … like …" Arfel said.

"Know you will, bluesman. Know … you can."

She was the first to walk down onto the creaky step and then took the second step. She was on the dirt road. Arfel followed her. Some of the road's dirt kicked up as they walked, her leading him up a road, and then another, one which wound.

"I—"

"T-talkin' ain't good. Leas' for now."

Arfel could feel the sex in her. The pure, raw sex in her. Arfel reached back in to his back pocket and pulled out the short bottle of whiskey.

She laughed indulgently, the night air catching it like fine, quick rain. "Got whiskey where we goin'. Ain't nothin' cheap 'bout it."

Blue Fire was slung across Arfel's back, the leather straps holding to the front of his chest.

"Drink all you want, bluesman. You need."

Arfel looked at her hips, her bottom, his eyes touching them, his hands thinking as much.

They moved out the moon, off the road. The owls kept them alert, the soft rustle of trees, night sounds. "Gonna have to 'member how to get back, bluesman. How we travel to off here. How I take you."

Arfel and Blue Fire knew that. They knew the roads, the woods, the details of travel. Yes, the roads and the late hours and how to stretch themselves across a lonely night and then find the best way home, like a note that's dropped out the sky.

"Know you travel, bluesman. Know that."

Arfel could taste her lips, the red on them.

"Know you make yo'r way from here to there—don't stay no one place long."

Arfel's eyes were memorizing everything; his ears, the sounds.

"Make me craz-ee, bluesman. You and Blue Fire, make me craz-ee, bluesman ..." She grabbed Arfel's hand, holding it hard, and then letting go. "Gonna, gonna love you, bluesman. Gonna give it all to you, all of it, bluesman."

Arfel's heart raced, and he smelled that sweat in her as if churning. And then they came out the wooded area. And it was as if the world had opened up to them once again. They were on flat, open ground, and Arfel could see the well-built wooden cabin just in the distance.

"Won' be long, bluesman. 'Fore we play y-yo'r blues." She grabbed Arfel's hand again, this time, not letting go.

Their footsteps quickened. Arfel could feel the man in him, the very thing which made him a man grow, lengthen more in his pants.

The moon shone down on the log cabin bright and full, realizing its absolute powers.

"I ... I ..."

And the blueswoman opened the log cabin's door.

"See!"

And Arfel, in the light, saw everything: the chairs, the sofa, the whiskey cabinet, the bed.

"See, bluesman!" And then this long cabinet running across the cabin's floor was unlocked; and the whiskey bottles, short and tall, stood together. "Drink all you want, bluesman. Doesn' mine ... mine atall."

But Arfel was looking at her, at the blueswoman, and she knew it. "Play Blue Fire, bluesman. Play Blue Fire," she said slowly, reaching Arfel. "Play yo'r blues," she said, idling there.

"Don' know nothing else," Arfel replied, his hands holding to the leather straps, easing Blue Fire off his back. And when he had Blue Fire in tow, had opened the guitar case and put Blue Fire in his hands, it's when the blueswoman halted him.

"Not now, bluesman. Uh-uh."

Arfel found a place for Blue Fire. And then he was holding on to this blueswoman as her body began this Jezebel dance, this snake torture, lighting a fast fire in him. His eyes closed. "Seen how you move …" Arfel's hand touched her buttocks, bringing her up in to him. "Seen how …"

Her breath stung his neck, flashed hot. And then she bit his neck, sucking at it.

"How you move, blueswoman …"

And her hand touched his leg, and she felt his bulge, this hard thing centered between her thighs. "Oh … bluesman. Bluesman …" Her flesh trembled as she moved him backward. His hand found more of her as they fell back onto the unmade bed.

"T-the lights, bluesman …"

But Arfel wanted to see her body, this magnificent black creation, this magnificent piece of black art that had been driving him crazy from night to night, up to now, in Sunny's Blues Shack. Her thighs, her butt, her—

"Oh … yes … uh … yes … the lights …" Arfel let go of her, and then there was a screen of dark, and then he heard her like the night air. He heard the sounds of her clothes leave her as her breath came in spurts, skimpily.

He knew where she was. "Let me," Arfel said. "L-let me …" He wanted to feel her panties, what covered her. He wanted to feel her bra, what held her in.

"Yeah … bluesman. Yeah … yeah …" she moaned softly.

And now he kissed her, her tongue sliding over his.

And now he kissed her, his mouth sucking in her nipple.

Now she unbuttoned his sweated shirt. And her breast came out his mouth, her mouth screaming vividly. And his clothes were leaving him as her hands *took* and *grabbed* as his breath jerked like a snapped line. Her tongue slid onto his chest, over his back; and his low moans echoed hers, freeing them into a blind pace. And the other breast was his to suck and make love to as he lifted her more up into him as he felt his manhood being searched for by her long, thin fingers.

And Arfel shut his eyes knowing where the blues, Sunny's Blues Shack, Blue Fire, Gin-Water Pete, and Brown Georgia had led him, to a log cabin out of nowhere where this blueswoman's back was a silver streak bewitching the moon.

"Bluesman!" the blueswoman screamed as deeply and long as any blues. "BLUESMAN!"

The sun warmed his naked body. Arfel had full range of the bed. His hand had no need to feel for her. Arfel knew the blueswoman wasn't there, that he was alone: that she'd gone.

Arfel looked for Blue Fire. "There you are, Blue Fire. There you are—girl," Arfel said. "Drank too much," Arfel said, lifting his head off the mattress. "Got my head bad." He felt comfortable in his own nakedness but then turned to look at his clothes. "Neat. She fix them neat on the chair, Blue Fire."

Arfel knew his clothes had been somewhere in the room, the floor—somewhere. But the blueswoman was good enough, nice enough to do the clothes right, put them on the chair where they could rest easy. The warm sun felt good on his skin. He remembered her, last night; all the blues he played in Sunny's Shack was worth it—she was a blueswoman all right.

He eased himself up, straightening himself in the bed as he reached for his pants. The whiskey bottle was gone, but the knife in his back pocket was there—folded neatly.

Arfel began to dress. "Feel a little dizzy-headed, Blue Fire. Head still ain't right. On … on straight." He remembered again. Her body warm as the sun, generous as a sea wave, rocking him in her warm waters. Arfel trembled: his and the blueswoman's sex was still in him, petitioning for more. "She's gonna be at Sunny's tonight, Blue Fire. She's coming back, Blue Fire. She ain't got any regrets about nothing."

Arfel sat back on the bed to put his boots on. With each shoelace threaded through the boot's eyelets, Arfel sighed. *I am a bluesman,* he thought. *You meet a woman, and you fan the fires of hell, and then you move on, pack your guitar, and move on.*

"There's other women down the road. You always find you one."

The way they made love last night … But this blueswoman knew the rules. She wasn't asking for anything—only the night. Arfel felt he and Blue Fire were about ready to leave the log cabin. Arfel looked at the liquor cabinet; a heavy metal lock locked it. "Wasn't gonna drink nothing no way, Blue Fire. Head's fixed too bad." Arfel laughed.

Arfel looked over to his right, something his back had been to the whole time. He saw it. "What did she do, go and do, Blue Fire?" Arfel picked it up off the table. "She left a note." He began reading it.

"'Aint cuming tanight. Blusman. Be heer. Blusman. Waitin heer, Blusman. Log cabeen.'"

Arfel's body was on fire.

"You hear that, Blue Fire," Arfel said, sticking the note down in his back pocket. "Hear that!"

Blue Fire was in Arfel's hands. Blue Fire was put in her black case. Now Arfel's hands were as soft as a velvet sky as he laid her across his back. He looked back into the room from the cabin's door. "She knows what time I'll be here, Blue Fire. What time I'll come," Arfel said, shutting the log cabin's door.

The barn door creaked some when it opened.

"Damn, Arfel, see you an' Blue Fire back in time for Miss Henrietta's breakfast. Damn, you know that much!"

Arfel entered Mr. Chester's barn, shyly.

"She a blueswoman, Arfel? Sex you up good?"

"She's a blueswoman, Gin-Water Pete. Sure is."

"Ha!" Gin-Water Pete was holding Brown Georgia. "Trouble though. Nothin' but trouble. Trouble written all over that colored gal."

Arfel began walking over to where his suitcase was. "Maybe so," Arfel said agreeably. "But wasn't last night."

Gin-Water Pete didn't seem to disregard what Arfel'd said but, just the same, seemed to pass it off. "Brown Georgia steady. Don't cause me no ill."

Arfel took Blue Fire off his back, putting her flat on top of the hay.

"Can't sex her though!" Gin-Water Pete laughed. "Ain't goin' for that!" Pause. "Play hard last night, Arfel. Blues was pourin' outta me. Outta places I don't know to fine." Gin-Water Pete struck a note on Brown Georgia. "Love playin' with you. Know it ain't gonna be long, though. Either me or you gonna be packin' soon. Headin' off. Makin' good distance."

"By tomorrow I'll be gone. Me and Blue Fire, that is."

"Figure as much. Where to, what town—you know?"

"You know I don't know where to, Gin-Water Pete. Wouldn't be a bluesman if I did."

"Uh-huh," Gin-Water Pete said, slapping his leg. "Ain't no mystery then. Set forth."

Arfel joined Gin-Water Pete on the ground. "How many towns I can't name, Arfel. How many women."

"I like it like that, Gin-Water Pete."

"Me too. Gotta move. Gotta feel like I runnin' after somethin'."

"With me—it … it's like I'm looking for something."

"A restless soul, is you?"

"Uh, yes—no, no, I think it's more like an experience, what it is for me. Something to sleep on. Tuck under my pillow."

"Pillow, yeah, uh, yeah—what, uh, what you can put in our music, that what you sayin', Arfel? Gettin' at?"

Arfel paused before he gave answer to Gin-Water Pete. "Yeah … yeah …"

Gin-Water Pete sucked in a labored breath. "Gotta know them blues 'fore you can play them in your fingers. Sing them songs off your tongue. Don't gotta know the town or the women in them towns, onlies' what you know." Gin-Water Pete had knocked hay off his boots.

"She's somebody's trouble though. But you ain't gonna be 'round long 'nough to find out. To figure so."

Arfel stretched out his legs.

"Goin' there tonight?"

"Uh-huh."

"Damn you, boy!" Gin-Water Pete laughed. "Damn you. Her pussy that good!"

"Same way as she dances, Gin-Water Pete."

"Got her own place, huh?"

"Don't know—couldn't tell."

"Nice though?"

"Yes." Pause. "Cabinet's stocked full of liquor."

"Man drink liquor like that. No woman, Arfel. Not even a blueswoman."

Arfel had to consider Gin-Water Pete's lucid observation.

"You be careful out there. Don't know who lookin' over your shoulder. A owl, what. Don't know who's where. Don't know who's 'round, standin' in a man's shadow."

Arfel did have to consider that too.

"But … you go 'head an' have your fun, Arfel. Ain't no crime in livin'. None at all in that."

Gin-Water Pete lumbered up to his feet. "Mr. Chester gonna be comin' through that door," Gin-Water Pete said, pointing at the door. "Soon 'nough."

Gin-Water Pete looked down at Arfel.

"Hungry, ain't you? Pussy ain't food, Arfel. Lessen you was eatin' it last night on an empty stomach." Pause. "Eat pussy too!"

Arfel laughed at Gin-Water Pete's remark.

"Miss Henrietta sure can—"

"Mornin', boys!"

"Mornin', Mr. Chester!"

"Morning, sir!"

Bessie's harness was in Mr. Chester's hand. "Get in late, Arfel?"

"Y-yes, sir."

"Figure you do." Mr. Chester smiled.

"Was out with, what, one of them—"

"Blueswomen?"

"Yes, Mr. Chester."

"Sow my oats long 'go, Arfel, Gin-Water Pete, 'fore Miss Henrietta an' me. Doesn' know them nights no mo'e. Jus' days, days addin' up to mo'e days. Days keepin' record. K-keepin' them rows straight, me an' Bessie. Plantin' an' tenderin' an' prayin' fer a good crop. Ain't bad days out in God's sun, boys. Me an' Bessie, boys."

"Not bad at all," Gin-Water Pete said.

"Nope, not bad at all, Mr. Chester."

"Miss Henrietta's waitin'."

Gin-Water Pete and Arfel smiled tooth to cheek at each other.

"Love cookin' for you, boys. Say she ain't lookin' forward to you leavin', but know the routine." Mr. Chester's head sloped off to the side of his shoulders. "You boys hear the music, follow it. Follow it jus' like I does with Bessie every mornin'. 'Ceptin' for Sunday—our day a rest, that is.

"Know every hair on her tail."

Chapter 3

The blues was virile, powerful up in Arfel.

"Leavin', huh, Arfel?" Gin-Water Pete whispered. "Leavin' for the blueswoman."

"Uh-huh," Arfel whispered back.

A bluesman, Jimmy-Spoon, had joined them on the small piece of a stage. "Jimmy-Spoon play it. Play it our way."

Sex was all in Arfel.

The music had filled him like liquor, and now he was ready to go off to the blues shack: the blueswoman was waiting for him. Blue Fire was on Arfel's back.

"Don't go out the front door,
When yah can go out the back. (Humpff!)
Know you leavin', ba–bee—
Ain't nothin' sad as that.

What I said last night,
Lookin' up at the moon.
Bury my head in my pillow,
Ain't left the room."

Gin-Water Pete's words peppered the air as Arfel entered into the dark space.

"Gonna find it, Blue Fire. Ain't gonna have no trouble with that. Gonna remember everything from last night. Every creak and crack in the night. Even the last owl I hear. That hoot. Even that, Blue Fire." Arfel was walking the dirt road, sure of himself, certain as to just how far he had to go—the color of the moon.

"Same moon as last night. Looks the same. Feels just the same." And into the wooded area Arfel and Blue Fire slipped as the moon could only peek through the branches not seeing much of the ground below. "Remember this, Blue Fire? Do you?" Arfel asked, sighting a tree much shorter in height than the others, shrunken, stunted: Arfel remembering it well, like a year of travel.

"See. And that owl, Blue Fire. It's singing the same song. Same song as before. As last night. In, in the air."

Arfel felt her all night in Sunny's Blues Shack. There was a tension in him, and then he'd release it, and then it'd build back in him again as high as a mountain, the tip of the sky. "W-who, Blue Fire? What, what blueswoman's gonna do this to me in the next town over. The next time around?"

Arfel was sweating, his black skin feeling it more and more. It was like he was back in Sunny's Blues Shack, he and Gin-Water Pete and Jimmy-Spoon not rushing through the music but riding on it, letting it ache up their bones, letting it say what it had to say, and then ache up their bones, settle, find space.

The way the blueswoman made love, the way she rocked his soul—the wind. "Remember that too, Blue Fire. And … and that too," Arfel said, pointing his finger at landmarks he'd sworn he'd remember, not to ever forget. "Getting closer, Blue Fire. We're getting closer." Because Arfel could smell the blueswoman, smell what was between her legs, her thighs—the oils.

And soon Arfel and Blue Fire were out the wooded area and into the clearing as if the world had opened out to them.

"T-the light's burning, Blue Fire." And so it was, the log cabin's lights were burning brightly. Arfel's feet were close to running, but

21

slowed. More than once his hand wiped his brow. "This ain't good, Blue Fire: us rushing so."

This was to be the last night for him and the blueswoman. This was to be the last night of this. There would be other blueswomen, plenty of them. There would be other towns, plenty of them. There was no rush, Arfel thought. *No need to rush.*

But with that said, Arfel's body still craved last night, the blueswoman's hips cracking like the tail of a wind. Arfel's body still craved that kind of raw night, as wild as the Fourth of July.

Knock. Knock.

It was the right thing to do, knock on the door. It was the most polite thing for him to do.

"It you, bluesman?"

"Yes ... me ... yes—it's me."

"Don't have to knock."

Arfel opened the log cabin's door. She was on the bed in a long, loose-fitting skirt with her legs pushed up and the skirt hiked up so he could see most of the flesh of her long legs until the skirt made a tunnel into a dark passageway. "You brung Blue Fire?" she said, as if she had to say something.

"I don't go no place without Blue Fire."

"She don't mind?" the blueswoman said.

"No."

"Knowin' what we do? How we do it?"

"No."

"Ha!"

Arfel understood what the blueswoman was doing: she wasn't at Sunny's Blues Shack, her body grinding out the blues, suffering it, but in the log cabin letting it run through the same ritual, motions.

"S-she ain't jealous none?"

"No."

"Ha!" Her fingers ran the edges of her skirt when it, idly, dissipated her interest. "Blue Fire tell you that, bluesman?"

She seems to be trying to get inside my soul, find its compass, direction, Arfel thought.

"She tell you that?"

"Always talk to Blue Fire. Blue Fire always listens."

"Tell you that, bluesman?"

Arfel took Blue Fire off his back, placing her on the same chair as last night. He walked toward the liquor cabinet.

"Don't gotta do nothin', honey." She sprang off the bed. "Let me." She opened the liquor cabinet (it was unlocked). "Ain't gotta do nothin' like that, bluesman." Her eyes darted right into Arfel's. "Know what you like, bluesman. How you like it." She had a bottle in her hand and was pouring from it.

"Come, honey." She was back in bed. "Know you gotta thirst—you walk far."

"Thank … thank you."

Her hand went up to his shoulder, and she pulled Arfel down to her. She kissed him full on his lips. And then her breath whispered, "Here."

Arfel took the glass of whiskey out her hand, his hand shaking. "Ain't … ain't you going to—"

"Had mine 'fore. 'Fore you come. Doesn' you smell it on my bredt, bluesman? Doesn' you?"

Arfel sat on the bed's edge. The blueswoman moved back to where she'd been, raising her legs up, hiking her long, loose-fitting skirt higher.

Arfel cocked back his head, and the whiskey ran down his throat.

The blueswoman was holding on to the bottle, her long fingers seemingly nursing it. She moved back up to Arfel, kneeling, looking over his shoulder. One hand held on to his right shoulder, and her head rested on his left one as she poured drink into his empty glass. "Don't run out, bluesman." She laughed again. "Ain't runnin' outta liquor. Don't never run outta that."

"Who … how … how you come by this? By—"

Her lips covered his lips as his hand reached for her sweet bottom. "Oh … bluesman. Last night, bluesman. L-last night." Arfel wanted to move her down in the bed, but she skittered from him—out of reach.

She was out the bed, on the floor.

"How you play tonight, bluesman wit … without me, bluesman?"

She's a Jezebel, Arfel thought. *She's a black Jezebel like Gin-Water Pete said she was.*

"Play good, bluesman on ... on Blue Fire? Play good?" she said, looking over at Blue Fire.

She still held the liquor bottle.

"Pour," Arfel said.

"Pour ... pour." And she held on to that long liquor bottle, teasing it so. "Get ... get good an' drunk, bluesman. Do that bluesman."

"Yeah ... yeah ..." Arfel said, mumbling the words. She stood in front of him and leaned over, and Arfel's eyes saw all of what they saw last night in her loose-fitting blouse: her black breasts as full as two black moons in the sky.

Her eyes saw where his eyes were fixed. "Yo'rs, bluesman. All ... all yo'rs ..."

But Arfel had questions to ask as she poured the whiskey in the glass. "Who ... whose liquor does this be—"

"You don't as' no questions! You know that, bluesman. You don't as' questions for the night. You play yo'r blues, bluesman. Play yo'r blues, an' move on!"

Arfel shut his eyes. *What's wrong with me?* He knew the rule, the agreement, the law. "Uh ... uh ... yes ... yes ..." Arfel cocked his head back and shot the whiskey down his throat. "No questions. N-no questions."

"Gonna be same life tomorrow, bluesman. Tonight don't change nothin'. Nobody. Yo'r blues same as mines," the blueswoman said wearily. "Play the same song, bluesman."

And for that brief moment, Arfel connected with her, with this blueswoman.

She snapped off the room lights. "Gotta fine me, bluesman!"

Arfel leaped to his feet and then stumbled. "Ha!" He laughed as wildly as her. "Gotta fine me if ... if you want me, bluesman ... Gotta fine me!"

And he could hear the subtle sounds, the things leaving her body, skin being stripped in silence.

"Down, down to my panties, bluesman. Down to my panties. Ain't forgot, bluesman. Ain't forgot." Pause. "Fine me, bluesman. Fine me!" Her voice shrieked.

But all Arfel had to do was follow her voice. It's all he said to himself over and over: *Follow her voice. Follow her voice.*

24

But she was the one to find him. To pull him to her. "Bluesman. Blue … bluesman …"

She was on the wall, up against it; he pressed himself to her. Arfel mumbled something into her ear. They were skin to skin; only Arfel's pants were belted to him.

They slithered down the wall and onto the floor. Her lips were kissing his chest, smothering it. She was riding him, holding on to him, riding his hips, holding on to his back. And then he pushed her back onto the wall, her head leaving his chest. And she loosened her legs' hold on him, for the blueswoman knew what Arfel was trying to do. And she heard his zipper open, and her panties being pinched open, and her legs tightened around Arfel's hips as Arfel inserted his penis into her wet vagina.

"Oh … oh, bluesman!" she screamed, her breath rising out her. And it's when Arfel smelled the blueswoman's liquor, what she'd said she'd drunk before, was sweet in her.

They'd made love twice: the second time better, harder than the first. In the dark, she found his lips with the lip of the glass. "Drink, bluesman. Drink all … all you want," she said, lifting the glass so Arfel's tongue could taste the rich whiskey. They were sitting upright in the bed, their backs against the wall.

"Mo'e? You want you mo'e, honey?" Arfel didn't decline.

It was a fresh bottle of liquor she poured from. "When my daddy say po'r, I po'r."

Arfel smiled, satisfied.

"Bluesman, you sure know how to make love …"

Arfel's tongue was tasting the freshly poured whiskey.

"N-nasty," she said. "Nasty, bluesman."

He could make love to her again, easily, if the blueswoman wanted to.

She hugged the warm bottle of liquor to herself, running it the full length of her body. "Miss me that kind a lovin'."

By tomorrow he and Blue Fire would be gone. After he and Gin-Water Pete played at Sunny's Blues Shack, they'd be hitching a train, getting out of there, out of this town for a new one. There was no need in him mixing in this. None whatsoever.

She kept rubbing that bottle on her as if it were his tongue licking her silky black skin, making it shine. Then Arfel's eyes looked over at her, her dark, strawberry-red nipples excited, stiffening. Arfel felt warm. She poured more whiskey into the glass.

"Here ... here, bluesman."

Arfel's eyes rolled in his head, him lightly laughing. Then he looked at his nakedness, nudity, and how hard his penis was and laughed fuller.

"Oh ... bluesman, you a colored man in my bed."

Arfel didn't understand what she meant—he didn't have to, he thought.

She lay flat. His head rolled over on top of her shoulder, and then he snuggled up to her breast, sucking it, the nipple, feeling her feel him what was for the third time. But then his head began swimming, dashing to and fro, not connecting permanently, not to anything solid, distinct, moving without oars, anything to anchor it. His eyes rolled more up into his head, his mouth releasing the blueswoman's breast, leaving it unburdened, unsheltered. His body curled up in the bed. It felt as if he were drifting upriver with his friend Tom Mickens on that handmade wooden craft they built one day in Tom's backyard and they took to water to christen when they were ten or twelve or something.

"Bluesman, bluesman." She was shaking him. "Bluesman, bluesman, b-bluesman."

But Arfel's head kept drifting upriver, he and Tom Mickens and that watercraft trying to discover adventure, fun, on a dry, sunless summer day back home.

"Bluesman, bluesman ..."

Arfel would not awaken. He'd blacked out in the bed from the quantity of liquor still stuffed in his belly.

Somehow Arfel felt cool, chilly. The blueswoman wasn't there. Arfel felt it right off. Her warm body was not there. And then at the bottom of his feet, Arfel felt something strange, like a lump. A terror grabbed him, a raw, coarse shock. The dark was blinding. He didn't know what it was. Nothing could be seen. His feet only felt something at the bottom of the bed. Arfel panicked. Fear leaped up into his throat. Arfel was on his feet. "Ouch!"

His skin, the bottoms of his feet, its skin was being torn, shorn, broken open by what was sharp, cutting, was down on the cabin floor.

Where's the light switch!

"Ouch! Ouch!"

Arfel didn't understand this. His hand was on the wall, tracing his hand across the roughed wall. Blood was pumping out his feet. Arfel didn't have to be told that. His skin was torn. He felt his nakedness, and he could see the log cabin's door was open, and even the silvery stars in the sky he saw. And then his fingers, feeling the wall, struck something, impeding them; and Arfel knew this was the switch, the light switch—what would make light, sense out of all this in this room.

Arfel snapped the light on. His back was to everything. He turned slowly.

"NO!"

He was dead. The white man. The short, pudgy white man was dead in the bed. He'd been killed. His neck was slit open. And there next to that white man's pool of blood was Arfel's knife as big as day. Arfel looked down on the floor and saw glass scattered everywhere, broken, littered—destroyed. And a wooden cane. Violence was everywhere in the room.

"It's the white man's ..." Arfel said in a hushed voice. "It's the white man's cane. I-I don't remember nothing. I don't remember nothing ..." Arfel cried out. His body shuddered at the horror, at the look of the bloody, grisly sight.

He was drunk. He'd blacked out.

"I-I don't remember noth-nothing."

But it was his knife—it belonged to him. "It's my knife. My knife ..." Arfel looked over at Blue Fire. "Blue Fire. Blue Fire—it, it's my knife. Blue Fire. My knife!" He looked down at the broken glass; he had to get back over to the bed.

Arfel got down on his hands and knees and began brushing the glass away, making a path to the bed. His hands kept brushing, him crawling on the hard planks of the tough wooden floor making a path to where the short, pudgy white man lay dead in the bed with his throat slashed open and his dried blood soaked into the white sheets where Arfel and the blueswoman had made love twice in one night.

Arfel was on his feet. He was afraid to look but did. The knife was right there on the bed, frantically angled. Arfel snatched the knife off the bed. "Oh god, god!" Arfel screamed. "GOD!"

He knew he was in trouble. He knew his horror. He knew this the entire time.

He took the knife's blade and wiped it on the bed's white sheets: wiped the bloodied blade clean. "Blue Fire … Blue Fire …"

He knew he and Blue Fire had to get out of there, get out of there, get out of there. His clothes were still on the floor, still there where he and the blueswoman first made love: the blueswoman hadn't laid them on the chair before she left the cabin.

"Where is she! Where's the blueswoman! The sheriff. The sheriff, Blue Fire!" Arfel's hand tightened to the knife's handle.

"The po … po-lice, Blue Fire. The po-lice. Law!" Arfel felt like a murderer now, like someone who'd slit a white man's throat open, clean.

He folded the knife's blade.

"Did the blueswoman go for the po-lice, Blue Fire? Did she!"

Quickly Arfel dressed himself, and at its conclusion was when he slipped the knife back down inside his back pocket. "They ain't finding nothing, Blue Fire! Nothing!"

Arfel looked back over to the dead body.

Arfel slung Blue Fire over his back. He was going to look back over there when he got to the cabin's open door but said instead, "The hell with it, Blue Fire! The hell with it!"

Arfel sped into the dark, looking up to the bright stars for guidance. "She deserted me, Blue Fire. The blueswoman deserted me. But why shouldn't she? Why shouldn't she …" But Arfel knew the blueswoman knew the story, knew what he'd done to that white man back there in the log cabin with his bloodied knife.

Arfel and Blue Fire were about to slip back into the wooded area. Arfel turned to look back. "She knows, Blue Fire. The blueswoman knows."

And Arfel knew from this moment forward that his life had turned for the worse, had skidded off into an ugly, ghoulish tale.

"*Psst … psst …* Gin-Water Pete," Arfel said, shaking Gin-Water Pete out his sleep. "Gin-Water Pete!"

"Ar-Arfel. Ar … Arfel …"

Even in the barn's pitch-black, Arfel felt fear in Gin-Water Pete's voice.

"Where you been!"

"I killed a man tonight, Gin-Water Pete …"

"Killed a man!"

"A-a white man, Gin-Water Pete!"

Gin-Water Pete grabbed Arfel's shoulders and shook him fast and powerful. "A-a white man, Arfel? A white man!" He was shaking Arfel as if he were trying to shake some new sense into him. "Make sense, Arfel. Make goddamned sense, goddammit!"

Arfel pulled his knife out his back pocket. The steel blade glistened in the dark.

"With this, Gin-Water Pete. W-with this. Slit his throat clean!"

Gin-Water Pete's hands stilled, froze to Arfel's shoulders solid like ice. "Arfel, has you gone mad!" Gin-Water Pete said, burying his head in Arfel's chest.

"Came back, me and Blue Fire came back to the barn for our things."

"That woman, that blueswoman mixed up in it, I know. That blueswoman, devil-woman mixed up in it."

"Yes, yes …" Arfel said, his hands breaking free of Gin-Water Pete's.

"Tell you she trouble. Tell you all the time she a devil-woman, gonna bring you—"

"It's done, Gin-Water Pete! Over—"

"A white man. You killed you a white man. You gotta get outta here, Arfel. Run, Arfel, run!"

"Blue Fire and me come back for our things."

"Yes, back for your things you … you an' Blue Fire."

There was no struggle for Arfel to find his things in the dark.

"Run, Arfel. Colored man gotta run. N-nigga gotta run."

"When, when they find out …"

"All hell break loose. Come runnin' after you. Po-lice, law down here." Gin-Water Pete pounced onto his feet. "Damn, Arfel!"

Arfel had every scrap of his belongings. "Gin-Water Pete, you and Mr. Chester and, and Miss Henrietta. Gin-Water Pete, you and—"

"Don't worry 'bout us."

The barn door creaked when it opened. The stars were the only light.

"Good luck, Arfel. You an' Blue Fire. God's speed." Gin-Water Pete shook Arfel's hand. "Won't be here when they come neither. Brown Georgia an' me goin' opposite direction than you an' Blue Fire, though, Arfel." Gin-Water Pete smiled. "Always was."

"But Mr. Chester and Miss Henrietta, Gin-Water Pete. What … what's gonna happen to them?"

"When them people come, the law, Mr. Chester an' Miss Henrietta know how to handle them. Mr. Chester live a lot of years, him an' Miss Henrietta on this farm. Mr. Chester an' Bessie be out there in the mornin' same way. Bessie an' him plantin' them rows. Miss Henrietta in her kitchen, cookin'. Them things keepin' to normal. How they been all 'long."

Arfel shook his head.

"Pleasure playin' with you, Arfel." Arfel and Gin-Water hugged this time. "You a helluva bluesman. Helluva bluesman!"

Arfel smiled into the starry night.

"You gonna get there safe. Where you goin'. You an' Blue Fire—wherever you travel off to."

"Thank them, Gin-Water Pete. Thank Miss Henrietta and Mr. Chester for me, please."

"Don't worry, Arfel. Worry any."

"They'll know why I left without …"

"Uh-huh." Pause. "You know how to travel, you an' Blue Fire, how—on the back roads, Arfel. Keep there. Always on the back roads. Don't veer. Hardly wander."

Arfel and Blue Fire were on their own. But they always traveled this way from town to town, only it was different this time, much. Arfel never felt Blue Fire on his back before as he carried his suitcase and his guitar in his hand—not until now. "Blue Fire. I'm tired. Tired." The run to the farm and from the log cabin to the farmhouse was long, arduous—and now this, this new movement away, into space and time.

"Tomorrow we was to leave, Blue Fire. T-tomorrow." Arfel darted into the woods, dense branches clouded everything, and the dark roared out at him and Blue Fire.

The trains, the trains, all Arfel could think about were the trains.

"The trains, Blue Fire. Can't think about eating or sleeping, Blue Fire—we have to get to those trains. Keep moving, Blue Fire. Keep moving, Blue Fire. Moving."

The trains roared like the darkness he and Blue Fire were wrapped in. They roared like engines churning black balls of fire. *When will they know?* Arfel thought. *When will they miss the white man? When will the blueswoman take them to him? To the log cabin?*

Arfel's hand slid back into his back pocket, touching the knife, and then fetching it, pulling it out. He stopped. "Killed you, white man. Slit your throat clean with it, white man. Carry it for protection." Arfel started back up. "Good with it." Yes, Arfel was always good with a knife. He and Tom Mickens. Carving things, making things out of wood. He'd stabbed someone with a knife before but not to kill him. But he ran his knife through his leg. He'd protected himself then too—on that occasion too.

"Tired, Blue Fire. Al-already tired."

He didn't want trouble for Mr. Chester and Miss Henrietta. He didn't want their lives any worse than what they were down here. "But you're right, Gin-Water Pete. Right. I know you're right about things."

Arfel wanted to cry out the blues, sing the blues—but then the trees shook. It was like a choir of tambourines shaking the roots of the trees. A choir of tambourines shaking them from up high in solitude.

Am … am I in church? Am I! Or were they the voices crying from the trees that'd hung them? What was it that he was hearing: black voices crying from out the trees that'd hung them? Bloodhounds. Bloodhounds on a leash, and some running free. Sniffing the ground for a scent. For something to pick up his scent in their noses. In the moonlight. In the brush. Trying to get closer to him. Some of them running free, unleashed. Some of them let go to run faster, more free, freer in the night wind on the hunt, the chase. "Coming after me. Blood-bloodhounds. Af-after us, Blue Fire. Af-after us. Bloodhounds."

Arfel's feet quickened. No longer did Blue Fire feel heavy on his back. She felt like always now. Blue Fire felt like always now, normal— Blue Fire hugging herself to his back.

Voices. Voices.

The grass was just below his knees. Arfel and Blue Fire were in tall grass, edging past, out of sight of the road, moving along, not knowing if a shadow was being cast or just this big black figure exploding in silence.

Voices. Voices.

Blood. Blood.

Was it the blood that lived in bloodstained grass—was it? Or were they the bodies that turned the waters cold, frigid—were they? Were they!

Arfel jumped like music to his own fear.

"Blue Fire. Blue Fire. How far to go, Blue Fire? How, how far to go before we reach them trains, Blue Fire? How, how far, Blue Fire? Ain't gonna die out here, Blue Fire. Ain't. Ain't. Ain't gonna die out here. Don't have no plans to die out here, Blue Fire. Ain't, Blue Fire. Ain't!"

Or were they bodies that turned the waters cold? The black bodies lugged in pinewood boxes in slow-footed funerals that had only the human choirs as choristers to scream out the death of the human soul ... Before ... before what, what?

"Killed him. Killed that white man with my knife," Arfel's voice erupted. "Slit his throat clean. And the blueswoman was gone, ran off, Blue Fire. T-the blueswoman ran off for the po-lice, Blue Fire. The sheriff. The law."

Arfel gulped.

"They're coming, Blue Fire. After a colored man. A nigger, a nigger boy. Chasing the wind. T-those bloodhounds are chasing the wind." Arfel's sweat was sucking up his skin. His skin couldn't breathe. Sweat was finding hollow pockets in Arfel's skin and not knowing how to

32

release them, let them go; find some silent, soft stream to follow, smooth course to run.

"We ain't gonna die out here, Blue Fire. Uh-uh. We ain't gonna die out here. In the grass. Following the road. On, on the edge of the road. But not so c-close."

But something was stirring on the back road. Arfel heard it. Heard—but it was the owls. Owls singing their nightly songs like birds of prey.

"It's what it is, Blue Fire. Nothing more. Nothing's following us but them bloodhounds, Blue Fire. Them bloodhounds nipping at the wind." Arfel looked over his shoulder as if to see just how much their feet had gained, looking, just looking ... Arfel shook and then gained better control of himself. For Arfel saw a light.

"A light, Blue Fire. There, there's a light, light coming at us. What it is. A light in the road, Blue Fire, in the distance—moving at us steady. Steady on us."

And Arfel realized it was traveling opposite from the direction he and Blue Fire came, that there was no way this person would know of the log cabin, the blueswoman, the police, the dead, bloodied white man in the bed.

The one-eyed truck drew closer and closer but traveling as if its tires were tired like the veins in the road. When the truck got closer to Arfel, Arfel blocked off his eyes with his arm, for that one light was as good and as potent as two. Then the truck stopped somewhere near Arfel's feet. It's when Arfel unblocked his arm from his eyes, but it was still as if Arfel were looking into the sun when it boasts all its power.

"S'pose you lookin' for a ride, boy?" the man asked.

If there was a face in the cabin of the pickup truck, Arfel had not seen one.

"Yes, sir. I-I sure am, sir."

"Then get in."

Arfel stepped out the truck's light.

"That door don't open so good. Here ..." The door was opened from the inside out. Arfel and Blue Fire got into the pickup truck. The cab of the truck was as black as a burnt-out sky.

"Seen what you look like in them truck lights. Reckon you willin' to see the same, then?"

It took little time before the flashlight in the man's hand turned in on his face and came on, and it's when Arfel saw black as black must've looked to a white man when he first saw black.

And then the flashlight shut off, and the colored man turned his head back to the road, and his neck cracked. The pickup truck started back up, feeling its way back up the road. There was no talk for a while, not until Arfel heard the bones in the man's neck turn to crack again.

"Hell, you ain't runnin' from nobody, is you, boy? Nobody 'round here? Hell, you ain't in no trouble? 'Cause we all be neighborly 'round here."

"No, sir."

"You a bluesman?"

"Yes, sir."

"Why you carryin' you that perty gui-tar strap cross yo'r shoulders?"

"Yes, sir."

"What you call it?"

"Blue Fire."

"What town you goin'?"

"North."

"You hitchin' them trains then? 'Bout but a few miles from there. Still be dark 'nough for to hitch the train."

"Thank you."

"You feel like playin' somethin' on Blue Fire to make the time go?"

"Sure, sure do." Arfel then strummed Blue Fire's strings, and it's when the colored man *hummed* along as light as rain.

Suddenly the pickup truck stopped in the road.

Scared, Arfel thought the colored man saw something he had not, the essence of something secret, clandestine out on the road.

"Ain't gonna get you there 'fore the sunrise, bluesman. Train come an' gone by then. Truck can't carry but so much weight fast. Better you go 'lone." The flashlight shone back on Arfel's face. "See yo'r worry. Listen to yo'r blues. What you play on Blue Fire to mark the time."

The colored man paused, and his voice sat down in his chest heavy like a furnace. "Gotta cross swamp water. Get over to the other side. You an' … an' Blue Fire." Pause. "Onlies' way you an' Blue Fire get there on time."

"Thanks. Thank you."

"Ain't no thanks, no thanks need be," the black man said sadly. Arfel opened the truck's door. "Just hope nothin' happen to you out there. All I hope. 'Cause you an' Blue Fire sure know how to play you a bluesman's blues."

Arfel with Blue Fire and his suitcase in tow could smell the swamp water from where they were.

"Know you smell it. Twenty minutes, most. Got you twenty minutes 'fore train come in on the other side. Come in an' leave. Seen worse I know. Uh, good luck now."

"Thanks."

The pickup truck started back up again, making the sounds it could to travel the dark road.

Arfel turned and stood and stared into the darkness. "How far are they, Blue Fire? Them bloodhounds? Them … The white man let them go?" And then Arfel felt as if he were encroaching on the dark. "Blue Fire. Blue Fire—you're always here, Blue Fire. By my side," Arfel said reassuringly.

And then Arfel realized that time was wasting. And then into a new set of dense woods he and Blue Fire plunged.

"Smell it, Blue Fire. Smell it. It … it's getting stronger and stronger."

And no moon sat on top of the swamp waters; it looked like a bed of black mud: thick, oily grit. Arfel held his breath at the water's edge. Then he bent and put Blue Fire on top of the suitcase. Then he sat down. He unlaced his boots' laces. He put the boots on top of the suitcase too. "Ain't gonna have leaky boots, Blue Fire. Ha. Not for up North. Uh-uh."

Arfel realized he'd just laughed: it felt good, solid in his chest. Arfel rolled up both pant legs. Arfel got up. He bent down again, lifting the suitcase far above his head. He turned and looked at the swamp water's oily black face. "Trains ain't far off from the other side, Blue Fire. They ain't far off once we get over there."

When Arfel entered the water, it rose to chest level, imposing a clear watermark. Arfel's eyes were shut as he kept walking with the suitcase high above his head, his arms up, stretched, extended, locked in rigid, rocklike position. "Stink, Blue Fire. Water stinks bad."

All Arfel's ears could hear was his heartbeat as if beating the waters, making them rush as if crocodiles were moving powerfully in them, in pursuit; wasting no time to gather, group, circle, probe … attack.

Arfel jumped, not knowing what below bit him in the waters, nipped his skin. Not knowing what was below him as long as it didn't drag him downriver, take him down the river's swift currents with it. Arfel's thoughts were of crocodiles, not that of a mob of white men. His eyes were still shut. He was too afraid to think, to know. And then—

"Blue Fire. Blue Fire. We're safe, Blue Fire. Safe. On land. Ground, Blue Fire!"

Arfel and Blue Fire and the suitcase had emerged from the waters. "Phew! Phew! Phew!" Arfel put the suitcase down at the bank of the water. "Ain't putting you back on my back, Blue Fire. Not now. Now."

Arfel's hands slapped at the water pasted to his clothes. And then he rolled down his pant legs and then picked up the suitcases and Blue Fire. And now there was only tall grass for Arfel to negotiate in order for him and Blue Fire to get to the trains. Grass not as tall as Arfel, but tall enough to hide in, not unless the dogs were set loose, freed from the farmhouse. Arfel moved through the tall grass swiftly. And then he looked overhead; the sky was lightening.

TOOT. TOOT.

"There it is, Blue Fire. Here she comes!" Arfel hid where he couldn't be seen, right below the train track's embankment. "She's slowing down, Blue Fire. Slowing down. Good and slow. And we're right where we oughta be." Arfel and Blue Fire had done this enough to know just where they should be positioned when they saw familiar physical designations of a railway station. "Got good length to her, Blue Fire. Ain't it, to show?"

Arfel could hear the train breathe in his ears. The train vibrated in his soul. The train as alive and loud as a load of thunder in the night's air.

"Good weight to her too. That too. Blue Fire. That too." And then Arfel looked over his shoulder. "Seems like we've been on the run a long time. What happened a long time ago?" Arfel sprang out his crouch, and he and Blue Fire dashed for the train, Arfel's feet dashing like deer feet through snow for the oncoming train.

"Oooo-we, Blue Fire! Ooooo-we!" Arfel's voice whistled clearly in the dark.

No one was in the boxcar but Arfel and Blue Fire. There was no one to share the boxcar with; both were alone.

"North, Blue Fire. North. We're heading North!" Blue Fire was already down on the car's floor. Arfel had opened the guitar case. "Let you breathe, Blue Fire. Y-you need to breathe. Know you've been cooped up all night except for when we played for the colored man. Man, Blue Fire, ha, that colored man sure was black." Arfel felt a chill penetrate him, causing him to sneeze.

The suitcase opened. "*Aaaah* ..." He held the bottle of whiskey in his hands. "Kill anything, Blue Fire. Whiskey'll kill anything in your soul." He took another good portion of whiskey from the bottle.

"Train's moving ..."

Arfel could feel the train's wheels and its steel tracks twist together. "Moving away from everything, Blue Fire. Heading North. From trouble, Blue Fire. From all the world's troubles."

Arfel's body lay naked on the boxcar's floor. He didn't know where the train's next stop on the line was or who next would board the train. The wet clothes were drying. Whiskey had kept him warm (the whiskey bottle was empty). Even though the boxcar wasn't cold, fear, Arfel knew, could ice your veins solid. It's what his veins felt like: ice in him.

Blue Fire is back in the guitar case sleeping like a baby, Arfel thought. It's something he couldn't do, not just yet. Sleep? It was bad enough looking into the eye of this black space and knowing his life had been turned, flipped upside down in the flicker of an eye, as sudden as a mad, frantic scramble. If he shut his eyes, what would happen to him next; what would his mind imagine, lead him to like a dark dream?

Arfel's hand touched the guitar case, and then he lay over it. "How much did I pay for you, Blue Fire? How many gui-tars did I have before you?" Arfel's eyelids drooped, were close to shutting, but snapped back up like tightly wound shades.

"Sleep ain't for me, just Blue Fire tonight. Don't see how. Uh-uh."

Arfel thought of the first time he saw Blue Fire. She was in another bluesman's hands. He'd walked into that blues joint that night with another guitar in his hands not for sporting but for playing.

"Thought so much about it, that gui-tar in my hands, don't even bother to name it. Don't even chance one." But Arfel wanted Blue Fire the moment he saw her. He knew he could play her better than that bluesman who was, better than any bluesman living.

"Dug into my pocket, Blue Fire. Dug down deep. And I looked at that gui-tar I brought in there with me. And I played it as sweet as any bluesman can play his gui-tar in that bluesman's ear. Like a harmonica, almost. Knew I was advertising it. Knew it had some decent sound in it.

"Remember?"

"What you call her?"
"Ain't gotta name for 'er. Too soon. She ain't broke in yet. Me an' 'er jus' strikin' up conversation."
"Got money in my pocket—and this gui-tar here."
"So what you anglin' on, boy?"
"Buy her from you."
"Oh, so you been playin' all night, an' now you wanna take my gal home with you, huh? That what you hittin' on?"
"No, just trade."
"Uh, an' you say how much money you got in yo'r side pocket, boy?"
"Blue Fire!"
"Huh!"
"Blue Fire. It's what I'm gonna call her!"
"Ha. Ha!"

And that was the story of Blue Fire and Arfel. It was their story: a bluesman and a blues guitar. "Was blue," Arfel said. "And played like fire!"

The train and track didn't seem to clatter as much now. The whiskey had settled in Arfel's belly. In fact, the train rocked gently over track now. And then soon, Arfel's eyes were touched by the beauty of sleep. And the night came to him, this night. Him and Gin-Water Pete in Sunny's Blues Shack. Him getting sweated up, ready for the blueswoman. His body on fire. Thinking of her, the blueswoman at the log cabin waiting for him, her body, the warm, wet juices that flowed just beyond her black bush of tangled hair.

He had to leave. He'd played Blue Fire enough for one night. He had to get to that log cabin, drink some more of its whiskey, get to the blueswoman; she was waiting for him. Black and long, breasts that heaved up to the sky when his mouth sucked them. Her black body trapped beneath his black body, crying like a dying angel. Into the dark, the woods, half drunk, smelling her, knowing the night before what he and the blueswoman had done: what was close to the gates of hell.

"Blue Fire! Blue Fire!" Arfel woke in a panic, in a deep layered, dripping sweat. "Blue Fire!"

Arfel's body scratched the boxcar's hard wood.

"I-I don't know what—remember what the white man looked like when I killed him. With my knife. With my knife!" Arfel's eyes strained to see Blue Fire. "Blue Fire. When, when I slit his throat clean through with my knife, Blue Fire. I don't even know. E-even know …"

Arfel's hand grabbed his pants off the train car's floor. His hand shot into the back of his pant pocket and pulled out the shiny knife. "Saw him, Blue Fire. Saw him—but … but don't remember nothing what he looked like when I killed him."

And the knife sliced the air, ripping into it as if it were a steel screen. "When my knife slit his skin, his throat, his throat clean."

The fear in him cramped his hand, and the knife fell onto the boxcar's floor. "The blueswoman was gone, Blue Fire. Gone." And then Arfel felt his nakedness; how lonely it all felt.

"Could-coulda died. But not there, Blue Fire. Not in a log cabin you and me. Not, not on Mr. Chester and Miss … Miss Henrietta's farm. Not there, Blue Fire. Not on a back road, Blue Fire. Not there. Not in a swamp, in, in swamp water, Blue Fire. Not there."

Arfel grabbed up his clothes and began hustling them back on. "I'm a bluesman, Blue Fire. I'm, I'm a bluesman. We play the blues, t-the blues, Blue Fire."

Arfel put his boots back on.

# Chapter 4

The trains … he and Blue Fire had stopped counting. The trains he and Blue Fire had hitched, Arfel and Blue Fire had stopped counting. The days and nights Arfel knew. Six days since that night. Six days since he'd killed the white man, slit his throat with his knife. He and Blue Fire's bones had had enough of train and track: they'd had enough for a lifetime.

There were other passengers along the way. He played the blues for them; they pleasured it. He didn't know what they were running from, or if they were running from anything, or if they were being chased, hunted, their story, but they pleasured his blues anyway. The train stopped. The boxcar's door opened. Arfel and Blue Fire leaped off the train and rolled down onto the embankment, Arfel protecting both Blue Fire and his suitcase in a special way with his body. When he hitched the train this morning in the other town, the sun was sharp in the sky. Now the sky was dark, flat. Arfel stood. He was told this was a big town, bigger than most. Already, it felt like a town he could hide in, get lost in, move amorphously in like a phantom.

Arfel brushed the fresh dirt off his jacket and trousers. He looked up at the dark sky.

"Blue Fire, we're safe. Blue Fire. Safe for now." Arfel walked up the embankment (the train was gone). He peered into the distance. He saw lights well beyond the tracks and wooden poles. "Look around, Blue Fire. We're gonna look around. Yeah, yeah, Blue Fire—it's what we're gonna do."

And now Arfel and Blue were at the edge of town about to enter upon it. He wanted to smell its fragrance as if the air belonged to him and Blue Fire alone. "Smell it, Blue Fire. Smell it. Smell how it smells. What she's doing." Arfel's feet moved lightly, politely dropping into the ground as if he were dust. And the more he moved into the town, the more he saw and wanted to see.

This is a city, he thought. *This is a city. This is what people who've been North and come back South call a city,* Arfel thought. Arfel saw buildings as tall as cornstalks and sugarcanes. Arfel's eyes widened. And then Arfel stopped and touched one of the tall buildings. "See, Blue Fire. See—it's real, Blue Fire. A-all real," Arfel said, looking up at the building as his eyes climbed at a gradual rate.

The night was slow in this city. People were walking as if mirrored images, reflections, one of the other. Arfel moved his head, slanting it downward at a sharp angle as if to hide it away, but no one passing taking notice of him; no one would know what he was doing and why. But then Arfel slipped in and out of another shadow since it seemed more comfortable there.

Already, for some reason, Arfel liked this city. Tall buildings, a lazy rhythm, eyes not looking farther than what they ought to. "Ain't gonna have to do no explaining, Blue Fire. At least not up North I ain't."

He and Blue Fire had never been up North. It's why he'd smelled the air: he wanted to know if it smelled any differently than what it did down South, hid away any secrets. But he'd sung about it and played about it on Blue Fire, about the "Freedom North," but really didn't know anything about what blues, if any, a bluesman could feel it had in its soul.

But everybody had a story, and he listened to those bluesmen tell theirs. And it spoke of freedom, always spoke of freedom as if there were no white men in the world. As if there were no rides taken in the dark, no white sheets, no trees for colored men to hang from. This was the "Freedom North" the bluesmen sang of, making him sing it too: the same song they sang from inside out.

"Blue Fire. D-did you hear it, Blue Fire? Did you hear it too?" Arfel turned around and looked back toward the train tracks. "It's going South, Blue Fire." Arfel turned back around. "Been there. You and me, we've been there."

Arfel and Blue Fire advanced more into this city. And to Arfel, the lights were bright (even though he still preferred the shadows), and the streets were paved better than what he'd ever seen. "There's something rich about his town and it don't mind showing it. Bragging on it." Arfel and Blue Fire were in another building's shadow shading them.

"*Pssst! Pssst!*"

And then this small balled figure leaped out from between the building's shadows, startling Arfel. Arfel's hand reached back to his back pocket. His hand was halfway down, when—

"Hey, Mister. Mister—you know how to play that thing, Mister!" It was a tiny colored boy who had a tweed cap on his head with its bill tightly rolled like a newspaper, who wore high-water britches and a blue-white windowpane shirt patched at the right elbow, and who had a smile that could knock the sun out the sky.

"Uh … sure. Sure do." Arfel felt relieved, his hand leaving his back pocket and what was in it.

The tiny colored boy's frail body (electric as a lightbulb) circled Arfel and Blue Fire once, and then twice for good measure.

"Y-you got a name for it, Mister?"

"Blue Fire."

"Blue Fire?"

"Blue Fire."

"It sure is a pretty name."

"Sure is, ain't it."

The tiny boy squirmed. "Call me Roadmap."

"Roadmap?"

"Roadmap. Ain't as pretty as Blue Fire, though."

"Ha! Pretty enough though, Roadmap."

"Yeah, guess so. Guess so. Thanks, Mister. Thanks." Then Roadmap rolled his cap's bill with his hand. He looked at Blue Fire as if, seemingly, hearing the music Blue Fire played being strummed out its steel strings and knew where the man and Blue Fire wanted to travel off to in this city.

"Mister, Mister—take you over to where you and Blue Fire can play the blues, Mister."

"Where's that, Roadmap?"

"Over on Barrel Street. Play the blues all night over on Barrel Street. Cost you a dime, though." Roadmap removed his cap, stuck it out to Arfel, and then put it back on top of his head.

Arfel chuckled mightily. "How about a nickel, then?"

"Nickel, nickel's fine by me."

"How far we gotta go to get over to Barrel Street, Roadmap?"

"Ain't but one mile … umm, but maybe closer to two."

Arfel laughed.

But before Arfel and Roadmap began their walk over to Barrel Street where the blues was played all night, Roadmap said, "May I touch her? Touch her, Mister? Touch Blue Fire?"

Arfel smiled.

Roadmap's head peeked behind Arfel's back, and his little hand swung out and touched Blue Fire's blue skin. "Oh … oh, Mister. Oh … oh, Mister …" Roadmap said as if his hand had been tickled. And then he began skipping up the street ever so blithely and absentmindedly.

"Roadmap. Hey, Roadmap."

"Oh, oh sorry, Mister. Sor-sorry …" Roadmap said red-faced.

Then Arfel and Blue Fire caught up with Roadmap for Roadmap could take them over to Barrel Street where the blues was played all night for a nickel.

Now Roadmap would drift a foot behind Arfel, keeping an eye on Blue Fire, so it seemed, and then speed in front of Arfel when there was to be a shift in direction. Now Roadmap was in front of Arfel, and now a foot behind Arfel.

"She shine, Mister. Blue Fire shine."

"Doesn't she, Roadmap. Doesn't she though."

"How … how you, how you come by her, Mister? Blue Fire, Mister?"

"Well …"

"Is it a long story, Mister? 'Cause … don't like long stories. Just don't."

Arfel laughed, covering his mouth. "Me neither, Roadmap. Makes two of us." Pause. "No, it ain't long, Roadmap—how me and Blue Fire come together."

"Good."

Pause.

"Well ..." Roadmap smiled eagerly.

Arfel had just finished telling Roadmap about the old bluesman who'd owned Blue Fire and how he and the bluesman had made a trade along with a cash payment for her.

"Wow, Mister! Wow!" Roadmap's eyes gleamed. Again, Roadmap's finger touched Blue Fire's blue skin. "Wow!"

"Yeah, named Blue Fire Blue Fire right there, Roadmap. Right on the spot."

"Nothing else come to mind?"

Arfel looked down at Roadmap. "Nothing, Roadmap. Nothing."

"Wow!" And then Roadmap's pretty face smiled like he had five rock candies in each cheek, evoking a sweet symmetry. "Betcha, betcha you really know how to play Blue Fire, don't you, Mister?"

"Sure do, Roadmap."

Roadmap's pretty brown eyes squinted as if they were looking into a bright sun. "C-can you play her some? C-can you, Mister? Can you?"

Arfel stopped walking, stopped right where he was, dead in his tracks. He put the suitcase down. Roadmap picked it up. "Ain't heavy," Roadmap said.

"Can carry it to where we're going, Roadmap?"

Roadmap's eyes shone like sapphires in Arfel's face. "Easy, Mister."

Arfel attached the leather strap to the guitar case he'd been carrying, slinging it across his back.

"Ready, Roadmap?"

"R-ready, Mister." And Roadmap picked up the suitcase again, and Arfel struck the chord on Blue Fire, and the look stuck to Roadmap's face told Arfel that the blues, what he played and knew, would never die in a colored man's soul.

Roadmap was a good travel guide, because Roadmap liked talking and explaining the different sights and sounds of the city to Arfel and Blue Fire (even pointing his fingers at things on a few, rare occasions after he'd stop to put Arfel's suitcase down) on the way over to Barrel Street.

"Mister, Randolph Lancaster Madison died in that building, Mister." Roadmap was pointing at a dour, depressing-looking building, to say the least. "Right there, they say, Mister, Mr. Madison died."

"He did?" Arfel said as if he knew the man.

"Yep, sure did." Roadmap had the suitcase back in tow. "Was a bad man around here, they say." Roadmap smiled handsomely. "'Course I wasn't born then, Mister."

"Of course. Before your time, huh, Roadmap?"

"Yep. You could say that. Yep."

"Ha."

"Yep, know a lot about this city. Some good and some not so good."

"Get around, huh, Roadmap?"

"Yes, sir: get around. Around this town." Pause. "Talking too much. Rather listen. Listen to Blue Fire."

And Arfel played on Blue Fire.

"Ever, ever get tired, Mister? T-tired of playing Blue Fire? Holding her in your hand for too long?"

Arfel kept strumming Blue Fire. "Uh-uh. Never. I'm a bluesman. You see, Roadmap, a bluesman plays the blues all day and night until his fingers either ache or fall asleep—whichever comes first. It's what a bluesman is."

"Thought so, Mister. Was just making sure." Roadmap winked. "Almost there."

"Ain't rushing you, Roadmap."

And then the air, suddenly, became different in smell, more raw in texture—and the appearance of things. And now a colored face was popping up here, and a colored face was popping up there. *Yeah, we're getting closer to Barrel Street all right, Roadmap,* Arfel said as if he didn't have to be told. And soon Arfel heard the music he and Blue Fire had heard in the South that'd traveled North.

"Hear it, Mister? See, Mister, we got the blues up here too. Got it singing up here too."

"Sure do."

Roadmap's little ears pricked. "Don't play it as good as you and Blue Fire do, though."

"Each man plays it his own way, Roadmap. No man's gotta make him an excuse for that."

"Guess, guess not. B-but it fixes me good—makes me cry sometime when I don't want to." Then Roadmap removed his tweed cap from his head and stuck it out to Arfel artfully, not putting it back on (almost how the trip had begun). It seemed Arfel and Blue Fire's tour with Roadmap was all but over, completed—spent.

"You and Blue Fire, Blue Fire, owe me a nickel, Mister."

Arfel smiled. "Thought it was a dime, Roadmap?"

"Don't matter." Roadmap smiled mischievously.

"You're a good guide, Roadmap."

"Yep, it's why they call me 'Roadmap' around here, Mister."

Arfel dropped the dime in Roadmap's cap as if accustomed to do so.

"Thank you, Mister." Roadmap took a graceful look at Blue Fire as he put his cap back on his head. "See … see you around, Blue Fire." Roadmap's voice had weakened. "I know you're gonna make a whole lot of people cry up here when the bluesman's fingers play on you, Blue Fire."

Arfel's suitcase was down on the ground. Shifting his eyes downward to retrieve it, when he looked back up, Roadmap was gone. "Go, little Roadmap go as he come," Arfel said amazed. "It looks like little Roadmap's got him some more nickels and dimes to hustle up before the night's out."

The blues music coasted up Barrel Street. Arfel's mind went off all his troubles, off Roadmap, off standing in a new city he would have to get to know and learn—navigate in.

"Sounds good, Blue Fire. Whoever's playing it." All Arfel saw now were colored faces, a steady stream of them like fish jetting upstream, not like on the other side of town where the railroad tracks and wooden poles were, ran and then divided.

"Don't matter: just wanna play when I wanna, it's all."

Arfel's gait on Barrel Street was slow, as if he had all night to walk the long, choppy stretch of block.

And there was one bluesman in the blues joint where the crowd breathed in the smoked-in smoke it puffed out. The bluesman had four fat diamond rings sitting on four fat fingers that played the lead melody on his blues guitar. The bluesman was making the blues glitter like gold; it seemed he was looking in the pit of his eyes.

Arfel's face had a look of profit. He and Blue Fire walked through the blues joint's open door, and the bluesman's wide-set eyes opened as soon as they walked in as though feeling them like magic pebbles had been rubbed across them.

"He reminds me of … of Gin-Water Pete," Arfel whispered off to Blue Fire, standing clear of whatever feeble light in the bar there was. The bluesman shut his eyes and moaned something which seemed as intimately felt as a tear tugging on a cry.

Arfel and Blue Fire entered more into the blues joint. It's when the bluesman's eyes slowly opened as if reliving the memory of a deep sleep; and the hand, with the four diamonds sitting on the four fat fingers, led out to Arfel and Blue Fire like a dear old friend—beckoning them both forward.

"You come to play?"

"Don't know much how to do anything else but."

"Then, pull you up a chair."

Arfel found an empty chair, and he and Blue Fire walked up to the stage.

"What act we billing ourselves?"

"Blue Fire and Arfel Booker."

"Sweet-Juice and Lemontree Johnson." Lemontree Johnson hung his head over Sweet-Juice, and Arfel hung his head over Blue Fire. "What we gonna play?"

"How about what we know."

Lemontree Johnson and Arfel then looked into the pit of their eyes to find just what that was for two bluesmen in this city's blues joint.

"Ooooo-we, baby. Ooooo-we."

Lemontree Johnson's head would bob and his guitar, Sweet-Juice, jerk on each syllable Lemontree sang.

"Throwed me out yo'r back do'r but don't get rid a me.
Memory chasin' yah lak a March win'
I long gone (OUCH!)
Ain't comin' back 'gin!"

Lemontree Johnson let his voice drift in the air some and then sang in an up-tempo.

"Cootchie-cootchie woman,
Wit yo'r backside out—
Nice an' slow, how yah move yo'r hips;
Cootchie-cootchie woman—
Wit 'er red lipstick!"

Then Lemontree Johnson switched straight into a midranged tempo blues.

"Died on Sunday mornin'.
Preacherman know my fate.
Say: Lemontree Johnson
Goin' straight to hell—
Just hope that train in the station, ain't late!"

And the blues joint kept rocking as Lemontree Johnson and Sweet-Juice and Arfel and Blue Fire just kept playing away like that.

It was time to quit.

Lemontree Johnson stole a look at Arfel from out the corner of his eye.

"Ha …" Lemontree rumbled softly. "Yeah, you can get the last note, Arfel. Tomorrow night, it be mine to order up for the keeping."

Then Arfel struck something on Blue Fire that made her guitar strings quiver.

"BAAA-BY!" Lemontree said, as if adding multiple exclamation points to it.

Lemontree turned to Arfel who was sitting just off to his right. "Let's make it of-ficial, Arfel," Lemontree said, sticking his bearlike hand out to Arfel. "Lemontree Johnson"—and then he looked down at Sweet-Juice—"and Sweet-Juice."

"Arfel Booker ... and Blue Fire."

They shook hands.

"She's yellow," Lemontree said, looking down at Sweet-Juice again.

"Blue," Arfel said.

"Make a pretty pair. Must look awful good from down there for anybody looking up," Lemontree said, looking down off the blues joint's stage. Then Lemontree stood. He was tall and broad shouldered—had a convincing power and spirit manifesting him.

"We played like crazy, Arfel. Was great!" Lemontree said, slapping his hands together. "Uh, 'scuse me, be right back. You an' Blue Fire don't go nowhere."

Arfel smiled. "Wouldn't know where to go in this city, if we did."

"Right. Just a expression. Expression. Be right back now."

Arfel looked over at his suitcase. It was still where he'd left it in the blues joint. "Guess they danced around it, Blue Fire. Them folk. You know where my eyes was most of the time: shut." Yeah, Arfel thought, coming off the stage—it felt good to laugh. First Roadmap put a chuckle in him and then Lemontree Johnson and Sweet-Juice, just being here in the jook joint.

A few minutes had passed. "Put you back in your case, Blue Fire. Or do you wanna stay—"

"Sweet-Juice don't wanna stay put in her case neither, Arfel," Lemontree said, bounding up on his toes. "That girl nosey. Ain't you, Sweet-Juice? Nosey as three womens. Sometimes four. Don't wanna miss out on nothing she can't see. Blue Fire same, Arfel?"

"Not quite."

"That leaves a whole lotta room for discussion, don't it?"

Arfel nodded and then smiled.

"Ready to go?"

Arfel felt like asking, "Where to, Lemontree?" "Uh ... uh yeah, Lemontree. Uh, yeah."

"Follow me, then," Lemontree said, laughing back at Arfel and his apparent apprehension. "Ain't gonna dump you an' Blue Fire in no river—you two play too damned good for that."

Arfel, suitcase and all, was right behind Lemontree as they stepped out the blues joint like late-night shadows.

"'Night, Last Round, ain't leaving off to the door with you tonight."

"So I see, Lemontree. 'Night."

"Bluebird Bar," Lemontree said, looking up at the Bluebird Bar's hand-painted name in blue over the bar's door frame. "Like its name, Arfel?"

"It's nice, Lemontree. Bluebird Bar."

"Is, ain't it?" Lemontree looked up and down Barrel Street next. "Must be late: slow as snails out here. Or worms turning." Lemontree laughed heartily.

"Uh, yeah, Lemontree," Arfel said, laughing as well, as if he knew the rituals of this city in one night of travel through its thick bulk.

"Ain't played this long an' late in a while." Pause. "Usually play with Knock-Kneed Kirkland. Knock-Kneed, he's a harmonica player, but play guitar too. Call her Purple Poison. Ain't seen him in two nights. Must be at Miss Millie's good-time house over on Dempsey Street. Knock-Kneed can't let them women go. Can't blame him much. He catch up with us soon enough.

"Arfel, which way we going, North or South? North." Pause. "North. North. Just funning with you. Love to tease."

Arfel continued to take in the city's sights.

"So who brung you over to Barrel Street, Roadmap?"

"Roadmap."

"How much he charge you and Blue Fire?"

"A dime."

"At one time was but a nickel, as of yesterday, that is. The rent's gone up, s'pose."

"Well, he, Roadmap, said a dime, and I said a nickel ..."

"So you work it out. Negotiate out the price."

"Yes, you might say that."

"Little Roadmap's a helluva guide. 'Course you know that by now." Pause. "Helluva guide."

"How much he charge you, Lemontree? Your first time over?"

"Don't tour me over. Was already here. But if he do—woulda paid extra too."

Both laughed.

"Smart as a chipmunk, Roadmap is."

"I wonder—"

"Know what you about to ask, Arfel. Ain't getting in to it with you. Not a tad. Let Roadmap tell you his story his own way. Keep it under his cap. He gonna be around. Ain't the last you seen of little Roadmap. Know he disappear on you and Blue Fire soon as you get up at the top of Barrel Street like the wind.

"But he be back—that the way Roadmap is. Operate. Handle his business out here on the streets." Pause. "Sweet boy. Got a way about him. Love the blues too."

"I know," Arfel said, remembering.

"Come by the Bluebird Bar. I know he there even if he don't think so. Time he set there. Know what I mean, Arfel?"

"Sure do."

"Can't no way hide on a bluesman. Know that. Not even little Roadmap. Bluesman smell you out like you a cootchie-cootchie woman who got too much perfume on. Sweetening your skin. Know that."

"Figure to know where little Roadmap is too when he's hiding in the Bluebird Bar, Lemontree," Arfel said.

"'Course you do, Arfel. You a bluesman. A bluesman *true and true.*"

"Roadmap carried my suitcase—"

"While you played Blue Fire? Uh-huh, that boy love him the blues all right. Love it to death."

How far Lemontree and Arfel had walked by now wasn't far. "Guess you still wondering where me and Sweet-Juice taking you and Blue Fire?"

"Yes."

"Already said, ain't dumping you and Blue Fire in no river, Arfel. No swamp water neither."

Had Lemontree smelled the swamp water in my clothes!

"'Cause ain't no swamp water around these parts. This the North, Arfel. City. No alligators neither—as much as I know." Lemontree cackled. "Taking you and Blue Fire to Stump McCants. Stump's got him a hotel called 'Stump's Palace.' Come here from up North. Stump a northern boy. New York City. Serve in the war. Got a wooden stump for a leg for his troubles. Come down here to settle. Make a go of it if he can."

Sweet-Juice was slung across Lemontree's back too, even though it was still out the case, exposed to the light night air.

"Tough as nails Stump McCants, Arfel. Old man grumpier than hell too. But got a heart of gold, just gotta scratch hard with your finger to find it sometimes—but it's there. Don't make no mistake about it. It's there." Pause.

"People die around you, faces you still see. Come. Show back like reflections in a damn pool."

Arfel's mind remembered the woods down there when he was being chased. The trees and the grass. The dead bodies in the waters turning them cold. His ancestors. Faces and voices that don't die: live in marsh and echoes and sacs of somber silence.

"Yeah, Arfel, war's an awful thing they say. Stump'll tell you about it. Ain't a day goes by he don't recall. Got a thousand stories to tell. Thousand memories that still linger."

Blue Fire had weight to her, just for that split second.

"And here we is, Arfel."

Stump McCants's "Stump's Palace" was nothing to look at in the daytime or nighttime either. It was a hotel built for whites, but only blacks rented rooms there now.

"Don't look like much, Arfel—but what does? Scratch two nickels to make a dime. Five to make a quarter. Hell, Arfel, what does?"

"It's all right by me. Right, Blue Fire?"

Lemontree's licorice black face smiled sweetly. "Gonna beat the hell out of a train ride. A mattress an' a bed. That train ride you and Blue Fire was on!"

Lemontree and Arfel were just about to enter Stump's Palace when Lemontree grabbed his arm, pulling him aside on the dirt-white stoop.

"By the way, Arfel, got something coming to you," Lemontree said, shoving his hand down inside his pocket and then coming out with something in it. "You was on the of-ficial payroll tonight. Time and date."

"But—"

"Take it, Arfel. Ain't much, I know. Not as much as I'd like. Only get real tough when we gotta three-way split, when Knock-Kneed Kirkland shows up."

"T-thanks, Lemontree. Thanks."

"Don't mention it. Ain't nothing."

Lemontree led the way into Stump's Palace.

"ZZZZZ. ZZZZZ. ZZZZZ."

"So there you are, Stump!"

Arfel saw Stump McCants's wooden stump; it was up on the hotel desk's long wooden counter.

Even if most of the lights in the hotel's lobby were turned off, Arfel still saw the most attractive artifact by far in Stump's Palace's lobby on a back wall behind the desk: a black-and-tan "R-A"-style wall clock in a slender case of linden wood solids and walnut veneer.

There were remnants of grandeur in the venerable old hotel, but with time and age and neglect, it had been worn down like a thin rope ready (at best) to snap.

Stump jumped out his seat like he was about to salute a first lieutenant in his old army unit's platoon.

"Brung you a guest tonight with me, Stump."

"Guest—long as he pays!" Stump McCants grumped.

"Arfel Booker, meet Stump McCants."

Stump McCants rubbed somewhat seriously at his eyes first before he took in and shook Arfel's hand.

"And—"

"See his guitar on his back, Lemontree. Eyes ain't failing me. Man, don't tell me he's a bluesman too!"

"True and true. True and true, Stump!"

"Shit. If it ain't just my luck!"

"Your lucky night, Stump. You mean. Arfel plays the hell out the blues."

"Last time I tell you, Lemontree: I'm from up North. New York City. Don't play the blues up there. Man's money talks up there. Black, white. Man's money talks. Green, not blue. Hell, blues don't pay no bills in New York City, boy!"

"Arfel and Blue Fire good for it though, Stump. They is."

Suddenly, Arfel felt out of step among his own kind, brethren, like he and Blue Fire had become a big burden to the two men he stood before—separating them. His polished smile faded.

"Sorry, Arfel," Stump McCants said. "Don't mean for us to start off wrong. Wrong footed. Just got to do business. Keep business business. Hotel keeping, it ain't no easy business."

"How much cash you got, Arfel?"

"Should have enough, Lemontree," Arfel said.

"Yeah, Arfel should have enough for one of my rooms, Lemontree. So why don't you leave this here business arrangement to me and … and Arfel," Stump said, smiling.

Arfel pulled cash money out his front pocket.

"That'll put you up for three nights in the Palace," Stump McCants said.

"Towels and sheets clean, Stump?" Lemontree laughed.

"Wash and iron them myself, between all the other things I do around here."

"Stump's a jack-of-all-trades, Arfel. And a master at not one of them. Ain't tryin' to talk—"

"Fix toilets too." Pause. "Talking about toilets and bath—ain't but one per floor. Uh, you on the second floor, Arfel. One flight up, to your left. Hot plate in the room for you to cook on," Stump said, handing Arfel the keys. "Room 2G."

"Well … guess you can go back to work, huh, Stump? Where me and Arfel found you when we come in."

"Long days, Lemontree. All I can say," Stump said, easing his body back into the chair. "Man's got to sleep sometime," Stump said, raising his wooden stump back up on top of the long counter. "My time comes when I make it."

Lemontree and Arfel were at the bottom of the stairs. "Ain't coming up with you, Arfel. Know your hotel ac-commodations fine. Know you have you a long night, you and Blue Fire. So I'm gonna mosey on up the road and keep pace with the moon."

"Thanks, Lemontree."

Arfel patted Lemontree on his shoulders.

"See you tonight. Knock-Kneed Kirkland be there. He good for two nights a catting in Miss Millie's good-time house, and then he finish—*kaput*," Lemontree said, his lungs deflating. "Them girls at Miss Millie's wear him out. Down all right." Lemontree rubbed his hands together.

"Hear him coming now. Them knees of his rubbing together. Why, you'll see tonight, Arfel. Oh, boy—ain't you!" Then Lemontree turned to go.

"'Night, Blue Fire," he said to Blue Fire over his shoulder.

"*ZZZZ. ZZZZ. ZZZZZ.*"

Arfel laughed. "Looks like Mr. Stump's making time like he said, Blue Fire."

Arfel looked up the bare-faced staircase and heard nothing. Except for Stump McCants's snoring, Arfel thought, the hotel was quiet. Arfel and Blue Fire proceeded up the stairs, practically tiptoeing, to find room 2G on the right. "Here it is," Arfel whispered proudly. "2G, Blue Fire." The number was painted on the door in white in a firm, stable hand. "Wonder if Mr. Stump did it?" Arfel giggled.

Arfel inserted the key in the lock and swung the door open. The dark rushed back at him. "Shades must be down, Blue Fire." Arfel's hand was on the wall reaching for the light switch, when it found it.

The room was big in size. And the bed was big enough for two good-sized people. And there was a washbasin and a mirror for shaving. And a hot plate for cooking like Stump McCants had mentioned.

"Not bad, Blue Fire," Arfel said, pleased by what he saw. "Not bad for a colored place." He put the suitcase on the floor. "Seen the bathroom, you too, Blue Fire? Yeah, I know you saw it—smelled fresh. Mr. Stump must keep it clean besides all the other things he does around here."

Arfel walked over to the bed. He worked Blue Fire off his back. Arfel put her down atop the soft bed. "We're gonna make it up here, Blue Fire." Arfel stretched out his legs and then lay back on the bed. "Found us another good bluesman to play with. They're up here. Can't hide. Nothing dies easy. Nothing. N—"

Knock. Knock.

"What, Lemontree and Sweet-Juice come back? They forgot to tell us something?" Arfel opened the door. "Mr. Stump."

"Everything okay, Arfel? Up here? In the room?"

"Fine, sir. Just fine."

"Just checking."

Arfel stepped back from the door. He'd sensed that Stump McCants wanted to come in.

"Ain't bad is it, Arfel?"

"No ... no, not bad at—"

"Ain't first class. Hell, ain't no castle. Palace like it's billed. But a man can lay his head down for the night and sleep good. I can guarantee him that much comfort for his money." Stump McCants's face was thin and grizzled. It seemed a kind face when it wanted to be, like now—but could probably change according to the time or weather.

"Don't hear me coming, huh, Arfel?"

"No, Mr. Stump."

Stumped glanced around the room. He wore suspenders that kept his dull brown baggy pants from hanging over the shoe top of his one good, hardy leg and a droopy white shirt.

"Get around damned good on this stump." Pause. "Used to 'thump' it around here. 'Thump. Thump.' People complained. Lost business. Guess maybe I was angry. Lost my leg in the war. Kneecap. Blew my kneecap off. Must've been. Right off. Splintered the bones clear to hell."

"Oh, yes, uh ... Lemontree told me, sir."

"One day here, next day gone. Yeah, I was walking around here still angry, I guess. But, hell, now, I can sneak up on people with it. Without them hearing a whistle. It just takes practice. It ain't nothin'—nothing hard to do."

"Yes, yes—Blue Fire and I didn't hear a thing, Mr. Stump."

Stump made his way (quietly) over to the bed. "What does she look like? Didn't see her, Arfel, when you come in. Know what Sweet-Juice looks like. Lemontree keeps her out on display. Always says Sweet-Juice nosey as hell. Probably told you the same."

Arfel looked down into Stump's eyes, gleamingly. Then he unfastened the guitar case.

"My! My!" Stump McCants said. "My—now, now if she ain't pretty! My! My!"

"Thank you, Mr. Stump." Arfel removed Blue Fire from her case.

"Now, can't play her now, Ar—"

"No, Mr. Stump. Wasn't planning to. Just like to hold Blue Fire when I can, sir."

"Like I get my sleep …"

"When you can."

Stump McCants laughed, patting Arfel on the back. "Mostly jazz in New York City, so don't get me wrong about the blues, Arfel."

"No, I won't, Mr. Stump. Sir."

"You know, it's what I like about you southern boys. Y'all boys still got manners. Breeding. Show an old man like me respect. His due."

"Thank you."

"Ever hear a jazz record?"

"Yes. But me and Blue Fire don't—"

"I know, I know. You blues boys roll out the bed playing the blues. The boogie-woogie, bottleneck blues. Don't worry none, Lemontree schooled me in on it."

Arfel covered his mouth to laugh. "It ain't so bad, Mr. Stump. Not as that."

"Man, sounds like a damned disease to me."

Both laughed.

Arfel yawned. "P-pardon me, Mr. Stump."

"Gonna let you get your sleep, Arfel. You and your guitar. Was just checking up on you. Making sure everything in the room here fits your style."

Even Arfel had to laugh at such an innocent remark made by Stump McCants.

"War, Arfel—it's an ugly beast—war. Nothing worse. People die around you like flies. Don't know nothing worse. Ain't seen nothing as bad."

Arfel thought of a white southern lynch mob hunting down someone who'd killed somebody who was somebody; slit his throat.

"Did you hear me, Arfel?" Stump asked, standing at the door.

"No, uh, no, can't say I did, Mr. Stump … sir."

"Ain't gonna hear me go down the hall neither. Make this stump sing. Besides, it was bad, bad for business the other way. Thump. Thump. Thump all the damned time."

Stump McCants shut Arfel's room door, and Arfel put his ear straight to the door, standing there for at least half a minute. "Uh-uh. None. I don't hear him none, Blue Fire. What about you?"

Arfel was achy, tired. He was at the big bed pulling back its plain-looking bedspread. "Ain't gonna look at the clock the first morning, Blue Fire. I'm gonna let the day set on its own. What about you?" Arfel struggled with his clothes, taking them off by memory and, now, what was demand.

Arfel got back up to turn off the room's lights. "How did I wind up here?" Arfel asked plaintively. He walked back over to the bed. Blue Fire was already on the bed. Softly, Arfel relieved himself of the day. It was his and Blue Fire's first night in this city, and already it felt better; those white men and their bloodhounds didn't feel as close to him now, Arfel thought.

"Blue Fire, you're sleeping on top of the bed tonight. But don't get spoiled. Ain't good to get spoiled."

# Chapter 5

Arfel slept like he'd had two days and two nights of sleep. The room's shades were pulled down. "If there's a sun, Blue Fire, it ain't shining on this side of the street this morning."

His bare feet landed on the floor. Arfel stretched and then lay back down on the bed, but across it this time. "Sleep good, Blue Fire. Solid."

Arfel still couldn't believe how well he'd slept last night. The train, the boxcar, the track—it was the first he'd slept this way. His body was at peace, his mind. It was the kind of night he'd prayed for, dreamed inside a dream. This city would be a new start for him, a new life: it held out enormous promise.

Now he'd have to learn the city and its ways. Navigate it. Learn more about this city to know it, learn its heart, know its soul. He was a bluesman. *True and true*, he was a bluesman. It was duty to know such things, put it in his fingertips, in the music he'd let wind out of Blue Fire when the time came. He saw some of the city last night but not enough. Today, he and Blue Fire wouldn't need Roadmap. There'd be no need for him to point his finger at things along the way, to tell him and Blue Fire the city's lore, the fine romance, honed intricacies, and details. For Arfel knew how to search through a strange new city, town—dissect it, digest it. All of this searching was in his blood; he was born with it. Each time he'd see, find something brushed over, overlooked from search to search. He'd find his own language and opportunity today. Just what was in this city, how it really looked with lights turned onto its dark skin.

By now Arfel was dressed. The room's shades were up. "Ain't no sun in the sky at all today, Blue Fire. On either side of the street." Arfel was strumming Blue Fire softly, limbering his fingers. "Feel like taking that walk I promised you?"

Arfel put Blue Fire on her back, but without the guitar case. "Know you're nosey like Sweet-Juice. Don't see any difference between you and Sweet-Juice, Blue Fire. Plus, you need the open air. Say you're about as awake as me this morning." And even though Blue Fire went with Arfel wherever Arfel went as a matter of course, Arfel always wanted anyone who saw him to know what he was: a bluesman.

"Ready, Blue Fire?" The room's door shut.

Arfel didn't know who his fellow hotel residents were. "Ain't been introduced to anybody yet, Blue Fire. Not that I know of." Arfel giggled. "We get in late last night, and we sleep late this morning. It don't make it easy for meeting people."

Arfel felt a hand atop his shoulder. He jumped.

"Done it again, Arfel. Damn if I don't!" Stump screeched. "Damn, if I ain't good with this thing," he said, looking down at the stump. "Damn, if I ain't!"

"G-good morning, Mr. ... Stump," Arfel said, still looking as if he'd been beset by a mob.

"Morning!" Stump McCants still wore the clothes he wore yesterday. "Hell, what kind of morning you know!" Stump said, moving to stand directly in front of Arfel. "A bluesman's morning? Man ..." Stump McCants said, exposing his wristwatch. "If you ain't got you a lot to learn."

"Uh ..."

"All right to sleep late, long as you're square with your money. Money don't get scarce—thin," Stump said, casting a suspicious eye. "Know what I mean?"

"Yes. Yes, sir, I do."

"Room's yours as long as you make it so. Make it as easy on you as you do on me."

Arfel stepped to the right of Stump and walked back up the hall.

"Don't mean anything by it: but you're a bluesman and I'm a businessman. There's no argument I see on the subject."

"Of … of course there—of course not, Mr. Stump. There's no argument."

"You and Blue Fire taking a walk? Strolling around town?"

"Uh, need some air, Mr. Stump."

"What, Roadmap don't show you enough of this place?"

Roadmap, Arfel said to himself. *Roadmap must own the city, all of it, every square block of it!*

"Know little Roadmap showed you in, was the one to steer you over to Barrel Street in the first place, the Bluebird Bar. Take you and Blue Fire by the hand. That Roadmap—he don't miss nothing I seen yet."

"It was Roadmap all right, Mr. Stump. Who got us over on Barrel Street, all right, sir."

"Jump out from out one of them tall white buildings on Gate Street like it's Halloween. I know. Scared the living hell out you and Blue Fire." Then Stump's voice quieted. "Boy got him ten different hustles he run at the same time. Boy's a businessman. Knows how to turn a buck out on the streets—all right."

Arfel was at the hotel's front door.

"Have a good walk. You and Blue Fire now. Good day for it."

"Thanks, Mr. Stump."

"Ain't much for you to see around here. Ain't much to it. You know, things always look much different in a city at night. Man, ain't got to tell a bluesman that."

Stump walked away. And Arfel and Blue Fire didn't hear a piece or even a splinter of him or his wooden stump.

"Here he come. Tell you his knees rub together. Sound like sandpaper scratchin' 'gainst wood!"

Arfel heard Knock-Kneed Kirkland's knees rubbing together like sandpaper from the front of the Bluebird Bar's door until now, midway, as Knock-Kneed Kirkland kept walking across the Bluebird's floor just as Lemontree said he was.

"Know where he been past two nights, not that Knock-Kneed ain't gonna admit it. Tell the world." Pause. "Knock-Kneed shoots straight, Arfel. Don't try to sell you something you got." Lemontree's four fat fingers with the four fat diamonds led out to Knock-Kneed now, as they did with Arfel last night.

"Why—welcome back, Knock-Kneed. Welcome back to the fold. The Bird."

Knock-Kneed Kirkland was short and as alert as a cricket hiding somewhere in the corner of his plaid shirt's pocket ready to chirp. His stingy brimmed hat was squared snug to his head. Knock-Kneed Kirkland walked fast, excitedly, as if someone had struck a match and set his shoes on fire.

"Was at Miss Millie's. Admit it, Lemontree. Catting for two days. Admit it."

Arfel tried not to laugh, trying to convince Blue Fire to do the same.

"Had a need."

"Appetite. A appetite, Knock-Kneed, you mean. A appetite."

"Uh-huh—yeah—that too, Lemontree. That too."

"Better leave Miss Millie's girls alone."

"Would kill myself first. Swear to God. Ain't lying, Lemontree."

"You must look like hell screwing a woman, Knock-Kneed. You and them damned knock knees of yours!"

"Who's—"

"My name's Arfel," Arfel said, standing.

"Good thing Arfel showed up last night. Kept a seat warm."

"Arfel Booker—"

"And Blue Fire," Lemontree said.

Knock-Kneed Kirkland and Arfel shook hands.

"Hell of a blues player, bluesman, but you'll see, Knock-Kneed. Blue Fire, she plays pretty like she look. No ways different."

"Pleasure to meet you, Arfel. Guess you heard my name enough times from Lemontree by now to know it. Lemontree won't put it to bed."

"Wear it out, you mean. Not with them knock knees, Knock-Kneed, you sporting. Even your momma knowed you was born crooked when you come out the womb."

Arfel sat back down.

"So you come in from—"

"Who the hell cares," Lemontree said, cutting Knock-Kneed off. "Just glad Arfel come here. Showed up. Him and Blue Fire. Train don't skip over this stop." Knock-Kneed took a seat. "Wasn't up there last night," Lemontree said, looking at the chair Knock-Kneed was sitting in. "Right, Arfel?"

"No, it wasn't," Arfel replied, smiling.

"Know your schedule, Knock-Kneed. Just how long a night for you at Miss Millie's good-time house is. Don't set a chair out for you last night. Keep it down nailed to the floor."

Knock-Kneed Kirkland laughed. Knock-Kneed began settling in on the Bluebird stage. He took his guitar out its case. It was purple. It was as shiny as glass. "Call it Purple Poison, Arfel," Knock-Kneed said, looking at Arfel. "Ooomph, if she ain't in my blood!" And clamped to Purple Poison's corpus was a metal rack with two harmonicas attached to it.

"By the way, Arfel, forget to ask you: how it'd go with Stump this morning?"

"Couldn't go better, Lemontree."

"Stump, he ain't got much, but he don't show it. Work hard every day pretty much like he panning for gold. But nothing in that hotel, palace of his but hard work. About as good as it gets. Stump, he ain't no fool."

Knock-Kneed Kirkland was strapping Purple Poison across his chest. And then she was on it.

"So who brought you over, Arfel, Roadmap? To the Bird?"

(*Darn't!* Arfel fumed. If he heard Roadmap's name mentioned one more time. Maybe he should've paid Roadmap a quarter instead of a dime for the trip over. At least a quarter. At least that much, with little Roadmap being so world famous and all!) "Uh, yes, Knock-Kneed, uh, Roadmap. Roadmap."

"Loves the blues."

"Tell Arfel that, Knock-Kneed. Already tell Arfel—"

"Roadmap told me too," Arfel said.

"And little Roadmap got you to play for him on Blue Fire—on your way over?"

"Uh-huh."

"Roadmap knows the blues like he knows this here city, Arfel."

"Tell Arfel that too, Knock-Kneed," Lemontree grumped.

Knock-Kneed Kirkland pinched the hat's stingy brim. "See we've got us a little crowd forming."

Arfel didn't look out into the Bluebird Bar. Instead, his eyes shot down to Blue Fire in her case.

"Night's just beginning, Knock-Kneed," Lemontree said. "Night's just beginning."

"Uh-huh," Knock-Kneed Kirkland said, hitting a sweet lick on Purple Poison.

"Two nights away feels like two years sometimes, Lemontree."

"Yeah—don't it now. Don't it … to a bluesman."

The three guitars' twangs were in everybody's ears. The three guitars, Blue Fire, Sweet-Juice, and Purple Poison, were working out some blues melodies.

"Workin' on it. Workin' on it now, Sweet-Juice. Workin' on it now, baby!"

Arfel was twisting a spate of short, jagged notes out Blue Fire's strings. He was making each of those notes shout out sweet-as-peach pie hallelujahs on a blue sky Sunday morning.

"Mah mommah ain't ug-lee,
She jus' mean—
Daddy say she de meanes' ol' lady
He dun evah seen.

Say de debil showed up 'fore she was bo'n—
Say God don't even wannah touch 'er,
Leave mommah 'lone.

Oh mommah ain't ug-lee—
Say she jus' downright awful mean,

Daddy say meanes' ol' lady,
He dun evah seen.

Have children,
Say mah mommah have ten children,
Won't sell 'em back.
Raise every las' one a dem ten childrens,
In a wooden shack.
Oh Daddy work 'is farm from dawn tah dusk,
Ain't no white man in dis white worl'—
A colored man can trus'.

Make me blue, Mommah, dis big ol' worl',
Wannah die lak a man,
Not lak a girl.

Yah tell me, yah tell, me, mommah:
Lemontree, stan' up, stan' up tah de white man
Son, stan' yo'r groun'.
Did, Mommah, put dat white man six-foot undah,
Onlies' take one roun'.

Oh, Mommah, mah mommah ain't so ug-lee, ain't so mean,
Jus' don't yah go askin' dat white man—
Buried down in New Orleans!"

Lemontree then spanked Sweet-Juice's yellow wood with his hard,
heavy hand, and Knock-Kneed Kirkland pinched a long squeal out his
ten-holed harmonica like it was ripping the skin off a Missouri mule's
ass well before the poor mule was ever born.

"Aww … go on an' play, Arfel—
Uh, Blue Fire, Ah mean,
Left from home at sweet sixteen.

Left runnin' from sumptin',

Denis Gray

Damn, man, Ah don't know—
Maybe sick—sick, damned sick an' tired
Of being po'r.

Now, got me runnin' watah each mornin' tah wash down mah back.
Onlies' feel lak Ah'm still back home,
In mah mommah an' daddy raggity ol' shack.

Ten littl' childrens wit no shoes,
White man win,
Colored man lose.

Awww—go on, go on now—shush now, boy,
Ain't so bad,
Can't give yah nuttin'—
Yo'r daddy ain't had.

Awww ... go on now, shush, now boy—
You got too much to say,
Ain't so bad,
Heck, boy, yah got 'way.

'Cept white man follah yah no mattah where yah go—
Rain, sleet, hell, man—
Even run thru snow.
Ain't nuttin' funny 'bout it,
Onlies' gottah chuckle sometimes, man, gottah fun.
Say dat white man own 'im a piece of a hell,
How he make de sun.

Burn a colored man till he turn black,
Say how he own de worl'—
Say, white man ain't givin' it back!

Aww ... go on, Arfel, Blue Fire—Ah mean—
Left from home at sweet sixteen."

And Arfel was playing Blue Fire, putting some kind of mighty, hefty sound in her body; and there was so much to feel, so much to sing about from within himself, volumes and volumes. There was a silence now heard in the Bluebird Bar's patrons as their soaked, sweat-filled black bodies swayed elegantly, even if torn in some way, marred in some way, surviving in some way. The blues music all but fulfilling, hypnotic, when drunk in slow—when in no rush to push deep, far into the night.

"Aww … go on play, Arfel, Blue Fire—Ah mean. Go on an' play."

"Played the hell out the blues tonight!"

"Sure did, Lemontree. Sure did!" Last Round, the Bluebird's bartender, said, serving Lemontree, Knock-Kneed, and Arfel. Last Round was a big man (bigger than most). He was a bartender/bouncer for the Bluebird Bar (efficiently performing the two jobs for the price of one). With a strong voice and shoulders that could balance the world, his beard was thick enough to hide away a key.

"Yeah, was fryin' fish tonight, Last Round. Fryin' fish!"

Last Round winked at Arfel while handing him his glass of whiskey. "It's what Lemontree calls it, Arfel: 'frying fish.'"

"Don't know why, so don't ask me," Lemontree said with a big, pasty grin on his face. "Guess I just like me fried fish."

They all agreed.

Lemontree opened his mouth and pushed back his drink. Then he stood. He hitched his trousers. "Know where I'm going," Lemontree said matter-of-fact.

"To see the man. Get our money for the night," Knock-Kneed said.

"Three-way split tonight," Lemontree said like his wallet had already sprung a leak.

"Sounds like your shoes are pinching your toes, Lemontree."

"Don't it though, Knock-Kneed."

"But it's worth it," Knock-Kneed said, packing Purple Poison and his two harmonicas away for the night. "Man …" Knock-Kneed said, looking Arfel dead in the eye. "Ain't never played with a bluesman like you. How you play the blues. In all my young years. Tonight, it was worth every second of my time here in the Bird."

"Thanks, Knock-Kneed. Thank you. Thought the world of you too."

"Hell, thought them folk was never gonna leave outta here tonight."

"Do have to work, Lemontree."

"Sorry, but the 'man' ain't getting much work out them poor souls this morning, Last Round," Lemontree said, heading for the bar's back door. "Not the way they dragged their dead asses outta here!" Lemontree then went off to do his money business.

Both Arfel and Knock-Kneed were packed. Knock-Kneed carried his guitar case across his chest. It looked cumbersome on Knock-Kneed at first glance—but then it didn't. Knock-Kneed pointed his finger over to Last Round. "Lemontree should be walking through the back door …"

"Right about … now!" Last Round's voice blasted out from behind the bar.

And just like that, there Lemontree was walking like he had money jingling in both his pockets (not unless they had holes in them).

"Hell, we ain't rich, but we ain't gotta tell nobody—do we? Can live us another day!" Lemontree laughed.

Knock-Kneed was the first to get his money. "Lemontree, you sure you counted this out right? This is too much—"

"No, it's correct, stack out right, Knock-Kneed. Ain't no misfiguring involved," Lemontree said, shoving his money down inside his front pocket.

"But what about Arfel?" Knock-Kneed asked anxiously.

"Arfel's all right too. He—"

"Lemontree …" Knock-Kneed said doubtingly.

"Don't worry any, Knock-Kneed—gonna tell you all about it. Get around to it. Will, by golly."

Lemontree then gave Arfel his portion of the three-way split, and even Arfel was surprised by the amount of money, for it was more than what he'd received last night when it was a two-way split between him and Lemontree. "Are … are you—"

"Time to lock up, huh, Last Round?" Lemontree said. "And we holding you up."

"You know it's no bother, Lemontree."

They were at the Bluebird's front door. Last Round's keys clanged.

"Locked up the back door, don't you, Last Round?"

Last Round wrapped up every inch of Lemontree in a fond bear hug. "Practically every single night you ask me that same question, Lemontree. Since you been playing here at the Bird."

"Do … uh … don't I?"

"Uh-huh. You do," Last Round said.

"Hell, must be getting old. Yeah …" Lemontree paused. "That's it."

The three were strung across Barrel Street, right in the middle of it. There was no traffic out on the street. The open street was pretty much Lemontree's, Knock-Kneed's, and Arfel's to do with whatever they pleased.

"Now, Lemontree, about this money situation," Knock-Kneed said, turning to him.

"Said I was gonna tell you about it," Lemontree said, looking over to Arfel who was to the right of him, and not Knock-Kneed who, of course, had asked the question. (Lemontree was in the middle of Knock-Kneed and Arfel.)

"But at your own convenience, is that it, Lemontree?" Knock-Kneed kidded.

"Man, if you ain't one smart city boy who plays the blues!" The three kept walking along the length of Barrel Street like they owned it, like three blues kings. "Okay. Okay, Knock-Kneed, hear you breathing out loud. Your heart aspirating—if there's such a word."

"Be-because I still don't see how I'm carrying this loot in my pocket, Lemontree. It's still a mystery to me. Confounding as hell."

"And I'm gonna clear it all up for you, Knock-Kneed. Right now, on the spot." Lemontree looked over at Arfel. "There's a system, you see, Arfel. Every night, uh, every night I go out the Bluebird Bar's back door and over to one of them buildings in the back."

Arfel hadn't been in the back of the Bluebird Bar yet, so he wasn't familiar with the buildings Lemontree just referenced, this unknown territory.

"It's a system. Me and the man got a system."

Who? Arfel was wondering. *Who? What man?*

"Philander Prince is his name. He's white. Don't have to ask."

"Never, I've never seen him, Arfel. I—"

"'Cause we got a system, Knock-Kneed. We two. Philander Prince. Me and that white boy."

"He's young."

"Young enough for me to put across my knee and spank."

"And white, and his name is Philander Prince. It's all I know about him," Knock-Kneed said lamentably.

"'Cause he work it out with me. Nobody else. Exclusive. You know that, Knock-Kneed. Ring the outside bell to the building." Lemontree paused. "Tall, thin, ghostly white man, his 'man,' answer the door. Man look like white plaster. Fresh made. Ain't set for long, all right."

Arfel could see him, this white man who looked like fresh made white plaster, who hadn't set for long, who was tall and thin.

"He's the money man for Mr. Prince. Wears him white gloves—"

"Yeah," Knock-Kneed said.

"Knock-Kneed ain't never seen … Yeah, just me—but knows what he looks like. Met Philander Prince."

"Lemontree's one of the few in this city who has, Arfel."

"Yeah. We shake hands. Talk. Drink a glass of cognac. Act polite. Sociable."

"What … what did he look—"

"Loves the blues," Lemontree said, cutting Knock-Kneed off. "Don't ask me why that white man, why Philander Prince loves the blues. Don't," Lemontree said like he was stitching through the question himself. "Boy was playing classicals. Classical music when I seen him though. Ever hear you one of them records, Arfel? Classicals?"

"No, no, I haven't, Lemontree."

"Don't understand it none. Know them classicals don't understand the blues. So guess we even on that score."

"But Mr. Prince—"

"He was listening to them classicals when I visit him, Arfel, not the blues."

"J-just … just a white man … A white man listening to the blues …" Knocked-Kneed said.

70

"He got queer eyes, Arfel. Strange. Queer blue eyes. Maybe the boy gone crazy, why he listen to the blues." Pause. "Could be the only reason."

"And about the money tonight, Lemontree: how'd the money come out the way it did?"

"Loved it, Knock-Kneed! Knew there was three of us tonight—his man said. White man talk for a change to say Philander Prince 'love it.' So he put, uh, stick some extra dollars in there. In the white envelope his man gives me."

"Oh … so that's how—"

"Said whoever that new bluesman is, play good. 'Damn good!' his man said."

Arfel's skin stiffened like cowhide.

"See we at your stop, Knock-Kneed."

"Got here too fast tonight, Lemontree," Knock-Kneed said, looking over at Arfel. "See you tonight, Arfel. Blue Fire."

Arfel and Knock-Kneed shook hands. Knock-Kneed patted Lemontree's shoulder.

"Better remember who the boss is. Who the white man pay at the end of the night, Knock-Kneed."

Knock-Kneed made a turn onto Lime Street.

"Got him and Blue Fire all to myself!"

"*Shhh* … Lemontree," Knock-Kneed said, putting his finger to his mouth. "Before you wake up the whole block."

"Hell, won't be the first time!" Without skipping a beat, Lemontree turned to Arfel. "You know Roadmap drop by? You and Blue Fire know that, don't you?"

"We heard him, Lemontree. Had our eyes shut but heard him."

"Stayed—"

"For about an hour."

"Yeah, about that. What it was tonight." Pause. "Boy miss out on some of his hustles 'round here. His payroll ain't so hot tonight. Slender by his standards. Boy gonna have to make up for it tonight. But he know how. Figure it out, Arfel."

"I hope so."

"Guess Roadmap wanna see if you and Blue Fire was for real. Was no fluke. Real McCoy. Play the same as you do when he brung you over to Barrel Street, the Bluebird Bar, same as Philander Prince, the white boy was doing from last night, suppose. Know it was somebody new. Not Knocked-Kneed nor Purple Poison playin' in the Bird."

"Hope, hope me and Blue Fire passed the test, Lemontree. W-with R-Roadmap, that is. Lemon—"

"You do, Arfel. More than so. Roadmap don't usually stay so long. Fifteen, twenty minutes—most. Eliminate that kinda time out his hustle."

Arfel smiled.

"See why he stayed on, Arfel—Roadmap do."

"You, you do, Lemontree?"

"You running from something or somebody—ain't you? You and Blue Fire?"

Suddenly, Arfel's forehead was caked in sweat.

"You don't have to tell me what or who. Roadmap hear it, Knock-Kneed, Last Round … Philander Prince. Even the white man, the ghostly white man. The white man with the white envelope, his hand shaking. Shaking when he speak for Mr. Prince."

And as Lemontree talked, Arfel was shaking as if every tissue in him was in a state of alarm.

"It's your blues. Your blues. Ain't gotta talk about it, Arfel. But I heard it. You and Blue Fire was talking. It's your blues, all right."

"I am running from something, Lemontree. From some—"

"You don't have to tell me what or who, Arfel," Lemontree said, holding his hands square to Arfel's shoulders. "Man, it's just another thing you can put in the music. You own it. Nobody can take it from you and Blue Fire, Arfel. Ain't nobody can."

Minutes later.

"Now it's my turn to say good night." Pause. "Must've felt like a tourist today. Sightseeing and all."

"Yes, Blue Fire and me."

"Yes, Blue Fire and you." Pause. "Fun to poke through a city. Soul of one. One big as this. Least one time for now."

"C-certainly was, Lemontree. It—"

"But it grows on you, Arfel. Sweet-Juice'll tell you that, right,

Sweet-Juice?" Lemontree said, talking to Sweet-Juice who was out her case. "Start feeling like weeds after a while. 'Bout as pretty as it gets. As good."

Arfel and Lemontree shook hands. "White man. Listening to the blues. Owning a blues bar. Listening to classical music, classicals. Got a record ..."

Arfel listened to Lemontree's voice trail off.

"Uh ... whenever you and Blue Fire got the time. Arfel, wanna listen to it, classicals, you let me know," Lemontree said, walking away. "Philander Prince, he give me a copy for playing."

"Uh ... will do, Lemontree. Will do."

"White man must know something, feel something. Swear his hand was shaking like a St. Vitus Day dance with that white envelope in it. Thought the white man was gonna drop it. Out and out drop it, the way he was carrying on so at the time."

Arfel and Blue Fire were alone, walking toward Stump's Palace, their new home. "We did wail tonight, Blue Fire. Did make the blues ..."

And then Arfel didn't want to face the thought he was thinking, things that brought the blueswoman and the dead white man back to life. Arfel didn't want to think about those things. The night was moist like air remaking itself. It was like a screen where the fog had rolled in from the waters; and now the worst troubles could hide, roll off, then sleep inside a patched dream. Arfel and Blue Fire seemed to be floating in it, moving like ghostly images into a new tomorrow with each bright, new beat of their heart in tune.

"ZZZZZ. ZZZZZ. ZZZZZ."

Stump McCants was in the chair. His wooden leg was propped up on the wooden counter. Arfel looked at Stump and then up the stairs. "We can make it if we're quiet, Blue Fire. Man has a right to sleep. Especially a man who works as hard as Mr. Stump.

"Hear you nodding your head off, Blue Fire."

Arfel was tiptoeing across Stump's Palace's hotel's lobby floor when—

"Morning, Arfel."

"Oh ... good morning, Mr. Stump, sir."

"You and Blue Fire have a good night?"

Arfel had no way of knowing whether or not Mr. Stump's eyes were opened or shut, since he couldn't see him. "Yes, uh, yes, we did, Mr. Stump."

Stump's eyes were shut. "Good."

"Me and Lemontree and Sweet-Juice and Knock-Kneed and Purple—"

"*ZZZZZ. ZZZZZ. ZZZZZ.*"

"Pois ... Poison, Mr. Stump."

Arfel's head fell back on his shoulders, and his laugh soared up to the heavens, but quietly so. And then Arfel laughed more when that beautifully crafted wall clock on the desk counter's back wall gonged, and for Arfel it was the first he'd heard it gong with such delicate preciseness.

"Clock sounds so nice, Blue Fire. Ain't gonna disturb me or nobody else in the Palace. Rest of the guests in here. Nobody, Blue Fire."

Arfel was on the second-floor landing. "Blue Fire, there must be a trick to that. To how Mr. Stump does that so easy. Easy as cake." Arfel was making his way down the hall. "Probably doesn't know himself how he does it—or ... or if he does. So maybe we'd better not say anything, just might ruin it. Put a hex on it." Arfel popped his room light on. He looked around and then laughed. "Just like we left it, Blue Fire."

Then Arfel noticed something about himself: his body didn't feel tired. After riding in those wooden boxcars for so many days and nights, his body had finally recovered. Arfel went to the basin, ran the water, and splashed water on his face like fresh cologne. "It feels good, Blue Fire. Cold—"

And then he turned the faucet's other handle.

"And hot. Cold and hot water, Blue Fire. Cold and hot water."

Arfel walked over to the windows and pulled down the shades. Then, tired or not, he began the nightly routine of undressing. He was still going to crawl into that bed of his, he thought. What else was there to do at this hour? Especially at this hour.

"Feet even feel fine after all that walking this afternoon. Feet need exercise, that's for sure." Arfel had put Blue Fire down on the floor. He got up and turned off the light and then returned to the bed. (Expertly, he'd threaded through the dark.)

Arfel was in bed. His eyes stayed open, not tricking themselves by any thoughts of sleep. "Played tonight. We played the blues tonight, Blue Fire." Arfel savored his words like he'd unshackled them, freed them from a routine labor, had been born fresh and new to a new life.

But had he played Blue Fire and his blues too good tonight?

"T-the white man understood, Blue Fire. Even Mr. Prince, Philander Prince, a white man, paid extra for singing the blues—our ... our blues for him tonight. A, a bluesman's blues. He paid our rent for the next night. Mr. Prince—he knows that kind of blues, Blue Fire. T-the white man."

Arfel's eyes blew up. "And ... and his man, the man with the money was shaking. The white gloves, shaking." And then Arfel saw Lemontree's powerful black hand as it had mimicked the white man's when it'd shaken with the white envelope in it.

"The blues. The blues did that ... The blues did that." Arfel felt anguished. He could smell the bloodhounds' scent as he knew they must be smelling his, he thought. "Smell it, Blue Fire. Smell ..." And Arfel, who was in the middle of the big bed, scrambled to the side of it and grabbed Blue Fire off the floor. "Tell him too much. Tell too much to the white man already. H-he's listening, Blue Fire. White man's everywhere!"

And Arfel held on to Blue Fire, putting her beside him on the bed just in case the white man came to steal him away at night, or if he came to him in his dreams: ghostly white, bloodhounds' panting at the moon, hunting, finding, and a hanging—*yes*—a hanging tree for a nigga, a black man to hang from. Blue Fire would be there to protect him, save him, Blue Fire.

Yes, Blue Fire beside him on the bed.

Chapter 6

Two days later.

Roadmap was on Lincoln Street. He'd been over on Gates Street, but business was slow over there. Maybe it would pick up on Lincoln Street. It's how he'd figured it.

The weather was turning, but he had a jacket—Roadmap always had something; somebody would provide for him. But tonight, on Lincoln Street, he blew on his hands.

Last night he was at the Bluebird Bar. He had a hiding place there, a spot, not that Last Round would throw him out of the Bluebird. It's just that he liked sneaking in there and hiding. It was fun—more fun that way. But last night, in the Bluebird, he really stayed too long. He could've kicked himself in the pants for staying so long, but he couldn't help it, not the way Mr. Lemontree and Mr. Knock-Kneed (and especially Mr. Arfel) played the blues. Man, he'd thought at the time, *What blues!*

And the Bluebird Bar was acting crazy like he'd never seen it. *You'd thought those folk were in church around here!* he thought at the time.

From the first night he met Mr. Arfel and he pulled Blue Fire out her case, he was fascinated by her. He liked Sweet-Juice and Purple Poison, yes, for sure, but not like Blue Fire. "Boy, if she, if she ain't pretty!" Roadmap gushed, standing in the shadows of the building's tall doorway. "Boy, if Blue Fire ain't pretty!"

Then Roadmap blew on his hands again. It was the second night Mr. Arfel and Blue Fire had taken him away from his nightly hustle. The second time lasting longer than the first, much. But even later if he had wanted to kick himself in the pants, losing out on half his night's hustle, it was worth it.

Blue Fire shone. She outshone a blue diamond, a blue sapphire, Roadmap thought.

The lights at the Bluebird were but so strong, but Blue Fire shone. She'd shone when Mr. Arfel had first pulled her out the guitar case. She shone right then, in the night, he could see her shine. How pretty Blue Fire was. Now he wished he were a bluesman. "W-wish I was you, Mr. Arfel. Wish." He wished he had someone to hold on to. Someone like Blue Fire just to hold on to.

Roadmap blew on his hands. He wished he had someone to talk to. "Bluesman talks to his gui-tar. Know they do. I-I seen Mr. Lemontree, he talks to Sweet-Juice. Seen it. Seen it a lot. Know they do."

A friend. He wished he had a friend instead of knowing everybody and everybody knowing him. A friend. Someone he could trust. Not that people weren't good to him, not that they weren't. "Wish I was you, Mr. Arfel. Holding on to Blue Fire. Pl-playing Blue Fire, Mr. Arfel. Talking … talking to Blue Fire. Wish I was you, Mr. Arfel. W-wish it was so."

Fifteen minutes later.

It is slow going on Lincoln Street too, even slower than Gates Street. Things are slow all over. Ain't going over to Gates Street. Just a slow night around here, Roadmap thought.

But Roadmap knew where he was going to go. While he was traveling to his new destination, Roadmap pretended, at times, he was Mr. Arfel.

"Twang, twang …"

And singing one of Mr. Lemontree's songs.

"Twang. Twang.

"Sounding good.

"Twang. Twang.
"My woman done leave me,

Twang. Twang.

Take the firs' train outta town,
Don't leave me angry,
Jus' leave me down.

Now Ah gotta make my own bed in de mornin',
W'en Ah get out de rack—
'Cause dat girl a mine say, 'Lemontree—
Ain't comin' back!'

Twang. Twang.
Oh, Lordie, oh Lordie—
Can't cook nothin' dat Ah don't burn,
Jus' seem I ain't had me,
No time tah learn.

Guess Ah'll drink muddy watah—bettah dan dyin'—
Dat colored gal sure could cook,
Oooooo-we, man, sure ain't lyin'!"

Roadmap giggled.
"Know a lot of Mr. Lemontree's songs. A lot." Roadmap was always good at memorizing things. He'd just have to hear it once or twice, no more, and his mind would snap onto it, not letting it go.
Roadmap kept true to his course.
It's how his mind worked. He memorized the city in no time flat

when he got here and wore down a lot of shoe leather (which he couldn't afford), but he learned the city in no time flat. Knew there was going to be a white side of town and a colored side, but wasn't prejudice: he was going to learn both sides of town equally. He knew the white man's money felt just as good in his hands, sat just as high and proud in his pockets as a colored man's—didn't make any difference to him; wasn't going to be prejudice—couldn't afford it.

Was he afraid of the streets out there? No, maybe at one time, but not now. He knew the streets, everything there was to know. There were no surprises for him, not a one. He knew when something was a good or bad situation. He'd been robbed, snatched up by the night, its evil forces, his money taken from him. But he could hear feet now, even a bird's, hear things before they happened.

"Plus, I can run like hell!" Roadmap had told someone who'd inquired about his personal safety.

Roadmap knew the sounds and rhythms of the night. He was a good-enough fighter but wasn't big. But he didn't rely on his fighting, for at any time that could fail him. Roadmap relied on his mind, that wouldn't. He Could outsmart a wiry-haired fox and knew it.

Mr. Arfel and Blue Fire came back to mind.

"Ain't going by the Bluebird tonight, bad for business—even though business already bad. Take two nights off, and it's like I take a week. Nothing happening out here, Mr. Arfel, Blue Fire. Ain't got but two nickels to make a dime to show for the night." Roadmap was seeing his destination clearly, straight ahead of him. "Gotta put another dime in my pocket. Them two nickels. I … I know—feel awful skinny."

Roadmap wished he had someone to talk to besides himself. Someone like Blue Fire. "Like Mr. Arfel does."

Roadmap was there. He walked through the front door. "Hi there, Mr. Stump!"

"Roadmap!"

"Come looking for work, Mr. Stump."

"What you doing, Roadmap, slumming?"

"Yep. Business is slow over on Gates Street."

"You try Lincoln?"

"Slow there too. Bad all over. People around here must be taking the night off, Mr. Stump. Gotta be."

Stump rubbed his grizzled chin and pulled down on his slim-styled suspenders. "Yeah, Roadmap: business is slow over here too. The hotel business."

Oh, oh! Roadmap panicked: no work around here either!

"But there's always something to be done in a hotel, Roadmap."

(Phew!)

"I ain't saying that, now."

"Yes ... yes—I know you ain't, Mr. Stump. Know you ain't."

Stump then looked around, his face puzzled as if it were something it liked doing when it had contemplative issues reserved for profound thought such as this. "Polish. I got me some brass polish ... some-somewhere, Roadmap. Some-somewhere." Stump's face stayed puzzled. "Some damned where."

Roadmap certainly wished Mr. Stump would hurry up and find the polish before his face stayed contorted the way it was, permanently.

"Here—no, be right back, Roadmap. Right back."

"O-okay, Mr. Stump." Roadmap watched Mr. Stump go down the hall. Mr. Stump and his wooden stump. "Sure is quiet. Don't make no noise when he walks with that wooden leg, Mr. Stump. Do he? Might not hear him in the night, out on the streets. Don't know if I do. Trust to."

"Have it, Roadmap. Have it right here! You can get to work. Polish the hotel's brass. Needs polishing. Ain't had the time. Be honest with you—forgot all about it, not until now. Seem like I forget more things than I ... well ... oh well ... You've got you a job, Roadmap. Put together a few pennies for the—"

"A dime, Mr. Stump. A dime. Cost you a dime. Ain't working for nothing less, Mr. Stump."

"A dime?"

"Said a dime," Roadmap said, crossing his arms over his chest, stiffly.

"Ain't giving an old man a break? An old hotel keeper, huh?"

"Uh-uh," Roadmap said. His head shook back and forth.

"A businessman. A businessman."

"Yep, Mr. Stump: a businessman."

Roadmap took the rag and big can of polish from Stump.

"It's what I like about you, Roadmap. Boy, you know how to turn you a dollar all right!"

Roadmap held on to the can of polish and the rag good and tight.

It was close to twenty minutes later.

Stump was inspecting Roadmap's work. At the moment, Roadmap was working on the hotel's front door handles. "Good, Roadmap. Good work." Pause. "Except you miss you a spot back there."

"I did, Mr. Stump?" For the time being, Roadmap was down on his knees. He got up and followed Mr. Stump and his wooden leg down the lobby's hall.

"There. See."

"Uh … yes … yes, Mr. Stump. Sure do." Roadmap and his brass polish and rag got to work rubbing out the spot.

"My eyes ain't so bad …" Stump said as Roadmap worked. "After all, for an old coot, huh, Roadmap? It's just all these years of cleaning," Stump said. "Just see things, I suppose, most people don't."

Roadmap put one more dab of polish on the spot.

"Good, Roadmap. Good. Now you can get on back."

"Yes, Mr. Stump."

"If I find something new, I'll let you know." Stump laughed. "Gonna get my dime's worth of work out of you tonight, Roadmap. That's for sure."

Roadmap was halfway up the lobby's hall when he turned and said, "You're a businessman, Mr. Stump—true and true, Mr. Stump."

"What I am, Roadmap. Why, that I am."

And then the wall clock gonged.

"I love that clock when it—" And then Roadmap caught himself, for he knew what that meant!

"Roadmap, when was the last time I told you about me and that clock?" Stump said, speeding back to Roadmap on his stump.

"I ain't forgot, Mr. Stump. Not—"

"Me neither. Fight in that war, against them Nazis. And the first thing I see when I step through that front door to look at this big-shot hotel they was selling me, Roadmap, was a German clock!"

"Yes, yes, sir, Mr. Stump, sir ..."

"Knew it was German. Wanted to shoot the living hell out of it right then. The living ... Can't make no sense out of it. Why it was the first thing I seen." Pause. "All that killing. War. But then, I said, 'What's war got to do with making a clock lovely as that?' What, Roadmap? Tell me?"

"D-don't know, Mr. Stump, I-I don't," Roadmap said, shaking his head nervously, confused too.

"A German clockmaker made it. All I know. Or could be a Jew. Just know I don't know what the Palace would look like without it. Or sound for that matter."

Now Roadmap looked more confused than Stump.

It was much later in Stump's Palace.

"Man, if this ain't work!" Roadmap wiped his brow; sweat was pouring out his cap like a waterfall. "But I guess a dime's a dime. I set the price, gotta stick by it. Ain't gonna cheat on it. Nobody on it. Nowhere near."

Doggoneit! Roadmap thought: *he* would *like somebody to talk to, somebody like Blue Fire.*

"May—maybe a dog. It ain't gotta be a big dog," Roadmap said. Then quickly he cancelled that thought out his head. "Gotta feed a dog no matter how big. Walk a dog. Don't gotta feed a gui-tar. Maybe walk it. Like Mr. Arfel does, but a dog can eat what you don't already have—if you let it."

Roadmap was on the second floor. "Wonder what room Mr. Arfel and Blue Fire stay in?"

But for some reason he knew they stayed on the second floor in the Palace, but didn't know why.

"J-just feel you do, Mr. Arfel, Blue Fire. Got that feeling. Best rooms on the second floor. First floor ain't bad—but second floor's better. Way." Roadmap looked up and down the hall; the doorknobs were shining like mirrors, plus whatever other brass he saw. Roadmap puffed out his chest.

"Done me a fine job I know, Mr. Stump. Polish good," he said, shaking the can of polish directly above his head. "Real good," he said, shaking the rag the same way. "Now to collect my two nickels, or dime, however Mr. Stump's gonna pay me."

Roadmap made his way down the hall.

"ZZZZ. ZZZZZ. ZZZZZZZ."

He heard Stump at the top of the stairs.

"Know you sleeping, Mr. Stump. But I came collecting. Ain't coming back. Gonna have to wake you. Sorry, Mr. Stump. Sorry … but I need my dime tonight."

Roadmap was halfway down the stairs when the hotel's front door opened.

"ZZZZ. ZZZZZ. ZZZZZZ."

"Morning, Arfel."

"Oh, oh good morning, Mr. Stump."

"You and Blue Fire have a good night?"

"Yes … yes, we did, Mr. Stump, sir."

"Good."

"Me and Lemontree, and Sweet-Juice, and Knock-Kneed, and Purple—"

"ZZZZ. ZZZZZZ. ZZZZZZZ."

Arfel covered his mouth laughing. "Same old routine, Blue Fire. Every night with Mr. Stump. Seems like."

See, Roadmap said to himself, *Mr. Arfel talks to Blue Fire. See, told you so, Roadmap. Told you so!*

"Bed's gonna feel good tonight, Blue …" Arfel looked up the staircase. "Roadmap."

Roadmap came down the stairs. "Morning, Mr. Arfel."

Then it was as if Roadmap's eye had rounded Arfel's back. "Morning, Blue Fire."

Arfel saw the can of polish and the dirtied rag in Roadmap's hands. "Been working, Roadmap? Mr. Stump got you working in the Palace?"

Roadmap looked around the hotel broadly as if he were looking at something really spectacular. "Do all the hotel's brass, Mr. Arfel. Polish the brass around here. All of it, Mr. Arfel."

Arfel looked down as if he were looking at something really spectacular too. "A lot of brass, Roadmap. A lot."

"Y-you can say that again, Mr. Arfel."

Then both Arfel and Roadmap looked at the stairs. Arfel was the first to sit, and then Roadmap. Roadmap sat one step above Arfel. "I'm awful tired too, Roadmap." Pause.

"Uh, but you don't come by tonight. By the Bluebird."

"It's why I'm working for Mr. Stump tonight, " Roadmap said businesslike. "Gotta make up for lost time. Uh, some."

"You were at the Bluebird a long time last night, Roadmap."

"Yep, and it was bad for business."

Long pause.

"You talk to Blue Fire, don't you, Mr. Arfel?"

"Uh-huh."

"Know you do. Know you do before I seen you from up top the stairs tonight, Mr. Arfel. Caught you doing it."

"Yeah, Roadmap, all bluesmen do, talk to their instruments like they're gonna talk back."

"Ever do, Mr. Arfel?" Roadmap giggled.

"Only when we play them, Roadmap. Talk up a storm then."

"Yes … I know, Mr. Arfel." Roadmap was looking down at Blue Fire lying in her case. "Got a lot on their minds, Mr. Arfel," Roadmap sighed. "Wish I had somebody to talk to."

"You get lonely, don't you, Roadmap?"

Roadmap seemed to be reining in his tears. "Yes … uh … sometimes, Mr. Arfel. Uh, sometimes."

"I know, Roadmap. I—"

"But I ain't complaining, Mr. Arfel. Ain't."

Arfel looked at Roadmap's cute brown-skinned face. "No, no—I know you ain't, Roadmap."

"But I was thinking tonight, ain't gonna try to fool you about that, Mr. Arfel. Was thinking tonight of Blue Fire. Of having somebody like Blue Fire to talk to. I was Mr. Arfel—truly was.

"Talk, talk to her a lot, don't you, Mr. Arfel?"

"A lot, Roadmap." Arfel laughed. "Knows all my problems, heartaches, and all the good that happens."

"It's why she plays the ways she does, Mr. Arfel. Blue Fire listens."

Roadmap stood. "Gotta go, Mr. Arfel."

Arfel was going to say, "Where to?" But realized Roadmap knew. "Yeah …"

"But first, gotta collect my money from Mr. Stump."

"ZZZZ. ZZZZZ. ZZZZZZ."

"Mr. Stump worked me hard, Mr. Arfel," Roadmap said, seeming not to forget. "To the bone."

Arfel stood.

Roadmap was moving toward Mr. Stump whose wooden stump was propped up on the wooden desk counter.

"Uh … Roadmap, don't wake him," Arfel said as Roadmap was about to tap Mr. Stump's shoulder. "Don't wake Mr. Stump."

Roadmap turned. "No, Mr. Arfel?"

"Let Mr. Stump sleep. Can only catch it when he can." Arfel's hand dipped inside his pocket. Roadmap was standing beside him, now. "How much Mr. Stump owe you?"

"Dime, Mr. Arfel. Dime. Don't matter how you pay it—two nickels, a dime—ten pennies, whatever. Don't matter."

"Got two nickels."

"That's fine, Mr. Arfel. Fine by me." And politely Roadmap's tweed cap came off his head as if he were tipping it to gentry. Two nickels then dropped down into Roadmap's cap for payment. Then the cap returned to Roadmap's head, the cap's bill rolled up tight like a newspaper. "Thank you, Mr. Arfel."

"You're welcome, Mr. Roadmap."

Both laughed at their little untitled act.

"Well … see you at the Bluebird tonight, Roadmap?"

"Maybe, maybe, Mr. Arfel." Pause. "Hear … hear me, don't you, Mr. Arfel? You and Mr. Lemontree?"

"Uh … feel you, Roadmap. More like we feel you."

"Know it, Mr. Arfel. Know it the moment I get in there. Can't hide from a bluesman any."

"Uh-uh," Arfel said, turning himself to the stairs and then back around again. "Ain't worth trying."

"K-know I can't. Not a blues …"

And Roadmap had disappeared, was gone, back on the road, making tracks.

Roadmap was out on the streets traveling along his turf.

This was a new day; but he was still angry with himself, steamed, since all the work he'd done for Mr. Stump, he should've charged him a quarter—at least that much! He knew he sounded like an ingrate, but Mr. Stump had worked him last night like nobody's business. The job was worth at least a quarter, nothing less. The next time he did business with Mr. Stump and Stump's Palace, he was going to find out what kind of work he had in mind. Mopping and sweeping was different from polishing brass, especially how Mr. Stump wanted the brass polished in Stump's Palace.

Roadmap rolled his cap's bill. "Busy night tonight. Real busy."

Roadmap was on Dempsey Street, and then Arnold Street. "Gotta keep a good pace: don't wanna get behind."

And before long, before Roadmap knew it, he was at the top of Barrel Street; and the blues music drifting out the Bluebird Bar was filling Roadmap's ears like angels in blue-painted faces. Roadmap couldn't get over to Michael Street if he tried. His body leaned in one direction but lured him in another. Roadmap's brown shoes kicked the curb.

"Darn't! Darn't!"

It was all Roadmap could say as his body began moving down the street about as fervidly as the blues Roadmap was hearing being played out the Bluebird Bar by Lemontree and Arfel and Knock-Kneed, lifting his spirits with ease.

"Oh … Blue Fire …" Roadmap said once he was in the Bluebird Bar, in his hiding place from where Lemontree and Arfel could feel him. And Roadmap heard the blues being played stronger, more powerfully than before on Sweet-Juice and Purple Poison and Blue Fire, as if a great tidal wave had risen above the world's head and was washing it clean.

"Blue Fire … Blue Fire …" Roadmap's eyes were closed as he talked to Blue Fire as Blue Fire was talking to him. Blue Fire had listened to him just last night when he sat down on the staircase in Stump's Palace just above her telling her secrets he'd only confessed to himself—secrets Blue Fire now played on the Bluebird's bandstand before a packed blues crowd.

Chapter 7

Miss Millie's body could fill out a tub.

But Miss Millie was wearing a very chic white dress of the highest quality and design. Miss Millie always wore a white silk dress of the highest quality and design with a white silk sash bordering its middle with a blue-and-white carnation tucked into it. Miss Millie was up on the third floor of the building's three-floor walk-up. Miss Millie's voice was rollicky, uncultured when she spoke.

"Told you not to wear that color, Venia. That it clash too much with them evil eyes of yours."

"Miss, Miss Millie …" Venia, one of Miss Millie's working girls, said demurely. "I ain't evil—just don't take no shit from nobody!"

"Sounds like evil to me. Life's full of that four-lettered word."

Miss Millie didn't curse, not unless she had to. "Well … change anyways, and maybe business will pick up on your end. Your night's worth."

Miss Millie was playing a record. It was a blues record. She liked the blues. "Mmm … Mmmm …" Her lips pressed together, and she was singing along with the music, but then stopped. "Don't know how to sing any of them blues songs good, but they sure do know how to mess with me." Miss Millie was making her way down to the second floor, but who should be running up the stairs at breakneck speed but Roadmap.

"Evening, Miss Millie!"

And who should be right behind Roadmap but Serena. Tall, dark, lusty, tasty-looking Serena, one of Miss Millie's working girls.

"Running to me or away from Serena, Roadmap!"

"T-to you, Miss Millie. To you, ma'am!"

"Thought so," Miss Millie said, casting a stony glare at Serena. "'Cause Serena knows the rules around here. Don't you, Serena? Girl!"

Serena began backing down the stairs, her long, sweet-looking black legs. "Yes, Miss Millie. Yes—I know the rules around here, ma'am," she said defeated.

"So get back to what you was doing. I ain't got to tell you."

"Yes, ma'am."

"Come on up, Roadmap," Miss Millie said, deciding to go back up to the third floor and not down to the second.

Roadmap was leaning on the banister. It was rickety.

"Before you fall over and sue me!"

"Not you, Miss Millie. Not you, ma'am," Roadmap said, scampering up the stairs behind Miss Millie who could hide him well from the front. Miss Millie stood off by a door which was shut, and some man's and woman's low moans came from out of it; even the blues music on the floor couldn't flatten them.

"Maybe we oughta ..."

"Used to them, Miss Millie," Roadmap said, acknowledging Miss Millie's discomfit.

"Uh ... uh, sure you is, Roadmap. But still ..."

"It's okay, Miss Millie. It is, ma'am."

Both moved farther back, closer to Miss Millie's room. Her bedroom door was shut (it's where the blues music came from).

"Come to work, Miss Millie," Roadmap announced.

"Heck, honey, I know that. It's all you know to do, Roadmap."

"Ain't complaining."

"Wasn't saying that you was."

"Work for Mr. Stump last night."

"What kind of work Mr. Stump have you do around the Palace?" Miss Millie asked facetiously. She pivoted her weight daintily.

"Brass, Miss Millie. A mile of brass. A ton of brass. Polish brass in Mr. Stump's hotel all last night, ma'am. Seeing brass. Dreamed nothing but brass last night. See it this morning. Nothing but brass all day." Pause.

"Uh, you ain't got brass to shine, do you, Miss Millie?"

Miss Millie fluffed her silver-white wig. "No, can't say I do, Roadmap."

"Thank you, Miss Millie. So much, ma'am."

"Mr. Stump worked you that hard, huh?"

"Yep, like a mule, ma'am. My tongue hanging out. Should've been there. Mr. Stump get every penny's worth of work out of Roadmap last night, all right." Roadmap looked at Miss Millie. "Mind if I ask, ma'am?"

"Ask what, Roadmap? You always polite in asking."

Roadmap looked Miss Millie up and down. "How many of them white dresses you got?"

Miss Millie laughed riotously. Her hand went to the door handle. She opened her bedroom door. "Come in, Roadmap."

"Never been in your bedroom, Miss Millie!"

"Know you ain't."

Roadmap was breathless. Fancy furniture, fancy drapes, fancy rugs, fancy wigs were in Miss Millie's bedroom. "It ... it ..."

"It's pretty, ain't it, Roadmap?"

"Yes ... yes—it's, it's what I was about to say, Miss Millie—pretty. Pretty. Ain't ... ain't ..."

"I know, Roadmap. You ain't never seen you no room quite like this one before. Not like mine. Uh-uh. Miss Millie's room."

"Never, Miss Millie. No wonder you don't show it off none. To nobody. I- I wouldn't either if I had me a room like this room, ma'am."

Miss Millie went over to the bed. Her hand touched the bed's silk bedspread.

"Private, Miss Millie."

"Private. Yes, private, Roadmap. I agree."

"Sleep good in that bed, I know."

"Like a dream."

"Soft, Miss Millie?"

"Soft as cotton, Roadmap." Miss Millie's hand pressed down on the bed. "Come over, Roadmap."

Roadmap did so cautiously.

"See …" Miss Millie said, pressing down on the bed again.

She took his hand. "You can press down on it, honey, if you want."

"Soft, Miss Millie. Uh-huh. M-miss, MISS MILLIE!" Roadmap squealed. Miss Millie had pushed him down on top of the bed.

"Knew you wasn't gonna get on it otherwise!"

Roadmap was scrambling to get off the bed, but Miss Millie's large hands braced him. "You already mussed it, Roadmap. I know domestic, honey. Worked as one. Know how to fix a bed. Lay back, Roadmap. Relax. Ain't but one of this kind. Only but one in the world. Miss Millie have it customed built according to her exact taste and design."

Roadmap lay back on Miss Millie's bed. "Like it, Miss Millie. Ma'am … do I."

Miss Millie stood before her long closet, parting its doors. "See, Roadmap!"

"Betcha you got a thousand of those white dresses. A, why, a thousand of them!" Roadmap was straightening himself out on the bed, rolling his cap's bill.

"Not a thousand, Roadmap."

"But pretty near, Miss Millie, I bet." Pause. "Why white, Miss Millie? Why you wear white dresses. Always wear white dresses around here, ma'am?" Roadmap was off the bed.

"Don't know why. Them women, white women I used to scrub for they wear white. Bright dresses. It's what I remember most. Alla them. I wash for them white women, Roadmap. Wash white dresses back to white."

Roadmap was busy. He was cleaning out one of Miss Millie's rooms. He heard the moans and sometimes grunts from both sides of the room's wall. He knew what the people in both of the rooms did.

He'd seen them. *Yeah, he'd seen them*, Roadmap thought. He'd opened doors in Miss Millie's good-time house. But nobody saw him or caught him. And he saw things. Like naked men and naked women. He saw what their bodies looked like naked. He saw how they moved when they did something he'd never done but wanted to so badly. He liked peeking but didn't do it often since he wasn't to get caught. And of course Miss Millie didn't want him to go near those rooms, even if she knew he did.

Roadmap had a broom and was sweeping and tidying the room. In the morning, this was Mr. Jack's job, but Miss Millie said she would find something else for Mr. Jack to do tomorrow. There was always something in Miss Millie's good-time house to do.

Roadmap, while sweeping, thought of one of Mr. Lemontree's blues songs. And like magic, the broom handle became Blue Fire, and Roadmap was ready with a song to sing, but reservedly so.

"Twang. Twang.

Got de blues, baby,
Don't know why,
Maybe 'cause my mule Nellie—
Go off an' die.

She don't complain, laugh sum—
Don't know nothin' 'bout dyin',
W'en it cum.

Funny, Nellie grunt one time 'fore she go,
Don't know if she sayin' good-bye—
Or sayin' hello.

Blues talk tah me, don't let me cry—
Dink ol' Nellie—
Was sayin' good-bye.

Twang. Twang."

Roadmap had his eyes shut as he began to hum the blues. But suddenly Roadmap heard the room's door open and then as suddenly close. His eyes popped open wide when he saw—

"Miss Serena!"

Tall, dark, lusty, tasty-looking Serena was in the room, her back against the door. "Thought I heard you, Roadmap. Thought it was you w-who come through."

"Y-yes, it was me, Miss Serena. M-me. C-cleaning up for Miss Millie, m-ma'am." Roadmap was sweating from out both sides of his tweed cap.

"Like it when you clean up for Miss Millie—when you come around, Roadmap," Serena said, her back not coming off the door. Serena's hand brushed at her long black hair. "Work better than Mr. Jack, know that, Roadmap. For a fact."

Politely, Roadmap nodded.

"Uh-huh, like it when you come around, Roadmap. Pretty young boy like you."

Suddenly Roadmap realized he had the broom in his hand. "Uh … better get back to sweeping, uh … uh, Miss Serena, ma'am. Uh, yeah. My sweeping, Miss Serena. D-duties. Miss Serena."

It's when Serena undid herself from the door. She walked over to the bed that wasn't as big as Miss Millie's but big enough.

Roadmap tried not to look at her but couldn't help but to.

Serena sat on the bed. She lifted her left leg, and all Roadmap saw was flesh. "Work hard, don't you, Roadmap?" Serena asked. Her hand brushed through her long black hair again.

Roadmap turned his back to her. He began sweeping hard with the wooden broom. Roadmap swept with a dedicated vengeance, keeping his head down and his eyes locked tightly to the floor. "E-every day, Miss Serena, ma'am. E-every day."

"Me too, Roadmap. Mostly laying on my back though. Hear them, don't you, Roadmap?"

Roadmap looked up from the floor. He nodded.

"You know what I do …" Serena said, making herself more contented on the bed. "Hear them moans. Know you peek. Seen you, Roadmap."

Roadmap gulped.

"Know you seen my body for a fact too. A lot, Roadmap. Seen my body, Miss Serena's body a lot."

Roadmap had a sick, frightened look on his face.

Serena's body was spread out on the bed. Then her long black body curled like a lazy cat in the sun. "Like it, don't you, Roadmap? Like it when you see it, d-don't you?"

Roadmap pouted.

"Say you do. Like Miss Serena's body. S-say you do, Roadmap. Say it, say it, say—"

"Y-yes, Miss Serena. Yes, yes, I do, I do."

"You never …"

"No, Miss Serena. No, ma'am. I-I don't."

"Not once?"

"No, no, Miss Serena. N-not once. No, no time …"

"Thought not," Serena said, yawning and then covering her mouth languidly. "Was a virgin your age too, Roadmap. Was," Serena said wearily. "But it ain't nobody's business what I do now. None, Roadmap," Serena said, her eyes lighting back up. "Or how much Miss Millie pay me. Between Miss Millie and me."

And then Serena eyed Roadmap and hard. "Come … come here … Roadmap. Come … here."

"Do I, do … do I have to, Miss Serena, ma'am?" Roadmap asked respectfully. "Ain't supposed to be in here—you know that. If Miss Millie catch you …"

"Come here. Come here to Miss Serena Roadmap."

And now Roadmap was advancing toward Serena.

"And the broom, you can put it, rest it against the wall easy, honey. That broom of yours. Ain't gonna need it, uh-uh …"

Roadmap did put the broom against the wall.

"Ain't gonna hurt you. A-ain't gonna do nothing bad to you, Roadmap. I'm gonna love you, Roadmap—what I'm gonna do, honey. What."

Roadmap shut his eyes as if in a trance, his whole body relaxing. He felt a sudden surge of exquisite exhilaration penetrate his pants. "Y-yes, Miss Serena, m-ma'am."

"Want your first time to be with me, Roadmap. With Miss Serena.

Ain't gonna hurt you. Do nothing bad to you. Nothing you won't want to remember."

Suddenly, Roadmap felt Miss Serena's hands touching on him. "First your cap, Roadmap. Gonna take your cute cap off for you. Your head."

"Thank you, thank you, ma'am." Roadmap felt his tweed cap come off his head.

"Then your shirt, Roadmap. Off that tiny chest of yours."

Roadmap felt Miss Serena's light fingers undo his four shirt buttons.

"Now for your pants, Roadmap. These tight pants of yours."

"Thank you, thank you, Miss Serena," Roadmap said, his knees knocking together and then stopping before Serena began removing his pants: Roadmap hoping Miss Serena hadn't heard them—his knees.

Then Roadmap heard his belt strap slip from around his waist. Roadmap's blood was at a boil.

He felt his pants slip off his waist.

He heard Miss Serena giggle as he stepped out his trousers.

"See you *is* ready, Roadmap. Oh ... is you, Roadmap. Is you ..." Miss Serena said, looking at the small but decisive bulge straining itself inside Roadmap's underwear.

"Yes ... yes, Miss Serena. Y-yes, ma'am—I-I is, ma'am." Roadmap, whose eyes were still shut, began imagining how Miss Serena's black body looked the times he saw it in wild motion: long, strong, lean—her jutting breasts.

Roadmap heard Miss Serena more, getting herself prepared.

"Look at me, Roadmap. L-look ..."

And it's when Roadmap opened his eyes, and there Serena was on the bed: naked.

"You're beautiful, Miss Serena! B-beautiful, ma'am!" Roadmap gulped loudly.

Her eyes shut with a sweet grace. And Roadmap climbed on top of the bed, moving toward this beautiful woman who breathed comfortably through her opened mouth. She shook her long black hair, letting it mess her face. Her eyes peeked through the screen of hair like cat eyes. Serena began crawling forward on her hands and knees, and her hands began to pull down Roadmap's underwear.

"SERENA!"

"MISS MILLIE!"

"MISS MILLIE!"

Roadmap jumped off the bed, pulling up his underwear.

"Damn you, girl!"

Serena grabbed her dress off the bed.

"If I didn't know you was up to no good. If I didn't know!" Miss Millie flew across the room. "Get out! Get out! Get out my house. You're fired! Fired!"

"But, Miss Millie. Miss—"

"Get out! Get out I said!" Miss Millie was shaking badly.

Serena was shaking.

Roadmap was shaking.

"Out the house! Out the house!"

"O-okay, Miss Millie. Okay." And then Serena looked at Roadmap. "He … he had to learn from somebody, Miss Millie," Serena said, brushing past Miss Millie. "Somebody was gonna teach Roadmap."

"Not in my house he don't!"

Serena said no more; she just made her way out the door.

Roadmap stood against the wall frozen.

Miss Millie wrung her hands. "Can't trust you, Roadmap. Can't …"

Roadmap was afraid to say anything.

"Girls tell me how you peek in the rooms. They know but don't say nothing to you, but me. But I don't say nothing to you—you a boy, Roadmap. A, a little boy. You curious. All children are. Just is by, by nature." Miss Millie walked over to the bed. She sat down on it. She looked at Roadmap.

"Probably my fault anyways. Don't belong in here, Roadmap. In a good-time house. You coming and going in here." Pause. "But you got to make it just like I do when I was on my own. On the streets. Same as Serena. Same as all the other girls who work in Miss Millie's house. Ain't nothing to be proud of, what we do—but this old world ain't making my bed easy. No softer to sleep in."

Roadmap came from off the wall. "D-don't fire Miss Serena, Miss Millie, wasn't her fault, ma'am."

"You don't tell me what …" And then Miss Millie stopped when she felt Roadmap's hand touch hers.

"Wasn't nobody's fault, Miss Millie."

"No, never have no children, Roadmap. Guess God plan it that way. Live a hard life. No, ain't much different from what you're living, Roadmap. But for a colored woman, like I said, it ain't much more than this. What I got to show here."

"I-I know, Miss Millie."

Miss Millie got up off the bed. She began walking toward the room's door. "Now you get back to work, Roadmap. I'm still paying you. You still working for me. You still got a dime coming."

Roadmap grinned. "Y-yes, Miss Millie, ma'am. I sure am. You sure are. Uh, yes, Miss Millie. Yes, ma'am. Sure. Sure."

Minutes later, Miss Millie came back into the room. "Everything's fine, Roadmap. Between me and Miss Serena. Okay now, honey."

Roadmap was mopping. The floor was damp. He and the mop strings were moving out the room.

"Be in my room, Roadmap. You can come for the money there, when you put everything back in the closet."

"Uh … uh, yes, Miss Millie. Be right there …" Roadmap said, his small body, with his cap back on his head, working like a demon, whipping the mop back and forth over the floor in exact tune with his backside.

Miss Millie was grooming one of her wigs (a shiny red one), when she heard a tap on her door.

"Uh, it's me, Miss Millie."

"Know it is, Roadmap. Well … come in."

"Yes, ma'am." Roadmap stepped into the room for a second time tonight.

"Finished, Miss Millie. And put everything away in the closet, where it belongs."

"Mr. Jack should be so good. Gotta stay on that man day and night to do right."

Blues music was filling the room. "Know somebody who plays better than that, Miss Millie. Do."

Miss Millie stopped brushing the shiny red wig.

"Know him good, ma'am. Plays at the Bluebird."

Miss Millie was about to open her mouth—

"Mr. Arfel and Blue Fire."

"Heard of them, Roadmap. Mr. Knock-Kneed told Miss Sandra about them the other day. Was about to mention their names. Arfel and uh—"

"Blue Fire, ma'am. Blue Fire." Roadmap's body began to really vibrate. "Play good, Miss Millie. Real good."

"I see they do, Roadmap," Miss Millie said, seemingly using Roadmap's body as a guide.

"Love Mr. Arfel, Miss Millie—but, but you should see Blue Fire, Miss Millie!"

"Prettier than Mr. Knock-Knee's Purple Poison? Mr. Lemontree's Sweet-Juice?"

"Yep, prettier, way prettier, Miss Millie." Pause. "Sings to me. All the time. Love the blues, Miss Millie." Pause. "Wish I was a bluesman. Just wish it. But can't sing nothing worth nothing, Miss Millie."

"Got me a tin ear too, Roadmap. Ain't no better. Can't hear nothing good beyond a good scream or a belch."

"You bad off as me then, Miss Millie."

"Yeah, Roadmap, we wind up on the same scrap heap. Paddling in the same boat. Heading down the same sorry stream."

"Sorry. Sorry about before, Miss Millie."

"Said what I had to say, Roadmap, before. Ain't gonna preach. Sermonize. Never been in my nature to."

"Want to apologize though—proper, ma'am."

"Accepted." Pause. "Guess if I was a mother, had me a young boy like you, Roadmap, wouldn't want him to learn about sex that way. In a good-time house."

"No, Miss Millie?"

"Uh-uh, Roadmap. Even though it's done all the time. So much of the time."

"Know that, Miss Millie."

Miss Millie stepped away from her collection of wigs out on the table. "You know a lot, don't you, Roadmap? Street teach me the same way, honey."

"Ain't complaining though, Miss Millie."

"No, no, me neither, Roadmap," Miss Millie said, sitting atop the bed.

"Soft, Miss Millie. The bed. It's soft. Sure is soft. It is."

Miss Millie motioned for Roadmap to come join her on the bed. Roadmap did.

"You don't have many friends, do you, Roadmap?"

"Don't have to, Miss Millie. Don't see any reason why I should."

"Me either, Roadmap. Not in this business I run."

"You're the boss, ma'am"

"Uh—yes, yes, I'm the boss all right."

"Gotta make sure everything comes out all right at night. The money and, and all."

"Yes, Roadmap, it's what Miss Millie has to do."

Roadmap looked at Miss Millie soulfully. "Sleep okay in this big bed, Miss Millie? Alone?"

"Oh … Roadmap, you do understand don't you, honey? You do, don't you?"

"The blues playing through me, Miss Millie. The blues always playing through me. Get sad sometimes—but I-I …" Roadmap withdrew his eyes from Miss Millie.

"Sing you a song, Miss Millie," Roadmap said excitedly. "Sing you a song, if you like!" Roadmap hopped off the bed.

Miss Millie slapped her hands together.

"Sing you one a Mr. Lemontree's songs—if you like!"

"Yes. Yes, Roadmap. Yes!"

Roadmap struck a pose. "Pretend, pretend I'm Blue Fire, Miss Millie. In, in the Bluebird. Just pretend, ma'am."

"She's pretty like you say, Roadmap?"

"Prettier than that, Miss Millie. Blue Fire's prettier than what I say." Roadmap paused to reposition himself. "So … so you pretending—right, right, Miss Millie?"

"Oh, I'm pretending all right, Roadmap." Pause. "Got my eyes locked shut, don't I?"

"*Twang. Twang.*

"Playing on Blue Fire, Miss Millie. I'm playing on Blue Fire now. At present. Right now. Present time.

"*Twang. Twang.*

"That's Blue Fire playing, Miss Millie, ma'am."

"*Twang. Twang.*

"'Course Blue Fire sounds better than that."
"Of course, of course," Miss Millie said.

"*Twang. Twang.*

"Much better.

"*Say Ah ain't hun-gry, baby,*
Just ain't ate.
Don't seem lak Ah can keep
Mah money straight.

Ain't ate no human food since,
Two sunups an' two sundowns—
Say mah stomach ain't growlin',
Say it jus' kickin' 'roun'.

Momma, she ain't wid me,
Momma's ol' pots an' pans—
Been out here scufflin',
Doin' de bes' Ah can.

But ain't goin' hun-gry,
Uh-uh—not fer 'nother day.
Gettin' rid a dat gray cloud,
Pushin' it on its way.

'Cause seen me a big ol' bullfrog,
Jumpin' out the lake.
Say a bullfrog leg tasty,
Say—it just ain't steak!

"Twang. Twang."

Miss Millie's eyes rang with laughter.

Roadmap was still stuck in his pose. Roadmap's hand gripped the cap's bill. Then he rubbed his stomach and licked his lips—he started back up singing.

"Twang. Twang.
Bullfrog's legs sure is good,
Wid a bottle a barbecued sauce.
Lemontree show that frog leg
Who was boss!
(OUCH! Help … help me, Jesus!)

Littl' tough in de middle,
Got a salt it down jus' right.
Slow-cook it in a big ol' pot a hot water—
Overnight.

Now frog legs on mah menu,
Six says a de week.
Why—eatin' me a barbecued frog leg now,
As we speak!"

Miss Millie was rolling with laughter on top of the bed. Tears ran out her eyes. "May-maybe you are a blues singer after all, Roadmap. May-maybe, honey."

"Uh-uh, Miss Millie, only Mr. Lemontree and Mr. Arfel."

"Guess so, Roadmap. Probably so."

"You should come by the Bluebird Bar, Miss Millie. Take a night off.

Know you work all the time—but just to see Blue Fire. Let somebody else run this place for the night. See for yourself, ma'am."

Pause.

"Surprised, uh … this Mr. Arfel—he ain't dropped by here, Roadmap. Miss Millie's good-time house. For one of the girls. How long you say he's been here in town?"

Roadmap grinned winningly. "Long enough, Miss Millie."

"Ain't got no needs? Hmmm …" Long pause. "He is a man, ain't he, Roadmap?" Miss Millie laughed innocently, then suspiciously.

"True and true, Miss Millie. Mr. Arfel's a man true and true, ma'am. Can't say he ain't."

"Then I'll see him if he stays around here long enough. Come by for one of the girls. If you say he's a man."

Roadmap sat back down on the bed. "Soft. Can't get over how soft it is, Miss Millie," Roadmap said, touching the bed expertly now. "Miss Millie …" Roadmap yawned as wide as his mouth allowed. "Can I …"

"Stay the night, Roadmap?"

"Yes, Miss Millie, ma'am."

"Ain't done it for a while."

"Uh-uh, ain't. My office is quiet. You know where the cot is."

"In the closet."

"Uh-huh. Just pull out the cot, Roadmap. Still folded up in there, away good, honey."

Roadmap got up off the bed. "Hate to leave it, Miss Millie."

Miss Millie thumped the bed once, and then two more times. "*Is* soft."

"Cot gonna feel good though. Real good." Roadmap looked around Miss Millie's fancy room one more time.

"Who do the cleaning in here, Miss Millie, Mr. Jack?"

"No. Don't have nobody clean in this room but me. Mine to do, honey. For my own self."

Roadmap started for the door. "Good night, Miss—"

"Ain't you forgot something, Roadmap?"

"*Oops!*" Roadmap said, closing his mouth, knowing he'd erred.

Miss Millie leaned over to her nightstand. "Laid it out for you, Roadmap."

"What, two nickels, Miss Millie?"

"Two nickels, Roadmap."

"Rub two nickels together to make a dime." Politely Roadmap removed his hat. Miss Millie dropped the two nickels in her hand down into the hat.

"Thank you, Miss Millie."

"Don't work you as hard as Mr. Stump do, do I, Roadmap?"

"Uh-uh. Not hard like that: not like a mule," Roadmap said stubbornly. "A old mule, ma'am!"

Roadmap was putting his cap back on his head, and he was putting the two nickels away in his pocket—mixing them with the others. "Gonna get details on Mr. Stump next time I work for him. Details, Miss Millie."

"Find out if it's sweeping or mopping—"

"Yep, or brass, ma'am, Miss Millie. Charge Mr. Stump a quarter next time. I ain't no mule, Miss Millie. Ain't, ma'am."

"Come here, Roadmap." Roadmap did.

Miss Millie's arms engulfed him and then kissed his forehead. Roadmap looked up.

"'Night, Miss Millie."

"'Night, Roadmap." Roadmap was at the door.

"Turn off the office lights. Don't have to burn all night."

"Yes, Miss Millie."

Miss Millie looked around the bedroom, and then at all of the many colored wigs. Miss Millie lay back on her big, soft bed. She shut her eyes, the lights staying on, the blues playing in the room from the record player in the background—tenderly.

Chapter 8

Everybody's glass in the Bluebird Bar had liquor in it. It was still too early for anyone to be drunk—not that anyone cared.

Lemontree had sung through two blues songs and was about to start a third, when his eyes hung on to a lady who had a butt like a pack mule.

"Arfel."

"Uh-huh."

"You see what's winking back at me?"

"Uh-huh, see it loud and clear, Lemontree."

"Umm—like me a woman with a big butt. Could sell hers for a bag of flour at the corner store. Maybe two. Damn, if it ain't packed tight, all right!"

Arfel took his eyes off the woman, letting Lemontree do all the looking. Lemontree's eyes shone like his four fat diamonds on his four fat fingers.

"Gonna play for her tonight, Arfel. Find a song inside me somewhere deep, me and Sweet-Juice. Yeah, gonna play for her …"

Knock-Kneed was late. It was just Lemontree and Arfel on the Bluebird stage.

"Knock-Kneed like them like that too: wide as a moon and thick as a brick. Just hope she don't go nowhere for the night." Then Lemontree shut his eyes. "Mmmm …"

"Got me a littl' dog (call 'im Sam).
He go blin',
Tell 'im, Sam, bettah yah lost yo'r eyesight,
An' not yo'r mine.

Sam bark two times on Sunday,
When Ah git in.
Sam don't see mah face—
Sam jus' smell mah gin.

Sam as' me: Lemontree—what kinda cootchie-cootchie woman—
Dis time?
Tell mah dog Sam: a perty brown-skinned woman—
Wid a big behin.'

Sam bark fo'r times mo'e lak God 'turn 'is eyesight back,
Lak dings jus' fine.
Swore tah God Sam seen dat perty brown-skinned woman—
An' 'er big behin'!"

"Play, Blue Fire—lak yah got gin in yah! Know yah see her too!" Lemontree's hands wrung more sweat out them.

"Losin' mah mine, baby—
Heared me—

Say Lemontree losin' 'is mine, baby—
De way yah shimmy-sham in dat short blue dress
(Don't seem fair.)
Oughta call de po-lice, lock yah up,
Put yah undah arres'.

Onlies' tell dem, tell dem po-licemens one ding 'fore dey do.

(Jus' one ding, baby.)
Can lock ol' Lemontree up in a jail cell wid dat big-butt woman;
Can make dem room—for two!"

"Hear you, Blue Fire."

"Hear yah, now."

And without warning, two loud voices pierced the air, and then a beer bottle cracked open.

"Cut your ass straight down the middle, nigga. Make two a you!"

There were two short men and one tall woman on the Bird's dance floor. The crowd had scattered, was looking on.

"Beer bottle don't tell you twice!"

"I come in here with her, Jimmy-Sweet. She—"

"But I'm takin' her home," Jimmy-Sweet said, the bottle's sharp, jagged edges Jimmy-Sweet's weapon. "Cut yo'r black ass six ways to Jesus!"

"Let go of that bottle!" Last Round shouted from behind the bar. "Let it go, Jimmy-Sweet. Don't start no shit in here!"

"Shit already start, Last Round!"

"Elam, bring Lou in here," Last Round said, coming from behind the bar (now being the bouncer, not the bartender). "Seems like Lou's Elam's girl now."

Jimmy-Sweet jabbed the broken beer bottle at Elam. Elam Bridges jumped back. "Well, I come in here tonight to take her back."

Elam began backing off.

"Ain't fair to Lou," Last Round said.

"Fight for her ... ha, this here nigga ain't!"

Elam Bridges continued to back away.

"Is you!" Jimmy-Sweet said again, jabbing the jagged bottle menacingly at Elam Bridges. "Is you!"

Nobody in the Bird moved.

"No ... no, I-I ain't ... I ..." Elam Bridges said, blending into the crowd.

"Gonna drink your liquor home tonight, an' leave Lou an' me to our own doings."

It didn't seem as if Jimmy-Sweet had to jab the beer bottle at Elam Bridges again.

"Drinkin' 'lone tonight, Elam," Jimmy-Sweet said coolly. "While me an' Lou dance to the blues in the Bluebird." And then Jimmy-Sweet's face darkened. "Get the hell outta here, scared nigga. Pay Last Round for what liquor you owe, an' then get the hell outta here. Don't wanna see you back!"

"Pay me tomorrow, Elam. Go on home now like Jimmy-Sweet tell you to. Your tab, know how much you owe."

Elam Bridges shook his head.

"Yeah, scared nigga!" Jimmy-Sweet said one more time.

"Yeah, g-guess you're right, Last Round," Elam said.

Jimmy-Sweet turned his back to Elam. Roughly, he grabbed Lou Paris by her arm. "You mine now, woman. Ain't leavin' this time'!"

Lou Paris didn't struggle; it was like she knew Jimmy-Sweet's right hand well.

It was little over an hour and a half later in the Bluebird. "Roadmap's here."

"I know, Lemontree."

Arfel and Lemontree hadn't taken a blues break. They were about to take one now.

"Better not to take too long a break. Roadmap don't like that," Lemontree said to Arfel who was sitting to his right. "Think sometimes Roadmap don't think a bluesman got nothing to do but play his gui-tar and sing the blues."

"Do we?" Arfel laughed.

Lemontree removed his straw hat (a thin layer of sweat layered his head). Lemontree fanned himself and then Sweet-Juice. And then with no surprise to Lemontree, at least, Knock-Kneed came bursting toward the stage.

"You late!"

"Heard you, Lemontree. Heard you."

"Looks like we gonna have to split our take-home pay two ways tonight." Lemontree winked at Arfel. "Get full pay when you render full service. Ain't cheating you out of nothing you ain't earned tonight, Knock-Kneed. What's fair for you."

"What'd I miss, anything?"

"Uh … not much—huh, Arfel?" Lemontree said as if he was hiding something like a parakeet under his big straw hat.

Then Arfel looked back at Lemontree as if he *was* indeed hiding a parakeet under his hat. "No … uh-uh, Knock-Kneed, not much."

Now it seemed as if Lemontree and Arfel had the lure after they'd served the bait.

Knock-Kneed was fussing with his guitar case. He pulled Purple Poison out the case.

"Come on now, Lemontree … Ar-Arfel … don't be like that."

"Like what, you late. If you was here, right, Arfel—woulda seen the *little* misunderstanding that took place in the Bird too. Right, Arfel?"

"'Little' sounds awful big to me right about now."

"Yeah, Knock-Kneed, was it. Jimmy-Sweet and Elam Bridges get in to a row. Dust up. Two of them. Over Lou, Lou Paris—"

Knock-Kneed looked out to the tables in the Bluebird and saw Jimmy-Sweet's arm holding Lou Paris.

"That … why that's right. Lou is—"

"Was."

"Was?"

"Was. Past tense. Ain't no present now." Pause. "Jimmy-Sweet fight for her. Break a bottle in here. Jimmy-Sweet squared off with Elam."

"Did he—"

"Cut him? No. Jimmy-Sweet don't do that. Waste no glass on him. No blood hit the floor. No, don't go that far, Knock-Kneed. Right, Arfel?" Pause.

"Don't have to. No, Jimmy-Sweet just chase him off with words. Elam was backing off, but Last Round encourage him to go home. Drink his liquor in peace. Stay clear of Jimmy-Sweet. Don't want to tangle with that young boy. Dance up close with him, like dancing up close to the devil."

"No," Knock-Kneed agreed.

"Mean as a one-legged hen!"

"And Elam—"

"Being mild mannered and all."

"I'm glad he came to his senses. Took Last Round's advice."

"Everybody is, right, Arfel?"

Of course Arfel didn't know either of them, Jimmy-Sweet or Elam Bridges, but he'd seen Jimmy-Sweet in the Bird before, but not Elam Bridges.

"Sweet boy, Elam." Then Lemontree looked at Sweet-Juice, who he now held in his hand. "Talking about sweet … Sweet-Juice getting impatient. Never mind Roadmap," Lemontree said, cocking his head over at Arfel. "Know Roadmap fidgety. Boy fidgeting like he got red ants in his pants!"

Arfel and Knock-Kneed laughed.

"We'd better play, and fast!"

The harmonicas were strung across Knock-Kneed's chest. "Know you missed my sweet harmonica, Lemontree."

"The way things was flying around here between Jimmy-Sweet and Elam Bridges, hell—we don't miss nothing, do we, Arfel? Nothing that make sense."

Arfel struck a B-flat chord on Blue Fire.

"Damn, Arfel," Knock-Kneed said. "Thanks a lot!"

Lemontree, Arfel, and Knock-Kneed were in a groove now. A slow grind kind of a thing where bodies could touch and feel one another, become almost like a blend of the blues and body heat.

It's how Jimmy-Sweet and Lou Paris were dancing on the Bluebird's dance floor, almost like a blend. Her body less resistant to his now, seemingly understanding it again, finding parts it knew, could fit to.

Lemontree was looking out onto the dance floor.

"Ain't forgot about that big-butt Louisiana blueswoman, Arfel. And she better not say she not from down there neither," Lemontree whispered to Arfel. "Yeah, she still out there."

Arfel saw her big butt too—fanning the air, making a breeze.

"Naw—Arfel, ain't forgot about that big-butt Louisiana woman, not one bit!"

Lemontree fanned his face, then Sweet-Juice.

"Awww …"

"Listen, baby, gotchah 'nough butt—
Built for two.
Think Lemontree seein'—
Leas' two of you.

One shake South,
Othah shake North,
Know yo'r butt homegrown,
Ain't sto'e bought.

Wan' me two scoops a yo'r ice cream,
For mah ice cream cone.
Play now, Sweet-Juice—
Takin' both dem big butts home!"

And so Lemontree was in more of a stormy sweat. "Uh-uh, Arfel, I ain't forgot about that big-butt blueswoman—not one bit."

But for some reason, Arfel had been thinking of Roadmap. For some reason, Arfel couldn't fathom himself.

"Jimmy-Sweet!"

The music in the Bird stopped dead.

"Jimmy-Sweet!"

And the Bluebird crowd, along with Jimmy-Sweet and Lou Paris, turned their heads.

"JIMMY-SWEET!" And Elam Bridges's eyes rolled around in his head like skittery marbles.

Jimmy-Sweet hadn't let go of Lou Paris. Her body still locked lightning-hot to his as if it were breathing a new sex into her. "What you want, nigga? Me an' Lou ain't finish dancin'."

Elam's body would tilt forward and then sway from side to side as if it were trapped inside a stormy day. "Ain't calling your name but one more time, JIMMY-SWEET!"

"Ain't gonnah have to!" And Jimmy-Sweet flung Lou Paris to the side. And he grabbed a beer bottle and was about to crack it open, when Elam Bridges went into his suit pocket and pulled out a gun and began waving it in the air, chaotically—as if he didn't give a damn if he shot the whole world to hell.

The crowd in the Bird ducked for cover. All of them except for Jimmy-Sweet and Lou Paris.

"Scared nigga! Scared nigga! Scared nigga!" Elam Bridges repeated over and over. "I-I ain't no scared nigga!" And then Elam Bridges aimed the gun at the Bird's ceiling.

Blam! Blam!

And this time Lou Parish and Jimmy-Sweet ducked for cover. "Ain't no scared nigga! Ain't! Ain't!" And then Elam Bridges pumped the air with bullets. Bullets were flying all over the Bluebird Bar.

And Arfel ran to where he knew Roadmap was hiding. "Roadmap!"

"Mr. Arfel, Mr. Arfel!" And Arfel rolled Roadmap onto the floor, covering him with his body just in case the bullets from Elam Bridges's gun reached them.

"You, you can have her, Jimmy-Sweet. You, you can have Lou … I-I just ain't no scared nigga. I-I just ain't that …" Elam Bridges said, walking out the Bluebird Bar, his gun drawn, its muzzle smoking—the bullets in the chamber spent.

It was just Arfel, Roadmap, and Blue Fire out on the road.

"I wasn't scared, Mr. Arfel."

"I know you wasn't, Roadmap."

Roadmap giggled. "Was my body shaking a little, Mr. Arfel? Some?"

"Just, uh, yeah, a little, Roadmap. Some."

"Y-you seen it too, Blue Fire?"

It wasn't as late as usual when Arfel and Blue Fire left the Bluebird for Stump's Palace. Things in the Bluebird Bar had kind of slowed down some after the Elam Bridges, Jimmy-Sweet, Lou Paris affair.

Lemontree didn't walk the road with Arfel tonight. After Lemontree had visited Philander Prince and was handed the customary white envelope by the white man in white gloves and paid Arfel and Knock-Kneed their due, Lemontree went off with that big-butt (Louisiana) blueswoman whom he was singing about and who, all night, had kept his body's heat at a high boil.

Arfel loved to look at Roadmap whenever they walked together, which was often, lately. With the rolled-up cap of his, and the way he just walked about the city streets as if he owned most of the world by pure imagination and the sheer genius of youthful invention—Roadmap was all of that to watch and far more. He'd learned how to make it in this world already. This, probably, was what made Roadmap so much fun for Arfel to walk with: this beautiful sense of order in him, intrinsic and genuine.

Roadmap kicked at something invisible to Arfel. "Seen worse fights than that around here, Mr. Arfel. Much worse in this town."

"Me too, Roadmap. But I don't like bullets flying over my head, not under any circumstances."

"Yeah, don't know Mr. Elam to do nothing like that. Usually find him sitting in church on a Sunday morning. In one of them pews."

Arfel laughed.

"Don't know liquor to do that to him," Roadmap said responsibly.

"Liquor's got a way, Roadmap. Too … too much liquor and too much anger."

"Miss Lou. Miss Lou, she … she's all right," Roadmap said as if trying not to find anything wrong with her—bad about her. "But she ain't nothing for two men to be fighting over."

It's when Arfel realized he was talking to a young boy of tender age. That he was talking adult things to a young boy who, by all rights, should be thinking about doing other things, not adult things. But this was Roadmap's life: adult things. Life had put it there, and then the blues, and now what Roadmap was beginning to mean to him and Blue Fire.

"Know about women, Mr. Arfel," Roadmap said while standing in the light from the lamppost on Lime Street that shone down on his face. "Know about them, Mr. Arfel."

Arfel looked at Roadmap, but not judgmentally.

"You don't know Miss Millie, Mr. Arfel," Roadmap said, looking up at Arfel. "But she knows about you." Pause. "Mr. Knock-Kneed comes into Miss Millie's good-time house. It's how Miss Millie find out about you and Blue Fire in the Bluebird, Mr. Arfel." Roadmap adjusted his cap. Pause.

"You don't go there, Mr. Arfel. T-to Miss Millie's good-time house."

"Uh … no, Roadmap."

Roadmap stared at Arfel hard before he said, "Uh … what—you ain't got needs, Mr. Arfel? No, uh, needs in you, uh, Mr. Arfel?"

"Don't worry, Roadmap—I've got plenty of needs."

"For a woman, Mr. Arfel?"

"For a woman, Roadmap."

They hitched back up.

"Know about women at Miss Millie's, Mr. Arfel," Roadmap said matter-of-fact.

"You don't—"

"But I seen them. Seen them when they do 'it,' do 'it' with the men who come in there."

"But … you've … you've never done anything with them, have you, Roadmap?"

Roadmap sucked his teeth. "Almost, Mr. Arfel. Come close. Real close with Miss Serena, Mr. Arfel. Real close."

"You—"

"Was last night. Was working for Miss Millie. Cleaning out one of her rooms with the broom and mop and all."

"Oh," Arfel said.

"Yep, she come in the room. Come at me. Scare me at first, never done it with a girl or … or a lady before, Mr. Arfel. But want to." Pause. "Tall and long, Miss Serena is, Mr. Arfel. She gotta eye for me. All along. Seen it, Miss Serena …" Roadmap collected his breath as if, if he didn't, it would leave his mouth sour.

"She want to know if I ever 'did it,' Mr. Arfel, but I say no. She stretch out on the bed showing skin. S-say she want my first time to be with her, Mr. Arfel, since she knew I never been with …"

Long pause.

"Then, then, Roadmap?"

"Oh yeah, Mr. Arfel, she begin taking off my belt. Hear it in my ears. Sound smooth like fish in—slipping through water. And when my pants come off, shut my eyes, Mr. Arfel. Shut them good. Imagine

Miss Serena. How I seen her, her body doing it with them men in Miss Millie's. In them rooms. Full, pretty breasts." Pause.

"She move. Hear her. 'Look at me. Look at me,' Miss Serena say. And when I open my eyes, Mr. Arfel, all the way up, Miss Serena was naked. D-down to nothing!

"'You're beautiful, Miss Serena! You're beautiful, ma'am.' 'Come to me, Roadmap,' Miss Serena say. 'Come to me.'" Pause.

"And when I do on the bed, crawl to her on … Miss Serena's hands was pulling down my underpants, but … but—"

"What, Roadmap? What!"

"'Serena, Serena'! Miss Millie scream, knocking back the door. She fuss, Mr. Arfel, Miss Millie. Fire Miss Serena. Fire her on the spot, Mr. Arfel. Chase Miss Serena off. Out the room."

They kept walking toward the Palace.

Why had he let himself get so sexually aroused, Arfel thought, when he knew Roadmap had said he was a virgin? But for some reason this Miss Serena woman excited him like the blueswoman he'd met and now was trying to forget each day as if she'd become a cancer inside his brain.

"Ask Miss Millie not to fire Miss Serena when things get better, Mr. Arfel, slow down some. Least I could do, Mr. Arfel." Pause. "Miss Serena don't mean nothing. Ain't nobody's fault. How I feel about it. Miss Millie take her back, though, don't fire Miss Serena."

"Good, Roadmap. Good. Was hoping so." Pause.

"But sure wish Miss Millie don't come busting through that door like she do with me and Miss Serena. Sure do, Mr. Arfel!"

Know you do! Arfel said to himself. *Know you do, Roadmap!*

A lightness was in both of them.

"Miss Lou gonna run off from Mr. Jimmy-Sweet again, Mr. Arfel. Just wait and see."

"Uh, don't know nothing about it. But I'd say you're right, Roadmap."

"Darn tootin'!"

Stump's Palace stood right before them like a lighthouse in the night.

"Blue Fire's quiet, Mr. Arfel. But she talked enough tonight."

Arfel and Roadmap were just below the three hotel steps leading up into Stump's Palace. Arfel stepped up onto one step, and then the second.

"Guess it's the end of the road, Mr. Arfel," Roadmap said softly.

Arfel turned to look back at Roadmap. "You might as well come in, Roadmap."

"I-I can, Mr. Arfel?"

"Ain't seen my room. At least not with me and Blue Fire standing in it."

"No, Mr. Arfel—not ever."

Roadmap hopped up the three steps.

"I'm a good leaper, Mr. Arfel."

"So I see, Roadmap."

They entered the hotel. Arfel's head swished to the left, and then to the right, so did Roadmap's.

"So what you think, Roadmap?"

"I don't know, Mr. Arfel, was expecting Mr. Stump's stump up on the desk too. Propped up there."

"It is earlier than usual, Roadmap."

"Uh, don't matter, Mr. Arfel: seen Mr. Stump sleep at this hour too." Roadmap was completely cognizant of time.

"Gotta be doing something ... Hmm ..."

"Just know it ain't the brass, Mr. Arfel." Roadmap turned and looked at the front door's brass knobs. " Still shines like a gold piece, Mr. Arfel."

Arfel put his hand atop Roadmap's shoulder in admiring Roadmap's handiwork too.

"Mr. Stump's gonna pay me a quarter next time, though—I swear!" Roadmap griped. "What I promised myself. Raising my rate."

"Good for you, Roadmap."

"Yep, Mr. Arfel. Raising my rate."

Arfel looked up the hotel's stairs, only, Roadmap was looking at the wall clock.

"Come on, Roadmap."

"Mr. Arfel, you know about that clock on the wall?"

"No, no, I don't, Roadmap."

"Mean Mr. Stump ain't told you and Blue Fire yet?"

"Just know it gongs pretty."

"It does, don't it, Mr. Arfel—nice and pretty." Pause. "But it's German, you know?"

"It is, Road—"

"Uh-huh. Where it comes from. Germany. All the way cross the ocean to here." Roadmap looked transfixed by what he said and when the white enamel dial swept across the Roman numerals and then stopped.

"Uh, you still, uh, coming, Road—"

"Right behind you, Mr. Arfel. Don't gotta kick me!"

They were up on the second landing. Arfel stopped at his door.

"Knew you was on the second floor, Mr. Arfel. You and Blue Fire. Don't bet myself—just know. Should've, though."

"Yep, Roadmap—you would've won."

Arfel was opening the room door.

"Just didn't know which room it was."

The room's light shot on.

"Been in this room before, Roadmap?"

Roadmap's eyes performed a quick sketch of the place.

"Sure have, Mr. Arfel." Roadmap hitched his britches. "Mr. Stump have me work in here before too."

"Mr. Stump sure keeps you busy, Roadmap."

"When I let him. Don't always come around to the Palace." Roadmap breathed in the room's air. "Like the outdoors, Mr. Arfel. Mostly. More so than the indoors. More to my liking."

Arfel put Blue Fire on top of the bed. Roadmap came over to the bed and looked at the guitar case. "Can I look at her, Mr. Arfel? Forget what Blue Fire looks like."

Arfel snapped open the guitar case. "Blue Fire, Roadmap wants to see you."

"Blue Fire …" Roadmap said, not being able to take his eyes off her. "Ain't … ain't—I ain't never asked to touch her strings, Mr. Arfel." Pause. "C-can I?"

Arfel sat down on the bed, and Roadmap sat beside him. "Blue Fire, she'd like that, Roadmap. Sure would."

Roadmap's little fingers came close to Blue Fire's strings, trembled, and then froze. "Don't want to now, Mr. Arfel." Roadmap's voice trembled with emotion. "J-just don't."

Arfel closed his eyes as Roadmap did the same. "Blue Fire understands, Roadmap," Arfel said, his fingers touching on Blue Fire's strings. Roadmap reopened his eyes.

"Blue Fire only belong to one bluesman, Mr. Arfel. You."

Both sat on the bed. Arfel hummed and patted his feet casually. Roadmap got his feet down on the floor, and he did similarly. Arfel was playing Blue Fire oh so softly and humming oh so syrupy (what with the late hour in Stump's Palace). "Mmmm …"

"You don't sing no songs in the Bird, Mr. Arfel," Roadmap commented. "Make them up, Mr. Arfel."

"But know plenty, Roadmap."

"Why don't you, Mr. Arfel, sing in the Bluebird?"

"Let Mr. Lemontree do that. Mr. Lemontree does good enough for both of us."

"Guess so, but I'd still like to hear you cut aloose with something, Mr. Arfel. Once and a while." Pause. "Ain't complaining."

"No, I know you ain't, Roadmap—complaining."

"Just stating fact."

"That you are, Roadmap. That you are." Arfel turned to his right (Roadmap was to the left of him on the bed). "Gonna put Blue Fire back in the case. Say she's tired, Roadmap."

"Don't look it, Mr. Arfel."

"Gotta respect her sleep, though, Roadmap—Blue Fire don't ask for much."

Roadmap watched as Arfel put Blue Fire back into her guitar case.

"Blue Fire's the prettiest gui-tar I ever seen, Mr. Arfel. Ain't gonna say different. Love … love you, Blue Fire."

"Likewise I'm sure, Roadmap," Arfel said.

Roadmap tried camouflaging his yawn but couldn't. Arfel yawned widely too. "Don't know why this night feel, pulling so long on me, Roadmap."

Arfel stretched his arms; Roadmap did the same. "Don't know why it feels that way, that way on me too, Mr. Arfel."

"Even though it's earlier than usual."

"Earlier than usual, Mr. Arfel." Then Roadmap's hand pressed down on the bed. It wasn't as soft as Miss Millie's custom-made bed; it seemed Roadmap knew that.

"So … where do you—"

"I sleep around, Mr. Arfel," Roadmap said, anticipating Arfel's question. "Sleep at Miss Millie's last night. In Miss Millie's office. On a cot. Had a good sleep, Mr. Arfel. Cot and pillow."

Arfel was taking off his coat jacket when, gently, Roadmap touched his hand. "Can … can I stay the night, Mr. Arfel? Won't get in nobody's way. Promise. Sleep here with you and … and Blue Fire, Mr. Arfel?"

There were singular rings of beauty surrounding Roadmap's eyes. It's the best way Arfel could describe it to himself. "Ain't nothing that would give me and Blue Fire greater pleasure, Roadmap. Nothing."

"Y-you mean that, Mr. Arfel? You do!"

Arfel shook his head. Roadmap hopped off the bed as if, suddenly, his britches were on fire. "Thanks, thanks, Mr. Arfel. Thanks!"

And then Roadmap calmed, and he walked over to Blue Fire who lay in her case, but the metal snaps had not been fastened. Roadmap removed his cap, holding it in his hand. "Thank you, Blue Fire," Roadmap said.

Then Roadmap hopped about as if he was doing a St. Vitus dance to a fiddle and drum. "Don't need nothing but the floor, Mr. Arfel!"

It was later.

Arfel had done Roadmap one better than the floor; there was a blanket on the floor and a pillow. Roadmap was lying right next to the bed.

"Won't have to pee till morning. So you won't hear me move none, Mr. Arfel. Like I said, won't be no bother. Ain't going in and out the door."

"Hope I remember you're down there, near the bed when I go and pee, Roadmap. Don't step on you. It's how I usually exit."

"Blue Fire don't have to, do she, Mr. Arfel? Pee?" Roadmap teased.

"If she does, been keeping it a secret from me all these years. Under her pretty hat."

Roadmap giggled. He stretched his neck up. Blue Fire was next to

Arfel in the bed. "This how a bluesman sleeps with his gui-tar at night, Mr. Arfel? Mr. Lemontree and Mr. Knock-Kneed too?"

"Probably only me and Blue Fire, Roadmap. Us two."

"Figured Blue Fire to sleep in a chair, Mr. Arfel, not—"

"Blue Fire knows what a seat of a chair feels like. Ain't always a lady of high privilege."

Like mist settling, Arfel and Blue Fire did the same.

"'Night, Mr. Arfel."

"'Night, Roadmap."

Fifteen minutes later.

"*Pssst.* Mr. Arfel—you wake?"

"Uh-huh."

"Me too." Roadmap frowned.

"Guessed that already, Roadmap."

Roadmap giggled. He'd been too excited to sleep and knew it. "Usually out like a light by now, Mr. Arfel. Know that. Nothing to stop me. But tonight ..."

"I know."

"What—you ... I ... you—I mean you excited too, Mr. Arfel?"

"Yes."

"What, you and Blue Fire?"

"Yes."

"Bet she ain't sleep either. Bet that too. F-for sure, Mr. Arfel."

"Nope, don't think so, Roadmap. Don't think Blue Fire is."

"Good." Pause. "What we gonna talk about, Mr. Arfel? Then?"

"What?"

"Gotta talk about something. Ain't losing sleep over nothing."

"Me either. Ain't wasting the night away."

Arfel rolled over to the side of the bed and looked down at Roadmap. "Sleep with your cap on, Roadmap?"

"Always, Mr. Arfel. Don't lose it that way. Even if somebody try to snatch it. Steal it in my sleep. Sneak up on me at night. Fight for it like I fight for my life."

Arfel could feel the energy in Roadmap's eyes and throat.

"Rough out there."

"It is, Mr. Arfel. Is."

"Life …"

"Say it ain't supposed to come easy, Mr. Arfel. That's what they say. The, the blues—everything."

"It's why you like the blues so much, Roadmap?"

"Yes, Mr. Arfel. Guess so. Yes. Mr. Arfel. Yep. Do."

Arfel didn't want to feel as if he were prying; but he wanted to know more about Roadmap, this young boy who, for him, had become practically son-like. But Roadmap, with his uncanny sense of things, timing, like the right blues riff, beat Arfel to the question Arfel was about to ask to uncover more of who Roadmap was.

"Thrown out, Mr. Arfel. Out the house. Onto the streets," Roadmap said with no pain, anger, or remorse—only a certain truth ballasting his voice. "Ain't the only person tossed out on the street in the middle of the night. Not my momma. Momma don't do it. She die when I was three. Don't remember Momma much. Don't. Know I loved her though, Mr. Arfel. Know that much." Pause.

"Daddy, he was a 'runaway man,' Mr. Arfel. It's what I call him. Run away before Momma die. Don't know him. Don't know if he's living or dead. Know I never loved him, Mr. Arfel. Know that much about him. He's a 'runaway man,' it's what I call him, Mr. Arfel. A-a 'runaway man.'"

Roadmap's sadness practically gutted Arfel.

"Was living with a cousin. Was with others, but was living with cousin Rebecca. But her husband, cousin James, after a while, don't take a liking to me. Said cousin Rebecca spend too much time with me, and I eat too much. Got me a appetite, like food, admit—but I don't, Mr. Arfel.

"I-I don't, honest." Pause. "Cousin James make it up. All up on me. Lie on me. All of it. Don't eat no more food than my share, Mr. Arfel. What cousin Rebecca fix, p-put on the plate. Honest. Don't eat no more than what's due me."

"Know you don't, Roadmap."

"Know we poor, Mr. Arfel. Me and cousin Rebecca and cousin James poor. Ain't nobody in the world need for them to tell me that, Mr. Arfel."

"It's how it all started, Roadmap?"

"Uh-huh, Mr. Arfel." Pause. "Arthur, Mr. Arfel."

"Arthur!"

"Yep. Arthur P. Little," Roadmap said with great pride. "Who I am."

"Like it, Roadmap."

"Me too."

"But ..."

"It don't work on the street, Arthur P. Little, but Roadmap does."

"Did you think of it right off, Roadmap?"

"Right off, Mr. Arfel. Yep. Come to me one day while I was showing someone around town. First time one of them strangers ask my name."

"And ..."

"I say, 'Roadmap, Mister. I go by Roadmap. They call me Roadmap around here, these parts, Mister.'" Roadmap's voice was ramped-up. "Right away it come to me. L-like a lightning flash." Pause.

"But still say it ain't as pretty a name as Blue Fire. Stick to that, Mr. Arfel." Pause.

"Uh, Momma go by Benita T. Parks. Daddy go by Edgerton E. Little. Momma and Daddy don't marry, Mr. Arfel. They give me my daddy's name though: Little." Roadmap laid his head back down on the pillow. "Ain't complaining, Mr. Arfel. Ain't."

"Know you ain't, Roadmap."

"Look at the stars at night. Smile pretty down on me. Don't know how things go. Ain't looking to change nothing."

Again, Arfel couldn't get over Roadmap's wisdom. Or was it resignation to some willed, foreshadowed destiny?

"Gotta make do with what you've got," Arfel said more like he had to say something that had years of aged wisdom in it too, no matter how well Roadmap had articulated it.

"Uh, Mr. Arfel ..."

"Yes, Roadmap?"

"Uh ... you and Blue Fire don't snore, do you? When you and Blue Fire finally get off to sleep, doze off good. You don't snore like Mr. Stump, do you?"

"Don't know, Roadmap. Blue Fire don't tell me, and I don't tell Blue Fire. Not yet, we don't reach that stage."

"Well … I hope not," Roadmap said worriedly. "Morning comes quick enough."

"Sure does, Roadmap. Sure does." Pause.

"'Night, Mr. Arfel. Blue Fire."

"'Night, Roadmap."

Chapter 9

The sun struck the window, and then Arfel's eyes. Arfel rolled the nasty saliva around in his mouth like a big plastic marble and then tasted it in his throat with a certain degree of dogged displeasure. It's when Arfel's body unwound to catch its breath.

"Sun's about to blind me. What about you, Roadmap?" Arfel asked, rolling over onto his side.

"Roadmap, Roadmap's gone, Blue Fire," Arfel said astonished, yet knowing he shouldn't be. "Little Roadmap's gone."

The blanket and pillow were off the floor, and Arfel's eyes followed the trail that led over to the chair. The blanket was folded neatly on the chair's seat. The pillow was on top. It was as neat as a feather.

"Love you, Roadmap. Love that boy, don't we, Blue Fire." Arfel's body arched away from the sun. His body felt like roasted peanuts.

"Last night it was a little cool, but this morning the sun's eager, Blue Fire." Arfel's body awakened more. "Time to rise and shine. Roadmap's already started his day. Already out the door." Arfel shook his head disappointedly though. "Don't even hear him go. Don't say nothing, Blue Fire—'cause you don't hear him neither!"

Arfel was dressed. Blue Fire was on his back. Arfel shut the room's door. Sprightly Arfel moved down the hall and down the stairs. Arfel saw one of the hotel guests slip out the hotel's front door. "Ain't seen too many people in Mr. Stump's hotel so far, Blue Fire. At least none to meet or mention." Arfel was heading for that same door, when he heard, "Roadmap beat you by a good … uh"—Stump checked his watch—"three hours by now, Arfel!"

Arfel's head turned.

The grin plastered on Stump's face had been blessed by, what seemed, timeless insinuation.

"Late, Arfel …" Stump said, coming toward Arfel. "You and Blue Fire late, according to Roadmap's standards." Stump's grin grew grander. "Shot out of here like a light. Don't think I don't see him—but I do. Has to be crazy if he don't think I don't see everything that goes on around here in the Palace.

"Just like I knew he was in your room last night—overnight, Arfel," Stump boasted.

"Uh-huh, me and Blue Fire put him up, Mr. Stump."

Stump put his hand out and as capriciously withdrew it. "Ain't charging you extra, Arfel. So don't worry."

"Phew … thanks, Mr. Stump!"

"Since it was Roadmap. Little Roadmap."

"Okay, Mr. Stump," Arfel said, turning to leave the Palace.

"Heard about last night too," Stump said in a lightweight voice. "The Bluebird. Heard about the ruckus in there. The gunshots. Jimmy-Sweet, Elam Bridges, and Lou Paris. Lovers' spat. Jealousy. All that crazy stuff. Hogwash!"

Arfel nodded.

"Youth wasted on youth," Stump grumped.

"Mr. Stump, you were young once, s—"

"Don't remind me," Stump said, favoring his good leg, standing. "Sometimes wish I could have it all back."

Stump's answer puzzled Arfel. "But why, Mr. Stump? Don't everything, good or bad, one day, count for something?"

"Hell, I don't know. Just wish it was different—that's all. Hell, an old man can wish, can't he?"

"Yes, yes, Mr. Stump."

"Nobody's chasing me ..."

Shock singed Arfel and spun his head in a thousand different directions.

"I guess—but myself."

Arfel was on Spring Street. His thoughts were running away with him. They were colliding together like two demoned planets in space.

"Don't want to forget why we're here, Blue Fire. Don't want to forget that. Don't want us to forget that dark night. Them roads, trains. D-don't want us to forget them, Blue Fire." Pause. "Ain't nobody chasing Mr. Stump, but ... but me—us ..." Arfel blocked the sun off his face. "Us—it's ... it's different."

Arfel was going to Lemontree's place. He'd never been to Lemontree's place; but Lemontree, before the commotion began at the Bluebird last night, invited him to drop by. Lemontree gave Arfel directions. Arfel felt comfortable enough with them and the town to be able to reach Lemontree's place on his own.

"Roadmap," Arfel said as if he'd struck gold. "Do he snore, Blue Fire?" Arfel asked, bemused. "Sure don't hear him." Arfel looked up the road. "Lemontree said Spring Street, and then, then over to uh ... uh, Congress, uh, right?"

Roadmap snuck out on him and Blue Fire as quiet as stars in the sky, Arfel laughed. But last night Roadmap told him and Blue Fire all about himself. His life had so many bumps and bruises in it already: thoughts beyond every day. Arfel tugged on Blue Fire's leather strap roughly. His head hung as if it'd lost its quality. There was shame in him, something that told him he was not living up to the truth: his past. *Who was he hiding it from? Why was he hiding it?* (Even before he killed the white man.) He always hid his life away. Sometimes even making things up just to fit in, as being some relative experience. His past, no one knew it, not even Blue Fire. He'd even kept it from her. Blue Fire only knew the life *they'd* lived since he'd traded cash and another guitar with the old bluesman for her in a blues joint. He and Blue Fire started then and there.

"Don't wanna tell nobody of my life," Arfel said, looking at a new street sign in clear view.

"What me and Tom … Tom Mickens used to do down by the river with those girls. Was-wasn't right, Blue Fire. Just wasn't right. No, Blue Fire. No."

By degrees, Arfel and Blue Fire were getting to Lemontree's place.

"Know you can't wait to see Sweet-Juice, Blue Fire." And then Arfel and Blue Fire came upon Lemontree Johnson's place. Arfel didn't think; he just reacted.

Lemontree is a bluesman, what else should I have expected? Not much else for Lemontree.

Arfel was about to knock on the flimsy door, when it flew open. "Arfel. Blue Fire!" Lemontree said, grabbing Arfel, Arfel trying his best not to upset Lemontree's straw hat during the brief exchange.

"Seen you and Blue Fire coming. Me and Sweet-Juice, that is. Couldn't wait for you two to get here, Arfel. Been grouchy all morning. Fussy as all hell. Ain't you, Sweet-Juice?" Lemontree laughed inside a barrel of a laugh. "Bitchy, for the record. Get that way sometimes when she want her way. Not always—but sometimes." Lemontree grabbed a chair.

"Arfel, sit down."

The floors were wood, hard, thick planks of roughed wood. "Expected you earlier," Lemontree said. "Probably giving a bluesman a bad reputation over at Mr. Stump's." Lemontree slapped his hands together. "Give him more to grump about—like we got to add more bacon fat to the pan."

Arfel looked around the room … wasn't much for him to look at that was for sure.

"What about you and Roadmap last night? How far he travel with you?"

"Spend the night in the Palace. Me and Blue Fire put him up."

"Ask to stay?"

"Yes."

"Saw you rush off the stage last night. Saw the direction you was headed, your body was turned off to." Pause. "Downright decent of you, Arfel. For you to think of little Roadmap first. Brave as hell."

"Thanks, Lemontree."

"Thought of him right off?" Lemontree asked, leaning forward in the chair.

"Don't—you know what, Lemontree, I-I don't remember."

"Sometimes when them things happen, you don't. Nothing comes to mind. You like those bullets flying out Elam Bridges's pistol last night: you just fly off. Helter-skelter. Say you just reflex. Instincts." Pause. "The night wasn't spoilt though, Arfel. Mr. Prince pay me—"

"And you still went off, got to go off with that big-butt blueswoman, Lemontree."

Lemontree slapped his hands together again. "Didn't I!"

Lemontree removed his straw hat. His forehead was in a sweat. "That gal's name was Bonnie. Was worth every note I played, and every song I sung. Her butt, that is, last night. Ain't hardly lying to you, Arfel." Lemontree opened out his big-cut hands. "Don't know nothing sweeter than holding a big butt, a gui-tar, and a ... a big BUTT. Hell ... do say that already, twice already, don't I, uh, Arfel."

"Uh, yes, Lemontree, her butt was—"

"Big. Big. LOUISIANA BIG. All I'm gonna say on the topic, for now. Time we got together."

Lemontree was putting his straw hat back on as he rushed across the floor. Then he bent over, and when he reared back up, he smiled as if he'd made a special catch of some intimate interest.

"Arfel, let's go fishing!" Lemontree was standing there with two wooden fishing poles in his hand, all of him looking like a long lake.

"How'd you know I—"

"You a country boy like me. Ain't no difference. Know you ain't done it for a while. That much of the country ain't left you. Know you miss it."

They were outside Lemontree's place. Lemontree looked at it with distant eyes. "Bought me this old piece of nothing. Ain't ashamed of it—but … you know. Just gotta find me a woman. That's all, Arfel. To share it with. Round everything off. Suppose it's why I bought it in the first place."

Lemontree and Arfel were fishing. They hadn't caught anything, but it hadn't been that long that they'd been at it. Their bait was good. They were at the water's edge. "No fish nibbling on them worms. What, these fish around here too good for our worms, Arfel?"

Arfel yanked lightly on his fishing pole. "Must be, Lemontree."

"Getting hungry, though. And one a them, no, uh … make it four of them fish in the sea gonna be on my plate before too long. Staring up at me. Eyes wide open."

"Maybe they know that already."

"Man, Arfel—ain't this living?" (If Lemontree and Arfel didn't look like two pigs plopped in Farmer Jones's slop.) "Never know, do you, Arfel?"

"About what, Lemontree?"

"Gotta watch them quiet ones. Daddy always tell me. It's true. Never know what they likely to do. And when." Pause.

"Huh, Elam Bridges: quiet as a mouse. A churchman. Go every Sunday. Don't miss a one. Mild mannered. Don't curse. Drink, but don't curse." Pause. "Raise him holy hell last night, though. Drink and the devil got a way to twist a man's arm, Arfel. Persuade, push the worse outta him. Drink, and the devil."

Arfel's hand rubbed his knee impatiently. "Lemontree, I-I don't see any po-lice on this side of town. Like last night with Elam Bridges. The commotion in the Bird."

"Po-lice?" Lemontree said, relaxing his fishing pole in the water. "Po-lice?" Pause. "Oh, this side a town po-lice pretty much leave coloreds alone. Let us kill ourselves kinda, pretty much how we, the rate we wanna. Uh … choose to."

Arfel felt his stomach crunch, then cramp.

"Don't bother much with what we do." Pause. "Knock-Kneed's quiet like that."

"Knock-Kneed, Lemontree?"

"Oh—when it come to the white man."

"Oh."

"Been in conversations with him. Me and him talk on the subject—quiet on it," Lemontree said, returning to fishing. "Knock-Kneed got them same experiences. South treat him and his daddy and his momma, uh, relatives, exact way—nobody get off the hook."

Arfel laughed, so did Lemontree—at the obvious.

"Ain't comparing people to worms now, Arfel …"

"But come to think of it—"

"Come to think of it …" Then Lemontree unwound his large body, for he could continue with this kind of talk of his. "Knock-Kneed got the South born in him," Lemontree said, going back to his careful observations. "When you don't want to talk about something, you trying to hide it, Arfel. Hide it from yourself."

"M-maybe, uh, maybe Knock-Kneed's trying—I mean maybe he's private, Lemontree. Real private with things, his feelings. Why he holds them in."

"Maybe so. Could be. But you can bury it, them feelings of yours but so far down in you, and then they come back to haunt you. Rise up. Seen it enough times to know. Don't talk about something, fester as they say. Festers. Knock-Kneed got something festering he ain't telling nobody about. Take but one reminding for it to explode. Get bad, real bad on him, Arfel."

It was two hours later, and Lemontree and Arfel were sitting at the water's edge with their stomachs filled to capacity. Lemontree had brought a skillet with him and seasoning, and he'd built a fire for himself to fry the fish (which he did), and he and Arfel had finished off two big catfish between them (the fish had been biting, all right!).

Both Lemontree and Arfel were laid out on their backs head to heel. Sweet-Juice lay in her case next to Lemontree, Blue Fire next to Arfel. Arfel and Lemontree were sucking at their teeth (Lemontree hadn't carried toothpicks); was the only thing to echo off the lake.

"Got the blues in me since … since young—what about you, Arfel?

Same for you?" Lemontree asked with a voice as lazy as someone who'd just caught, fried, and eaten two big catfish.

"Came as natural as sleep, Lemontree," Arfel said, resting his eyes.

"Got religion in it from the start. Every time I touch the gui-tar when I was five ... or was it six—don't matter much, feel religion in my fingers. Least what I come to know as religion."

"I was eight."

"Started late. Late for you." Lemontree giggled. Lemontree reached for Sweet-Juice. He removed her from the case and then hunched his powerful torso over her. "Travel with you far and wide—don't I, Sweet-Juice?"

Arfel smiled at the two of them.

"When I die, don't know what they gonna remember about me, Arfel. What they gonna one day recall. Good or bad." The brim of Lemontree's hat tipped enough to touch the edge of Sweet-Juice's yellow wood. "Ever think about dying?"

"S-sure, Lemontree."

"What man on earth don't. Ain't a question to ask just one to know." Pause. "The world on an axis, Arfel. Keep revolving. Don't stop. Keep spinning like a top. Top of a top."

"You're not tired, are you, Lemontree?"

"What, of living? NAAH ... Ain't tired a that, just sometimes wanna make sense out a all of this. All a this running around we do."

"It does seem crazy sometimes."

"Crazy. It does, Arfel. Feel religion, that it coming from somewhere. Someplace."

"Uh, me too."

"Especially you, Arfel. Especially you. True and true."

"But you aren't religious, are you, Lemontree?"

"Believe in God as well as the devil. Just don't go to church. Uh, gotta have someplace you can go off to to pray for yourself. Give money to. Support the church. For what a man stand on." Pause. "But ain't got much else to do with religion but what I believe." Lemontree's eyes set hard on Arfel.

"Uh—I believe in God and the devil too, Lemontree. Don't have much of a philosophy like you ..."

"But you believe in the holy word and such. What the gospel preach. Jesus say for living a good, clean life? The catechisms and all?"

"Uh, uh-huh."

"Tough to follow though. Especially a bluesman."

"It is," Arfel said, smiling.

"Don't expect us to, Arfel. God. 'Cause a bluesman built for sinning, good times. Ain't got nothing else to say about it, come to mind—less you do."

"God's got to do us better than that, Lemontree."

"Don't know so by my life. Uh, life and times. And many other bluesmen I see." Pause. "Why I bought that house. Want a woman. Too old for children, even then. Just wanna wife, Arfel. Just to say I was here. Had me somebody. Don't leave outta here alone."

"C-children …?"

"Yeah, they carry it on, keep it going, but it's too late for me. Gotta settle for what I can get, and even that looks like it's gonna be too late. The clock's ticking down on me. Getting late. Too set in my ways. Even a mule's better company, less trouble to clean up after. Time's moving by, Arfel, for me."

Arfel looked back up into the fading sun.

"Ever think about it, Arfel?"

"No, Lemontree. Uh, no," Arfel said quickly.

Lemontree's eyes draped over Arfel as he sat where he was and Arfel was looking up into the sky.

"One day you gonna tell me why you and Blue Fire running. Why you come here, to this town. Can't stay safe but for so long."

Arfel's eyes skirted away from the sky. "C-can't, L-Lemontree …" Arfel's voice shivered. "Can't … can't."

"Don't wanna know till you ready to tell me. Your insides gonna run out of patience—turn on you—or it's gonna be scared something bad—where it needs to be heard."

"I'm away from it, Lemontree."

"Ain't had to run. Just get away from things that don't please me. Keep me back. Or I see I can't change." Pause. "But you're running, Arfel. You and Blue Fire is running from something or somebody. And the rail train bring you on a two-way track: from South to North and back."

131

Lemontree stood and stretched. "Been a good day for fishing, Arfel. Started off slow."

Arfel got up and brushed himself off. "I know, Lemontree."

"Fish was lazy. Worms was turning slow too."

"Lemontree ..." Arfel said, muffling his laugher.

"I know: some days I just need to stop talking. Know when I'm well off. Just shut my big trap the hell up."

Lemontree looked over at Blue Fire. "Well ... at least Blue Fire don't mind."

Arfel patted Lemontree's back as both began making their way back to Lemontree's place.

"Blue Fire'll tell you tonight, Lemontree, how she feels about that."

"Know she will. By the way, Roadmap sneak out on you this morning?"

"Like a whisper, Lemontree."

"Know he do. Wasn't a hard guess to make."

Lemontree and Arfel were just about to cross a dirt road.

"Don't know if Bonnie's butt gonna show up at the Bird tonight, don't say she was. Just know—she sure wore me out last night. Cracked my spine." They'd crossed the road. "Never did like my blueswomen thin."

Chapter 10

Arfel was on fire.

There was this woman. It was the blue dress, what her body put in it.

Arfel was on fire.

His eyes were closed, but he could smell her like rainwater. He wanted to run out the Bluebird Bar but couldn't. It was like before with that other blueswoman—it was like that, just like that; this woman was running her flesh through him, stoking up giant fires in it.

"Woman—shake lak a rattlesnake
Yah 'bout tall as a day.
Lak it w'en yah mouth ain't got it,
Much tah say.

Take yah home, woman—
Yah know how it go,
Seein' what yah doin' tah me,
On dat dance flo'r.

Ain't dinkin' 'bout yah, baby—
Uh-uh, not much.

Jus' sweatin' all dis bad whiskey out me—
An' such.

But yah mine all Saturday night,
An' mostah Sunday mornin' too—
Till de sky turn from black,
Till it turn back ... tah blue."

And Knock-Kneed's harmonica squeezed out a sensuous squeal like a woman's moan that'd climbed to a fever pitch.

Arfel was afraid to open his eyes, afraid the woman, this new blueswoman might be there. Arfel thought, *But I would be taking her home to Stump's Palace, to my room back there. I know what's back there like the lines in the palm of my hands.*

Arfel opened his eyes; and she was out on the dance floor, the blueswoman, moving but so, waiting for Arfel's blues guitar to lock into Lemontree's and Knock-Kneed's. Probably her not knowing their names: Blue Fire, Sweet-Juice, Purple Poison. Probably her not knowing that bluesmen give their guitars names, just that they play the blues and comprehend the mapping of the human soul.

Arfel made a gesture to her; she responded in kind.

"Know I sung it right, Arfel. For you," Lemontree said through his thick grade of sweat. "Seen how you like them, Arfel. Do."

Later.

Arfel came back on the Bluebird stage.

"The girl say she's coming back? Seen her leave."

"Uh-huh," Arfel said, pushing back a whiskey. "Said she's got something to do, Lemontree. Then she's coming back to the Bluebird."

"The Bird." Pause. "Don't wanna know your business, Arfel, but already do." Lemontree chuckled. "But you ain't had none of this city's cunt, has you?"

Knock-Kneed giggled at Lemontree's remark.

"Not you, Knock-Kneed. You and Miss Millie keep a regular date!" Pause. "No northern pussy, Arfel," Lemontree said.

"Same as southern pussy," Knock-Kneed chipped in. "Just travel farther to get here."

The three laughed.

"Has been a while, Lemontree, Knock-Kneed," Arfel said, addressing Lemontree and Knock-Kneed.

"Man can't do without but so long. Ain't in his constitution to."

"A woman's either," Knock-Kneed said, countering Lemontree's remark.

"Yeah, a woman's neither." Lemontree removed his straw hat and fanned his face with it, then Sweet-Juice's. "Tried to go two weeks without any, without a woman one time. Me, Lemontree Johnson." Pause. "Was looking at dogs after five days. Now you know that ain't right!"

"Man and a woman, what does it mean, anyway?" Knock-Kneed said. "We all had us childhood sweethearts. Someone we said we … we'd love forever. It's what we said. Promised ourselves."

Lemontree's eyes looked downright soulful.

"Someone who touched us where we was most—"

"Pure."

"Yeah, Lemontree. Most pure."

"Long time ago, Knock-Kneed. Uh, when feelings was new, was just beginning." Pause. "What was her name for you, Knock-Kneed?"

Knock-Kneed's sleepy eyes brightened. "Louisa Carter. Called her Lou. Like Lou Paris who was in here the other night."

"Harriet Flowers for me," Lemontree said.

Knock-Kneed's and Lemontree's eyes shot over to Arfel.

"Oh … uh … Esther. Esther James for, uh, for me."

"Don't know somebody to be so downright pretty as Harriet Flowers was," Lemontree said. "Was loading my daddy's rusty piece of a truck with crates when I seen her, Miss Harriet Flowers. Can't recall what was in them crates as of today but can recall Harriet Flowers skipping up the road just so. Say right off: Don't want her shoes to get no dirt on them. Dusty them up. Think that right off. Uh-huh. How it come to mind at the time," Lemontree said, his hat no longer fanning his face, nor Sweet-Juice's for that matter, having stopped since he'd mentioned Harriet Flowers's name.

"How many of those things work out, Lemontree?"

"Not many, Knock-Kneed. Uh-uh. Probably count them on one toe. No more." Pause. "But you keep dreaming of that moment, don't you? Uh-huh. Keep dreaming it'd be the same no matter how old you get. Heart got something in it that burn bright and beautiful and true."

Pause.

"So you and that gal gonna go off to Stump's, gonna get you some northern pussy, huh, Arfel?"

It's when Knock-Kneed nudged Arfel. "Like I said, Arfel: it just had farther to travel north to get here—that's all."

The blueswoman was back in the Bluebird Bar. She had on a different dress, but the same body squeezed in it.

"Gotta go," Arfel said, looking first at Knock-Kneed and then at Lemontree.

"She come back for you. You ain't short on cash?"

Arfel shook his head in the negative to Lemontree as he began packing Blue Fire away in her guitar case.

"Give you Mr. Philander Prince's handout tomorrow night, Arfel. Have it in my pocket, ready for you."

"Okay, Lemontree."

"Night, Arfel."

"Night, Knock-Kneed."

Arfel was off the Bluebird stage. He walked over to the blueswoman. She took his arm, and both walked out the Bluebird Bar.

Arfel and the blueswoman were about to turn left on Barrel Street, when Arfel saw Roadmap wheeling down Barrel Street.

Arfel waved to Roadmap. Roadmap waved back.

"Mr. Arfel got him a woman tonight! Yep! Yep! W-was beginning to wonder about Mr. Arfel. Was." Roadmap laughed. Then Roadmap's little face soured. "Ain't gonna hear Blue Fire tonight. Sweet-Juice and Purple Poison, but I ain't gonna hear Blue Fire tonight."

Arfel was still afraid, even though he knew where he was taking this blueswoman off to. He was still afraid, even though he was walking city pavement, not country road, not moving through dense woods but looking up at lampposts lighting each step he and Blue Fire took toward home, Stump's Palace. The blueswoman breathed easily. Her skin had been splashed with perfume, the night carrying its scent warmly. She was full-bodied like the other one, long like the other one—but yellow—this blueswoman was yellow-skinned, not black-skinned like the other one. She didn't want to talk it seemed. Arfel could feel her yellow skin still had the blues in it, a fire, a red autumn. He didn't want to love her, just make love to her. Esther James was a long, long time ago.

Arfel stopped and pointed his finger ahead of him. "There's the—"

"Know the place, bluesman. Know where you was taking me to when we start. From the get-go."

They started walking again.

The blueswoman seemed to be in a hurry; only her body betrayed her, walking softly as if there was a flow in her natural as a southern river spooling.

Arfel and the blueswoman were in Stump's Palace.

Stump's wooden leg was up on the counter. Arfel anticipated their usual nightly exchange but stood there in silence. Arfel and the blueswoman made their way up the sturdy staircase.

"Just down the hall," Arfel said as if he had to say something that was in order, in order to produce sound—something solid. "G-got my key."

"You play good ... bluesman," the blueswoman said, repeating what she'd said in the Bird. "Touch something real deep inside me."

Then Arfel stared at her yellow face. *She is yellow*, he thought. *She is yellow. She is a yellow-skinned blueswoman!*

The key opened the door. Arfel let the blueswoman pass him. She knew where the light switch was as the light popped on. Then she walked over to where a floor lamp was with a plain lamp shade. "Can turn that one off, bluesman. If you wanna."

Arfel did. The room's light became more contained, shaded in. "Like it like that," she said, her body sweetly indulging its shiver. "Oh ... can you play the blues, bluesman."

Arfel wanted to strip her down. It'd been so long, so long he'd been without a blueswoman, strip her down, without sex.

She was on the bed. Her black nylons ran high up her legs. "Went back to put them on, bluesman. Last pair I got out the box."

Arfel's body was on fire.

"See you in a rush," she said, lifting her leg above her head to take the other black nylon off her long, shapely leg. "All night I seen that— what you was doing."

Arfel put Blue Fire in a chair.

"Been drinking all night—but don't feel no way drunk now," she said, her tongue licking her red lips. "Any." Her pocketbook lay flat on the bed. She reached for it. It was purple. She opened it. "Feel like drinking now, some." A short bottle of gin emerged from the purple pocketbook. "Want some?" the blueswoman said, twisting the gin bottle's cap.

"The Bluebird filled my bill. You go ahead."

"Sure …?" she offered again.

"Sure." The bottle went up to the blueswoman's red lips, and then she made some traceable sound as her head tilted back, the bottle and her mouth focused as one. "Sweet, bluesman. Sweet …" she said as her mouth returned to the bottle for more.

Ain't gonna drink this time, Blue Fire. Ain't gonna drink this time. Black out. Ain't gonna kill no white man this time, Blue Fire. Tonight! Tonight!

The bottle was empty. The blueswoman placed it down on the floor and then kicked it over with her three-inch heel. "Ha. Ha. Ain't you coming for me, bluesman? D-don't you want it? Don't you, now?"

Arfel wanted to strip her … But she was already peeling off her clothes. "Want you, bluesman. Want you. Want you bad."

Arfel's body was moving in a frightful way, kinetic, practically poetically mad.

"Hurry, bluesman. H-hurry. Hurry, bluesman."

"Yes. Yes. Yes!"

She was a yellow-skinned woman, skin as yellow as butter. There was more for her to take off—but she seemed to be waiting. "You can see me in the dark … know you can, bluesman."

Arfel understood. He moved over to the floor lamp. "Oooo … I want you, bluesman. Ooooo … I want you. You and that gui-tar playing to me all night. Ooooo … P-playing a blues. Ooooo … bluesman—you coming, ain't you, c-coming?"

And Arfel was there.

"Ain't no rush is there, bluesman? Ain't no rush—is there?"

"Uh … uh … uh …" Arfel said as his long tongue licked her shoulder.

"Make love like you play. Know you do. Make love like you play. Know it …"

Arfel slipped off her panties; the blueswoman moaned deep. "Lick me, bluesman. L-lick me …"

Arfel could see her skin change from rich yellow to warm red. "On fire, bluesman. My body's on fire."

Arfel came down on her, their bodies pressed down to the mattress. Her breasts throbbed against his. "Suck them, bluesman. Suck them hard, bluesman. HARD!"

Her throat gurgled with joy when Arfel did.

Arfel let go of a moan as his mouth rested on her nipple, and then it took it in again—sucking it hard. The blueswoman's hand reached for Arfel, finding him hard. Her hand was warm as it stroked his hard penis.

Arfel's eyes danced inside a blue moon.

And then Arfel's body lurched and then reared back, and her hand touched the full of him as Arfel waited for her legs to spread open.

But the blueswoman's back raised off the bed, and her mouth went deep into Arfel's, sucking in his tongue as Arfel's mouth had sucked in her nipple, and when this was through, her mouth veered into the canal of Arfel's ear.

"Want it from the back, bluesman …" she said, leaning into Arfel. "Want your blues from the back …"

This blueswoman was in his bed, and now Arfel didn't know what to do with her. He moved without her moving with him. There was more light on her, the morning coming faster and faster, but it was still night.

Arfel looked over to the chair where Blue Fire was. Arfel's eyes were burning. There was a new fever in him; the blueswoman was not enough. Not for him.

Arfel opened Blue Fire's case, and there the whiskey bottle shone like a trapped diamond. "Need you now." Arfel grabbed the bottle. It was full. It was new. The bottle was in the air, and it dipped into Arfel's mouth, Arfel sucking the liquor down his throat, finding new ways to drink it. "Blue Fire, Blue Fire. I-I gotta sleep, Blue Fire. I-I gotta sleep. But don't want to. W-want to, Blue Fire."

The bottle was empty. Arfel was able to make it back to the bed. The blueswoman was still naked, not moving, gin and sex, gin and sex, something about the night.

The blueswoman was breathing. Arfel listened to her. Some rhythm was playing deep inside her, the same that was on the dance floor and in Blue Fire when he played her in the Bluebird. Arfel wanted to sleep like her, but he was afraid—when he woke—the white man would be there dead in his bed with his throat slashed open, the sheets as red as a blue sea. When he came to. His eyes opened.

"The liquor. The liquor will make me sleep. It'll make me sleep."

He touched the blueswoman's smooth yellow skin that felt like black velvet. He looked at her, her black hair splashed back against the white pillow. Arfel put his head down on the pillow so his breath could join hers, his face facing hers. Arfel's eyes began to slow down. He could feel some space in himself, some separation as if floating in air. He felt comfortable, relaxed, his breath echoing hers like a blues fugue, the blueswoman's.

Shortly, Arfel rolled his body away from her, seemingly confident he could keep this up, echo the only sound on earth he heard that was in the room, make do with the liquor slowing him, dulling his senses.

And then it happened without any resistance, Arfel taking off to sleep as easily as the blueswoman had in the big bed.

Arfel was traveling in this sleep of his until he woke, his eyes red, white fear shaking through his mind like willowy ghosts had gathered to mark his grave. "The white man … The white man!" Arfel said in a hushed terror. "W-who was he! Who was he! What did he look like w-when I killed him! When I slit his throat clean with my knife!" Arfel now shouted out into the room. A million white ghosts in his mind. A million white ghosts in his soul.

"When my blade found his blood … r-ran through his skin. When I killed him!"

It's when Arfel remembered the blueswoman now in his bed, the blueswoman lying next to him.

Arfel reached down for his pants on the floor and pulled out the knife in the back pocket of his pants and held it in his left hand as tight as his breath and shifted his weight to the blueswoman, and he moved the knife masterly in the dark, for the knife could find the slimmest part of the blueswoman's throat, a single vein.

But the blueswoman was still sleeping. She hadn't stirred from her mix of liquor, sex, and sleep; and Arfel dropped his head down to his naked chest and cried out.

"Blue Fire, Blue Fire—what's happening to me, Blue Fire! What's happening to me!"

And Arfel dropped the knife off to the floor and began to cry. For Arfel knew, he just knew he was going to kill the blueswoman, the yellow blueswoman who was now in his bed. If she'd heard him, the many words he'd just used, the confession he'd just made, the blues now killing his soul—he was going to kill her the same as he'd killed before: slit her throat clean.

"I-I was going to kill her, Blue … Blue Fire … Blue Fire …" Arfel said, his voice sparking the air. "As sure as day turns into night. I was gonna kill her. Slit her throat. Her yellow skin clean through with my knife, Blue Fire!"

Now Arfel wondered what he'd become. What kind of bluesman he was.

Arfel listened to the blueswoman breathe out her scented breath to him. And he knew he would've killed her. He knew as sure as there is a god and a hell—he would've killed her as he'd killed the white man

141

in that southern town. This was what the white man was doing to him. This was how far he'd traveled, gotten from him, as far as the chase had taken him North.

Arfel picked up the knife off the floor and pressed its razor-thin blade to his throat. His hand was shaking like before, fitfully, frantically. "I-I don't know. I don't know what the white man's face looked like. Don't know what it looked like t-to this day …" For the dream, the nightmare he'd been in (deep as a well) took him but so far in distance: the sex and the liquor and nothing more. It couldn't take him beyond that, beyond that point of discovery and revelation and fact in the story where he'd killed the white man in the log cabin. It couldn't take him beyond that foggy bottom, that ugly, reprehensible regret.

"I-I don't know," Arfel said, the knife put back on his throat, his skin. "I … I don't know … to … to this day …"

The blueswoman was gone from the room, but Arfel was in a wild panic.

How he was able to hold on to his calm, sanity when the blueswoman awoke and dressed and left, he had no idea. But now he was in a state of panic, lost inside himself, in between time, finding the horror of what he did down in that southern town, down in that log cabin's room, more and more.

How was he going to make it through the rest of the day when it was already four o'clock in the morning? Arfel thought.

Chapter 11

Roadmap executed a right-hand turn on Spring Street. Soon, he was to step on Lime Street. "Mr. Arfel go off with that woman, that blueswoman last night," Roadmap said playfully. "Know her name, just ain't saying it. Know it good. Call her a blueswoman now. She go off with Mr. Arfel and Blue Fire. Yep, call her a blueswoman now."

Roadmap had a few nickels loose in his pockets. They jingled cheerfully.

"Had me a good night," Roadmap bragged. "Better night than what I expect. Thought to have." Roadmap was on Lime Street staring down Stump's Palace. "Wonder what Blue Fire does when Mr. Arfel ... when him and a woman ..." And then Roadmap became self-conscious, as if he was about to ask himself a silly, childish question.

"Oh—never mind."

Roadmap was at Stump's Palace.

He went through the door. Mr. Stump wasn't at the front desk. Roadmap looked up the stairs. He rolled the cap's bill. He could sense the blueswoman was gone, that it'd been just sex between her and Mr. Arfel. Roadmap was on the second-floor landing. His body kind of edged the wall, walking stealthily, almost purposefully out of character.

When he reached the room's door, he kind of listened for sound anyway. Satisfied it was just Mr. Arfel and Blue Fire in the room, Arfel knocked.

Knock.

"Mr. Arfel!"

"Roadmap!"

"Mr. Arfel … w-what's wrong, Mr. Arfel! What's wrong!"

Arfel let go of the doorknob and tried to slow down his panic.

"The blueswoman, M-Miss Lucy Roy—she don't rob you? Steal from you last night? Miss Lucy Roy don't—"

"No. Roadmap. N-no."

Roadmap saw Blue Fire on the chair. Roadmap was in the room as Arfel's body began to spin. "Mr., Mr. Arfel …"

"I-I've gotta, but I've gotta see Lemontree. Mr. Lemontree, Roadmap!"

"Mr. Lemontree, Mr. Arfel!"

"Yes … yes …" Arfel said, reeling backward and then falling back onto the bed. "Yes, yes, Roadmap. Mr. Lemontree. Mr. Lemontree, Roadmap!"

"Yes, yes, Mr. Arfel!" Roadmap said, now looking at the empty whiskey bottle and then the gin bottle down on the floor.

"Gotta talk to someone, Roadmap. To somebody."

Roadmap didn't hesitate in running; he was gone out the Palace.

Knock. Knock.

"Mr. Lemontree! Mr. Lemontree! It's me, Mr. Lemontree! Roadmap! Roadmap, Mr. Lemontree!"

"Roadmap!"

"Had to come, Mr. Lemontree. Mr. Arfel, Mr. Arfel's in—"

"Calm down, Roadmap. Calm down, now."

"Can't, Mr. Lemontree. Can't!" Roadmap's breath spat out his mouth. "Mr. Arfel needs you, Mr. Lemontree. Said he needs you. Run to get you—come to get you!"

Lemontree scooted back into his house and then came back with Sweet-Juice.

"Don't think you gonna need her, Mr. Lemontree. Not Sweet-Juice, Mr. Lemontree."

"Gotta take her, Roadmap. Sweet-Juice with me, Roadmap."

Lemontree and Roadmap were walking as fast as they could to get to Stump's.

"Mr. Arfel don't tell you nothing!"

"Uh-uh, Mr. Lemontree. Wasn't like that. Mr. Arfel was in a panic. Eyes was wild. Real wild. Was in a panic, Mr. Lemontree. Wild-eyed."

"The woman … Lucy Roy, 'cause I don't know her to—"

"No, Miss Lucy Roy don't do nothing to him. Mr. Arfel said she don't."

"Then what!"

"Don't know, Mr. Lemontree. Don't."

Their walk became even faster executed, agitated, and then silence pervaded. Lemontree began to think, to put thought with inquiry, and then finally came to a certain conclusion: Arfel being on the run up North. *Why is he here? Come to this town?*

"That's it, Arfel. That's it."

"Y-you say something, Mr. Lemontree?"

"N-no. Uh, no, Roadmap."

"Don't hear you too good if you did. Guess I was concentrating. Thinking. Concentrating bad. Hard. Mr. Lemontree. Thinking."

Lemontree began preparing himself for the worse, for he knew the news would be bad. Whatever Arfel was to tell him—he knew it was to be bad. He'd heard it in Arfel's playing on Blue Fire from the first night he arrived in the Bluebird, when it was just him and Arfel on stage, when Knock-Kneed was over at Miss Millie's catting for two nights straight. He heard the blues that was in him played through Blue Fire like a tragedy, like the bluest of what a bluesman can play anything on his guitar when humbled and harried by fear.

Lemontree forced Roadmap to walk even faster, close to a good gallop.

"Gotta get there, Mr. Lemontree. Gotta get there fast."

"Lemontree?" Stump said surprised. "Ain't no trouble, is there?"

145

"No ... n-not that I know of, of, Stump." Lemontree said reasonably—but huffing and puffing just the same.

"You don't normally come messing around the Palace this early in the day, Lemontree."

"I know," Lemontree said laconically.

"And what about—what you have to do in this, Roadmap?"

Roadmap shrugged his shoulders. "J-just following Mr. Lemontree. I guess, Mr. Stump."

"Guess so, Roadmap. Guess you are. Ha," Stump said.

Lemontree was on the second floor. He leaned against the hallway's wall. His body and all. "Wait ... wait a minute, Roadmap. Gotta catch my breath. Get it right, Roadmap." Lemontree took off his hat and then fanned himself.

"Making a breeze, Mr. Lemontree. A good one."

Lemontree stopped fanning himself. His body was bunched up. "Ready, Roadmap?"

"Ready, Mr. Lemontree."

Knock.

"Arfel."

"Lemontree," Arfel said relieved. "Lemontree."

Lemontree was in the room.

Arfel's and Roadmap's eyes quickly locked. "Gotta, gotta talk to Mr. Lemontree alone, Roadmap. Gotta be between me and him."

Roadmap half bowed his head. "Understand, Mr. Arfel. Understand that. I-I do understand."

"Thanks for ..." Arfel went into his pocket.

"Ain't gonna let you pay me, Mr. Arfel."

Arfel felt embarrassed by the thoughtless gesture.

"Owe you and Blue Fire that much, Mr. Arfel." Then Roadmap began walking up the Palace's long hallway.

"Thanks, Roadmap."

Roadmap turned and tipped his cap. "Don't mention it, Mr. Arfel."

Arfel shut the room door. Lemontree was sitting in a chair. Arfel turned to him. "See the bottles, Arfel. On the floor. Seen you ain't cleaned up." Pause. "Roadmap say the woman, that blueswoman don't give you trouble. Try to rob you or—"

"No, no—she don't, Lemontree. E-everything go, went fine. Like planned."

Lemontree took Sweet-Juice off his shoulder and put her on his knees. He held her there. He rocked her some. "See it do, Arfel."

"It's me, Lemontree!"

"You?"

"Me, Lemontree. Why I'm here. Why me and Blue Fire came to this town. C-came this far North."

"Thought so. Figured it on the way over."

"It's been haunting me, Lemontree. But last night ..."

"Was the worse. Worse to come. Come out of nowhere. Hit you like a bolt out a hell."

"Yes. Yes. I ..."

"Take your time. Me and Sweet-Juice ain't got nowhere to go," Lemontree said, still rocking Sweet-Juice in a soft lullaby. "Ain't in no hurry. So early in the day. So tell it right, Arfel. What's good, best for you."

Arfel sat on the bed. "Yes good, good for me. Best, Lemontree. Good, yes ..." Arfel looked up at the ceiling. "Seems like it happened so long ago, but it don't. I know it don't."

"It was a woman, Arfel? Then? A blueswoman?"

"Yes."

"Woman, blueswoman last night remind you of that blueswoman? That it?"

Arfel took a sufficient breath.

"Yes, Lemontree." Arfel's eyes danced around Lemontree, not looking at him straight on. "I was playing, Blue Fire and I was playing with ... with Gin-Water Pete, Lemontree. Gin-Water Pete and ... and Brown Georgia at Sunny's Blues Shack. Gin-Water Pete, you, you kinda remind me of Gin-Water Pete, Lemontree. Right off. All along. All this time me and Blue Fire been here."

"What about Brown Georgia and Sweet-Juice?"

"No, no. Can't say the same, Lemontree. Not that."

"Hell, who don't I look like? Think I look like every colored bluesman in the world—long as he's tall, black, and carry some good meat on him. Carry it well."

147

"Yes. Yes." Pause. "Tall, Lemontree. She was tall."

"Like the one last night?"

"And black."

"Not yellow-skinned …"

"Like the one last night." Pause. "Come into the place a couple of times."

"Like a mystery?"

"Yes."

"Seen them kind of woman. Been to them kind of places. Seen them kind of blueswomen. W—"

"Gin-Water Pete called her a, a devil, a 'devil-woman,'" Arfel said as if Gin-Water Pete possessed some magic eye.

"What she was. Slink like a devil. Yeah, a devil-woman," Lemontree said as if indeed he'd seen this kind of blueswoman before.

"Said to stay clear of her."

"Uh-huh. But you don't. You don't pay him no mind. Never mind. Gin-Water Pete, that is. Advice he give you."

"Gotta go with her, Lemontree. Gotta."

"Any man is, Arfel. Any bluesman is."

"Just a matter of when."

Silence.

"Don't know the town—"

"Passing through."

"Don't know the town, really."

"She lead the way."

"Yes."

"Take your hand, Arfel. Gotta follow the blueswoman off."

"Roads. Back roads, Lemontree. Woods. Go through thick woods."

Lemontree was shaking his head.

"So on … and so on, Lemontree. So on and so on—until we hit an open patch."

"Glade?"

"Yes. Glade." Arfel's eyes widened as if seeing something.

"What was it, Arfel? What the blueswoman lead you off to? Off—"

"A log cabin, Lemontree. Standing alone. By itself. Apart from everything else out there."

"Blueswoman, she still got your hand, Arfel. Leading you. You still feeling things. Multitude of them."

"Uh-huh. Was drinking, but she said, said there was plenty of liquor in the cabin. Plenty of ..."

"So ..."

"Yes, we get there, Lemontree. We ..."

"Open the door."

"It's fancy."

"Fancy?"

"Nice, Lemontree. Nice. And there was a cabinet, a cabinet stocked full of liquor."

"Fancy."

"Uh-huh, fancy," Arfel said. "Don't waste time. None."

"Don't expect you to. Not with no she-devil. Not with no blueswoman like you saying she was, waiting on you," Lemontree said huskily.

"She was everything, everything she was on the dance floor, Lemontree. Everything," Arfel said, remembering, not bragging.

There was a long pause.

"So ..."

"Oh ... so, so she was gone when I woke."

"From the cabin? Don't say nothing before she go?"

"No. Just wrote me a note. Left a note. Said she wasn't gonna be at Sunny's Blues Shack, but the log cabin. Said I was to come for her. Didn't write all of that out—"

"But you know what she was saying. How she was saying it. Putting it. Sense she was making."

Arfel shook his head.

"And ..."

"The next night me and Gin-Water Pete play at Sunny's Blues Shack like before."

"Uh-huh."

"Until—"

"That hour of the night."

"Yes."

"And you hit them back roads and woods till you get to the—"

"Glade."

Lemontree, now, was at the edge of his chair, rocking in an edgy, uneven motion with Sweet-Juice.

"The light was on."

"She was there."

"Uh-huh."

"The blueswoman was there."

"We, me and her go at it different than before. D-don't use the bed. We on the hard floor. It's where we start. Up against the wall in … in a corner—then slide, go down to the floor."

Then Arfel ran his eyes off from Lemontree. "Drink too much, Lemontree. Drink too much."

"A-afterward, Arfel?"

"Drink too much, Lemontree."

"But you and the blueswoman …"

"We do it again. My drinking, it don't stop nothing. Don't change my appetite. Appetite for wanting. Sex. Sex." Arfel's eyes were fixed back on Lemontree. Tears filled his eyes. "And now I don't, I don't remember nothing. Nothing," Arfel said, in a voice that he was struggling to control, since his mind couldn't find the truth of anything. Nothing. "I-I go and black out. Lemontree. Black out!"

Lemontree's huge hands rubbed together, then he clenched them up into a big bale of a fist.

"When I wake, Lemontree … the white man was dead. DEAD!"

"White man! The white man! What, what white man!"

"Slit his throat! Slit the white man's throat with my knife! With my knife!"

"White man! White man! What, what fucking white man you talking about!"

Arfel leaped to his feet. "I don't know. I don't know what white man," Arfel cried out.

"His blood was in the bed. The sheets. I-I wake and feel a lump below my feet. B-beneath my feet. H-his blood was soaked in the bed!" Arfel dipped his hand down into his left pant pocket and drew out the knife for Lemontree's full view and observation of what was now the "murder weapon."

"I killed him with this. With my knife. Slit his throat clean," Arfel said, his voice dropping off.

"The blueswoman!"

"Was gone. Long gone, Lemontree!"

"So you run, run, Arfel!"

"Run. Run. Run back to where me and Gin-Water Pete was staying. Mr. Chester's. Run to Mr. Chester and Miss Henrietta's farm. Run off to there. Run."

"Know what you gotta do."

"Yes."

"Hit them back roads and them woods."

"Stay out of sight."

"Hitch a ride to get to the trains, Arfel."

"Yes."

Arfel walked back to the bed and sat down on top it. The knife lay next to his leg. "Me and Blue Fire had to go through swamp water to get to the trains to get away."

"Them bloodhounds was on the chase. Move. Bloodhounds was probably chasing you by now, Arfel. Got good reason to. Sniffing the ground. For, for …"

"A, a white man. The blueswoman got her a sugar daddy. A white man to pay for her liquor down there. Stock her liquor. Damned fancy log cabin. You sex in." Silence. "But who was he, Arfel? Own a log cabin stock with liquor and a colored woman to lay down with him at night. Who was he!"

"Don't know, Lemontree," Arfel said, snatching the knife. "J-just know I killed him, Lemontree. Slit his throat clean. Clean through with my knife!" Arfel's tears glistened anew. The blade of his knife flashing with nasty intentions.

Later.

"Don't think it was that, Arfel. Just don't," Lemontree said, sitting in the same chair. "Don't think a white man was in it. Y-your troubles."

"Can't change it, Lemontree."

"No, you can't do that. White man's dead. Throat slashed. No, can't do that." Pause. "Had me a cousin who do that. Kill a white man. Run a pitchfork straight through him one day on a farm. Down in Georgia. Savannah. Run off. Ain't heard from him since. Don't know if Vernon dead or alive. Just know he's gone. M-make tracks."

"They'll be—"

"Coming for you. For sure. Sounds like this white man important. Got something to do down there. Where you was, with things."

Arfel nodded.

"Ain't gonna let a nigger get away with nothing. Know that for sure. Somebody coming for you. Out the mist. Come show up." Pause.

"A bounty hunter?"

"Probably. Hire out somebody. Somebody who's professional at it. Know how to hunt. Travel alone. On his own. How to hunt down a nigger. Follow him to the last stop on the train even if he drop—another bounty hunter have to pick up your trail. Scent. Ride the rails."

"They must—"

"Know your name by now."

"Arfel Booker."

"Find out someway. Somehow. Mr. Chester, Miss Henrietta. Sunny's Blues Shack. Burn down they place. One or two or both. Law on they side. Since they make it." Pause. "You been here for a while so, well … we'll just have to wait and see." Lemontree looked at Arfel. "You staying? You and Blue Fire staying on, ain't you? You ain't running off—is you, Arfel?"

"Yes, I'm staying, Lemontree. Me and Blue Fire are staying on. Ain't running off."

"'Cause if there's trouble, we'll handle it. If any comes your way, we'll handle it."

Lemontree stood. "Arfel, see you feel better about things."

"Do. Feel a lot better, Lemontree. Had to talk to someone."

Lemontree stood. "Had it bottled up, I know. Something as bad as that. Drive a man crazy. Need confession, what's good for the soul. But now it's out in the open. Got air in it. Plenty. Ain't but one of you now, but two." Lemontree began walking off to the door.

"Thanks for coming, Lemontree."

"Roadmap was all a dither."

Arfel laughed too. "Poor little Roadmap."

"Like the boy got worms in his belly: he squirm so."

Arfel laughed a second time. They were at the door. Arfel and Lemontree shook hands.

"Handshake's strong, Arfel. Rock solid." Arfel opened the door for Lemontree. Lemontree began walking up the hallway and then turned.

"Miss my cousin Vernon. Miss him to this day. Nobody knows if he's dead or alive."

Arfel closed the door, and his body caved in. But he did feel better that it wasn't just him but Lemontree now: two was better than one under any circumstance.

Chapter 12

Three weeks later.

Arfel had settled more into this northern city. Since his talk with Lemontree, it was like a big weight had been pulled off him, and he could exhale again. Just last week he and Lemontree played at Knock-Kneed's relative's funeral. Knock-Kneed was too emotionally torn to play with them. His relative had died of ptomaine poison. She was a young girl, fifteen years of age.

"I wasn't going to come tonight," Knock-Kneed said. "But had to."

Lemontree laid his hand down on top of Knock-Kneed's knee. "Been a tough three days on you, go of it, Knock-Kneed. I know."

"Food poisoning. Food poisoning. Being poor."

"Poor," Lemontree said with authority. "Feel it in every way. Pinch my soul."

"She was so young."

"She was, Knock-Kneed."

"Pauline. Was named after my auntie Pauline. She died giving birth, during childbirth, Auntie Pauline. Was young too. Nobody knew the same would happen to Pauline."

"Hell, nobody knows nothing. Especially a colored man, Knock-Kneed. A colored man living this life."

Arfel came back on the Bluebird stage. He'd just come from the bathroom.

"Toilet's not stopped up, is it, Arfel?"

"Uh-uh, Knock-Kneed."

"Guess I'm next to go." Knock-Kneed was up out his chair. "Be right back."

"Okay," both Lemontree and Arfel said.

"Knock-Kneed's still in pain, ain't he, Lemontree?"

Lemontree strummed Sweet-Juice harmonically. "World of it."

Arfel picked up Blue Fire and strummed something out on her strings harmonically.

"Still wondering why," Lemontree said compassionately. "Lost folk thataway. Relatives in my family. Rotten food. Ain't refrigerated proper. Know rats in the field eat better." Pause.

"What about you, Arfel?"

"It's happened in my family."

"Girl dying young like that for no reason can hold up to nobody. Holding a funeral for her for no reason. No just cause. People crying for no reason. Man, hell, don't know who flip a coin over our heads to give us colored folk such bad luck."

Lemontree had a whiskey glass at the tip of his shoe. He picked it up and drank the whiskey down. "He's such a good boy, Knock-Kneed. Don't bother nobody. Keeps pretty much to himself. Sociable, but don't get too much into politics and the such—white and colored."

"Yes, I know ... we've—"

"I know, Arfel. I know. We discussed it before—so I ain't getting old, just, ha, reemphasizing. You got what was bothering you out your system, but Knock-Kneed ain't got his out yet. Ain't come to terms with it. It's festering still. Ain't left him yet."

"I'm back."

"See that, Knock-Kneed," Lemontree said.

"Ready to play," Knock-Kneed said, picking up Purple Poison.

"Harmonica's gonna sound nice on what I'm about to play," Lemontree said. "Sing. Knock-Kneed. Harmonica's gonna sound awful nice."

And already, starting the tune, Knock-Kneed's harmonica was skinning back the Bluebird's air with a mournful tone.

155

Denis Gray

"Die young,
Die old;
Don't always know—
W'at's killin' yo'r soul.

Die so tomorrow don't—
Evah come;
Lak a fresh flower—
Die young.

Life ain't no bargain—
Fer nobody bo'n';
Funeral wagon come fer yah—
At dawn.

Luv yah dat night—
Luv yah still;
Feel lak it my soul—
De day dun kill."

It was a chilly, misty night on Lincoln Street.

"*Psst. Pssst*, Mister ..." Roadmap had been ignored.

Tonight had been a bad night for Roadmap. All night. He was sheltered, but still, the mist and the chill had bore into his clothes, and his toes were getting cold, felt as brittle as icicles. So Roadmap did his usual when he was faced with this kind of predicament: he hopped on one leg (right then left) in place in order to try to get his blood to circulate—boil a little bit hotter.

"Ha. Ha. Ha ..." Roadmap laughed, hopping about in the dark shadows, hoping to discourage the cold. "Ha. Ha." Roadmap laughed as he kept at playing his game.

Roadmap hadn't regained his full voice when he said, "*Psst. Pssst.* Hey—"

And it's when Roadmap slapped his hand to his mouth hard, as hard as he could to seal it.

The white man was tall and wore a big brown hat. And he passed by the opening between the two tall white buildings on Gate Street, a short distance from the train station.

"He … he don't belong here," Roadmap said scared, frightened. "That, that white man don't belong here!" Roadmap could hear the white man was gone, and it's when he ran off like he was chasing the wind on this night of chill and heavy mist on Gates Street.

And while speeding off for the Bluebird, Roadmap's mind reeled back to three weeks ago. What he heard outside Mr. Arfel's door when he had not descended the staircase, when he stood in the lobby alone, quietly, thoughtfully (Stump was elsewhere in the Palace); and at that precise moment, all he could think about was Mr. Arfel and Mr. Lemontree in room 2G and what Mr. Arfel had to tell Mr. Lemontree that'd made him run to Mr. Lemontree's residence to get him.

So he'd pressed his ear against Mr. Arfel's room door as hard as steel, for Roadmap had to know what Mr. Arfel was running from, what had brought him to this northern town.

"H-how could you, Mr. Arfel!" Roadmap had said when he heard Arfel say he'd killed a white man with his knife. That Mr. Arfel had slit the white man's throat. "How could you kill anybody as pretty as you play Blue Fire, Mr. Arfel!"

"Slow it down, Arfel, Knock-Kneed. Slow it down to a minimum. A walk. Want everybody to hear this. Slow it down. Gotta blues song to sing for everybody, Arfel. Everybody gotta hear this blues."

"Go tah church on Sunday,
Say Ah go tah church on Sunday—
Got tah pray.
Still gonnah dank God,
Fer 'nothah day.

Ain't angry at 'im
(Ouch, Lord have mercy!)
Fer handin' me dis life.

Can't always tell
If Ah'm livin' it right.

Always some trouble kickin'
At mah do'r—
Don't bothah bill collector—
Dat Ah po'r.

Oh ... Jesus, Jesus!—
Don't let me kill no one—
(Nobody, please, God.)
Don't let me havetah use mah knife.
Lemontree go tah church on Sunday.
Still tryin' tah do it right."

"Keep it slow, Arfel, Knock-Kneed, at a minimum. A walk. Got something else to say. Something else bothering me. Eating at me. From inside out."

Lemontree was sweating through his straw hat like it was black skin in a pot of boiling collard greens. "G ... good, Arfel, Knock-Kneed. Good. At a minimum, a walk."

Lemontree began.

"Jus' 'cause a dog ain't trained
Tah bite,
Don't mean,
It ain't ready to fight.

Jus' 'cause a colored man,
Git ol'—
Don't mean he
Dun los' his soul.

Still know white man,
Dun 'is daddy wrong—
Was way back w'en,

But weren't dat long.

Mess wid dat dog,
In de wrong way—
Tell yah, man, one day—
Gonnah be some hell tah pay!"

And then Lemontree turned to Arfel sharply. "He's here, Arfel. Roadmap's here."

But Roadmap wasn't in his usual "hideaway" spot but was charging toward the Bluebird stage.

Lemontree and Arfel were aghast. "Road—"

"Gotta see Mr. Arfel. Mr. Arfel and Blue Fire, Mr. Lemontree. Gotta see them, Mr. Lemontree. Gotta see them!"

Neither Arfel nor Lemontree knew what this was about, the current of fear buzzing through Roadmap's eyes.

"Take over, Knock-Kneed. Spotlight's on you."

"But, but—"

"Play something. Sing something. Dammit. Do something, man!"

Roadmap ran off to the back of the Bluebird knowing Mr. Arfel and Mr. Lemontree would follow suit.

"W-what's gotten into the boy, Arfel! In-into Roadmap!"

Lemontree carried Sweet-Juice in his hand and Arfel Blue Fire in his, as they left the Bluebird stage to seek out Roadmap.

When they got in the back room with the dangling light, Roadmap was shaking something fierce, something clear, vivid.

"Out on that corner. In that cold, damp rain, Roadmap."

"Ain't that, Mr. Lemontree. Used to that. Ain't that." Then Roadmap's pretty brown eyes looked up at Arfel. "A-a white man come to town, Mr. Arfel. A-a white man. He's tall with a big brown hat, Mr. Arfel. Tall with a big brown hat."

Arfel and Lemontree looked at each other befuddled.

"Heard you, Mr. Arfel. Heard you through the room door. Know I wasn't to listen. But couldn't sit still. Heard you tell Mr. Lemontree, Mr. Arfel. About everything," Roadmap said as if he should've been told all along. "Know what you done to that white man down there, Mr.

Arfel. In that town. Know you killed him. How you killed him. Slit his throat, Mr. Arfel. The knife you carry. Y-you carry in your back pocket, Mr. Arfel. Know why the white man come. And who he coming for!"

"He's—"

"On the other side of town, Mr. Arfel. The white man. Cross, cross town for now. Leave him there. Take shortcuts, Mr. Arfel. But he's soon gonna know where they play the blues. Blues come from in this town."

"Y-yes …" Arfel said, his voice in deep trouble, and feeling as if the last note in his life had been struck.

"Don't see his eyes, Mr. Arfel, but know he got a mean stare. Glint. K-know that."

"He ain't gonna find you, Arfel. Nobody know you!"

And then Roadmap was about to take off.

"Where you going, Roadmap!"

"To tell Miss Millie, Mr. Lemontree!"

"But Miss Millie's girls—"

"Don't know, Mr. Lemontree. Don't. He might come with money, Mr. Lemontree. White man might be coming with money in his hand."

"Right, Roadmap. Right. Real smart of you. Make sure Miss Millie don't let none of her girls see him. Don't know what they might do for money. See, see money."

Then Lemontree turned to Arfel. Lemontree handed him his house key. "My place, Arfel. Staying in my place." Pause. "Don't burn no lights. Gotta latch on the floor. A rug covers over it. Stairs lead down to a space. Can burn a light down there. All you want."

"What about Mr. Stump!"

"White man looking for you, Arfel. All Stump got to know. Know what to say. He don't gotta know the story. None of it. This a pleasure for all of us colored folk!"

Lemontree and Arfel shook hands. "Be in at the usual time. Ain't switching the night around."

"No … no."

"Gotta make it ordinary, routine—no different."

Lemontree was back on the Bluebird stage.

"Where's Arfel, Lemontree? Saw Roadmap run out of—"

"A white man's coming, Knock-Kneed. A tall white man with a brown hat's coming. He's looking for Arfel. It's all I got to tell you. Nothing more. What you should work from."

Knock-Kneed shut his eyes solemnly, in an electric silence, and then opened them. "Knew Arfel was in trouble. Didn't know what for, Lemontree. But you can tell when a man's on the run from something."

"Uh-huh," Lemontree said, moving Sweet-Juice in position for his fingers to play on her strings. "Uh-huh."

Sometime later.

The harmonica pealed through the air along with Lemontree's dark-cast voice anchoring it.

"Aaaaaah!"

"Hang me from a tree,
Ah can feel it still—
Tree don't lie none,
W'en it kill.

Neck snap lak a chicken's neck … bone,
Was dead by den—
Say yah let me hang dere,
Blowin' in de win'.

Know why Ah hate yah,
Need no excuse—
Aaaaah,
Go on an' tell 'im,
Tell the man—Sweet-Juice!"

And even with his eyes shut, somehow, Lemontree knew he was there. The tall white man with the brown hat Roadmap had described had entered the Bluebird Bar.

"He's here," Knock-Kneed muttered to Lemontree.

"Know so," Lemontree muttered back.

Lemontree and Knock-Kneed just kept on playing on Sweet-Juice and Purple Poison.

"Tell me woman, w'at yah say,
W'en Ah git drunk in town—
Ah don't come home,
'Cause Ah sleepin' 'roun'?

Mule-man, yah calls me,
Mule-man—
Say (haha) Ah built lak a mule—
Uh, Lemontree, don't come near me,
Wid dat big ol' tool.

Ah, shut up, woman,
It all a colored man know
How tah do.
Git drunk,
Ah say git drunk—
An' ... screw!"

Lemontree's tile-of-white teeth smiled out at the tall white man who'd ordered a drink at the bar.

"He gonna be talking to Last Round soon," Lemontree said through clenched teeth to Knock-Kneed. "A cheap drink ain't gonna buy him nothing."

And suddenly Lemontree felt Roadmap's presence once again, and he knew Roadmap was there to keep an eye on this new stranger in town, that Roadmap would follow him wherever he went—and the white man wouldn't even know it. Have a clue.

Got you a shadow tonight, white man. Following you, Lemontree said to himself. *Hot on your tail.*

Lemontree shut his eyes as his fingers continued to strum on Sweet-Juice. *Ask all the questions you want. Nobody know Arfel Booker and Blue Fire in this town.*

"Ooooo … luvs yah, baby,
Ain't gonna lie.
Doctor say—Lemontree, got five mo'e good years left in yah,
'Fore yah die.

Said, thank yah, Doctor,
Thought mah heart was weak (from all dat drinkin' an' runnin' 'roun'),
Blood circulate slow in de mornin',
Gittin' from mah head down tah mah feet.

You a mule-man, Lemontree,
A mule-man, Ah say—
Ooooo, Doctor,
Baby laks me dataway!"

It was as late as it gets in the Bird. Lemontree had stuffed the white envelope in his jacket (courtesy of Philander Prince). Knock-Kneed had his take for the night. Lemontree was holding on to his share and Arfel's.

Last Round was cleaning off the top of the bar with the wet rag. "Ha. It was fun, Lemontree. Fun. Acted like a real monkey. Monkeyshine. Dipped in monkey do-do."

"Know it was, Last Round!" Lemontree said, slapping his hand down on the bar.

"See no evil, hear no evil, speak no evil. That's all the white man gotta know." Last Round laughed.

"Sung him that song, all he wanna know. All he think a colored man can do: drink whiskey and screw a woman."

"Well … he got bamboozled tonight, Lemontree," Knock-Kneed chimed in.

"Uh-huh. Miss Millie and Stump got the same tune for him: white man's on the wrong side of town in this town tonight. No … nowhere where he belong," Lemontree said, patting Knock-Kneed on the back.

"Tell Arfel the same. See him tomorrow night."

"Will do, Knock-Kneed. Will do."

Knock-Kneed bid Last Round good night.

163

"Whiskey taste good, extra good tonight, Last Round."

"Ask me who run the bar. Tell him a white man who hate niggas but don't care where his money come from. How he gets it."

"Can't say that about Philander Prince, Last Round. Can't put that white lie on that white man, though."

"I know, Lemontree, but his white face, it's when it smiled pleasant, Lemontree. *Reeeal* pleasant. The most pleasantest. Shined like monkeyshine. Do-do do."

Lemontree was out the Bluebird Bar. He was walking down Barrel Street. For some reason he was humming. When he realized what he was doing, he didn't stop. He just pressed on more. He had to laugh at Roadmap: his ear must've stuck to Arfel's room door. Neither he nor Arfel heard him. They weren't in the Bird playing the blues, but in Stump's Palace. But it was a lucky thing Roadmap knew Arfel's story. He'd saved Arfel tonight. God was with him tonight. Roadmap and almighty God.

"Roadmap speed right over to the Bluebird. Take off like a shot—I suspect."

Lemontree could see Roadmap's little legs churning, spinning, turning as fast as a speeding bullet. "Fast as a bullet."

The air was dark, the heavy mist still there—fully plated. The four fat diamonds on Lemontree's four fat fingers shone out into the dreary dark. Lemontree thought of Arfel down in that space in the house just below the stairs. "Ain't warm down there on a night like tonight. Can't say it is," Lemontree said, hugging his coat better to his burly body.

"But that's all right: Arfel's running hot, can't help but. Running hot like a stove top."

Lemontree was about to round the corner, when he saw a shadow of something, a piece of something deliberately jump back behind the building. And then Lemontree smelled him like the mist, and his laugh came out as pure as a black snake's. Lemontree's hand raised up to his straw hat, making sure it stayed straight, was securely squared in place.

"He following me. The white man. He following me." Lemontree laughed, but not too loudly. "Well, good for him. Good for him. Gonna walk him in the rain. Mist. Ain't going straight home. Get there when I want. Wanna. Ain't doing him no favors. Walk him like a dog on a leash. Get him shaggy as hell. For his tail to drag."

Lemontree had been walking slowly—but now he walked even slower. "Take you for a walk around the block. Let you see how coloreds live up here. North. Rain ain't gonna hide nothing. Just wash it down some." And then Lemontree wondered where Roadmap was while he tailed the white man who was tailing him; what kind of distance Roadmap was maintaining between them.

"Sorry, Roadmap. Real sorry," Lemontree said. "You gotta get more wet too. Know you know these streets better than any of us do."

By now, even Lemontree was getting tired. He could just imagine how Roadmap felt, what he was going through. "The white man about to catch on by now." Lemontree was on Cross Street. Ain't gonna keep this up. Even Roadmap know it's time to play it straight. White man gonna know I'm hiding something.

"Ain't so dumb."

Baron Street was only two blocks from Cross Street. Lemontree's clothing was soaked through and through, but there was no chill in him—just a fine fire feeding his belly, circulating him. Sweet-Juice was in her case, so her wood was in no way at harm.

"Sweet-Juice, you the only one keeping warm."

The white man was doing a good job of following him, for a white man, Lemontree thought. If it'd been an Indian or a colored man—he'd never seen him in the first place, Lemontree laughed.

Lemontree was on Baron Street. "We home, white man." And then Lemontree looked at his house from the distance he maintained: it was pitch-black. "Know you and Blue Fire down in the basement, Arfel. Nobody else."

Lemontree walked to the house unassumingly. "Live right here, white man. Nowhere else. Right here in broad daylight. See, it's dark for now. Nobody home. Know you don't want to come in. Ain't nothing for you to see. Don't want to venture but so far, no way." Lemontree went into his right back pocket and pulled out his spare key. He opened the door, flipped on the light, and then shut the door.

"You can stand out there as long as you want, though. Through with you. With my business for the night." Lemontree put on another light to illuminate the room even more. Then he stood by the house's front window and achingly pulled off his jacket. His hand hesitated with his straw hat before removing it. Then he shook himself like a wettened cat, Lemontree seemingly trying to free himself of whatever wet blanketed him. Seconds later, Lemontree stretched.

Arfel was below the floor of the house. He'd heard Lemontree come in. He didn't know the situation, so he would rely on Lemontree to control things. Lemontree knew the situation; his judgment was all that mattered for now.

Roadmap had his eyes set more on the house than on the white man. "Doing fine, Mr. Lemontree. Doing fine. Just fine. Don't mind the long walk, do my legs fine. Good. Walked farther for a night."

It was possibly five or six minutes later. The house was pitch-black. Roadmap's eyes were pinned back on the white man as he still hid himself away.

But then there was movement. "W-what you doing, white man?" Roadmap queried, his voice quivering. "What you doing? What? What!" For Roadmap was watching the white man approach the house, his height diminished, shortened; his boots fell softly in the soggy dirt.

"Don't say nothing, Mr. Lemontree, Mr. Arfel. N-nothing. Don't … don't talk!" For Roadmap knew Mr. Arfel was in Mr. Lemontree's house, him and Blue Fire. Both down below the floor, the space Mr. Lemontree had shown him way back when, from the past.

"The, the white man's there. H-he's at the door!" And Roadmap's eyes could see the white man take off his big brown hat and pin his ear quickly to the door.

"Know you ain't talking. Saying nothing. Know that!" Roadmap said gleefully. Then Roadmap saw the white man take his ear from off the door and place his big brown hat back on his head. "Knew it. Knew it. Knew you and Mr. Arfel ain't saying nothing, Mr. Lemontree!"

The white man kept to his crouch and the softness in his boots as he began moving in the dark, creeping silently away from Lemontree's house.

"Right behind you, white man. W-where I am. Right behind you. Seeing you off to the trains."

Lemontree got up and turned on the light.

"If that white man still out there, somebody gonna die tonight." Lemontree looked down to the floor, at the Navajo rug covering part of it. "Know he been gone. Roadmap too." Lemontree kicked the rug aside.

Arfel jumped.

The latched door opened.

"Arfel ..."

"Lemontree ..." Arfel said, his eyes looking up into this oily, shiny black face. "White man's gone. Been."

Arfel began climbing the ladder.

"Arfel ..." And it's when Lemontree hugged him.

"F-feels like heaven, Lemontree!"

"Families used to live that way when they was on the run. Being hunted down. Slaves. How it was."

"I ... I know, Lemontree."

"Some days don't see the sun rise or set—forget what the moon look like." Pause. "Hungry?"

"Starved!"

"Ha! Rustle you up some ham and po-ta-toes." Lemontree had the black cast-iron skillet in his hand (they looked odd up against those four fat diamonds on those four fat fingers of his). "Roadmap with him." Lemontree washed the skillet down. "Been with him all night. Step for step. All night all right. Making tracks."

"Are you sure Roadmap will be all—"

"Don't worry about Roadmap, Arfel. Roadmap could follow a Indian scout out on open plain, no trees, and that Indian don't know Roadmap following him to this day. Him or his shadow." Lemontree wiped the skillet. "White man got a bloodhound on his tail and don't know it. Track him straight to Alaska."

Arfel sat down at the table.

"Ain't pinning no medals on heroes, Arfel, but little Roadmap was one tonight."

"I was lucky, Lemontree."

"That you was. It's what I tell myself, Arfel. God's lights shining down on you. Holy an' all. All around you."

"But now, Lemontree. What, what should I do now?"

"Wait. Wait. Stay put," Lemontree said, the bacon grease popping high in the skillet. "Man pushing farther North. Got a long stretch of road and track left before he push back here."

"Do you think ..."

"He's getting a feel, a smell for every town, Arfel. Ain't no young man, ain't old—but got enough experience to know when the time comes. Present itself." Lemontree's eyes looked down into the skillet. "He's gonna figure things out in time. No sense you running right behind him. You and Blue Fire ain't running this time. White man ain't robbing you of no more sleep."

Arfel nodded but wished he could be assured of that, that sleep would come easier for him: this long stretch of blue.

"Besides, who can you trust, but the folk in this town. Us. Nobody else, Arfel. Along the way. Traveling."

He hadn't thought of that, not that—only—Lemontree had!

"By the way ..." Lemontree said, digging into his back pocket. "Got it all here."

"I ... me and Blue Fire—"

"Take it—even though you cheat the night. Ain't, ha, honest with it. At all."

Arfel had to laugh.

"You and Blue Fire." Pause. "When I go for the money, Philander Prince man's face puzzle. Know what he thinking. Know that man good by now. Tell him you, 'the bluesman—got himself a toothache, sudden. Quit early.' Ha. 'Be here tomorrow night.' Ghost-white face don't look so damned white, then. Got some color in it."

The house's lights were still burning.

Knock. Knock.

Arfel and Lemontree knew by the knocks on the door who it was. They were expecting him—it's why neither had considered sleep.

"Roadmap!"

"Mr. Arfel!"

Arfel grabbed Roadmap, picked him up high off the floor, and hugged him. When Arfel put Roadmap down, Roadmap strutted like a proud peacock with a stock of newly bought feathers sprouting out his short body as he walked into Lemontree's house to announce to Lemontree and Arfel—

"Walked that white man to the trains. Seen him get on, and the train leave the station. Even seen the last smoke leave out the stack, Mr. Arfel. Look pretty in the night. Do. Gray, Mr. Arfel. Gray. A pretty gray. Pretty sight."

Lemontree laughed riotously.

"Last train out the station for the night."

"Toot one time too, Roadmap?"

"Know it did, Mr. Lemontree. Know it did too." Pause.

"Hungry?"

"Starved, Mr. Lemontree!"

Lemontree and Arfel winked at each other. "Mr. Arfel save you some po-tatoes and honey ham, Roadmap."

Roadmap pulled off his jacket. It was still loaded with rain. "What, you ain't eating, Mr. Lemontree?"

"Too nervous to, Roadmap."

Arfel's and Roadmap's insides split open with laughter.

Arfel was sitting next to Roadmap at the short table.

"Mr. Arfel, you … you and Blue Fire, you and Blue Fire … well … you ain't going nowhere, is you? You ain't leaving, leaving town, is you!"

Roadmap had grabbed Arfel's arm when he asked him. "The white man ain't chasing you away is, is he, Mr. Arfel? You and Blue Fire, is he!"

Arfel's hand fell on top of Roadmap's reassuringly. "Uh-uh, Roadmap. Staying put. Me and Blue Fire ain't running this time."

Roadmap kissed Arfel's hand.

"Roadmap ..."

"Had to, Mr. Arfel. Had to. I'm so happy!"

Roadmap was eating his ham and potatoes off the plate now, but between bites he was updating Arfel and Lemontree, both looking intently at him. "We ... he got to Miss Millie's. We ... he get there, but don't get far. Miss Millie say at the door, if he ain't there for one of the girls, then he have to go. Ain't no loitering on the property. Her house ain't for that. Say she don't know Arfel Booker when he ask. Ain't heard of Arfel Booker or a gui-tar called Blue Fire—and don't like the blues anyhow. None of it. If it, the blues, what Arfel Booker play."

Arfel didn't know Miss Millie but thanked her nonetheless.

"White man ain't used to being talked to by coloreds like that. The North do have a little charm about it. Can say that much for it," Lemontree said.

"Mean, though. That white man," Roadmap said.

Lemontree didn't flinch.

"He get to Mr. Stump's. Get over to the Palace."

"Can't wait to hear what Mr. Stump tell him, huh, Arfel?"

"He inquire polite—"

"Trying to use sugar even though Mr. Stump know it about as sweet as pepper, Roadmap," Lemontree said.

"Use Mr. Arfel's name." Roadmap cracked a smile. "But Mr. Stump say he don't rent out rooms to bluesmen."

Arfel still grimaced at the sad news.

"Say they run out on him. Say when they come through the door with a blues gui-tar, he tells them the hotel is full. No rooms for rent. Sends them bluesmen off packing. Seen too many of them sneak out the back door the next day!"

"White man—"

"He don't smile, Mr. Lemontree. His face hard like stone. Ain't got no humor in him. Fun. Just don't."

"No, I expect not, Roadmap. No—I expect he don't. Ain't here for none of that. Come to town for that."

Roadmap scooped half a potato onto his fork. "Well, he gone now. Ain't never been so glad to see a train leave town, Mr. Lemontree. Ain't."

"With a white man on it, Roadmap."

The three of them were sleeping in Lemontree's one room. Lemontree in his bed and Arfel and Roadmap on blankets on the floor. Lemontree had two pillows, one for him and one for Roadmap.

"Ain't pretending I'm sleeping, asleep, 'cause I ain't," Roadmap said.

Roadmap realized he wasn't waking Mr. Lemontree or Mr. Arfel—since he could hear how they breathed: not at all hypnotically.

"Can't seem to fall off neither, Roadmap," Arfel said, yawning wide.

"White man still sitting in my mind, Mr. Arfel. Ain't gonna lie." Pause. "What make him so mean, Mr. Arfel?"

"It-it's a long story, Roadmap."

"A long story," Lemontree echoed Arfel.

"Ain't sleeping neither, huh, Mr. Lemontree?"

"Uh-uh, Roadmap."

Silence.

"Just come here the wrong way."

"What you say, Mr. Lemontree?"

Lemontree repeated himself. "Yeah, come here as slaves. Come here to do the white man's work. Build things up for him. Work his farms, fields. Till his soil—anything to break a man's back, and his spirit." Lemontree's body shifted quietly in the bed. "When everything start off on the wrong foot, hard to change it. Turn it around."

"It doesn't want to get better, Roadmap," Arfel said. "Don't. White man wants to keep you down—"

"It to his benefit," Lemontree added. "And by now, he thinks it's his right to."

"I ain't afraid of him though," Roadmap said. "Ain't a bone in me afraid of him, Mr. Lemontree. Mr. Arfel."

"You see, Roadmap, Mr. Arfel run not 'cause he afraid of the white man. Uh-uh …"

"I ran, Roadmap, because I'm afraid of his law."

"Ain't no justice for a colored man, Roadmap. Ain't none down there in the South. Ain't no law gonna stand up for a colored man. Set up for him. Ain't no justice wrote down in them books for him. Uh-uh. Books of law for a colored man."

"Sounds bad, Mr. Lemontree."

"Decent people make the law, Roadmap. But them other ones, seems like, the ones who carry it out."

Pause.

"How far the man gonna go, Mr. Lemontree, till he come back?"

"Far as the trains take him. Ain't looking back till he have to. Ain't. Not until." Lemontree's weight was now heard in the bed. "And then when he come back for a second time, go, look—he gonna figure out things far better than what he do the first time he was here."

"He's gonna be meaner, Mr. Lemontree?"

"Say so. Been on the road so long. Say so, Roadmap. Meaner. Much." Pause. "Mr. Arfel got a price on his head—ain't coming down. Worth the man's time but ain't worth his worry."

"When he comes, I'll see him, Mr. Lemontree. Yep. At the train station, Mr. Lemontree. Sure as day."

"Know you will. That's so, Roadmap."

"Mr. Arfel, how, how it feel to kill a man, Mr. Arfel?"

"Don't know, Roadmap. Black out."

"Drink make you lose your senses, lose sense of things, Roadmap. Liquor."

"Don't drink, Mr. Lemontree, say that much for myself."

Arfel and Lemontree laughed.

"Ain't gonna say I ain't tried to. But spit it out. No, I ain't much for drinking, Mr. Arfel, Mr. Lemontree."

"Don't solve nobody's problems, Roadmap. Sometimes think it make them worse."

"So why—"

"Sometimes you wanna forget things, Roadmap," Arfel said. "Nights, if you depend on memory, uh, what you know, Roadmap, you die."

"Drink kills you too," Lemontree said. "Only, at a slow, dragged-out pace."

"You think about dying, Mr. Lemontree?"

"Oh, yeah, Roadmap. Ain't a option."

"What about you, Mr. Arfel?"

"Wasn't thinking about that tonight at the Bluebird. But the night I killed the white man, it's all I was thinking about, Roadmap, dying. When I run through them woods, swamp water, me and Blue Fire, I could hear the ancestors, the people I don't even know, Roadmap, turn in their graves. Spirit of them breathe out. What—feel them turning in the waters, ice cold—blood blue as a bluebird's."

"Scared, Mr. Arfel?"

"Was scared, Roadmap. Was. Was thinking about dying, Roadmap. Not living. But wasn't gonna die down there. Don't know where they're gonna bury me when I die, don't know that. Don't care to know that ..."

"But ..."

"Not that night, Roadmap. Not down there. Wasn't going to bury me down there."

"Sometimes a man gives himself a choice, Roadmap."

"Would've killed again, Roadmap. Me and Blue Fire wasn't about to die out there. Wasn't." Pause.

"Can sleep now, Mr. Arfel. Know I can!"

"Me too, Roadmap," Arfel said.

"Ain't gonna be the odd man out," Lemontree said. "Since it's my floor you two sleeping on, and my house."

Pause.

"But one thing, Roadmap, before I go off ..."

"Yes, Mr. Lemontree?"

"Gonna sleep in that soggy cap of yours all night? Ain't taking it off your head?"

"No, Mr. Lemontree. Ain't."

"Forgot what your head look like these days, Roadmap. Swear. Ain't got bumps, sores in it, do it? All bumped up?"

"No, Mr. Lemontree. It's still clean as a whistle. Know it is!"

Chapter 13

The sun was out in the sky. It struck Roadmap right dead in the eye when it shone its best.

Roadmap looked around; he'd been the only one sleeping.

"Morning, Roadmap!"

Roadmap's yawn was broad. "Good morning, Mr. Lemontree!"

"See the sun shine in your eye."

"Yep." Yawn. "Where's Mr. Arfel? See Blue Fire but not Mr. Arfel, Mr. Lemontree."

"In the bathroom."

Then Roadmap heard the bathroom water run. "Oh—hear him now." Roadmap enjoyed another bloated yawn. "Been up long, Mr. Lemontree? You and Mr. Arfel?"

"Don't beat Mr. Arfel up by much, but you—a lot."

Roadmap laughed. "Sorry, Mr. Lemontree. Don't usually sleep this late. Don't put no trust in time last night, Mr. Lemontree. Figure I'd let it come … and go."

"Good morning, Roadmap!"

"Morning, Mr. Arfel! Heard you was up before me, not like"— Roadmap winked—"before, the last time we was together. At the Palace." Roadmap got to his feet. "Quiet as a spider then, Mr. Arfel, before I leave. Blue Fire ha … don't even see me when I go." Then Roadmap's leg began shaking.

"Gotta go! Gotta pee! Be right back!"

Quickly Arfel stepped aside, out of harm's way.

Roadmap shut the bathroom door.

"Cook up something, then for you and—"

"Gonna ask Roadmap to go over to Knock-Kneed's place, Lemontree," Arfel said, cutting Lemontree off.

"You don't wanna get in the way of Roadmap's commerce, Arfel."

"Lemontree, I got a few loose nickels in my pocket."

"My pockets jingling awful good too, Arfel."

One looked at the other. "Though Roadmap do it for free, he's so much involved in this thing with us."

Roadmap was out the bathroom; he was zipping up his pants.

"Wash your hands, Roadmap?"

Roadmap looked up.

"'Cause we gonna eat soon," Lemontree said.

"Ham and … and po-tatoes, Mr. Lemontree?"

"Uh-huh, Roadmap. And sausage, eggs, and grits."

"How about it?" Arfel asked.

"Ain't complaining, Mr. Arfel. Ain't." Roadmap grinned. "Yep, ain't had two meals solid like this in a while. Like Mr. Lemontree's cooking. Like it a lot."

Later.

Roadmap wasn't with Arfel and Lemontree. He had gone to get Knock-Kneed at his place. All of them were to convene over in Arfel's room in about an hour. Lemontree and Arfel were heading over there now to Arfel's room.

"Arfel, looks like you put a few pounds on overnight instead of losing some."

"I like your cooking too, Lemontree. Must admit. Don't squeeze me out. Roadmap ain't the only one."

"Skillet. Skillet and some grease. Ain't nothing more than that. Pop it light in the pan."

They were out the door.

"Today ..." Lemontree said, his eyes looking up at the sun, "ain't nearways like it was yesterday."

"Dry out my clothes, Lemontree."

"You is changing when you get back—ain't you?"

Arfel took note of his disarray.

"Do sleep in them all night, Arfel."

"On your floor, Lemontree."

"On my floor, Arfel."

"Thanks, Lemontree. Thanks for last night. Me and Blue Fire don't have a chance to thank you with all that went on, the commotion and all."

"Long as you and Blue Fire safe, Arfel."

Arfel looked into the sun and then back over to Lemontree. "Gonna tell them, Lemontree. Tell them everything. The whole story. Leave out nothing. Mr. Stump's gonna know why he had to alibi for me last night. And Knock-Kneed's gonna know. Want him to know too."

"They all on the record now, Arfel. On the of-ficial record. Gotta scratch them in to include them."

Arfel and Lemontree were in the Palace's lobby. Lemontree looked to where Stump should be.

"He ain't here, Arfel." Lemontree grinned.

"That clock 'bout to gong any minute now—but know how to get him."

Arfel looked at Lemontree mischievously.

"At one time was a hog caller back home, back then. Know how to call hogs. Something you don't never forget."

It's when Lemontree planted himself in the middle of the hotel's lobby like a big sequoia tree. "STUMP!"

Arfel nearly jumped out his skin.

"STUMP MCCANTS!" Lemontree chuckled.

"That'll get him here. New York City, or no NEW YORK CITY."

And before you could blink twice, Stump came out of a room just down the hall. "Hell, who you trying to wake, Lemontree—the DEAD!"

Stump didn't seem to be surprised to see Arfel with Lemontree. "So there you are, Arfel. Morning, Arfel."

"Good morning, Mr. Stump."

"And don't think I ain't charging you rent just 'cause you and Blue Fire don't sleep in your room last night. Ain't got nothing to do with that. Business is business." Then Stump turned his attention back to Lemontree—exclusively to him.

"This is a respectable hotel, Lemontree—if you ain't gotta be reminded. Hotel guests ain't suffering fools," Stump said, pressing forward on his wooden leg. "Now, what you want!"

"Mr. Stump," Arfel spoke up, "I want to tell you about last night."

"It's over and done with, Arfel," Stump said matter-of-fact.

Arfel cleared his throat. "You alibied for me, and I want you to know why, Mr. Stump."

"Don't have to know, Arfel. Ain't none of my business to know. Just a hotel keeper around here."

Arfel cleared his throat a second time. "It, Mr. Stump, sir—I beg to differ, uh, it would do me good to let you know. I want you to know."

"Meeting up in Arfel's room, say in"—Lemontree looked at his timepiece—"twenty minutes. Soon as Roadmap get Knock-Kneed over here."

"Knock, Knock-Kneed's coming, Lemontree? Ain't seen Knock-Kneed and his knocked knees in a while. His knees still knock, don't they?"

The lobby's wall clock gonged. "So you coming up to the party?"

"Sure am, Lemontree. Soon as Knock-Kneed and Roadmap get here." Then Stump's eyes turned as sweet as his smile. "Thanks, Arfel. Thanks for including an old grouch like me in on it. Thanks."

Arfel and Lemontree were in Arfel's room. Arfel was fidgety. "Nervous?"

"A lot, Lemontree."

"Best they know."

"It's hard to say you killed someone."

"Not when it's a white man, Arfel!"

"Ain't proud though, Lemontree. Ain't proud of the fact."

"You a bluesman, Arfel—I know."

"A bluesman, Lemontree—not—"

"A murderer."

Arfel nodded.

"Ever, ever think about that woman? The blueswoman? Think she on the run too?"

Arfel's eyes appeared perplexed. "Never thought that far ahead …" Arfel said, frustrated.

"Could be on the run. Hitched a train. Come North."

"Yes … yes."

"Same as you."

"Yes."

"She seen everything. Was a witness to everything. To a killing. A white man's murder. She gonna take some blame in a white man's court. White man's nigger woman—colored woman ain't no better off than you." Pause. "How many people know about her down there, Arfel? Know about them? Her and the white man? How many you count on to know that?"

Arfel was pondering. "The log cabin hidden away like it was. I …"

"Secrets. Secrets. How many to know your secrets?" Pause. "S-somebody always do. Somebody always stumble across them without them even looking, knowing. Putting any such thought toward the matter."

"So you think someone, somebody knew of their—"

"Arrangement?"

"Yes."

"Could be a lot of folk—could be no more than one or two. Most."

"And she could be on the run."

"You got the weapon."

Arfel was sitting on it as he sat in the chair. "Could just as easy blame it on her. They—"

"Ain't gonna hang her like they was gonna hang you. But put her away—and she wish she was hung: die so fast … easy."

"Hope she ran, g-got away."

And then logic kicked in.

"Had to, Arfel. They send the white man for you."

It's then when Arfel realized that he and Lemontree, they'd been merely picking at straws.

"Ain't knocking on my own door—just coming in, Arfel!" Stump said, pushing Arfel's room door open.

Knock-Kneed and Roadmap trooped in right behind Stump.

"Here for the meeting," Stump continued.

"Hi, Arfel, Lemontree," Knock-Kneed said.

"Caught Mr. Knock-Kneed heading for Miss Millie's—"

"What, this early, Knock-Kneed!" Lemontree asked with a queer look on his face.

"Had the urge, Lemontree. T-that's all. Uh, had the urge."

"You about as sexed up as a old, horny hunting dog, Knock-Kneed, with hanging balls. Who don't know no hour of the day to get in his way."

Arfel got up out his chair. "You can sit here, Knock-Kneed." Arfel went and sat on the bed.

"Sit on the floor, Mr. Arfel."

"Don't have to, Roadmap. You can sit on the bed with—"

"Want to, Mr. Arfel."

It was as if Roadmap was giving this stage, this place for Arfel to have to himself.

Now that Arfel had Stump, Lemontree, Knock-Kneed, and Roadmap staring at him like they were staring down the muzzle of a gun, Arfel was more nervous, petrified.

"Ain't used to this," Arfel smiled nervously.

"Just pretend you at the Bluebird playing on Blue Fire, Arfel. Stroking Blue Fire with your eyes shut," Lemontree said.

Arfel picked up Blue Fire off the bed. "Maybe if I hold on to Blue Fire." He smiled crisply. Then Arfel's mouth began forming the words. He looked exasperated. "I ... uh ... uh I ... I killed a white man."

And Stump and Knock-Kneed hushed.

"It's why that white man came looking for me last night. I killed a white man down there. Down South. Town down South. Slit his throat clean through with my knife. W-what I did." And then Arfel yanked the knife out his back pocket. "A white man's blood was on it. A white man's blood crusted to it." Lightly Arfel's fingers trod across the blade's razor-thin edge.

"Ain't proud of killing a white man. Of killing anybody. Don't remember anything. Black out. Good. Good. All I remember. Black out. Was drunk. Drank too much. That night. Was with a blueswoman. Was in a log cabin she take me to. Went there for two nights to have sex with her. Second night was when I woke, and the white man was down at my feet in the bed, and his blood was, was in the bed, and I seen the knife—and the blueswoman was gone. Had gone off."

Arfel shut his eyes in pain. And he let the pain have its way, until its throbbing, pounding finally left. "Ran from there, t-that town, and been on the run since."

"He's coming back, Arfel."

"I know, Knock-Kneed."

"Gonna offer money up next time. Share in what's due him. Spread it around. The price on your head."

"Uh-huh, Knock-Kneed."

"Then you're going to find out who your friends are around here, Arfel," Stump said. "Yeah, money's gonna be his bait. What he got to work with."

Lemontree agreed. "By then, he just gonna want the journey to end. To bring his nigga in. Bring him home."

"When you think he's coming back?" Stump asked.

"Ain't gonna be long," Lemontree said.

"He'll get to New York City—"

"And see they don't play the blues there. White man smart enough to know Arfel gotta play the blues."

"Uh-huh," Stump said.

"Gotta know that, Lemontree."

Arfel sat on the bed blank-faced as all this conjecture swirled around him concerning his circumstance.

"Spot him as soon as he steps off the train."

"Know that, Roadmap. Your eyes and ears."

Silence.

"Gonna remember the Bluebird Bar, the one blues bar in town. Gonna remember how me and Knock-Kneed was playing the blues. Purple Poison, Sweet-Juice—and the like," Lemontree said.

"Probably the one town he remember before all the others: as long as the road's been for him."

Arfel and Blue Fire were alone. Arfel's head was down on his pillow. He felt like a hunted man again, back on the run again. Arfel felt every bone in his body, one ache after the other. Maybe if they broke, he could just lie there, he thought. Maybe if they broke, they wouldn't ache.

Did he have friends in this town? Did he have to worry when the white man came back? Would someone sell him out, take the white man's money, use his name when asked? He would go back to the Bird tonight. He was a bluesman: it's where the blues was—at the Bluebird. Lemontree sang the songs he and Blue Fire knew, that had carried them this far. There was no pretense in the blues, no other story it could tell, make work to fit. He was never to have freedom, maybe it's what the blues was telling him. Maybe it's what it'd been telling him all along when he played it from town to town, from day to day, from one year into the next.

Arfel was dressed and ready to go. His slacks were pressed. It was time to go to the Bluebird. Arfel closed the door behind him.

"Good evening."

"Oh, good, good evening," Arfel said to the person he'd seen maybe once or twice before.

The person's door opened and then closed.

Would that be the person, when the white man came back, who would sell him out, down the river for the money the white man will have buried in his pant pocket? Arfel asked himself. Or would the man be there, behind that door, in that room when the white man knocked?

"Going crazy, Blue Fire. Going crazy. Got to do better. I've got to do better than this." Arfel took in a deep breath and when he let go, it was like he was trying to extinguish all the lights lighting the world. "How far have I gotten, Blue Fire? How far have I gotten from down there, Blue Fire? The South? T-that town?"

The chase, hunt—it was up North now. The chase from down South had come up North. The chase had extended itself, stretched itself; and now the white man was stretching himself farther North, farther into regions, territory he didn't know. Making himself more and more generous, available. But a colored man, a nigger, if he said he was looking for a nigger …

Arfel and Blue Fire were in the Palace's lobby. Arfel could see Stump, even though Stump was bent over, doing something. But then he looked up as soon as he saw Arfel. "Hoped you was going out tonight," Stump said with a delightful smile on his face. "Hoped you and Blue Fire was playing tonight."

Arfel nodded off to Stump. "Uh-huh, Mr. Stump, Blue Fire and me are going off to the Bluebird."

"Life goes on, Arfel …" Stump said, straightening his back, grimacing just so slightly, "no matter what." Pause. "Got a muscle ache, Arfel. Might've strained something, don't know. Have any idea where it came from." Stump's hand touched the aggravated spot. "Ain't a muscle spasm. Know what they feel like. Just work it out. Take my time. Ain't had it but a day. Just hard to get rid of at my age."

"So take it easy, Mr. Stump. Don't rush things."

"Easy for you to say. But a buck around here don't come easy. Need every buck I can turn to run this place. Can stick in my pocket. Tricky, risky business—the hotel business. Hotel keeping. For anyone. Ain't for the weak-kneed," Stump laughed, looking down at his wooden leg.

"Money, they say, is the 'root of all evil.' But when you run a hotel business"—Stump winced again, and Arfel didn't know if it was from the muscle aching his back or from what Stump was about to say next—"there ain't enough 'evil' to go around. Money talks—it's all I got to say. Money solves most problems a man's got." Pause.

"Uh—see, see you tonight then, Mr. Stump. Blue Fire and me will see you tonight when, when we get in, sir. T-then."

"Ha! Same routine, Arfel. You, Blue Fire, and me."

Arfel was out the door. The night's air felt dead to Arfel. It lacked fragrance. Arfel felt stiff, lacking fragrance. "Money. Money, Blue Fire." And now Arfel was back to that notion again. Stump had opened that can of worms again, pried it open—that notion that could have only the most dire of consequences.

"Colored man doesn't have much money, Blue Fire, but, but what about his soul? A c-colored man's soul, Bllue Fire?"

Arfel could feel a blues playing in his brain; it hadn't reached his fingertips yet.

Lemontree was looking at an old rusty gun.

He didn't kill the man, just nicked him in the shoulder. He didn't aim to kill, just disarm him; but because of all of what had foreshadowed it, he often wished he'd aimed the gun higher, more specifically. Killed that no-good sonuvabitch with one round out the chamber. The gun was kept in a sack in a drawer.

"Yeah, shoulda aimed you higher," Lemontree said, shoving the gun back into the sack and then shoving the desk drawer shut.

"Let that white sonuvabitch live another day." Lemontree looked at his huge hands. "Rather beat a man. Beat his brains out. Shoot him, the bullet do it for you. Spin out the chamber. Make it easy on him. Beat him, he feels everything in your hand. The power. Personal, real then."

He was back to thinking like this again, the violence that once flared in him, unchecked, unmitigated. "Every man got a violence in him, Sweet-Juice," Lemontree said to Sweet-Juice, picking her up, preparing her for what would be another night with Arfel and Blue Fire and Knock-Kneed and Purple Poison.

"Every man I know. Try to run away from it, but can't. White man's always there. A stick. A shadow. Something standing in the way."

Lemontree put his straw hat on. "Wonder sometimes what I'd be, Sweet-Juice. Guess I was just built to be a bluesman. Don't know if the white man make me one or God. A bluesman uh … guess it ain't so bad. Ain't killed nobody yet—just come awful close at the time."

Arfel, Knock-Kneed, and Lemontree were on the Bluebird's stage.

"Oh—
Ah lak jelly beans.
Hear me now—
Hear w'at Ah gottah say.
Eat dem outta big glass jar,
Near mos' every day.

Said Ah lak me some jelly beans,
Eat dem lak pork chops.
In brown gravy—
W'en mah money gits lean.

Jus' don't yah as' me 'bout dem black ones—
Ain't lettin' dem ruin mah mouth.
Ain't lettin' dat ol' Alabama cracker trick me—
Why, Lemontree run North—not South!"

Sweet-Juice's bass line was cracking in the air like the tip of a bondsman's whip splitting open the skin of a colored man's back. The bass line had a colored man's blood in it and jagged scars that'd been left behind like ghostly rail tracks running off to nowhere.

"Dyin' in a coffin—
Not in a grave.
Don't yah shovel none a yah dirt on me—
Ain't yo'r slave.

Got dem childruns, build it nice,
Sweet-Juice.

Bury me in mah straw hat—
An' wat's mah Sunday suit.

Gottah look perty fer 'im,
At dem pearly white gates.
See, Lemontree—
Can't be late!"

It was late in the Bird. Most of the Bluebird patrons had left for the night.

"Peeling out, Arfel. Everybody got somewhere to go off to."

"Like home," Knock-Kneed joked.

"Put a rock in them all night. They gonna sleep good tonight."

And then the music stopped.

Arfel looked cursed, as if reality was back at him as quickly as the last note he'd played. Arfel shrugged his shoulders and reluctantly unstrapped Blue Fire.

"Whiskey taste sour tonight, Last Round. What you put in it!"

Last Round yelled something back to Lemontree, which made him howl.

"Was a good night."

"It was," Arfel said. "Was like last night never happen."

"But it did, Lemontree," Arfel said.

"Ain't canceling it out, Arfel. Just saying we rocked the blues soft tonight. Got some anger in it, hurt—but it still come out soft. Ain't scared of tomorrow coming. What it might bring. What we wind up with."

The three, Arfel, Lemontree, and Knock-Kneed, waited for Last Round to lock up the Bird. Then they all bid Last Round good night.

"What, ain't heading our way tonight, Knock-Kneed?"

"Uh …"

"Seen it all night, Knock-Kneed, what you up to. Seen you waggling your knees like you gotta pee. A bad bladder. Know you know where the Bluebird bathroom is in the Bluebird Bar. Used it before."

Lemontree's eyes fixed themselves straight onto Knock-Kneed's crotch. "Heading over to Miss Millie's, ain't you? Ain't—"

"I've got an urge, Lemontree." Knock-Kneed glanced at Arfel. "Ar ... Arfel."

"Boy must have a long dick on him—all I gotta say. To need pussy the way he do!"

All three laughed.

"One day, one day you gonna catch something from that establishment Miss Millie run, and it ain't gonna be the common cold."

Knock-Kneed kept chuckling.

"Miss Millie's girls are clean." Then Knock-Kneed sighed. "Lemontree, can't I spend the little money I've got the, the way I want?"

"Sure, sure you can, Knock-Kneed. Go on. You young. Got the night. Money don't count for nothing to a bluesman—not till he's old."

Knock-Kneed had bid them good night.

Lemontree and Arfel were walking slow tonight. Bed held little prospect nor practicality for either—so it seemed. "Arfel, been thinking all day."

"Me too, Lemontree.

"You go first, Lemontree."

"Had a gun in my hand."

Arfel flinched.

"Take it out the drawer. It's where I keep it, stuffed in a sack—away from everything." Pause. "Couldn't stop holding it. Be honest with you. Looking at it. All I could do."

"Last night brought this on, didn't it, Lemontree? Didn't it? That white man!"

"Forgot what that gun look ... feel like in my hand, Arfel. P-plain forget," Lemontree said, transfixed. "Good. Feel good. Ain't gonna lie and say it don't." Pause. "Was remembering back."

"To when, Lemontree?"

"Not so long. To when the last time I used it."

"You used it?"

"Wasn't nothing," Lemontree said softly. "Even though trouble come from it." Pause. "Coulda killed him. Shoulda. Can be a violent man, Arfel. It was what I was thinking about all day. Ain't gonna lie to you and Blue Fire. Like any colored man who seen enough."

"When he comes back, when that white man comes back,

Lemontree, how many people around here are gonna know me then? My name, Lemontree? When the white man goes into his pocket, and what's gonna come out is … is gonna be more than a colored man can make in … in one, two months around here, Lemontree. Pull-pulls out his pocket."

"It's how you been thinking?"

"All day, most of the day. Know money's the root of all evil—Mr. Stump reminded me of it today."

"Gotta believe a colored man hate a white man more than he love his money. Gotta believe that, Arfel. In your heart. What you—"

"But it's my neck, Lemontree. Me and, and Blue Fire's neck. We're the ones on the run—being chased by him, all this time."

"Mind was thinking about something else too today."

Arfel waited on Lemontree.

"Was born a Baptist."

"Me too."

"Ain't one for going to church much, but believe in God, Arfel, like we talk before. Need peace in our lives, you and me need, just now. Fear ain't good."

"But I … I'm not afraid, Lemontree. I-I …"

"Just afraid of what you might do, just like me. Got that feeling sunk in your heart. So today I was thinking …" And then what came out of Lemontree's mouth was as smooth as a shaved stone. "Church. Let's say you and me go to church, Arfel!" Pause. "Can take Blue Fire and Sweet-Juice along. Ha. They been to church about the last time we was!"

"Wasn't Knock-Kneed's cousin's funeral—"

"That wasn't no church. That was a funeral. Somebody dying. Passing off to glory land."

"Sure, Lemontree. Sure."

"We gotta take our minds off things," Lemontree said slowly. "Relief, Arfel. Can't keep up like this. Our minds going at this pace. Going too fast. Gotta slow down some."

Arfel held on to Blue Fire's leather strap. "Hear that, Blue Fire? You and me and Lemontree and Sweet-Juice are going to church."

"Might just shine my shoes up. Put some spit on them. Or at least kick the country dirt off them some."

187

"Uh … you've got dress shoes, Lemontree?"

"Two pair. Ache like hell. Feet ain't really broke them in yet. Give them a chance."

"Well …"

"Here we are talking about church and Knock-Kneed's over at Miss Millie's."

"Still haven't met Miss Millie or any of her girls, Lemontree. Hard, hard to believe."

"Never did have to go and do what Knock-Kneed's doing—not unless I was strange to a town and was no woman for me to find to latch onto. Sex with." Pause. "But I spend what money I make from playing like it was water too, when I was young. (Diamond rings on my fingers prove that!) Wasn't saving money to spend on a mule, a plow, and forty acres of land and the mule dying on me the same day. Nope.

"Uh-uh. Yeah, was thinking today, was born to be a bluesman, Arfel—nothing more. If I was born rich, might as well've been born poor. Got God to thank for what I am. Nobody else. Don't think a colored man ever have to talk to him, not until the blues come along and can do so."

Chapter 14

Lemontree had kicked the country dirt off his shoes, all right. A polished apple couldn't shine more divinely.

Arfel was at Lemontree's. It was the morning for them to go to church. Arfel was tieless—it's why this kind of conversation ensued.

"Gonna find you a tie to go with them socks, Arfel. Don't worry. Gonna match you up right. Top to bottom."

Lemontree had a tie on, fat and wide, fancy looking too. Arfel's dress shirt was buttoned up to the top button. Arfel didn't look uncomfortable but far from normal. A box was out on the scratched-up kitchen table. It's how Lemontree kept his ties, in a box that was in the closet that now was on the kitchen table. Lemontree yanked a tie out the box.

"What about it, Arfel? This one?"

Arfel looked at the wrinkled-up mess Lemontree held as if not a bone in him approved of such a downright raunchy sight.

"Darn't, Arfel—you know I'm gonna press the damned thing. You ain't wearing it with ten miles of bumpy road in it."

"The color matches," Arfel said.

"Raise—pull up your trousers again, Arfel."

Arfel did.

"Yellow socks. Yellow tie. The preacher gonna see you coming up the road two miles back."

They'd had breakfast. The dishes were in the sink. Lemontree looked over at them disdainfully. "Wash them when we get back from church. Ain't washing dishes now—in my Sunday suit."

"I do feel dressed up," Arfel sighed, feeling the suit's soft threads against his skin.

"Figured my cousin Eli was about your size and weight. Left three suits behind. Don't come back for neither. Knew he was gone when he leave. Said he was going to New York City. Guess he thought them suits wasn't good enough for New York City weather. Hope New York City make him rich by now. Been gone a long time."

Lemontree had pressed the ten miles of wrinkles out of what had been the unsightly tie. Arfel had the tie in his hand and was looking at it confused, as if to figure out which end went where and how.

"Arfel, don't tell me you don't know how to tie a tie. Don't know which end goes where."

"Uh, just, just plain forgot I guess, Lemontree."

"You young boys. Y'all need a daddy. Still gotta show you things. How to do … Aaaah …" Lemontree took the tie. "It goes like this. Now look and learn. 'Cause I ain't gonna show you but once."

Even with their dress suits on, there they were: Blue Fire and Sweet-Juice strapped to Arfel and Lemontree.

"Arfel, ever see snow?" Lemontree asked Arfel, stepping out the house's door.

"Snow?"

"Heard of it though?"

"Yes."

"Hit down on us." Lemontree looked up at the sky. "Say a month. In a month's time. No more than two. It's when I miss down South. Looks pretty, snow—but you know the cold's to come."

Lemontree's eyes vacated the sky. "Well … we ain't gotta worry about that today. There's a good wind, but not much more."

Arfel felt good about going to church this morning. For the past few days he'd entertained the thought—what Lemontree had suggested. It was time to sit down with God, take some record of himself. It was time for some kind of spiritual reconcilement to take hold.

"Don't know how good this preacher is, gotta go strictly by reputation, since my backside ain't warmed a pew on any Sunday morning I know of. People around here say he's good. Real good with words."

"Hope so, Lemontree."

"Uh-huh. Say he preach the gospel good. Dig into the 'Good Book.' Know it from cover to cover."

"I … I like any good preacher."

"Say he can stir up a hornet's nest. Chase the devil's monkey," Lemontree said, draping his arm around Arfel's shoulders. "But I heard many a man call himself a bluesman, guess you do too, Arfel, and don't got nothing to show for themselves."

"It's gotta be all about life, ain't it, Lemontree?"

"Life. Can talk about something, Arfel, if you been living something that mean something." Pause. "Same with religion. Don't want no preacher preaching to me if he don't know nothing about life. Just words in a book. Ain't lived some details, margins of it, to understand it."

"When someone shuts his eyes—"

"In church, they're praying, Arfel," Lemontree said.

"But in the Bluebird Bar—"

"Same damned thing, Arfel. Your spirit. A bluesman's spirit shining *true and true.*"

Lemontree's hand came off Arfel. "It's how you can tell a preacherman and a bluesman." Pause. "When both preaching the gospel."

Arfel had a dance in him, so did Lemontree. A blues band. A sanctified shake. "Could shake my backside like a tambourine, Arfel. Ain't gonna lie!"

"Pastor Cumberbatch could preach, Lemontree!"

"And the choir—sing!"

Arfel and Lemontree were a block removed from the "All Hallows Sanctified Church of God."

"How much you drop in the plate?"

Arfel grinned. "Not telling."

"That much!"

"About!"

They laughed.

"Good preacher ain't nothing without a great choir, though, and, uh, a good choir ain't nothing without a great preacher."

"Lemontree …"

"Got it worked out for myself, Arfel," Lemontree said, removing his hat to scratch his head. "All worked out to my thinking. Do. All you gotta do is take it upon yourself to listen." Pause. "Now see … a good preacher can preach all day, but if the choir ain't singing right …" Long pause. "And … a good choir can sing all day, and if the preacher ain't preaching right …"

Arfel's body was rigid.

"Aaah—you ain't got nothing to say, Arfel, you and that yellow tie you wearing, got stuck around your neck!"

"Got it out your closet, Lemontree!"

"Arfel—don't even try none of that!"

And out of the bush he jumped.

"Mr. Arfel! Mr. Lemontree!"

"Roadmap!"

"Roadmap!"

Between them, Arfel and Lemontree hugged Roadmap mightily.

"Been to church?"

"H-how'd you know, Roadmap?"

"Look like somebody preach to you, Mr. Lemontree. How. Yep, might as well be Pastor Cumberbatch."

"Know him?"

"Yes, Mr. Arfel. Sure do. Kind man. Decent man. Sleep on Pastor Cumberbatch's pews at the Hallows Sanctified Church of God more than a few times."

"Mouthful, ain't it, Roadmap? To say, ain't it?"

"Uh-huh. Pastor Cumberbatch's church's name sure is, Mr. Lemontree. All Hallows—"

"Don't have to say it again," Lemontree grimaced. "Need to, Roadmap."

Then Arfel got Roadmap's attention. Roadmap looked Arfel up and down like Arfel was a drain pipe. "Raise your, uh, pull your trousers up, uh, please, Mr. Arfel."

Arfel did.

"Yep, thought that tie hadda match something on you, Mr. Arfel. Yep."

"Don't tell me, Roadmap, you're gonna go after me—now." Arfel laughed.

"Come out of Mr.—the tie come out of Mr. Lemontree's closet, don't it, Mr. Arfel?"

Arfel happily turned toward Lemontree.

"Mr. Lemontree likes yellow. It's why I knew it was his. Knew it right off."

The three were walking.

"Ain't seen you the past few nights, Roadmap. In the Bird. How come?"

"Getting my money straight, Mr. Lemontree."

"For what, Roadmap?"

"Don't know. Ain't thought about it much. Just going on—"

"Instincts?"

"Yes, Mr. Lemontree. That."

"Best thing you got, Roadmap, instincts. You got on you. Fail you sometimes, instincts—but ain't nothing perfect, so don't take me wrong."

"No, Mr. Lemontree."

"But your brain ain't always got answers for you, so you gotta turn to something else. Ain't always right, instincts. Don't always have the right answers, Roadmap, but they always there."

Roadmap's hand rolled the bill of his tweed cap. "Good preaching today, Mr. Lemontree? Mr. Arfel?"

"Good, Roadmap."

"Yes, it was," Arfel said.

"And the choir?"

"See ... see, Arfel, Roadmap knows!"

"Church services ain't good unless there's both, Mr. Arfel," Roadmap said, his eyes looking up innocently at Arfel.

And here I am, Arfel said to himself, *learning a lesson from Roadmap I'd just been taught by Lemontree, and here Roadmap is only—oh, ahh, never—*

"Yes … yes, Roadmap."

"Mr. Arfel's a Baptist, Roadmap. Born a Baptist. Reared a Baptist. Know them kind of things for himself," Lemontree said, winking spiritedly at Arfel. "About a church choir and a Baptist minister."

Roadmap had been invited to dine at noon at Lemontree's residence.

"Seconds, Roadmap?" Politely, Roadmap coughed into his hand. "It … uh—if it ain't too much of a bother, Mr. Lemontree. Ain't too much trouble." Roadmap withdrew his hand from his mouth. "Know I can eat, Mr. Lemontree. Yep. Know that."

Blue Fire was propped up on a chair. Roadmap couldn't keep his eyes off her. "Hi, Blue Fire. Hi."

Lemontree laughed. "Don't make Sweet-Juice jealous now, Roadmap. She a woman too. Know you know that. Aware."

"I know, Mr. Lemontree. I know." Roadmap watched as Lemontree served his plate with food. "Why's …" Roadmap said, still looking at Blue Fire, "it a woman? Why a bluesman's gui-tar gotta be a woman? Carry a woman's name with it?"

"Watch your hand now, Roadmap. Food's hot."

"Uh, right, Mr. Lemontree. Thank, thank you," Roadmap said, extricating his hand from the plate.

Arfel was scratching his head for answers. But really, he was waiting for Lemontree to answer Roadmap—it's what his brain was actually doing.

But Roadmap's eyes remained fixed on Arfel.

"Enough, Roadmap?"

Roadmap looked away from Arfel and to his plate of hot food. "Fine, Mr. Lemontree. Thank you."

Lemontree gestured to Arfel.

"Full, Lemontree," Arfel said, his hands grabbing his stomach to demonstrate.

"Had me enough too," Lemontree said. Lemontree put the food back on top of the oven.

"Bluesman always gotta have a woman around with him, Roadmap. Seems so. Don't matter whether she's real or unreal," Lemontree said, taking to his chair. "It's like a stream running right straight through you sweet and nice. So much like Macon County nights in Alabama, Roadmap."

Arfel and Roadmap had made a little distance between them and Lemontree's house.

"Thanks, Mr. Lemontree." Roadmap was waving back at Lemontree. Lemontree waved back. "Full now," Roadmap said softly. "Know I like to eat, Mr. Arfel. Yep. But Mr. Lemontree's cooking … encourages me some."

Arfel's yellow tie was off his neck and back in Lemontree's closet where, Arfel had said, it belonged. He was still wearing Lemontree's cousin Eli's suit since Lemontree had dropped it by Arfel's room yesterday. Before Arfel and Roadmap left Lemontree's, Lemontree told Arfel he could keep it; was sure his cousin Eli wasn't coming back from New York City for it.

"Could sell that suit for you if you want, Mr. Arfel."

Arfel kind of looked at it, the suit, again. "Hangs on me that funny, Roadmap?"

"Ain't saying that, Mr. Arfel. Just saying I could sell it for you. Could, if you want."

"Don't think I'm going back to church, me and Blue Fire, huh?"

"Ain't saying that either, Mr. Arfel."

"So what are you saying, Roadmap?"

"Don't know, Mr. Arfel—just following my instincts like Mr. Lemontree said to do."

Arfel felt as if he'd been had as Roadmap giggled incessantly.

"So what have you been doing, Roadmap?"

"Know it ain't time to look now, Mr. Arfel, yet. But soon."

Arfel was rocked back on the balls of his feet by what Roadmap had just said.

"Know that, Mr. Arfel." Pause. "Take more time than this for the train to run up and back. Up North and back, Mr. Arfel."

Arfel unbuttoned his shirt collar even though the wind had picked up steam.

"Don't wanna rush things, Mr. Arfel. Insides gonna know when it's time. When the white man come back into town. Gonna be at the rail station, Mr. Arfel. Waiting."

Arfel was back in his bed.

His body was shivering up a storm. It was like he had a bad cold in him. He'd gone to church today to gain some peace, decorum, some sense of reconcilement; but now he was quaking with fear and terror. He hadn't confessed anything. He'd shut his eyes in the pews to pray; but he'd felt empty inside, without grace, without compassion or redemption—no better than a heathen, a savage, than someone with a knife in his back pocket and who felt its hard steel on the church pew's dense wood.

"Minister was preaching, Blue Fire—and the knife, the knife was still in my back pocket. Sitting there. Carry it everywhere, Blue Fire. Carry it everywhere. To church. Everywhere, Blue Fire. I go, Blue Fire. I go."

When he put on Lemontree's cousin Eli's suit, he'd wondered whether or not he should carry it—the knife. But it'd become a part of him—like an arm, a leg, a limb.

Arfel held on to Blue Fire. "Gotta have it, Blue Fire. Gotta have it. Where's the blueswoman, Blue Fire? Where'd she run off to? Did she get away, Blue Fire? Did she get away too?"

Church.

He and Lemontree clapped and prayed. The music swayed and buttressed their bodies magnificently, made them feel like they'd been saved by the Holy Ghost, by the spirits descending down from Calvary.

"For a second, Blue Fire. For … for a minute—it was like a flood, Blue Fire. I was lost. It was like a flood. I'd been saved. It was like holy water that was being poured over Arfel's body by God. God, Blue Fire. GOD!"

To kill a man, any man—God's house. God knew. In his house, the preacher knew, Pastor Cumberbatch. "He was touching my head, Blue Fire."

Trying to redeem him, rid him of the devil rousting inside him. Clapping and swaying and his and Lemontree's bodies feeling like they'd been saved by the Holy Ghost, born again.

"I know the white man's coming, Blue Fire. God ain't got nothing to do with it. Don't confess my sin, Blue Fire—just got to live with it."

Arfel wasn't in Eli's suit. He was in his underwear.

"Snow, ain't gonna see snow, not the same snow Lemontree's gonna see. We ain't gonna see it." Arfel's fingers gripped the bed's sheets. "White. White like these sheets, say it is," Arfel said, seeing white in his eyes even in the dark room.

Arfel shut his eyes. "Can feel it though, like a warm July night. Go off to her, Blue Fire. The blueswoman. Her body, them sheets, Blue Fire, was warm, Blue Fire, warm. It's only when I wake, when my eyes come around do it feel cold. Snow. Blue Fire. Snow in my soul. The cold—it come, Blue Fire. The cold come …"

Arfel buried his body more into the bed. Blue Fire not as cold or suffering or scarred.

Chapter 15

One week later.

If there were two things Roadmap would like to do right now, they were sleep and sleep. Roadmap yawned impressively. "Don't know what got in me." Roadmap was in an abandoned building. It wasn't far off from the train station.

Sleepies were in Roadmap's eyes, so he picked at them with his thin fingers to clear them. It'd been a cold night. The cold was in Roadmap's flesh. Roadmap felt it. It was cold like this the other morning before it took a turn in the early afternoon and warmed. Already Roadmap was thinking today would do the same. And then it struck Roadmap: today, today is the day, the start, the beginning of things.

"Instinct, Mr. Lemontree. It's … it's instinct, Mr. Lemontree." And like that, without any real thought but gut feeling, Roadmap was ready, prepared to start the day, push it forward.

From the crack in the side of the building, Roadmap could see the day. Roadmap headed for the crack. It's how he got in the building and how he would exit it. When he got to the crack, he poked his head out and looked both ways before pressing forward. "Coast is clear. Ain't nobody about for now."

Roadmap's body wiggled through the building's crack. The sky

Roadmap looked up at was ominous, foreboding. "Gonna hang around the train station all day if I have to. Yep, find something to do to make money. Always do. Ain't going broke. Uh-uh."

Roadmap had been at the railroad station all day. The station wasn't anything fancy to look at. Roadmap was outside the station. He'd been jumping around like a Mexican jumping bean before to keep his feet warm, but now the day was warming (as it had the other day).

A train came and then went.

Roadmap was blowing his warm breath on his hands more because of his nerves than anything else. He had a big responsibility and knew it. To Mr. Arfel, to Blue Fire, to Mr. Lemontree. He had a job to do, and they all trusted him with it. He wished Mr. Arfel and Blue Fire's situation wasn't the way it was—only, it was. He couldn't change it, nor could Mr. Arfel. Mr. Arfel killed a white man no matter how gentle and tenderly his fingers played Blue Fire. Still the thought of Mr. Arfel slitting a man's throat "clean," slashing it, still disturbed him.

"Mr. Arfel's a good man, decent man like Pastor Cumberbatch. Ain't no different that I can see. Mr. Arfel got a good soul. What makes him good."

And a train came and then went.

"Got cargo on it. Goods. Ain't got a white man riding it."

Roadmap didn't want to feel disappointed but was: he wanted to get this thing over with between Mr. Arfel, Blue Fire, and the white man who was to come to town. He sensed it in Mr. Arfel and Mr. Lemontree too: this wasn't easy medicine to swallow.

It was later.

A train came and then went.

It was later when Roadmap's heart jumped.

"The WHITE MAN!"

Roadmap's heart jumped again. "The white man—as tall as day!"

And there the white man was as "tall as day" (as Roadmap had said, described him), his brown hat seeming able to touch the sky. "Gotta long coat. Long brown coat to keep him warm, though it's warm now. Day's better now." The white man got off the train, and his coat flung open, and Roadmap saw the big gun sitting up in the holster.

"He hide it last time he was here. Hide it away from sight—even though I know he got it. "But ..." The coat was open, revealing the holstered gun. Roadmap had scrambled, did whatever so not to be seen ... detected.

"Walking faster. He know the town better now. Get around better now. Ain't forgot. Walk straight through it. Ain't no stranger to it now. White man think ... he thinks he owns it now. Can see that. Plain. Plain."

The white man had the same big leather satchel sitting high on his shoulders, and he was heading North. Roadmap, in his discreet, hidden way, was following him step for step as his heart pounded and quickened with each new step taken. "He ... he ain't going over to our side—the colored's side."

Right off Roadmap knew he'd have to keep an eye on the white man. That catching up with Mr. Arfel to tell him the white man had arrived in town, for now, could wait—was small potatoes compared to what was actually happening. "What you up to, white man? How smart you think you is? Can play cat and mouse with you all day if I want. Can, white man. Can."

The white man's strides lengthened more evenly over the ground, reached more, gaining more direct distance into this city. Roadmap mixed into crowds, clusters of people and then came out of them, feeling his body gesticulate as slippery as an eel's. And then the white man stopped and looked up. He stood in front of a refined, grand-looking hotel with old brick in it and terra cotta of beautifully hand-carved classical lines and Greek-figured forms.

"The Paladin Hotel. Gotta have money, white man. The Paladin Hotel. Gotta have money in your pocket, white man, to stay in that rich hotel. Cost a pretty penny a night." The white man entered the Paladin Hotel. "Sure you gonna stay this time. Knew you was. Ain't had one minute's doubt swimming in my mind. Gonna rest your head good and tight."

Roadmap crossed the street and peeked through the Paladin Hotel's revolving door's glass. The white man stood at the Paladin's front desk. And within seconds, the desk attendant handed him keys, and a burgundy-capped bellhop came for him, but he waved him off. "Don't need nobody. Just that gun. Under … beneath your coat. Just that gun. Just that gonna do."

The white man's body was turning. Roadmap slipped out of sight, totally out of view.

Roadmap knew all about this hotel, the Paladin Hotel. He knew where the elevators were located inside the hotel. He pushed through the Paladin's glass revolving door. He was in its lobby. He slipped over to where the elevators were, keeping his distance in calculating how the white man's body was positioned for it not to see him.

The white man stood by the elevator alone. The elevator came. The elevator operator pulled the iron gate open. The elevator operator pushed the iron gate shut. Roadmap ran to the elevator and looked up, following the red light at the top of the elevator as the elevator traveled through floors.

"Eleventh floor! Eleventh floor!" Roadmap's hand rolled his cap's bill. "High up, ain't you? Ain't but two more floors up." Roadmap blew on his hands. "Ain't going no place. Be right here." Roadmap began walking away from the elevators.

"Roadmap!" Roadmap turned.

"What you doing in here!" The young man's face was turning a nasty, rotten red.

"Hey, leave him alone, George!"

"Don't have to: coloreds don't belong in here. That colored boy knows that!"

"Hiya doing, Roadmap?"

"Ain't complaining," Roadmap said to the shorter young man. Roadmap knew his name was Donald but never used it.

"You ain't getting no handouts in here, Roadmap," George said. "Coloreds in the kitchen and laundry. Ain't no coloreds work out here." George laughed.

"The hell with you!" Roadmap cursed.

"What you say! What you say, you little fucking nappy-headed jigger-nigger!"

201

"Shut up, George!" Donald yelled.

"The hell with you!" Roadmap repeated.

"See … see—can't be nice to them niggers! See! See!"

Donald grabbed George. "You-you'd better, you'd better go, Roadmap!"

George's face was straining.

"Ain't afraid. Fight him right here. Yep, fight that boy right here. Ain't afraid. Turn him loose if you wanna. Kick that boy's ass right here!"

But Donald held on to George as George's eyes strained painfully in his head.

"Turn him loose—beat that boy's ass black and blue!" Roadmap said again, holding his ground.

"No, you'd better go, Roadmap. It ain't worth it. Ain't worth the trouble."

Roadmap sucked his teeth and then realized that that boy Donald was right: "wasn't worth the trouble." That he was in that rich white man's hotel, the Paladin, for a purpose, and what he was doing now wasn't it, not whatsoever.

But Roadmap still issued his final challenge. "Better hold that boy, if he knows what's good for him. Telling you. Better!"

Hours later.

It was dark. Roadmap was jumping around in one spot like a Mexican jumping bean again. It'd turned cold.

"Blown on my hands a thousand times today. Sometimes I want to, sometimes 'cause I don't." Pause. "Ain't complaining." But Roadmap was wondering what the white man was doing. "Know you mad. What you was before, first come here—been on them trains for so long. Meaner than spit. Snake oil. Rattlesnake."

Roadmap was across the street facing the Paladin Hotel. "Wait here all night. Into the morning, if I have to. Gotta. Don't care."

Only Roadmap wouldn't have to for suddenly, through the Paladin's revolving glass door, Roadmap could see a tall figure in a brown hat and long brown coat emerge from the Paladin. "There you are, white man! There you are!" Carefully Roadmap hid himself.

"About to go for a walk?"

The white man came out the hotel. But to Roadmap's surprise, he didn't head South (to where Roadmap just knew he was going to go), but North—again. Roadmap scratched his head through his cap— was befuddled. "Don't understand, white man. Don't understand what you're doing. Any, any of this."

Roadmap stood there where he was frozen in place but soon realized the white man and his long, steady strides afoot were taking him elsewhere—and fast, separating them. "Ain't that smart. Ain't that smart. Ain't leaving me behind!"

Roadmap scurried along. And now this walk through the city, Roadmap and the white man were on, increased more in distance and thrill.

Then, suddenly, Roadmap laughed from the pits of his small belly, for—

"Now I know where you're going, white man. Now I know where you're taking me to. Ain't no surprise now what you're doing." For soon the white man stood in front of the Bow Street Bar. They didn't play the blues there in the Bow Street Bar—but country and western music.

The white man entered the Bow Street Bar.

Two hours later.

"Good and drunk now. Know you is. Know so."

Roadmap could see a weave, a bend, a sloppiness in the white man when he left out the Bow Street Bar. A pattern. The night had turned colder, but Roadmap didn't feel it: his bones were as warm as a knitted sock. "You're going now. I know you going now. Liquored up. You're good and mean. I know you are. Know you are, Mister."

And with no doubt, the walk began in earnest in the new direction. In a direction Roadmap knew too well, and the white man knew too well. Roadmap and the white man were linked in this dance, this tangle of juxtaposed souls. "Gonna get to Mr. Arfel, Blue Fire before you do. But I'm gonna follow you. Follow you but so far."

And the white man's walk stayed unsteady—but clean, resolute.

Roadmap could see him on the road, going from town to town, from city to city, hunting, searching, trying to find this nigger called Arfel Booker and his guitar called Blue Fire. Knocking on doors, inquiring—snooping. Getting this answer and that answer. Wondering when the journey was going to end (if ever), the long stretch.

"This is your night, Mister. Think this is your night—when your asking's gonna end. When your searching stops."

And once again Roadmap was puzzled, for the white man was taking on a different direction, different route of action. "Thought you knew the way. D-don't need a guide. Don't need nobody to show you the way." Pause. "Thought you knew the way to the Bluebird Bar, Mister. Thought you'd never forget it. Not the Bluebird. Not …"

Roadmap didn't know where the white man was going. He couldn't make heads or tails of it.

"You that drunk!"

The white man swung open his long coat. And from the back, Roadmap could still see the gun, that big hunk of metal that could kill a buffalo or any big animal dead in its tracks without it making a billow, a cloud of smoke.

They walked. And they walked. And now Roadmap was catching on, realized where the white man was taking him. "M-Miss Millie's. Miss Millie's!" Roadmap screamed out in a controlled whisper.

Within minutes, Roadmap and the white man were there at Miss Millie's. But now it's when Roadmap did something risky.

Knock.

Knock.

The door swung open.

Within seconds, the voices were loud, large, snappish, at top scale. It was like a short fuse had been lit and now it was about to go off, explode in a person's ear to take up a big, awful space. Roadmap had snuck out into the back of Miss Millie's. And now his eyes could see Miss Millie at the door, and suddenly the white man shoved Miss Millie aside. Miss Millie stumbled backward into the room, hit the wall—then bounced off.

Roadmap smelled trouble. Miss Millie's voice was still raised—she'd regained her footing.

"Told you before, when you come, I don't know him. Never seen him!"

He said something. Miss Millie said something back. He grabbed her from behind. His arm cocked her beneath the neck. The gun came out his holster. Roadmap saw the gun flash hard in the light. Miss Millie's voice got louder, more excited.

"Go and kill me! Kill me, white man. Kill me!" The nozzle of the gun pressed against Miss Millie's right temple. The white man cocked the gun.

"Ha! Ha! Can't die but once!"

Roadmap felt the springs in his legs: he was going to run and leap on the white man's back—die in Miss Millie's good-time house for Miss Millie if he had to. But the white man released Miss Millie. His face, with his choppy beard, the wear and tear in it, an evil Roadmap could feel like the devil he was told Pastor Cumberbatch preached of in his church on Sunday mornings. When he preached about the world when it was at is worst, not its best. And the white man's eyes, drunk—shone with whatever had been his drink, he'd favored at the Bow Street Bar all night. Then he shoved Miss Millie, whose body hit solidly against the back wall this time, but showed no pain in her face and no loss of temper in her voice.

"Now get out! Get out!" Miss Millie screamed at the top of her lungs at the white man. "There ain't no bluesman here! No bluesman here!"

And the white man flung open his long brown coat. And he stuck his gun back down inside his holster and mumbled something like it roared beneath his whisper as he headed for the open door just before him.

Roadmap and the white man were back on the road. They were back to what they'd been before: Roadmap, this white man's tiny shadow (no matter how elusive), invisible, just enough of him to make do, to justify. "The Bluebird, Mister. The Bluebird …"

And Roadmap was about to use his shortcut that would save him ten, twelve minutes time, when the white man took up the wrong street again. "W-what you doing, Mister? What you doing!" Roadmap said, questioning the white man once again, this conundrum.

"Ain't the way to the Bluebird. Bluebird Bar. Ain't. Ain't!" Roadmap protested. But the white man was turned back to how he came, the route that got him over to this side of town.

Roadmap had no choice but to follow him, but to continue this silent dance, this thing that'd turned into exotic escape, imagination. Roadmap could tell by the white man's walk that the liquor in him no longer infected his equilibrium in the worst way. The walk before, the walk at the rail station and to the hotel—was back in him. And they slipped along silkily in the night air, the two of them chained together— Roadmap and the white man. Roadmap and the white man crossed the line from one district of town to the other. A Mason–Dixon line, a separation of territories, districts. The physical allotment of the town and its treasures and trade and commerce and income.

"Crossed over. Crossed back over to your side of town," Roadmap said. "Yep, Mister, you're going back. Back," Roadmap said in a hushed voice. A voice fresh with surprise. "The Paladin Hotel."

The Paladin Hotel stood there with all its lights shining from top to bottom out onto the street. And there the white man stood iron-stiff looking up at it and then entering its beauty.

Roadmap took off his hat, and his head sweat as the steam from the hot and cold rose off Roadmap's head intensely, climbing—hissing as if it'd been stoked by hot coals.

"Seen a man up an' die,
An' still git 'im no res'.
Not when eight a 'is wives show up at 'is funeral—
Dat same day, tah protes'.

Claim he owe dem chil' support,
Onlies' reason why dey was dere.
Come, say dey come,
Tah collect dey fair share.

Tell de preacherman: ain't none a dey business,
Why he die.
But dat dem six pallbearers wasn't takin' 'im nowhere,
'Cause right in dat casket he was gonna lie.

Oh ... Sweet-Juice—
A woman mean as a jug a gin,
An' nasty as a rattlesnake;
Man dead—"
But jus' as well be 'wake.

Dem six pallbearers den turn up de church aisle (not one got a smile).
An' go.
But dem eight wives still waitin' fer dat dead man tah wake,
An' pay dem de child support—say—he owe!

"Oh ... Lordie, LORDIE. Talk to me, JESUS!
But Sweet-Juice'll do.
Tell old Lemontree w'at he jus' said ain't—
True an' true."

Lemontree switched over to a new blues tune.
"Gottah dusty dollar,
A pig an' a poke.
Gottah pretty woman,
An' a pile a broke.

Woman don't keep you down,
She jus' don't pay de rent.
(None I know),
Ever be heaven sent.

Jus' sing the blues,
All day all night.
Lemontree Johnson ...
Now, dat's ALL RIGHT!

And for some reason it was like there was a harmonica wail in the Bird, but Knock-Kneed wasn't there, so Lemontree pitched a wail out his mouth that resembled one of Knock-Kneed's pained harmonica wails anyway. "Eeeeeeee! Eeeeeeeeee!"

Bodies in the Bluebird jumped and then lay quietly back like a new day had come. And then Lemontree and Arfel felt him through their shut eyes—Roadmap, his footsteps that raced the heart. Their eyes opened wide. Roadmap stood before them at the foot of the stage.

"He's here, Mr. Arfel. The white man's here!"

Lemontree's and Arfel's fingers croaked on Sweet-Juice's and Blue Fire's guitar strings.

They were in the Bird's cluttered, stuffy back room.

"C-catch … now catch your breath now, Roadmap," Lemontree said.

"Come in today, Mr. Arfel. Afternoon train. Was on the afternoon train." Roadmap was fanning himself with his hand. "Spotted him. Seen him, Mr. Arfel. Seen him!"

Lemontree smiled. "Me and Mr. Arfel delighted, Roadmap. Delighted. The wait—"

"It's finally over," Arfel said relieved.

But then a panic lit Lemontree's face. "Where's he now, Roadmap? How far away!"

"Ain't coming, been with him all day, Mr. Lemontree. Ain't coming for Mr. Arfel tonight."

"Ain't coming!" Lemontree said.

"He go to the Bow Street Bar—get drunk."

"Drunk!"

"Yep, drunk, Mr. Lemontree. The white man tie himself on one."

Arfel was the first to laugh of the three.

"It's what he did, Mr. Arfel. Sure did too. Tied himself on one at the Bow Street Bar."

"White man having him a little fun in town."

"Yes, Mr. Lemontree. Seemed that way." Roadmap stopped fanning himself.

Lemontree hopped up on a big wooden beer keg to sit.

"Oh, forgot to tell you—he checked in the Paladin Hotel first. Staying there for now."

"Spending his money free and easy now ... Living it up fancy," Lemontree said, rubbing his hands spiritedly.

"Yes." Pause. "Said the same thing, Mr. Lemontree. The same thing when I seen what he was doing. Up to. The same thing."

"Yeah, he thinks this is his last stop, all right, Arfel. Know where he belong. Last stop on the train. Up and down the tracks. Tell somebody the same. Wire him money to burn in his front and back pockets with. Making a hole in them. Rest his head when he get in.

"So you was standing out—"

"Don't worry about me, Mr. Lemontree. Bones warm as the sun. Jump around but wasn't cold. Uh-uh, Mr. Lemontree. No way." It's when Roadmap blew on his hands. "Oh ..." he said, embarrassed. "Uh ... been doing that all day. Uh, habit."

"And from the bar, when the white man come out drunk—where'd he take you to, Roadmap? Off to?"

"Funny. Funny—Mr. Arfel—funny, thought, honest—thought he was trying to fool me."

"But he didn't know you were—"

"No, no, Mr. Arfel. B-but I still thought the white man was trying to fool me—like he knew ..."

"Knew you was following him?"

"Yes, Mr. Arfel. It's the only way I can say it. Explain it."

"W-why, Roadmap? Why!"

"He don't come toward the Bluebird, Mr. Lemontree."

"Then where, Roadmap!"

"Takes me time, Mr. Arfel—but then I know: M-Miss Millie's."

"Miss Millie's!" Arfel and Lemontree said.

"Miss Millie's."

"What the—"

"The white man knocked on the front door of Miss Millie's, but I was already through the back." Pause. "Got money in his hand, Mr. Arfel, Mr. Lemontree. He wants to know about Arfel Booker and Blue Fire. All he say."

"But—"

"Miss Millie don't tell him nothing. Told him to put his money away, back in his pocket. They argue. Get loud. He pushed Miss Millie back from the door. Miss Millie knock into the wall. Stumble and, and all."

Lemontree's black skin burned orange. "I oughta—"

"She's strong, Miss Millie. But the white man grabbed her from behind and put the gun to her head, and ..."

"I caused this, me! Me!" Arfel screamed.

"Gun cock. Cock. But Miss Millie said go and shoot, kill me—I can only die one time. But one time—or, or something like that. And then let Miss Millie go and throw her into the wall again.

"And Miss Millie told the white man to go, get out of here, that she don't know no bluesman."

"Oh ... he's enjoying this—ain't he, ain't he!" Lemontree said. "Wanna cause as much ruckus for colored folk in this town he can. Bring his bad habits from the South North. Still think we scared jackrabbits on the run."

"M-Miss Millie's all right, is-isn't she, Roadmap?"

"Miss Millie's all right, Mr. Arfel. Fine, Mr. Arfel. Couldn't be better. Had something to say and said it."

"He's back in the Paladin, Roadmap?"

"Back, Mr. Lemontree. His walk coming back to him too. Straight. Walk off to the Paladin straight once he leave Miss Millie's, Mr. Lemontree. His drunk was gone. Liquor and all. All soaked up."

Lemontree whirled his body into action. "The white man's a cutie-pie all right. A real cutie-pie. Got whisker's like a bunny rabbit."

"He knows word's going to get around."

"Sure he does, Arfel. Knew you wasn't at Miss Millie's but here. Was announcing, advertising his arrival, his coming. Knew what he was doing at Miss Millie's all along."

"I just hope she's all right."

"You don't know Miss Millie, Arfel."

"I know."

"Miss Millie's all right. Roadmap sized it up: Miss Millie got a lot off her chest—not all, though. Uh-uh. Not all."

And then Knock-Kneed came charging through the door.

"Arfel! I heard!"

"See!" Lemontree said.

"I-I was over at Miss Millie's," Knock-Kneed stammered.

"See—"

"Vonnie-Mae and I, the girl I was with—"

"Know her," Lemontree said coolly.

"Heard a commotion. I hustled my clothes on, and—"

"And so you know," Lemontree said, cutting Knock-Kneed off.

"Yes."

"We was just talking about him. The white man. He was just under discussion. Roadmap's been following that white man all day. Been with him since he step off the train. Since then. In the afternoon."

"Good for you, Roadmap."

"Thank you, Mr. Knock-Kneed."

"Had breakfast with him, you might say." Lemontree laughed.

"S-so everything's all right!" Knock-Kneed asked Arfel.

"He's back at the Paladin Hotel."

"Stay-staying there, huh?"

"Yes," Arfel said, not knowing where the Paladin Hotel was or the Bow Street Bar for that matter.

"He didn't come here?"

"Uh-uh. Nope, Knock-Kneed. Nope. White man's having fun. Spike of it. Bowl of it. See right through him now. Trying to put a scare in us coloreds. A fear. Been out on them trains, that track, body tight as a board now. Plank of wood. Now he where he wanna be all along. Knows where Arfel and Blue Fire is. Know they gotta stop somewhere. Where the blues feel comfortable in Arfel's fingertips. And for a bluesman to take his last stand," Lemontree said, touching Blue Fire affectionately.

"Gonna talk money tomorrow when he wake. Gonna raise the stakes. Gonna see who the rats are in this town. Who's gonna come out the woodwork. He's sleeping on it. Right now as we speak." Pause.

"White man always thinking." Lemontree laughed. "Why he thinks he owns the world. Ain't got no soul in him—just think all day. Always think he got the wind at his back—and fortune straight ahead." Pause.

"When you going back for him, Roadmap?"

"Afternoon, I guess, Mr. Lemontree. Ain't doing much till then."

They all laughed.

211

"You're staying with me and Blue Fire tonight, Roadmap. At the Palace."

"I am, Mr. Arfel!"

"Sure are."

Roadmap jumped off the wooden beer keg. "Ready, Mr. Arfel, Blue Fire!"

"Now, Roadmap, me and Mr. Arfel got a few more songs to play before the night's gone, lights go out—now that Mr. Knock-Kneed and Purple Poison is here. Finished catting. Besides, Mr. Philander Prince is listening, that white boy wants his money's worth from us colored boys. Know that much!"

Arfel was barely through the Palace's front doors.

"Arfel! Heard!"

"How, Mr. Stump?"

"Don't matter. Don't matter how, Arfel! You're here!"

"Thought I—"

"Would've run, and quick. W-what's Roadmap doing—"

"With me?"

"Yes."

"Roadmap followed the white man all day. He's over at the Paladin Hotel, Mr. Stump."

"Paladin? Doing what!"

"Sleeping, I guess," Roadmap said nonchalantly.

"He was over at Miss Millie's but never got over to the Bluebird!"

"No," Arfel said.

"What kind of game's he playing?" Stump said, stamping his stump to the floor.

"A old possum game, Mr. Stump. Southern boys like me know it. We hiding, but both of us know where. Ain't played it in a while, Mr. Stump. But it's as old as the Mondays and Sundays that make up a week."

Stump eyed Roadmap. "So you brought Roadmap with you, to the Palace—your Indian scout."

"Might be dead today if it wasn't for Roadmap," Arfel said, hugging Roadmap to him.

"Thank you, Mr. Arfel. Thank you."

"You're welcome, Roadmap."

Stump walked back to his chair and sat. "Well, have a good night's sleep, you two, 'cause I am." Stump's wooden leg was back on top of the wooden desk.

"Know you will, Mr. Stump. Know you will," Arfel said.

Arfel and Roadmap were climbing the staircase.

"By the way, your rent's due in two days, Arfel. Got it marked."

"I-I know, Mr. Stump."

"You're paid through Tuesday," Stump said through a few short snorts out his broad nose. "Tuesday, Arfel. Tuesday."

The way Roadmap snapped his head back to look at Stump, it bothered Arfel.

Arfel was on the floor and Roadmap on the bed with Blue Fire.

"Ain't the first time I've been on this bed in this room, Mr. Arfel." The room's lights were off.

"Bet it ain't, Roadmap."

"Just the first time with Blue Fire."

"Know Blue Fire's happy."

"Yep, she looks it, don't she, Mr. Arfel?"

"Probably kiss you if she could."

"Mr. Arfel …" Roadmap blushed.

"Don't mean it, Roadmap."

"Wouldn't mind, Mr. Arfel."

Arfel was on the floor, but it was like a starry night. It was like a night when the best of things in life crown the day and blessings feel tenfold.

Roadmap's head was propped up by his hand (hand to his cheek, elbow fixed to the bed). Roadmap's cap remained on his head. "Wasn't scared tonight, Mr. Arfel."

"You wasn't, Roadmap?"

"No, Mr. Arfel, wasn't." Pause. "Think of you. What you tell me before. How brave you was when you was on the run from them bloodhounds, Mr. Arfel. When you kill that white man in that town. How you—"

"Don't know if I was brave, Roadmap. Just don't feel like dying that night. Don't feel like I've used up my time here on earth. Wanna give my life some more credit. Credit due it, I suppose."

Roadmap laid his head down on the pillow. "When I get married ..."

"M-married, Roadmap?"

"Married, Mr. Arfel. Married. Been thinking about it of late."

Arfel suppressed his laughter as best he could.

"Thinking about it a lot lately, Mr. Arfel. Marriage."

Arfel coughed to alleviate the tickle trapped in him. "Marriage, Roadmap?"

"Yep, marriage, Mr. Arfel."

"And ...?"

"Well ... gonna have children, Mr. Arfel. Decided—a lot. That's a fact. Ain't much to think of."

"What, uh, four ... five, may—"

"Uh-uh. No, maybe nine, ten."

"Nine, nine or ten, Roadmap!"

"Uh-huh. Decided, Mr. Arfel. Yep. Gonna have children all over the house. Everywhere. Everywhere your eye can aim." Pause. "Gonna be good to them, Mr. Arfel. Cross my heart."

And Arfel could hear Roadmap in the dark as his fingers crossed over his heart. "Promise, Mr. Arfel. Promise, Blue Fire. True and true I do." Pause.

"And, Mr. Arfel ..." It was a long pause. "Mr. Arfel, I-I ain't gonna throw none of them out, out on the street. Not none of them. Gonna love them the day they come into the world to the day they leave. Gonna do that. Promise."

And Arfel heard Roadmap's finger cross his heart in the dark again.

"Know that much about myself."

Arfel shut his eyes.

I know you do, Roadmap. For sure.

Chapter 16

"Roadmap!"

Roadmap was on his way out the hotel door on the dead run.

"Can't talk, Mr. Stump. Know it ain't noon—but I got things to do." Roadmap glanced up at the wall clock behind Stump's desk as proof.

"O-okay, Roadmap."

Roadmap was out the hotel's door. He ran at a snappy pace and then stopped to look back at Stump's Palace. "Thanks, Mr. Arfel, Blue Fire, for a good night. Sleep good, me and Blue Fire. Ain't gonna forget last night. Ain't about to." Roadmap started back up.

"Wonder what that white man's doing. Don't wanna wake him too early—ain't that eager or nothing."

Knock.

"Come in, Mr. Stump. Know it's you."

"It's gotta be me, huh, Arfel?" Stump said, entering Arfel's room.

"Nobody moves as quiet as you, Mr. Stump. Nobody I—uh, except for maybe Roadmap."

"Roadmap, the boy sounds like, damn, Arfel—ain't nothing like Roadmap. Can't say there is and mean it."

"Glad everything worked out last night," Arfel said relieved.

"Me too."

"Know Roadmap's good at what he does, but it still worries me. I try not to show it around him, but Roadmap is taking a chance. A big chance."

"The boy is," Stump agreed, pulling down on his threadbare suspenders.

"He called me brave last night, but it's Roadmap who's taking a chance, Mr. Stump. I ain't no hero."

"But Roadmap don't see it that way. He's looking for one, Arfel. And you're the nearest to it."

"But I ain't, Mr. Stump," Arfel said caustically. "Don't wanna be. I'm a bluesman. A bluesman on the run from the law, looking over his shoulder, Mr. Stump—trying to run as far as I can so not to run out of too much territory."

Stump's hand was still fastened to the doorknob—but then let go of it. "How much money you think he's gonna throw around today? The white man. Tell me?"

"Why, why Lemontree said the same thing last night, Mr. Stump."

"How much you think?"

Arfel shook his head. "Don't know, Mr. Stump."

"Staying at the Paladin. At that big, fancy hotel. Cost him a pretty penny, don't it? Don't seem to be in a rush. Money …"

Arfel eyed Stump suspiciously.

"I'm uh … uh, a businessman, Arfel—like you a bluesman. All I am. Talking strict-strictly as a … businessman. Who's been around. Knows what money can do to a man, Arfel …" Stump's lean favored his wooden leg. "I ain't gonna be rich. Wouldn't know what to do with a tub full of money if it come my way. Fell out the sky.

"Run this place, this hotel," Stump said, spreading his arms out in front of him as if to take it all in, "night and day. "Run it on more fumes than gas. Spit than glue. Tomorrow, gonna take in your rent. Don't know how many days more you gonna stay, but whatever money you give me, will do. Will keep you paid up for them number of days you here." Stump's hand rubbed over his scratchy beard.

"My life don't go beyond this hotel. The Palace. Don't want it to. The man made me bitter, I know, admit. Fight for something and see people die for it, and you want to honor it and all—but can't. You know it ain't yours. Was never yours. Ain't ever gonna be yours." Pause.

"I hate him as much as you, Arfel." Pause. "Tomorrow's gonna look like today. I'm gonna collect my rent money for however long you and"—Stump looked over at Blue Fire affectionately—"Blue Fire staying. And I'm gonna mark the days till you owe me again, and then come back with my hand out for collection. I saw coloreds die in the war. They still in my eyes. Memory of how.

"Sleep a lot, see them then. Money can't bring them back. Nothing can. Only keeping busy makes you feel you doing something worth the day. Your time. Sweat. Work, Arfel. Work. No matter how little it pays. S-some days my spit even got hate in it."

Arfel was at Lemontree's place.

Knock.

"Good timing, Arfel. Good timing."

Lemontree removed Arfel's coat. Arfel's body shook.

"Cold out today."

"You can say that again, Lemontree."

"Don't you worry none, Arfel. Ain't gonna put you down in the basement tonight."

"No?"

"Uh-uh. You laying low tonight. But not that low."

Arfel sat down at the kitchen table. "Hungry?"

"Uh—sure, Lemontree."

"Must be my cooking." Pause.

"Roadmap should be with him now. Ain't nothing going wrong 'less Roadmap say so. But I already know what the white man up to. Just gotta prove itself out thataway." Lemontree grabbed a skillet. "Arfel, let's talk. Been thinking about some things. Got a lotta things on my mind. Thoughts. A lot when it come to this situation we in. How to maybe better control it and all … I think."

Lemontree was looking Arfel dead in the eye and rubbing Arfel's shoulder at the same time.

"Care to listen?"

Arfel was curious as to what Lemontree was getting at, his thinking and his feelings.

The day for Lemontree was speeding along like a dog off its leash. He was hunched over Sweet-Juice in the Bluebird Bar.

"A chicken look both ways,
'Fore he cross the road.
Learn from 'is momma—
Ain't gotta be told.

Know if Farmer Ben or Jim hit 'em,
Wid 'is one-hundred-dollar bill truck—
Ain't got nobody tah blame on, but hisself—
Fer 'is own bad luck.

Why Ah looks both ways 'fore Ah cross de road,
North ... South ...
'Ain't gottah be told.

Smart jus' lak dat chicken is,
Ain't gonna git hit by a truck.
But probably be a bus—
Hell—man, be jus' mah luck!"

The Bluebird Bar's crowd rocked. Lemontree had been making up a number of cute little blues song ditties like that one for most of the night in the Bird.

"Dog burn down mah house,
An' mah bed.

Mad—
Wanna eat two 'squares' a day,
W'en he git fed.

How he strike dat match—
Till dis day, don't know—
Wid 'is paws?—
Lord knows, he ain't got no toes.

But watch, as the house burn down,
Wag 'is tail—
W'en it finally hit de groun'.

But we be de bes' a friends, my dog an' me—
Till this very day—
'Cept don't feed 'im once now,
But—twice a day!"

And before Lemontree could straighten his back back to normal, there was the white man looking at him—tall and with no signs of even a drop of liquor in him. Lemontree's black skin glowed like an autumn fire, smirking. He strummed Sweet-Juice. Knock-Kneed played along on Purple Poison with a barreling passion.

"Know why yah come,
Know why yah here,
Drink yah whiskey—
Don't lak beer.

Travel light; saddlebag, money, an' gun,
Got yah a nigger—
A nigger on de run.

Bluesman carry gui-tar,
A song in 'is heart—
Don't know nothin',

Denis Gray

'Bout w'at he start.

Onlies' yah can chase 'im
Tah de end a de sun,
An' a bluesman'll outrun—
Even a bullet—
Out a fuckin' white man's gun."

Lemontree's eyes and the white man's locked again, until one canceled out the other, both deciding to get on with the business at hand.

"Roadmap." Lemontree knew where Roadmap was in the Bluebird. "Knock-Kneed and me gonna play this one for you, Roadmap." Pause. "Come on, Sweet-Juice," Lemontree said to Sweet-Juice, coaxing her. "Come on now, girl."

"Come tah town,
Bound tah catch up wid 'im.
Say—'Mister, Mister,'
How it all begin.

Don't as' fer much, not mo'e dan a nickel, dime—
Drop it in 'is cap,
At de end a de line.

Know dis town lak de back a 'is hand,
Travel thru it—
Bettah dan any growed-up man.

Know w'at yah do,
How long it take.
Don't know 'im once—
Tah make a mistake.

Oh … but if you miss 'im—
W'en yah comin' thru,

Don't evah dink—not fer a minute, Mister—
Haha …
Dat he missed you!"

"Lemontree!" Already Lemontree could feel the pent-up tension in Arfel when he got in the house.

"The white man come, Arfel!"

"Good!" It's when Arfel relaxed.

"He come by the Bluebird." Lemontree slapped his hands together. "Cold. Water we fished in not too long ago, gonna turn into ice soon, Arfel. Solid ice." Lemontree took his time in taking off his coat like it had a block of ice in it.

"How long he stay, Lemontree? In the Bluebird?"

Everything Lemontree did was slow moving—at least for Arfel. "Not long." Pause. "Prove me right. Flash his money. Use your name like it catching fire. Like it set a fire to his tongue—he hate it so much."

Arfel laughed.

"Trying to turn colored on colored. Know it all along. Trying to turn colored on colored. Separate a field nigger from a house nigger. The southern way. Wanna find a nigger to snitch on you, Arfel. Buy him with money."

"Did-didn't want it to get to this, Lemontree."

"Don't say nothing on the other side of town. Don't wanna say nothing. People curious why he here. For what business he hold out. Only come on this side of town with his money, your name burning on his tongue like a house on fire, Arfel. Wanna play this game to its end, its conclusion. Don't care about nothing else. Have your own kind betray you. Give up your name. A nigger. Another nigger."

Pause.

"Hungry? Know you is. Been that way since I look on him. Don't even touch a drop of liquor in the Bird tonight, just got a hunger in me, Arfel—no thirst. Uh-uh, not of no kind."

"Roadmap's on—"

221

"He's still on his tail. That white man don't know how bad he been cursed."

"I was thinking about what you said earlier, Lemontree."

Lemontree had moved over to the stove. "Did all the talking before, Arfel. Know you had to soak it in. Wasn't rushing you. Not one bit. Thought it through like I told you, Arfel. Don't wanna throw nothing at you that gonna fly in the wind. Gotta be solid. Rock solid."

"T-thanks for that."

Lemontree held the skillet. "So what's it gonna be, Arfel?"

"Ham and—"

"Now come on, Arfel—hell—you know what I'm getting at."

Arfel shut his eyes.

"In or out?"

"In, Lemontree."

Lemontree sliced meat off the ham's bone with the big-handled carving knife. "Bluesman eating ham and chitterlings at"—Lemontree looked at his watch—"one forty-five in the morning." Lemontree sliced another slab of ham off the bone. "Should be off with a blueswoman. What I should be doing. A big-butt blueswoman."

"I don't know about that, Lemontree. You still ain't sold me."

"You don't know about nothing, Arfel." Lemontree chuckled, cutting Arfel off. "Arfel, don't want me nothing but—but a big-butt blueswoman. Nothing but!"

Roadmap was on the road. It was early. Charlie Snarlings had come for him. He was sent by Mr. Stump. Charlie Starlings told Roadmap Mr. Stump paid him to find him, a dime, Charlie Starlings said. Charlie Starlings said Mr. Stump said he was to drop everything no matter what and go to the Paladin Hotel to get him. At first Roadmap hesitated about leaving, but knew the white man wasn't coming out the Paladin until late, so standing there all morning made no sense.

If Roadmap touched his brain, it'd singe his fingertips. His brain was hot. Overheated. Hot as boiling water. "What do you want, Mr. Stump? What you angling? What's so important, Mr. Stump?" It had something to do with the white man, Roadmap knew that—but what? Just what?

"What do you and the white man gotta do with each other, Mr. Stump? I-I don't see the connection, Mr. Stump. Don't." Roadmap stopped long enough in order to catch his breath. Before, Charlie Starlings couldn't keep up with him; and besides, he didn't use the same shortcuts as Charlie. Charlie Starlings had parted company with him a couple of miles back.

Stump's Palace loomed in the distance. "Don't like this. Uh-uh," Roadmap said. "Don't like this, Mr. Stump. Don't like any of this. Not at all, Mr. Stump."

Roadmap was in the hotel but didn't see Mr. Stump. He stood at the counter. He wasn't going to look for him. Mr. Stump called for him, he knew he was coming—he wasn't going to look for Mr. Stump.

Roadmap had been standing at the Palace's counter for no more than a minute.

"*Pssst. Psst.* Roadmap." Roadmap looked down the Palace's long hallway.

"*Pssst. Psst* … Here, Roadmap … here …"

"Hear you, Mr. Stump," Roadmap whispered. "C-coming, Mr. Stump."

The closet door was open (where the brooms and mops and pails and rags and other cleaning items were). *Why are we meeting here?* Roadmap queried. When Roadmap entered the closet, Stump looked both ways before shutting the door. It was a tight … an awfully tight fit. A light dangled from the ceiling in there; oily blue sheens covered their skins.

"Glad you came, Roadmap," Stump said, still in a whisper. "Told Charlie where to look for you. If he don't already know."

Roadmap's eyes stayed glued to Mr. Stump's, afraid if he lost eye contact with him, he might begin thinking why he was in the broom closet, again.

"Have a favor to ask of you, Roadmap."

"A favor? Cost you, Mr. Stump."

"Know that, Roadmap." Stump smiled. "Know you're a businessman. Gotta take care of your business first and foremost. That end of things."

It's when Stump paused, and his long deliberation created anxiety in Roadmap, for Roadmap wondered if Mr. Stump wanted him to do the brass again, because if he did, he was going to charge him a quarter this time—nothing less. *But why in a broom closet? Why, if it's what Mr. Stump wanted to discuss?*

"Roadmap …"

"Yes, Mr. Stump, sir …" And then Stump's eyes seemed to withdraw themselves, only to, again, refocus in on Roadmap. "I want you to go into the Paladin Hotel and knock on the white man's door."

Roadmap was shaken back into reality as if a tidal wave had hit him. "Wha-what you, what you say, Mr. Stump? Wha-what, Mr. Stump?"

"You heard me, Roadmap."

"Knock, knock on the, on the white man's door, Mr. … Mr. Stump? On his door!"

"Ain't going crazy, Roadmap. Ain't, if it's what you thinking. I see that look in your eyes. There's business I've got with him."

"Business w-with a white man!"

Stump laid his hand on Roadmap's shoulder. Roadmap felt like knocking it off. "Hear me out, Roadmap. Out now."

Roadmap's small body was still vibrating from the news, something seeming so ominous and foreboding.

"Gotta pack of lies to tell him, the white man. Ain't gonna play it straight, no way straight with him. Not for one minute. A pack of—"

"A-about Mr. Arfel and … and Blue Fire, Mr. Stump?"

"Uh-huh. Cor-correct."

"Oh."

"And I need you to get him."

"Me?"

"You, Roadmap. White man's gonna buy into this hook, line, and sinker." Pause. "White man likes intrigue, Roadmap. Mystery. Northern white man. Southern white man. All the same way, Roadmap. Don't matter much."

Now Roadmap's chest heaved out what seemed a mile. "Thanks. Thanks, Mr. Stump."

In the light, Stump's grin glowed. "Now for information you've gotta deliver, give him—goes like this, Roadmap." Pause. "He's to meet Stump McCants, the owner of Stump's Palace, hotel keeper (he'll remember me), at the Bluebird Bar at eight o'clock sharp tonight, before Mr. Lemontree and Mr. Arfel go in. Play."

Roadmap nodded.

"Got it, Roadmap?"

"Uh, g-got it, Mr. Stump. G-got it, sir."

"Okay, Roadmap. Okay." Then Stump pulled down on the thin string to turn off the broom closet's light. Roadmap felt the dark instantly cloak him as quickly he thought of what was ahead of him with the white man in that dark, closed-in space. But then Stump opened the door, and he and Roadmap stood back in the hallway where there was sufficient light.

"Ain't scared, is you, Roadmap?"

"No, no, Mr. Stump—ain't, ain't scared."

"White man's gonna get a kick out of this," Stump said, still in a faint whisper—as if the hotel's walls had ears.

"Yes, sir, Mr. Stump." Roadmap laughed. Roadmap, who'd been a step or two in front of Stump, had stopped as Stump had passed him.

"Roadmap, go ahead now—shoo. Off with you!"

Roadmap stood there in the middle of the lobby like a roadblock. "Not without my dime, Mr. Stump," Roadmap said, suavely removing his cap. "Mr. Lemontree write a song about me, Mr. Stump. Mr. Lemontree. In the Bird last night," Roadmap gushed.

"Heard, Roadmap."

"Made me ... made me near world—"

"Famous. Heard, Roadmap."

"Just don't use my name." Pause. "Need my dime, Mr. Stump!" Roadmap's cap hung out there in the air.

Stump roared with laughter. "Businessman, businessman. How ... how you country boys say it?"

"*True and true*, Mr. Stump. *True and true.*"

"Yes, yes, true and true, Roadmap. True and true," Stump said, digging his right hand into his pocket to find some loose change swimming around in it.

"Ain't complaining, Mr. Stump." And Stump's dime dropped down into Roadmap's cap. "Ain't."

Roadmap was scared again: he was on a mission but didn't know the extent of it. The parameters of it. How it played out in the larger scheme of things. Did Mr. Arfel and Lemontree know about this, Mr. Stump sending him off to the white man? The Paladin Hotel? He hadn't asked Mr. Stump. He couldn't think at the time. All of this had been thrust on him too sudden for him to think, make serious, profound inquiry.

But now he was. Now it was all he thought about—whether Mr. Arfel and Mr. Lemontree knew what he was up to, what Mr. Stump had sent him off to do. Roadmap spun one time, then twice, feeling like a spinning top—very much baffled, bewildered. He had a solid dime in his pocket, not two nickels. Mr. Stump gave him a solid dime. Roadmap took it out his pocket. He laid it flat to his palm. It could stick there solid to his skin; it was so cold today. Roadmap, with a bent thumb, flipped the dime in the air. When the dime descended, landed back down in his palm, Roadmap slapped his other hand over it shouting, "Heads!" Then Roadmap undid his top hand from his bottom hand and used his eyes as if they were peeking into an underground cave.

"Tails …" Roadmap said, the column of air depressing his lungs. "Tails," Roadmap said, even more deflated by the occurrence. "It come up tails."

By now Roadmap had everything worked out just in case he ran into George. Just in case—Roadmap said to himself, once again.

Roadmap was in the Paladin. He was by the elevators but was showing no outward sign of what he was about to do.

"Nigger, I told you last time!"

It was George. Donald wasn't around—so it appeared.

Roadmap balled his small fists.

George rushed him. "Sassed me the last time. Didn't you. Didn't you!" George said, standing in front of Roadmap with a nasty glare in his eyes.

"Talked tough," George said, shoving Roadmap back.

"Sass you this time too!" Roadmap shouted back. And then Roadmap unleashed a kick, kicking George straight in the shins.

"Oww! Oww!" George shouted.

So Roadmap did it again, kicked George straight in his shins.

"Oww! Oww!" George grabbed his leg, was hopping around. Then he came at Roadmap, but Roadmap ducked his clutch and laughed.

"Slippery nigger. Slippery nigger, ain't you? Slop pig nigger! G-grease pig nigger!"

Roadmap was behind him, and he punched George hard in his back. George yelled again. It's when Roadmap kicked him in the behind— George's head butting into the elevator wall.

"Roadmap!" It was Donald. "What are you doing!" Donald saw George was rubbing his head and his behind simultaneously.

"Kicking that boy's ass!"

"So I see!" Donald laughed.

"Let me at that little coon-eyed nigger!"

"Seems like you've had enough, George," Donald said, blocking George off.

Angrily, George pointed his finger at Roadmap. "Ain't through with you, nigger! Hardly! Don't think we're through!"

"Kick your ass some more if you want. Don't matter to me!"

"Go, George. Go on."

"Yeah … yeah …" George said, walking away, attending to his aches and pains.

Then Donald turned to Roadmap. "Roadmap, what are you really doing in here? I know you didn't come to kick, ha, George's ass."

Roadmap was holding tightly to a brown paper bag. Something he carried with him into the Paladin, which he'd dropped onto the lobby's rug because of George. And now Roadmap could swing his plan into motion.

"Come to bring Miss Emma something," Roadmap said, looking at the brown bag.

"Miss Emma?"

"Uh-huh."

"You know where Miss Emma works, right?"

"It's where I was going, until that boy—"

"George."

"Yeah. That boy stopped me."

"Miss Emma's in the laundry room."

"Right."

"If you have any trouble, tell them I said it's okay ... Donald."

"Know that."

"That they can page me."

"Right."

"Gotta go, Roadmap."

Roadmap passed the elevators. "Know that."

Roadmap continued walking, but as he did, he turned around to spy on Donald as Donald hurried off—making a left turn into the Paladin's grand lobby.

It's when Roadmap executed a sharp about-face as he smiled like he was a big fish who'd caught a little fish whose tail tickled the lining of his tummy. But then that white cold returned, that scare in him. Roadmap's finger pressed the bright brass button and waited.

Folk had gathered at the elevator bank along with Roadmap, who looked down at him. Roadmap held on to the brown bag as if there were something important in it even if it didn't throw off an aroma, that there could be food in the paper bag he, presumably, was delivering to someone on one of the Paladin's floors.

The elevator was there, and there was a colored elevator operator, Mr. T. C. "Cappy" Hopkins. "Roadmap," Mr. Hopkins said with surprise. He pulled open the elevator's iron gate as the other three passengers boarded the elevator.

"H-hello, Mr. Hopkins. Uh ... good afternoon, sir."

"Fifth floor, please."

"Third."

"Eighth."

"What floor you want, Roadmap?"

"Eleventh, Mr. Hopkins. Delivering something."

"Oh."

Everyone, along with Mr. Hopkins, seemed satisfied, perfectly relieved. Mr. Hopkins pushed the iron gate shut.

The last passenger was getting off the elevator.

"Thank you."

"You're welcome, sir."

And then Mr. Hopkins's attention turned to Roadmap. "Delivery? What—you in the delivery business now, Roadmap? Got a new job going?"

"Yes, sir."

"Delivering what, Roadmap?"

"Something."

"Something?"

"It's what I said, Mr. Hopkins, something, uh ... uh, sir," Roadmap said, his fingers digging sterner into the bag.

"Must be something special."

"It is, Mr. Hopkins. Sure is."

"In a paper bag, Roadmap?"

"It is."

Cappy Hopkins removed his spectacles, only to rest them back on his angular nose. "Ain't nothing so sweet you delivering to a guest of the hotel, that's curling up my nose any, Roadmap."

Roadmap didn't answer.

"Eleventh floor it is."

"Thanks, Mr. Hopkins."

Roadmap hopped off the elevator.

Cappy Hopkins, who sat in his handsome-looking chair in the corner, stood. "Want me to wait?"

"Uh, no—you can go, Mr. Hopkins. Uh, ring for you when I'm through."

"Oh ... okay, Roadmap. You calling the tune."

Roadmap was heading North in the hall but didn't know if he should be heading South, for he didn't know in what room the white man was staying, and it hit him like thunder.

Mr. Hopkins was about to push the elevator's gate shut, when Roadmap said, "A, a white man, Mr. Hopkins. A—"

"Plenty of them around here, Roadmap. The Paladin, Roadmap." Mr. Hopkins laughed.

"Tall. Wears a ... a brown hat, Mr. Hopkins. Tall—and wears a brown hat."

"Oh, him. That white man. Room 1110. To your left, Roadmap. Eleven-ten. You mean, nobody told you the room?"

"Just the floor, Mr. Hopkins. Guess they forget. Guess I let them."

"You, Roadmap?"

Roadmap didn't reply as he heard the iron gate to the elevator shut, and the metal door closing—

"Be back for you, Roadmap. Ring now. Be right up. Give you special service."

—then the elevator's engine worked.

And Roadmap felt alone, completely alone—terrified. This was the first time since all of this had begun, Roadmap wanted to cry out of fear. He wanted to roll his cap's bill but didn't. He wanted to walk but couldn't. His eyes looked straight ahead. He was at room 1102. He had four more rooms in front of him.

"Ain't been this scared. Ain't been this scared. Never. Know he's there. In there. That room. Know he ain't going nowhere. Mr. Stump sent me. Mr. Stump wanna see you, white man. Mr. Stump sent me—want to see you at the Bluebird Bar. Wants to see you at eight o'clock, at eight o'clock sharp. Mr. Stump sent me, white man. Don't know why—but he wants to see you. Said you'd remember him from before, the last time you was here, before when you come to this town to inquire on Mr. Arfel Booker and Blue Fire. Somebody nobody in this town seen or heard of. Mr. Arfel Booker. Blue Fire. Runs the Stump Palace. Said you remember. Mr. ... Mr. Stump paid me a dime, Mister. Got it sitting down in my pocket. Feel it. Got it there. Got it down in my pocket. Feel it. Solid. Ain't spent it on nothing. N-nothing ..."

Roadmap's hand dropped the bag; it fell to the floor.

"Ain't nothing in it but air. B-but pretend. Ain't nothing in it but pretend." Roadmap began walking. "Mr. Hopkins is coming for me," Roadmap said, looking over his shoulder, back to the elevator. "Just gotta ring him—he's coming back. Coming back, Mister. Know I'm up here. On this floor, Mister."

Roadmap was at room 1108.

"Knows I ain't stealing nothing, Mr. Hopkins. Knows that for sure. Don't do that. Don't steal. Mr. Hopkins knows that. Why I'm up on this floor. Hustle. Just hustle. Hustle the streets. Hustle a nickel, a dime, mostly. Mr. Stump send me, white man. Something to do with Mr. Arfel Booker and Blue Fire. Don't know yet. Don't know nothing. Just gotta dime in my pocket. For spending. Sitting solid. Ain't no nickels hitting together. Ain't a noise to make in my pocket. One dime don't make noise; got a real nice quiet to it, Mister. Quiet like the streets, sometimes."

Roadmap was at room 1110.

Roadmap felt tears watering his eyes but fought them back. And then he thought of George by the elevators and how he'd kicked his ass good. Out and out kicked his ass good. "Kicked that boy's ass. Kicked that white boy's ass. Was bigger than me, much, Mister. Still kicked that boy's ass!"

Knock.

Knock.

And Roadmap waited for something, anything—looking back to the bag on the floor, and then off to the elevator.

And then Roadmap's eyes became riveted to the door with the number 1110 chiseled finely in it as it began to open out not more than an inch or so at a time.

Roadmap heard himself swallow the hot spit in his mouth, and his head bubbled in knocking, concussive pain.

Time had passed, but Roadmap was recalling it all again from the moment it happened until now, the day as long as a howling wolf's night. How the hotel door opened and he saw that white man with his brown hat still on his head, and his knees did shake, Roadmap thought. But he got the words out his mouth as quick as spit.

"Come to see you, Mister. Come to tell you something, Mister. Tell you something."

And though there was a terror in him, a throbbing fear, the words tumbled out his mouth as clear and pure as if he were talking to just anybody, any passerby on the street, and not the tall white man with the brown hat whose face had a wear in it—almost pathetic—and a gun on his hip.

"Ain't gotta know my name. Ain't gotta know my name, Mister. Mr. Stump send me. Stump's Palace. Mr. Stump McCants, Mister. Wants to see you tonight. Tonight, Mister. At eight o'clock sharp at the Bluebird Bar. Mr. Stump said he wants to meet you tonight. Eight o'clock sharp at the Bluebird Bar, Mister. He's got some—"

The door had shut.

"… information for you, for you, Mister."

And he'd stood there in the hallway looking at the door, room 1110, and then walked up the hall and picked the brown bag up off the floor folding it, tucking it inside his shirt, underneath his jacket, hiding it, and then walking down the Paladin's long hallway and past those other finely chiseled numbers and got to the elevator and rang for the elevator for Mr. Hopkins who was waiting for that ring; and here he was now, following the white man step for step for the Bluebird Bar … Step for step like a dark, creepy shadow in the road.

"Don't matter now if he sees me or hears me. Don't matter now," Roadmap said dejectedly.

But Roadmap was following him as he'd followed him before, his movements as creatively organized, still in secret. Roadmap hadn't seen Mr. Stump since this afternoon. He hadn't reported back to him. Mr. Stump knew he'd get back to him if there'd been trouble between him and the white man. It was like it was understood implicitly between him and Mr. Stump all along.

"Mr. Stump knows the white man's coming to the Bird. Don't look to be late."

Chapter 17

Stump glanced back at the old, grand tan RA clock and smiled. He knew just how long it would take for him to get over to the Bluebird Bar (had had it timed out). He hadn't been over there in a long, long time, he thought. When was the last time he saw Last Round anyway? He couldn't remember. *Last Round's going to be surprised to see me,* Stump thought.

"Gonna have a drink before I look that white man in the eye. Gonna feel a shot of whiskey gird me. Gonna feel good about this."

Stump had made a crude sign from a cardboard and propped it atop the hotel's countertop.

Gone for a while (aint gone fishing!)
Back soon.
Stump McCants Propietar

Stump brushed lint off his powder blue suit jacket as he put his big coat on. Stump felt like a businessman, a person who knew about the nature of people and things. He could look the white man dead in his eye with or without a shot of whiskey in his belly; but for what he was

233

about to do, he'd feel a lot better with a shot of whiskey in him, coating his belly, something to stabilize him for the course.

"Mr. Stump!" Immediately, Stump got Last Round's attention when he entered the Bird.

Stump and his wooden stump moved quietly across the floor (same as the stump did in Stump's Palace).

"Dang, Mr. Stump, ain't seen you in here in ages!"

"So they tell me, Last Round." Stump sidled up to the bar.

"How's the hotel business?"

"Ain't as good as the bar business—I see," Stump said, looking around the bar, seeing there was already a good crowd in the Bird. "But everybody's rent's paid up to date. It's about all I can say for the hotel business. As long as your rent's paid—my squabble ain't with you but somebody else."

"Uh … who's minding the store, Mr. Stump?"

"It's minding itself for the time being. Only for a short while, though. Ain't gonna be here long."

"Oh, what, you got business here tonight?"

"Might say that. Uh, so." Then Stump figured he'd not be so vague—it wasn't in keeping with his style or image. "Yeah, business, Last Round. Business."

"Wanna drink before—"

"My date shows up?"

"Right, Mr. Stump!"

"On the house, Last Round? Considering I ain't been in this estab—"

"Now, Mr. Stump, you've got your business to run and I've got mine. Both of us got to add up the tabs at the end of the day. Same bookkeeping."

"Can't twist your arm?" Pause. "The usual then, Last Round. If you still—"

"I remember, Mr. Stump!"

"Still remember the price?" Stump asked, slapping the dollar bill down on top of the bar.

"Got change coming, Mr. Stump." Last Round laughed. "Bar business ain't that good!"

Last Round served Stump's drink and laid Stump's change out on the bar.

Quickly, Stump downed the drink.

"Dang, Mr. Stump, you have been away from the Bird in a while!"

Stump pointed his finger at the empty glass.

"Gotcha."

This time Stump looked down at the glass as if he were looking through it as Last Round weeded out the Bird's share of money off the bar.

"You counted right, Last Round?"

"Sure, Mr. Stump. Ain't a penny more or less."

"Buy a box of bulbs." Stump seemed to be savoring his drink this time, drinking it nice and slow.

Last Round had been watching Stump for a while now. "Ain't you going to finish off that drink, Mr. Stump?"

"Just biding my time with it, Last Round," Stump said, taking a peek at his timepiece. "Treating it like doctor's medicine."

It was two minutes to eight.

"Got more in the bottle, Mr. Stump."

Stump's money was still out on top of the bar, his loose change. "Ain't that thirsty, Last Round."

Stump lifted the whiskey glass but hadn't drunk from it. Stump didn't have to turn his head but did, since the Bluebird's crowd's ugly mood had signaled to him (beyond a shadow of a doubt) that the tall white man was in the bar.

The white man looked down at Stump's wooden leg, a stump he seemingly hadn't forgotten since his last visit to this town.

The colored folk in the Bluebird cleared away as this white man approached the bar. The only one who stood his ground was Stump McCants.

"Stump. Stump McCants," Stump said, reaching out his hand to the white man. "You remember me?"

Last Round's head had turned, and what he saw was Stump McCants shaking the white man's hand.

(Roadmap had slipped into the Bluebird.)

Stump began talking in a low, whirring voice. Stump pointed his finger to his glass. "Another one round, Last Round. This man's paying!"

Last Round was further shocked, looking at Stump with animus, disgust, shaking his head, but pouring the drink into Stump's glass for the third time tonight.

Roadmap's stomach sank. What had he gotten himself into? Roadmap thought as he saw the white man's face shine, smile again and again as Mr. Stump kept talking. The white man hadn't ordered a drink, hadn't touched one; drunk a drop of liquor.

Roadmap wished he could get closer so he could hear better, but couldn't: he was confined.

And the people in the bar continued to keep their distance between the white man and Stump.

Roadmap's eyes bugged out his head when he saw what happened next between Stump McCants and the white man, for the white man went into his back pocket and pulled out a big wad of cash, ready money.

"No, no, Mr. Stump. NO!" Roadmap said, his hand muffling his cries.

The white man had done it in a way as to demonstrate to everyone in the Bluebird Bar that he and one of *their* kind had just transacted some kind of dirty, sordid business, had just been bought off, that there had been a payoff.

Last Round snatched the liquor bottle off the bar as if he'd snatched Stump's neck; was going to squeeze out his last breath.

The white man had spread the cash out on the bar, and Stump looked at it and then scooped it up.

Last Round took an empty liquor bottle and cracked it, leaving a jagged piece in his hand.

"Get out goddammit, Mr. Stump! The fuck outta here!"

"Me and the gentlemen, we was just leaving, Last Round. Just now," Stump said tauntingly. "We got some business to conduct back at Stump's Palace."

"You fucking Uncle Tom nigger, Mr. Stump! You fuck—"

"Come from the North, boy. Hell, don't know nothing 'bout no Jim Crow, what y'all southern niggers been fighting over since the goddamned Civil War!"

"Get your black ass outta here—nigger! NIGGER!"

And across the Bluebird's Bar Stump walked with the tall white man, hanging back in his shadow, who'd flung his long coat open, brandishing his gun.

Roadmap just stood there in the Bluebird. He couldn't move, he couldn't believe what he'd just witnessed: Mr. Stump selling Mr. Arfel and Blue Fire out to that white man for money, for something he hustled the streets night and day for, his entire life revolving around it.

"Think, Roadmap. Think!"

Sweat poured off Roadmap's face. Black sweat. "I-I've gotta trust him. I-I've gotta trust Mr. Stump!" It was all Roadmap could say.

"Gotta get going before they get too far on me!"

Roadmap tore out of the Bluebird like a blue streak. He wasn't looking to take shortcuts, not a one: he was going to catch up to Mr. Stump and the white man. Follow the two of them—this time.

"I've gotta trust him. I've gotta trust Mr. Stump!" Roadmap repeated, huffing and puffing.

And within minutes, Roadmap had caught up with Stump and the white man. And now Roadmap was following Mr. Stump and the white man. "Feel funny. Aw-awful funny," Roadmap said. "Don't feel right, Mr. Stump. Feel funny, Mr. Stump. Awful funny."

Stump's Palace loomed in the distance.

"We're here, Mr. Arfel. Blue Fire."

Mr. Lemontree had said Mr. Arfel and Blue Fire weren't hiding out tonight, that they were going to the Bluebird, that the white man could come—that tonight it wouldn't matter. But they'd be leaving for the Bluebird any minute now; it was routine—Mr. Arfel and Blue Fire.

"If you're in there, Mr. Arfel. If—a knife against a gun? The, the knife you slit the white man's throat clean with a-against a gun, Mr. Arfel!" Roadmap said hidden, bundled in darkness. "What you carry in your back pocket?" Pause.

"Gotta believe. Gotta!"

Stump and the white man continued their walk, pressing forward ever quicker until they'd reached the Palace.

On his wooden leg, Stump hopped up the hotel's front steps. Courteously, Stump opened the hotel's front door for the white man, allowing him to enter the Palace first.

"Like I said—I know I lied to you before, when you first come. But I'm from the North. New York City—colored man, nigger, don't know no better. Ha!"

The white man's voice, when he answered Stump, was tall and deep but not as tall and deep as a bluesman's when slowed down to sing of the world's hardships and heartaches, nonstop.

Stump looked at the sign he'd concocted before leaving for the Bluebird and then took the back of his hand, slapping it to the floor.

"The boy owes me rent! Didn't come up with it two days ago. Wanna slide by. First time since he's been staying here. Arfel Booker. First time he come up short with his rent. Don't pay." Then Stump's face turned a beet red.

"Gonna be his last time—I'll see to that!"

"Oh … yeah—he's, the boy's in room number 2G. Arfel Booker's in room 2G. Him and Blue Fire should be heading off to the Bluebird Bar any minute now. Any … Ha. Ha. Ha …" Stump sneered. "Routine." Pause.

"How you want to work this? Do this then?"

"Yeah, I got a spare key."

"So … when I walk in, I'll step away, away from the door and you'll …"

"Yeah—I get the picture. Yeah. Shoot that nigger, uh, boy right there. Yeah, I get the picture. Serves him right. Jumping rent. I get the picture—all right. Ain't gotta paint it for me. I-I …"

"Yeah, I'm ready. Don't want to shoot him—shoot Arfel Booker? I, yeah—I heard you. Yeah … y-yeah …"

Stump came from behind the counter. And he led the white man to the staircase and looked up. Then he began walking, climbing up those stairs with the white man following him from behind, every step taken showing some sort of regret, burden. The white man seemed to sense this, smiling broadly for the first time since they got in the hotel, this town, in fact, his hand touching the gun's hard metal.

They were there, in front of Arfel's room door, room 2G.

Roughly, the white man grabbed Stump's arm from behind before Stump did anything—seeming to want to size up things for himself. He bent low to the ground, for he could look under the door where crisp light streamed out. Now the white man smiled and drew his gun out the holster. And with his gun, the white man gestured to Stump what to do.

And now Stump saw all the days and nights of travel in the white man's face manifest, the hunt—the chase for a "nigga" named Arfel Booker brought to bear—who thought he'd outrun the white man's justice, from the white man's law, jail, and gun, as if a nigga would have to run to the end of hell; no less far, no less tormented, tortured, persecuted by fate and color and subjugation and degradation.

The wall clock in the lobby gonged.

Mr. Stump spit in his hand, rubbing them together before speaking.

"Arfel, Arfel—it's me. Me … Mr. Stump. Don't gotta be reminded. I've come for my rent. Two days' worth, boy!" Stump inserted the spare key into the door's lock. "You can lock the door, don't matter. Got a key. Know you and Blue Fire in there. See the light. Know the routine. Know you and Blue Fire ain't going to the Bluebird to play with Lemontree and Knock-Kneed tonight until you square up with—"

And the door swung open—

"ME!"

The white man charged into the room.

The lights snapped off.

"GOT THE WHITE MOTHERFUCKER!"

"YEAH, LEMONTREE!" Knock-Kneed held the white man's legs as he tried kicking them free.

"GOT HIM, STUMP! GOT THE CRACKER!"

Then the door slammed shut, and the room lights snapped back on.

Lemontree had wrapped his burly arms around the white man's neck, pinching off his circulation, and his hand covered his mouth. The white man continued to struggle, trying to break free—but Lemontree and Knock-Kneed kept him locked in place.

"You ain't gonna go nowhere, white man. Only to where we're taking you!"

"Tie him up like a hog! Hog-tie him!" Lemontree said as Knock-Kneed gathered the heavy corded rope off the floor. "I'll gag him. You ain't saying nothing for now, white man. Already said too much already tonight!"

"The pickup truck's in the back, Lemontree!"

Lemontree acknowledged Knock-Kneed. It's when he looked over to Stump as the white man continued to struggle, not giving up, strenuously protesting his captivity, cursing, entrapped.

"Good work, Stump. Good damned work. Shit, the plan worked!"

"The drinks at the Bluebird tasted like poison, Lemontree. I had to make it look real for the white man would buy it. Buy into it … but Last Round …" Stump's body slumped. "Like poison."

"Don't worry—we gonna take care of that piece of business. Square that. Last Round's gonna know. Folk around here too."

The white man was bound and gagged. "Yeah, good work, Stump," Lemontree said, patting Stump's back. "Now—let's get the hell outta here!"

When Lemontree lifted the white man up onto his shoulder, the white man's big wide-brimmed hat fell to the floor. Knock-Kneed wrapped him up in a brown blanket. He was folded over Lemontree's burly shoulders like a piece of rolled-up carpet.

"Coast is clear, Lemontree," Stump whispered out the side of his mouth.

"Ha. Don't matter, Stump. Coloreds live in this hotel. Coloreds." But then Lemontree ducked back inside the room. "You ain't going with us, Knock-Kneed."

"But I've got the pickup truck, Lemontree. My, my granddaddy's pickup truck."

"It's why I'm asking for the keys."

"But …"

"Give them to Stump."

Stump's hand opened.

"Don't need this kind of trouble for yourself. Me and Stump old, ain't got but so much to lose—if there's anything else for us to. Not you. Ain't the end of the line for you."

"But—"

"Just give Stump the keys. Hand them over. We'll park the truck in your granddaddy Curtis's backyard tonight when we done with this."

Knock-Kneed dropped the truck's key into Stump's hand as it trembled.

"You go ahead now. You and Purple Poison. You was in the Bluebird tonight. Everybody seen you, Knock-Kneed. You and Purple Poison got an alibi if things go sour."

It's when Stump and Lemontree moved smartly up the hall with that hunk-of-something under the blanket, folded over Lemontree's shoulders, flouncing like a bundle of mad cats.

Knock-Kneed stood at the room's door, silent.

Lemontree and Stump were down the landing's stairs, heading for the hotel's back door.

"Mr. Knock-Kneed! Mr. Knock-Kneed!"

Knock-Kneed's head turned. "Roadmap!"

"It's me, Mr. Knock-Kneed. It's me—you ain't seeing a ghost."

"What you …"

"Been following the white man all this time!"

"So you heard? Saw? What we did!"

"Yes, yes, Mr. Knock-Kneed. Was at the door and then run off before Mr. Lemontree and Mr. Stump leave." Roadmap grabbed Knock-Kneed's arm. "Where're they going, Mr. Knock-Kneed, taking him off to!"

Knock-Kneed hesitated.

"Tell me. You gotta tell me, Mr. Knock-Kneed. I gotta know!"

Knock-Kneed was shaking.

"Now, Mr. Knock-Kneed. Before they get too far ahead!"

Knock-Kneed whispered it into Roadmap's ear.

"Thought so. Thought so, Mr. Knock-Kneed!" Roadmap ran up the hallway.

"You be careful. You be careful out there, Roadmap." Knock-Kneed's voice faded in Roadmap's ears. Then Knock-Kneed's big fist punched in the wall, punched straight through it.

"H-hope that Mr. Stump and Lemontree do what's right for all of us. Us colored people. Just hope." Knock-Kneed looked down to the floor and picked up the white man's big brown hat.

241

"Know it don't belong to you, Arfel. Not to anybody I know!"

Roadmap was out the hotel's back door. The pickup truck had started up; its back was pointed to the back of the hotel. Even through a rearview mirror, Roadmap could not be seen.

The pickup truck started moving with more of its lights on. It was moving slowly. The hunk-of-something was gated in, not going anywhere.

"I'll beat you there. I'll outrun you, Mr. Lemontree! Mr. Stump. Know all the shortcuts. All of them!" Roadmap said, rushing out into the dark.

Roadmap's breath had left his mouth, dashing out into the dark night air. He wasn't breathing hard now. He'd been at the "Lucy Caton River" for a while waiting on Mr. Lemontree, Mr. Stump, the pickup truck—the white man.

"Run in the cold, but ain't winded. The wind pushed me along."

The wind kicked up.

Roadmap hid behind a clump of tall full bushes.

"Set near by the water, ain't I? Can see real good from here."

"Good thing you did with Knock-Kneed back there, Lemontree."

"Thought it through, Stump. That's all. If trouble comes, Knock-Kneed ain't in it. Ain't got a speck a nothing on him. Not a follicle."

The truck's lights were turned on.

"Arfel and Blue Fire—"

"Damn if I don't miss them already, Stump!"

"We're almost there, Lemontree," Stump said, looking ahead.

"Almost."

"Was thinking about things on my way over from the Bird. About a lot of things. A world of them, Lemontree." And then it was like it was all Stump wanted to say to Lemontree on the matter—for it to begin and end with that.

"It's cold tonight," Lemontree said, his naked hands gripping the truck's steering wheel, his skin being skinned back by the cold. "White man ain't used to this kind of cold."

The pickup truck stopped. Lemontree looked at Stump, and Stump at Lemontree. "Ready, Stump?"

"Been."

Each door opened.

"This night was coming, wasn't it, Lemontree?"

"Was singing it at the Bird all these months, Stump: Sweet-Juice, Arfel, Blue Fire, and me."

Each blew on his hands.

"Your hands'll be able to untie the knot, won't they?"

"Uh-huh. Fine. Ain't that cold, Stump. Not for that." And the wind whipped up—almost blowing Lemontree's straw hat off the top of his head. Lemontree pushed it farther down.

"If you believe in the devil, Lemontree, it's his wind blowing tonight. What's blowing. Howling straight outta hell. The devil's wind in the air."

Stump and Lemontree were out the truck, out in the wind and the cold. Lemontree snatched the blanket off the white man, and in the dark his face was red with cold, fear; stiff as the wind, as cardboard. Lemontree threw the blanket to the ground. "Gonna prop him up straight," Lemontree said to Stump, grabbing the rope and doing just that—propping the white man's body up in the pickup truck.

"Look like a frozen stature. Cold shivering through him, Stump. Ice in him. Don't he?"

Lemontree pulled the white man over to him and then hoisted him up onto his right shoulder as he'd done before at Stump's Palace. "Ain't no heavier. Ain't no lighter. Ain't no change in him. Slight or otherwise.

"Yeah, knew this day was coming," Lemontree said as if he had to bring that theme back into play, make it howl in the wind like a blues song. "Hoped it would come, Stump. Prayed so to."

And they were at the water's edge. Their shoes sank down into the muddy ground.

Lemontree took the white man off his shoulder and laid him down onto the muddy ground.

"Ain't had my baptism in the water, Stump, but in the church. But I seen it done. Seen it so many times, so many by so many preachers of God's kingdom. When the minister got more than nine, ten to baptize, to save in the water in the name of the Holy Ghost. King of Kings."

Lemontree shut his eyes and then opened them. He yanked on the rope, pulling the white man closer to the water's edge. "Knew this day was to come, Stump. Knew it," Lemontree said as if in a spiritual haze, an ocean of fire.

Lemontree's hand yanked the rope again, dragging the white man forward, willing him to move. Then he untied the gag, and he heard something from the white man for no more than a split second before submerging his head down slowly into the chilly waters.

And Stump, suddenly, picked up a big rock lying there in the hard caked mud, holding it high above his head.

"Bash his head in with it, Lemontree! They'll say his head hit up on one of them rocks. On them rocks in the water, when they find him!"

"No, Stump!"

"I remember them, Lemontree! Dying in that war for the white man. Jones, Goodyear, Carter, Wiley—Sergeant Bell. Sergeant Bell, Lemontree! Dying in that fucking war f-for the white man. F-for no fucking good reason!" And in Stump's fury, he lost control of the big rock, the rock falling into the hard caked mud, Stump crying, his body cracked by pain.

"Good luck, Arfel, Blue Fire. Good luck," Lemontree said while his black hands, the four fat diamonds on his four fat fingers, glittering in the dark at the bank of the Lucy Caton River, was pushing the white man's head farther and farther down into the waters ... drowning him.

There was gurgling as the water gurgled.

"Take your money! Take it!" Stump said, pulling all the white man's money out his pockets. "T-take y-your f-fucking money! All of it! All of it!" Stump said, tossing the money out onto the waters as if they were burnt ashes.

Lemontree stood and yanked the rope again, lifting the dead man, lying him crossways in the water so that his body could drift down it, obeying the natural law, genius of the river.

"Come, Stump," Lemontree said. "It's over."

Stump was still crying, his body bent over. "Sergeant Bell. He was a good man, Lemontree. A good man. All of them, Lemontree. Every one of them I fought with in my army platoon, were good, good …"

Lemontree put his arm around Stump, aiding him, not listening to the water's swift currents carry the white man along with it, him and Stump heading for Knock-Kneed's granddaddy Curtis's pickup truck.

The pickup truck started up, and it tracked away from everything out there blind, without headlights guiding it. The truck's cab as quiet as an empty church with Lemontree and Stump sitting inside it.

Roadmap listened to the truck labor away from the Lucy Caton River, but he did not look. "They're gone." Pause. "They killed the white man."

"Psst. Psst."

"Hey, Mister. Hey, Mister—you know how to play that thing, Mister?"

"Uh … uh, sure do."

"You … you gotta name for it, Mister?"

"Blue Fire."

"Blue Fire?"

"Blue Fire."

"It sure is a pretty name."

"Sure is, isn't it?"

"Call me Roadmap."

"Roadmap?"

"Roadmap. Ain't as pretty as Blue Fire, though."

"Ha. Pretty enough though, Roadmap."

"Yeah, guess so, guess so. Thanks, Mister. Thanks."

Roadmap was running, buffeted by the wind. The night was his to run in, the wind that always carried him back to the day. The night that was reliable, where he met strangers that came off trains, new to the city, sketchy, uncertain, feeling their way around it, not always knowing how long they'd stay. The night was his in this town, *his, his*—Roadmap's.

Roadmap stopped running. The dark was now keener than before. The uncut grass higher, at knee level. Roadmap was in an open field, a space free in shape and space. He was somewhere where children played in sunlight, where God struck a giant match in the sky—lighting it, and it glowed out onto the world.

"Been running. Running!"

Roadmap was walking now, almost at a slant, almost crooked-shaped. His head not near the sky. "Don't matter, Mr. Arfel, Blue Fire," Roadmap said, approaching the railroad tracks, far away from the station. "If another white man comes looking for you, Mr. Lemontree and Mr. Stump gonna do the same: kill him. Gonna never catch you, Mr. Arfel, Blue Fire. The white man's never gonna catch you!"

Roadmap was drawing nearer to the iron rails, his body almost at a slant, almost crooked-shaped, his head under the sky, submitting to the knowledge he knew. The beaming wisdom he carried with him in to each sorrow and gloom.

When Roadmap reached the rails, he sat down on top of them. "Ain't tired. Ain't, from running, Mr. Arfel. Blue Fire. Not that. Run for a reason. Just kept running till I got here." Pause. "Know I'm late. K-know it." Pause.

"Know you gone, Mr. Arfel, B-Blue Fire. Know the train, the train long gone. Long gone. Know that. Ain't complaining. Ain't. Ain't, Mr. Arfel. B-Blue Fire. Ain't …"

Roadmap fought back the tears settling thicker and thicker in him. "White man ain't letting you come back. Gonna never let you and Blue Fire come back here, Mr. Arfel. Hate him. Hate the white man.

"Mr., Mr. Arfel, know you ain't coming back … Blue Fire. Never, Blue Fire. R-remember you, Blue Fire. Remember you so …"

Roadmap drew his legs up and then put his hand down on top of the railroad track, touching it—his fingers feeling for something that might radiate, that was possibly left behind, a lucky trace, maybe.

"Love you, Mr. Arfel, B-Blue Fire. Love you so. I do …"

Then Roadmap rolled up into a tiny ball and cried as the wind whistled, sweeping up the long tracks ahead, in a hurry.

Was this what he was going to do for the rest of his life, think? Was this to be what was left of his life?

It was dark. The train rattled. The train rattled his bones. The train rattled like a thousand miles or more … ten thousand miles or more. The white man rode first class. He was riding in a boxcar. He'd hitched a train; he was back to where he'd been before, taking up where the white man left off.

"We don't have to worry about the white man any-anymore, Blue Fire. W-we don't have to worry about the white man anymore—we know that, Blue Fire. Know that, Blue Fire." The moment he and Lemontree concocted the plan rushed back to Arfel. Arfel knew that Lemontree wasn't going to let the white man get out of town alive.

"Arfel, been thinking. Thinking everything through. About that white man. How to handle that situation. Thought it through."

Arfel was at Lemontree's place, sitting at his kitchen table.

"It's my situation, Lemontree. Mine, Lemontree—not yours."

"It ain't, Arfel. The world ain't made up like that. The white man come to this town for you and Blue Fire as well as me and Sweet-Juice. Ain't no time for me and Sweet-Juice to be running from nothing, Arfel. Especially a white man. Not now. Today.

Arfel's head was down on his suitcase. Blue Fire was in her case, opened out. "Felt like crying then, Blue Fire." Lemontree unreeled his plan to Arfel (with some help coming from Arfel), how to spring a trap on the white man.

"Mr. Stump—are you sure …"

"I'm okay, Arfel. You don't have to worry about an old coot like me."

Lemontree, Knock-Kneed, and Stump were in Arfel's room together.

"I know what I got to say and how to say it at the Bluebird. Ain't gotta act mean, ornery—no different than what I already am, already act." Stump had cackled. "Comes natural."

"A-MEN," Lemontree had said.

"And you'll need transportation. My granddaddy Curtis's old pickup truck, Lemontree. Granddaddy Curtis, he'd like that."

Arfel could see the plan unfolding right before his eyes.

"A rope," Lemontree had said.

"And something to gag him with."

"I'll take care of that, Mr. Stump."

Pause.

"Roadmap."

"Roadmap?"

"Don't worry any, Arfel, Roadmap ain't in on this. Ain't gonna know nothing about nothing. Stump, you get Charlie Starlings to fetch little Roadmap. Can do that. And you tell him this: he's to go to the white man's hotel, to the Paladin, and tell him to meet a Mr. Stump at the Bluebird at eight o'clock sharp."

"Yeah," Stump had said, swallowing his spit, hard. "I know what to say."

"And we gonna be waiting, Knock-Kneed and me, in Arfel's room. Ain't gonna use a word between us till you get there, outside Arfel's door. 2G."

"Knew, Blue Fire. Knew—so, so did you." Arfel felt sick to his stomach: he'd stayed in that town too long. It'd felt too much like home. He could smell its water, its pearly breath; and then when the nights came, he was as joyful as it to wake up to a new day, to play a blues song to it at the Bluebird Bar.

And Last Round … He'd made friends, true friends.

"And … and I didn't get a chance to say good-bye to …"

"No … Roadmap don't gotta know nothing. Already think me and Arfel going into the Bird tonight to face up with the white man over this. Ain't no reason to change his thinking now."

Stump and Knock-Kneed had left Arfel's room.

"Just you and me now, Arfel."

Arfel had stood.

"No, sit, Arfel. Ain't leaving so soon."

"Thanks, Lemontree … I need the company."

"Besides Blue Fire?"

"Yes."

Arfel had smiled.

"Suppose so. It's been a long haul, Arfel. Ain't been easy. But ain't no looking back now. Takes time for a man to feel a part of something, and when he do—well …"

"It's time to leave, Lemontree."

"Yeah … it seems that way, afraid so, even though I been settled in. Got roots in the ground. A bluesman true and true ha. But got roots in the ground."

Arfel's mind had thought the obvious question then but couldn't ask it as if Lemontree were a fortune-teller, a bluesman with a crystal ball in his hands and not a blues guitar.

Lemontree had fanned himself and Sweet-Juice with the straw hat.

"When I was young, I was like shifting sand, Arfel. Here, there—damned near everywhere. Aaah—we been through that already, know that, Arfel. Covered that ground well back. Set of circumstances."

"Don't worry, Lemontree, you'll find a woman."

"Don't wanna blueswoman, Arfel." Lemontree had chuckled. *"Just a woman. Plain and sweet. A decent, Christian, God-abiding, God-fearing woman."*

"You'll find you one," Arfel had said encouragingly.

"And I meant it, Blue Fire. And I meant it."

Arfel said again in that dark box rolling along something like a cage rolling on iron wheels with momentum, velocity, a push forward down metal, clanking tracks.

Time had elapsed. Arfel had gotten up. Lemontree didn't object this time.

"Knew the blues you was singing, your soul was singing, Arfel, seemed like the minute I seen you. You come through the Bird's doors. Fit right in."

"Tried to hide it, Lemontree. Tried, tried—God knows I tried like heck to hide it."

"A man on the run catch hell, Arfel. It's like a disease: infect everything you got. From head to toe. Turn green."

Lemontree had hugged Arfel.

"Pushing ..."

"Farther North, Lemontree. Stretching farther North."

"You and Blue Fire," Lemontree said, stepping over to Blue Fire. "Sweet-Juice fall in love with Blue Fire too."

"The same for Blue Fire."

"Wasn't jealous. Day or night. Used to be the boss, the big Boss Lady in the Bluebird. Play circles around Purple Poison—but not Blue Fire. Not for one time in the Bluebird. Ha!"

"Ha!"

"Well ... Arfel, good luck," Lemontree said, extending his hand to Arfel. "God's speed."

"Thanks. Thanks, Lemontree."

Then Lemontree's hand touched on Blue Fire. "You sweet as blueberry pie my aunt Jessie used to bake, Blue Fire. On top her brick oven. Could eat Aunt Jessie's blueberry pie all day, seven days a week, if she let me."

Then Lemontree started for the door, and Arfel was holding on to one of Blue Fire's leather straps gingerly.

Lemontree'd opened the door. He turned.

"W-what's wrong, Arfel?"

For Lemontree had seen a face butchered by pain.

"Roadmap, Lemontree. Little Roadmap. Blue Fire and I won't be able to say good-bye to Roadmap, Lemontree. Roadmap—he's gonna ..."

And Lemontree wasn't a bluesman with a crystal ball but a guitar.

"Bye, Arfel. Bye now. Safe sailing."

And that's where Arfel was now in his thinking, thinking of Roadmap, the train gaining greater distance, stretching itself more and more from the town he and Blue Fire had begun to call home.

Arfel brought his knees up to his chin. He lowered his head.

"Roadmap, Blue Fire. Little … little Roadmap …" Arfel's hands closed Blue Fire's case. "Know you wanna sleep, so do I. We're, we're just beginning again. Have a room and three squares a day and a place to play at night—we have that, Blue Fire." Arfel brought his head back down to his suitcase.

"Don't know what's ahead. Lemontree and Mr. Stump and Knock-Kneed killed that man. Don't know what's ahead. He ain't coming for me. Wanted to say good-bye to Roadmap too. Was on the train at eight o'clock when the white man walked into the Bluebird, Blue Fire. We was on this train. Don't miss a toot or a whistle. Riding North. Making our way. Knowing everything was okay back there, Blue Fire. Blue Fire. P-put right." Pause.

"Roadmap … wished I could've tipped him a quarter for what he did. At least a quarter." Pause. "Wouldn't care if it was the last quarter we got between us. In, in the whole wide world. Roadmap could have it, Blue Fire. Wouldn't cost him a dime."

Arfel laughed. "No … not a day of sweat."

Time had passed.

Arfel was pushing farther and farther North. He'd been to New York City (Stump's town). It wasn't enough for him. It couldn't hold him in its glamour, its sway. They didn't play the blues in New York City (Stump had said as much). Jazz, they played jazz in New York City. They knew the blues in New York City but played jazz music. It wasn't a city for a bluesman but a jazzman. New York City was a modern city: youthful and eager well beyond its budding years.

The more Arfel and Blue Fire pushed North, the more strange and elusive things had become. He and Blue Fire seemed to be out of rhythm, out of pitch, sync with the day. Playing the blues. They were the South living in the North—trying to find their way, to tell old stories in new ways, with fresh realism, urgency, variety, but adding on to their story, struggle, day by day in quiet, desperate ways.

Arfel was shocked out his sleep on the rail train.

"Tom!" Spontaneously, Arfel's hand grabbed the whiskey bottle. Even in the dark Arfel knew where it was. He was feverish, shaking badly. His hand twisted the cap off the bottle—to open it. "Tom ... Tom ..." Arfel said more soberly, the mouth of the bottle open—the cap in his hand.

Arfel took a drink and wiped his mouth with the back of his hand.

Arfel took a drink and wiped his mouth with the back of his hand.

"I am a murderer. I am!"

It was him and Tom Mickens taking the girls off to the bushes down by the deep water. He was the one who held the knife to the girl's throat. *"Don't tell nobody—or else!"* It was Tom's idea all along, not his, but he was the one who carried it out. He was the one with the knife. He was the bold one—daring one. He was the one who held the girls from behind, who punished them with fear. *Don't tell nobody—or else!*—threatened them, menaced them, the worse side of him; there was an evil note in him.

It happened only a few times, but it was enough. He always carried this with him. This secret. He'd never told Blue Fire.

"But now you know, Blue Fire. You know what I was. My, my mind. My soul's letting you know!"

Arfel took a drink and wiped his mouth with the back of his filthy hand.

"Ashamed, Blue Fire. Ashamed. I've been ashamed all these years."

Arfel and Blue Fire were in another boxcar, another cage rolling on iron wheels, down metal, clanking track. Another dark space where there was no light, only the solitude of thought and silence. He and Blue had been in two boxcars in one day.

"Slit his throat, Blue Fire. Slit the white man's throat. My violence came back to me, Blue Fire. T-that night. What was always in me. Ugly note. What me and Tom did when we was twelve, Blue Fire. Twel-twelve ..." And now Arfel thought of Lemontree, Knock-Kneed, and Stump. "Mr. Stump didn't kill him. Not Stump McCants. Knock-Kneed,

Knock-Kneed didn't either. It was Lemontree. Lemontree killed the white man," Arfel said confidently, comfortably narrowing down his choice.

"Lemontree, Blue Fire." Arfel took a drink and wiped his mouth with the back of his filthy hand. "Did you shoot him with your gun, Lemontree? That old, rusty gun of yours? D-did you!" But then Arfel shook his head, thinking differently, remembering Lemontree's powerful hands. A bluesman's hands. "You killed him with your bare hands, Lemontree. C-choked him, did-didn't you, Lemontree? Didn't ..."

There was no more liquor in the bottle, so Arfel's hand felt for another bottle and found one. And he took a drink and wiped his mouth with the back of his filthy hand. "Made you a killer too, Lemontree. Made you a murderer too!" Arfel wailed. "Like me, Lemontree. Like me!" Arfel swallowed a lot from that bottle.

"See, Blue Fire. See!"

Arfel and Blue Fire had traveled farther North.

"Good luck, Joe." The white man opened the heavy car door. The sunlight sped fast into the car. "Don't know where you're heading, huh?" The white man looked as disarranged as Arfel.

"No. No."

"Same as me. Traveling to nowhere, Bub." And then the white man leaped off the train only to disappear; was gone, a white streak vanishing into the dark as if Arfel had been dreaming, hallucinating. He stood on two weak legs. He was on another train, in another boxcar. The sun was damaging his eyes. He looked at the heavy door and tried walking to it as straight as he could to collect himself.

Slam!

The door was shut. Arfel leaned his back on the back of the door and then, putting his boot back against the door, pushed himself off it. "Liquor bottles, Blue Fire. Liquor bottles. All we know. All we know," Arfel said, kicking a liquor bottle with his ragged boot. "Everywhere. Every damned where!"

It was the life he and Blue Fire lived, Arfel thought. "Drinking myself to death. It's all I know." Arfel dropped down onto the train floor. Blue Fire was opened out in her case. "Don't wanna drink. Don't wanna feel sorry for myself, Blue Fire. B-but the North …" It's not what the bluesmen who'd come from the North had sung about it in their songs. The North, the "Freedom North" wasn't about that.

"Saw it back there with Lemontree. Seeing it now. It's the same. Exact same. M-made to look different, dis-disguised. We … we live on one side of town and they live on the other. Ain't a difference, Blue Fire. Ain't."

It was Arfel's first impression when he got North, what he'd just said. But running from the law, from the white man, knowing he'd left him far behind (at least them), overrode what he saw, what no city could hide or disguise or disfigure. "Tried not to see it, Blue Fire. Tried not to. Didn't want to," Arfel said, drinking freely from the bottle.

"Tried—but it wouldn't let me. Them lights, them big city lights. Could see it, Blue Fire. I don't know what freedom is even now. Don't know what promise of freedom is. The … the 'Freedom North' is."

Arfel picked up Blue Fire.

"Wanna play you, Blue Fire. Wanna play a song, but not blue, Blue Fire. Don't wanna play nothing blue." Arfel's fingers were crimped from the cold, from the ride. "Got a name, Blue Fire. Got a name. Down South they call you 'nigga' to your face. Up North m-my name ain't 'Joe.' 'Bub.' Ain't. Ain't. It's Arfel. Arfel Booker. Don't know my name, Blue Fire. Lost it somewhere along the line. Long time ago. G-give it up … for good."

Chapter 18

Arfel looked up at the sky. Arfel hopped off the moving train.

Arfel and Blue Fire were in a new town.

"It's quiet, Blue Fire. It come down quiet. S-silent."

It was snowing.

Arfel stepped into the snow. "Peaceful."

It was the first time Arfel had seen snow—he'd heard about it, yes—but never had seen it or touched it or been in it before. "It's white, Blue Fire. White. All white. It's a white sky." Arfel stuck out his tongue, tasting the white particles falling out the sky, so much of it. "Light. Powdery, Blue Fire. Light and powdery." Then Arfel took his hands out his pockets and stood there like a statue gathering snow on its broadbacked black metal. "Like it, Blue Fire. Like it," Arfel squealed with childish glee. "Light. Light. Nice and light."

He just let the snow fall into his hands, catching it and then watching it melt away.

"Look at this, Blue Fire. Melts. More melts than what stays. See that. See that!" Arfel said, blowing what snow that was in his hands, out. Then Arfel stuck his tongue back out. "Ha. Ha. Ha …" Arfel had a suit jacket with a woolen sweater underneath. He hadn't shaved in four days. His head was bare. The snow was sticking to his clothes now, populating there. Arfel slapped his coat sleeve. "Can't get rid of it now. Won't let me. It's clinging to me like swamp grass, Blue Fire." Arfel looked left and right; he shrugged his shoulders.

"Don't matter. Don't. Just need us some shelter. Somewhere to stay the night. T-take up." Arfel looked back up into the white blanketed sky. "Snow. Snow. Everywhere. Falling out the sky. It's prettier than rain, Blue Fire. Much, much prettier. White. White. People just talked about snow. Said it was white, but don't ever say it was white as this. N-not white as this …"

It was dark. It was snowing. Now Arfel didn't care for the snow—not any of it. It was heavy to his feet. Walking through it was difficult, and his feet were cold, felt practically frozen solid. Arfel was shivering; all of this was grossly unfamiliar to him, cruel on its own behalf, motivation. It was punishing him.

"What have we gotten ourselves into, Blue Fire? The sun down South is hot, burns like a hot flame right through your skin, but there's shade. Somewhere to hide, somewhere to get away—go off to. A tree, a … a brook."

Arfel was covered in snow. His hair was frozen. His eyebrows and eyelashes too. He looked white, covered in this white, clinging to him better than swamp grass. For Arfel it was becoming hard to breathe. The air felt thin in his lungs, so Arfel was struggling, his lungs actually burning—trying to take in more oxygen in the air than there was. Arfel stopped but knew he shouldn't. Stopping, he'd found out before, a ways back, was a mistake. When was the last time he'd had a bath? Arfel posited. And then Arfel had to laugh at his own sense of humor. Soap, water?—he had to laugh at his own savage, wicked humor.

He kept trudging along, creating fresh, new footprints in the snow and images in his mind.

"Carry the blues in my back pocket,
God in my shirt.
Die in the ground tomorrow;
Packed deep in dirt."

"Lemontree! Lemontree!"

Arfel's voice echoed out in the open air like a bluesman's wail in winter. Like a bluesman's cry in the wilderness. All too unfamiliar to him, all too tragic in his bluesman's soul. An animal, a bluesman, a colored man, wailing the same wail into a white nothingness, into a white canvass, a white wall of grief and grieving and hysteria and haunting.

Arfel had to pee. But even that—he thought—would freeze in the air like a long, thin yellow stain.

But then there was a light that Arfel could barely see through his slit eyes.

"A light, BLUE FIRE! D-don't feel nothing on me. Nothing, Blue Fire. No body parts. Thumb or toe." Arfel kept walking in the fresh bed of clean white snow toward that light, something bright in the distance, beautiful for the eyes to behold. Arfel knew it promised something of wonder in this white wilderness.

Finally Arfel and Blue Fire were there.

"It's a farm, Blue Fire. A farmhouse. What luck, Blue Fire!" Arfel said, his lips numb, purplish, feeling as swollen as his thumb. There was a gate. The farmhouse was covered in snow. The farmhouse looked as neat and dainty as a white hat box. "What luck," Arfel said again, through numbed, purplish lips. "A bluesman gets lucky now and then, Blue Fire. Now and then!"

Arfel opened the gate.

The farmhouse was about fifty yards in distance. Arfel felt relieved there was such a short distance to navigate. Arfel looked at the sky benignly—as if he were looking up into the face of an archangel, for now, smiling down on him, peaceably, without fangs or threat or retribution. His stomach ached. He felt pangs of hunger, the how-many-days he'd been without food, only drink—his bottle of liquor to sustain him, keeping him alive. He was at the door; but as he stood there looking at it, staring at it, his nerves crawled over him like spiders over cold, dead skin.

"Blue Fire—I'm a stranger in the night. I look like a ghost, Blue Fire. A ... a ..." Arfel tried flexing his hand, its stiffness, in its bones, even defeating that. But soon, by some small miracle, he was able to ball his hand into a perfect knot-of-a-fist.

Knock. Knock.

Arfel stood in front of the farmhouse's door unblinking, knowing that all the farmhouse's lights were turned on, that someone was there inside the house.

He balled his hand into a perfect knot-of-a-fist.

Knock. Knock.

Why would someone expect me? Arfel thought. *Why!*

Knock. Knock.

The knock became more insistent, hefty.

Knock. Knock.

"Heard you!" the voice said, ringing from behind the thick barn door.

"Heard you!"

Arfel felt relieved.

"Who are you? What you want!"

"Mr. ... Mr. Booker," Arfel said, his mouth barely able to pronounce his name.

"Don't know you," the voice replied.

"Me ... me and Blue Fire."

"Don't know you," the man said.

"We ... we ..."

"Know all my neighbors—up here. Don't know you."

It's when Arfel heard a slight but stern voice in the background.

"My wife, my wife wants to know how—"

"Got lost in the snow."

"Said he got lost in the snow." The voice was more soft but no less stern.

"My wife wants to know from where you came?"

"Off ... off the trains."

"And why you here?"

"Traveling. Me ... me and Blue Fire are ... are traveling."

"Traveling where?"

"North. North. More ... more North."

Then Arfel heard the woman's voice again—the woman this man called "Martha."

"Don't take to strangers up here. T-to strangers knocking in the middle of the night. At this hour. Opening our door at night at this hour to strangers. But my wife, Martha, said to open the door, anyways. Said I should anyways."

And so the farmhouse's front door began opening; and when it was completed, there stood a tall, sturdy, square-jawed white man (the length of Arfel, but built more like Lemontree Johnson and Gin-Water Pete) and, standing a few feet behind him (as if hiding behind this trunk-of-a-man), a short, stocky white woman with a kind but old face. A missionary face, her hair pinned in a disciplined bun.

"Come in. My wife, Martha, said come in," the tall white man said, seemingly without any verbal communication between him and his wife, Martha.

Arfel stepped into the farmhouse; but once inside, he felt strange, at odds with everything in the house.

"Come from the trains?"

"Yes."

"Long walk from them trains."

"Yes."

"In a snowstorm."

Arfel was caked in snow. The white snowflakes that'd fallen out the white sky had whited everything white.

Arfel Booker was white.

Then the white man leaned his body over, and the short white woman (Martha) whispered in his ear. (*Whisper. Whisper.*)

"Got a barn in the back."

Arfel had not seen it, not with his eyes at times being practically blinded by the snow.

"Good shelter from the storm."

"Yes."

"Can't stay here."

"No."

"Not in this house."

"No, not in this house."

The white woman (Martha) smiled, and the white man smiled along with her.

"The barn door creaks. Been meaning to fix it. Fix it by spring. It's good shelter. Good till the storm breaks. Passes. For you to know."

"Thank you," Arfel said, looking at the white man. "And ... and thank you ..."

"Martha. My wife's name's Martha."

"... m-ma'am."

Arfel walked out the farmhouse's door, and soon it shut.

Arfel looked up at the sky, and the snow was still tumbling down recklessly. *It is an angel,* Arfel thought. *It is an angel. A white archangel.* "Behind the farmhouse, Blue Fire. The white man said behind the farmhouse. Ain't gonna be hard to find—not even in this snow." Arfel laughed good-naturedly. Clean, fresh footprints were tracking through the bed of clean white snow. And with this sudden knowledge of relief imminent, Arfel felt his skin warm, bubble, and then surge hot.

"There it is, Blue Fire. There's the barn. The white man's barn!"

For Arfel, the white man's barn stood there like a miracle, an oasis, something three miles back his mind couldn't conjure. "When the door creaks—don't, now don't say, let out nothing: Pretend we don't hear it. Like it don't happen. Uh-uh."

By now, Arfel and Blue Fire were at the white man's barn. It was caked in snow too, but instinctively Arfel found the barn's door handle. He began knocking the snow off the handle. "Here, here goes ..." Arfel teased Blue Fire, his voice practically winking at her.

Creak.

"Ha. Ha ... Can't help but hear it, Blue Fire. Can't help but hear the barn door creak!"

The barn was tidy. Everything in it had its own particular place and order. There was a kerosene lantern, but Arfel had no matches to light it (he was disappointed). Arfel put the suitcase down. There was a pile of straw in the barn like any barn. Right off, Arfel knew how he was going to utilize the straw. Arfel began shaking the snow off himself by brushing at it with his cold, crimped fingers and stomping his feet around so the snow could shake off him chunk by chunk.

"It's coming off, Blue Fire. Slowly, Blue Fire. Slowly."

In a flash, Arfel thought he was back in the Bluebird with Lemontree and Knock-Kneed (Roadmap somewhere off in "his" corner) playing his blues music, coloreds dancing to it; but not in the same syncopated rhythm his body now was in (shaking off the snow), not jerky, but clearly tuned without flaw or imperfection. Pretty much all the snow was off Arfel. Then Arfel went over to the pile of hay, gathering it in his arms and then sitting down in it. There'd been no hat on Arfel's head, so Arfel's head had looked like a crown of snow. He was without an overcoat, just a lightweight patchwork sports jacket with a bulky woolen sweater underneath.

Arfel shut his eyes. "Thank you, God," Arfel said between thin, pink, split-skinned lips.

Right off, Arfel's body took notice of the shelter: it felt good.

"Gotta thank that white man too," Arfel said as if he'd been remiss in doing so. "Oh …"—Arfel laughed—"and his … his wife— his wife, Martha." Arfel's fingers were good enough to unstrap Blue Fire from him. By being on his back—for Arfel—it was still as if Blue Fire and he were traveling in some curious, cryptic way. "Need your rest, same as me, Blue Fire. Do. Train and track—now … now snow."

Arfel unstrapped the guitar case, and he just looked at Blue Fire and nothing more. But he looked at Blue Fire the way Gin-Water Pete had, Mr. Chester and Miss Henrietta had, Roadmap and Lemontree and Mr. Stump and Last Round and Knock-Kneed had. He looked at her like he had when he first saw her, when money and his other blues guitar bought her from the old bluesman in the jook joint, was barter; made her his for the keeping. The memory of each episode, lightened his load.

"Still gotta pee," Arfel said, wiggling his legs, looking for a possible location in the barn where he could finally satisfy himself.

"There, Blue Fire. Back there. See a spot." Arfel smiled.

Arfel had returned to the spot where he'd been after relieving himself. "Now … guess we can settle in. Guess we'll settle in till this storm—"

Creak.

Arfel saw the white man enter the barn. Now the tall white man was covered in snow. Immediately, Arfel noticed the white man had a jar and spoon in his hands. He walked over to Arfel. He handed both to him.

"My wife, Martha, send me down here. Thought you might want something hot to eat."

Arfel couldn't believe his eyes. His hands took in the large jar and spoon. "Thank you. T-thank you kindly." Pause. "And will you thank your wife for me too."

The white man nodded. He looked around the barn. Then he walked over to the kerosene lantern hanging on a wooden post. "Got matches …" he said, going into his overall's pocket for them. "My wife, Martha, told me to bring them. Don't forget." He lit the lantern. "Just be careful, don't want no fire in the barn. Not that. Worse thing to happen: barn burning down."

Arfel opened the large jar. He saw it was soup. "K-know how long this snowstorm's gonna last?"

The white man walked over to the barn door; he opened it—

Creak.

—and looked out. He craned back his head. He had on a big hat, big coat, big gloves, and big boots. "Oh—looks like it'll likely break by, I'd reckon, early morning. Not before."

Arfel blew on the spoon with the soup in it. He tasted it. But it as quickly bit his tongue.

"My wife, Martha, make it hot. My wife, Martha, always makes it hot."

Arfel decided to use the jar of "real hot" soup as a hand warmer for his still chilled hands.

The white man's eyes cast around his barn again. "How long you gonna stay, do you reckon?"

"Oh—gonna leave, should be gone when the snowstorm breaks," Arfel said, now using a new language he'd learned.

"Where to?"

"Canada."

The white man closed the barn door and walked back over to Arfel. "You ain't far off. About three miles more. Not more than three miles more." The white man suddenly began looking closer at Arfel since Arfel didn't have the white snow sticking to his black skin. "Don't see Negroes up around here. Coloreds. Indians, sometimes, but not Negroes—coloreds." Pause.

"What kind of work you do?"

Arfel's hands were no longer frozen stiff to the bone. His hand had reached for the guitar case. Arfel pulled Blue Fire out the case. The white man said nothing when he saw Blue Fire—he just stood there as blank as the snow falling in big, chunky white flakes outside the barn. Arfel didn't strap Blue Fire on; he just held her freely in his hands. Arfel's eyes practically kissed Blue Fire as if they were magic.

"I'm a bluesman," Arfel said. "I play the blues. T-true and t-true."

The white man stood there like a marbled statue, white, silent, immobile.

Arfel's fingers began strumming Blue Fire. Arfel hadn't sung a blues song in a long, long time. It was always Gin-Water Pete or Lemontree who sang (as Roadmap had noted to Arfel about Lemontree at one time), who had blues songs spin on the tip of their tongues as bright as moon rings. Arfel cleared his throat; there was a collection of pain in him, like a full dam ready to burst at the seams and flood the land.

"Oh ... oh ...
Got ... got de blu ...
Sufferin' ...
Run ...
Been ...
Runnin' ...

Tears down mah
Oh ... oh ...
Back ...
Sun ...
Ain't but bad luck 'hind de silvry moon.

Momma, Momma—
Lord, Lord, Momma ...
Shine yo'r light ...
Sunday church up de road—
See de debil.

Oh ... oh ...

Come git me,
Die lak a man.
Cat ... catch me, white man—
Catch ... catch me, white man,
If ... if yah ... can!"

Arfel's eyes had been shut while playing; then they popped open and looked onto the white man's. The white man said nothing. He walked off to the barn door.

"I ain't tracking back out in the snow tonight. Won't be coming back for that jar and spoon till morning—when the snowstorm breaks." Pause. "My wife ... wife, Martha, don't mind. Told me not to wait. My wife, Martha, got plenty of jars and spoons up at the farmhouse." He opened the barn door.

Creak.

"Thanks again," Arfel said, putting Blue Fire back in her case, seeing there were to be no more blues songs to be sung to the white man, to come out his soul, out of Blue Fire. "And ... and be sure to thank your wife ..."

"Martha ..."

"Miss Martha."

The white man knocked snow off his hat. "Reckon you'll be gone when I track back in the morning—so good luck to you."

"Thank you. Thank you again." Pause.

"Don't have any Negroes, coloreds in Canada neither. Been up there a few times. Seen Indians, though." The white man closed the barn door.

Creak.

Blue Fire was back in her guitar case. Arfel left the case open. Arfel was in a frenzy, in a frantic, fantastic fit.

"That's the trouble, Blue Fire! No-nobody understands the blues up here!" The suitcase was near Arfel's fingertips, at arm's length. And in the suitcase were the liquor bottles. Arfel untwisted the bottle's cap and sucked in as much of that cold liquor as his throat could contain. His eyes blazed when his mouth split away from the bottle.

"N-nobody up here un-understands a-a bluesman's blues, Blue Fire! Nobody understands a bluesman's blues!" The bottle was back in Arfel's mouth. And there was a sting in his mouth from the cold, how it had sliced slits in both his fleshy lips.

"Don't matter where we go now—nobody knows what we're singing, Blue Fire. Nobody knows the blues. T-the blues up here, Blue Fire ..."

And so that was the problem for Arfel and Blue Fire: the more North they pushed, the more white men there were who didn't understand a bluesman's blues. Arfel and Blue Fire were surrounded by white men now, white men who blinded the eye like the white snow outside the barn, on top of that rising landscape. "But down South they ... a, a white man understands the bluesman's ..."

Arfel looked at the large jar of soup.

"Don't want it, Blue Fire. D-don't want that soup in my mouth. Soup's maybe good for warming a bluesman's hands to play on, on his gui-tar, but ain't good for warming a bluesman's soul!"

Arfel laid his head down in the snow. The liquor bottle was empty. Arfel shut his eyes, he thought of—

"Lemontree ..."

Arfel saw Lemontree's black face again: black as mud, black as a hole dug deep in the ground. He heard his laughter: thunder ringing in treetops. "Lemon ... Lemontree ..." Arfel's eyes were packed into his head. *Lemontree Johnson was a bluesman true and true*, Arfel thought. *True and True.* The first time he saw Lemontree up on the Bluebird Bar's stage, his four fat diamonds on his four fat fingers, he knew, knew Lemontree was a bluesman *true and true.*

Was it with his gun or his powerful hands that Lemontree killed the white man? The four fat diamonds glittering because of a different kind of blues. And now, simply speaking, Arfel thought, *Lemontree had blood on his hands.* "I put blood on Lemontree's hands, Blue Fire—me." Pause.

"And ... and Mr. Stump, Blue Fire. Mr. Stump—"

Mr. Stump had served his country in World War I. Mr. Stump saw white and colored men dying, how they looked, sounded, smelled—no matter their race, their color. Stump McCants had seen death, was a witness to it, a participant in it. But it was war, the white man's war. Him fighting for the white man, his country, his government, his society—but now a white man was dead, a bounty hunter hired by somebody, chasing a "nigga" over land, from the South to the North. Killed. Murdered. And now Stump had blood on his hands, only a different kind of blood this time, not from a war—fighting his country's enemy—but *the* enemy.

Arfel reached for another liquor bottle in the suitcase.

"G-gotta have it, Blue Fire. Liquor … whiskey in my soul. Whiskey in my soul."

There seemed to be a desperation in Arfel, something ticking inside him so true and certain and defined and direct and menacing and foreboding that it was frightening to him. "Gotta sleep, Blue Fire. Sleep …" Arfel cried out. But then he thought of Roadmap.

"Following the white man, Blue Fire. Roadmap following the white man like his shadow. A-attached to him. Little Roadmap." Roadmap getting caught up in this thing too, in this plot, terror, horror—in this awful dance, circle of fear. "Little Roadmap, Blue Fire. Having to be a man. N-not a bluesman, Blue Fire. Not a bluesman, b-but just the same. Just, just the same."

He and Blue Fire never said good-bye to Roadmap.

"Running. Running like we came, Blue Fire. Afraid to look back. Not saying good-bye to Roadmap. Gotta sleep, Blue Fire. Sleep," Arfel cried out. "Till … till the storm breaks, Blue Fire. Till … till the storm breaks." Arfel rushed the liquor bottle up to his torn, ragged lips, sucking whiskey in, down his throat, in giant gulps.

"Know when the storm breaks. Know. Don't … don't know snow. Know. Gonna know. Feel it in my bones, Blue Fire. Already feel it, Blue Fire. Feel it!"

The back of Arfel's hand kept wiping at his mouth, repeating it over and over as it kept wiping at his mouth, feeling this sting in his lips, how the cold cut it—made it that way: carved its pain.

"Can't even sing the blues to the white man. Can't. Can't explain our song, Blue Fire. Don't know how. Our … our blues … The blues been cut out my soul, Blue Fire. Cut out my soul."

Arfel's hand trembled. He glanced at the liquor bottle.

"Don't need it, Blue Fire. Don't need it—it's empty!" He shrieked, throwing the bottle against the barn's wall, smashing it into many separate, distinct fragments of gleaming glass. "Gotta … gotta …"

Arfel knew he had to calm himself, that he was in a bad state, fix, that things weren't going right for him. "We're in a barn, Blue Fire. Got shelter. In a white man's barn. Shelter from the storm. F-for the night."

Arfel was thankful to God for at least this much fortune, sense of a miracle. In the snowstorm, he quickly reminded himself, he'd never thought he'd find shelter, that he and Blue Fire would track on and on through the snow until the very end, until the night or day, or day or night took him and Blue Fire into its loving womb, to let them rest. It's how he'd thought out there on the landscape when the snow guided him and Blue Fire on and on in a blind fury and Canada was ten more yards and ten more yards and ten more yards away … away … away … away …

"Thankful, Blue Fire. Thank … thankful …" Arfel said, laying his head back down in the hay, shutting his eyes, seeing visions of a human lump trapped in snow, buried, breathing, lost—silent as any wild animal left there to be found, stumbled upon, and then examined.

"Ain't dying, Blue Fire. Ain't … ain't dying. Don't want to die. Don't know how. Want to live. Live. Live."

Softly, Arfel's eyes shut. Softly, a pretty blues melody began winding through his mind, some kind of truthfully tuned testimony of who he was: a bluesman. Arfel's pores began to gradually ease open. "I want to sleep, Blue Fire. Sleep. Just rest. Rest in the white man's, the white man's barn."

Suddenly Arfel laughed.

"The white woman, Miss Martha, she runs things on this farm," Arfel said. "Not the white man." Arfel laughed even more. "She runs the farm, not him, Blue Fire." Pause.

"Had him bring me the soup. Had him walk in the snowstorm to the barn. Was kind. The white woman. Wasn't his idea, Blue Fire. It was the white woman's—her. Miss Martha … Miss Martha's."

Outside the barn the snow still unfurled from out the whitened sky. The snow in the sky was in a stable tempo of silence. A white sky churning out more and more snow, its work quietly amassing—diligent, patient, responsible, making piles of it, mountains of it; a soulless, heartless creature of habit at work.

Arfel was snuggled in hay, finding a peaceful sleep, nothing more extraordinary.

Gotta get to her.

In just one night she had been in his blood. In just one night, the blueswoman had been in his blood, racing through it like a wild, unfettered fire. He was looking up at the moon, following its compass there in the sky. And the owl, with its song, singing its nightly song.

He'd felt her in Sunny's Blues Shack—the blueswoman. The blueswoman kept swelling his body, filling it more and more with her sweet wine and bared limbs.

Gotta get to her, Blue Fire. Gotta get to her.

And he and Blue Fire kept traveling.

Getting closer, Blue Fire. We're … we're getting closer.

Knock. Knock.

The blueswoman was in the log cabin, and last night became tonight as Arfel opened the cabin's door, and the blueswoman was waiting for him with her skirt cut high at her fleshy thigh.

"Bluesman …"

He was cool, chilly, the blueswoman wasn't there—gone. He felt it right away. It's then at the bottom of his feet when Arfel felt something in the bed with him, a lump at the bottom of his feet.

"The man was in the bed, Blue Fire!"

Arfel had awakened.

"His blood was on them sheets with me. My knife, Blue Fire. Blood, blood was on my knife!"

Arfel felt a chill slash his spine.

He reached for another bottle of whiskey from the suitcase and drank all of it down. He drank it down to its end, some of it running down the front of his jacket. "The blueswoman was gone. It was me and the dead white man in the bed together. Me and his blood, Blue Fire. Blue Fire." Arfel's eyes glazed over, remembering, putting his story back together in sequence.

"His—the white man's throat was slit clean through, Blue Fire.

Clean through! I slit the white man's throat clean through with my knife!" Arfel grabbed one more bottle out the suitcase. He drank some, but not all of it. He shut his eyes again and stretched all of himself out in the dry hay. All of himself in a sprawl.

"The blueswoman was gone, Blue Fire. She left me in the bed with the … the dead white man and … and his blood …"

The barn became quiet.

Snow still tumbled outside the barn; the white snow was everywhere.

Some hours passed. Arfel was still stretched all the way out in the hay. His body was stiff as a board, a plank of wood. But then he began coughing.

"Cough … cough … cough … Cough … cough … cough …" Arfel was pitching blood out his mouth and into the dry hay. He put his face down into the blood and then lifted his head with blood and clumps of straw mashed in a mask to his skin. His eyes felt like a bloody stump.

"I killed the white man, Blue Fire. Cough … cough. Killed him with my knife. With, with … cough … cough my KNIFE!"

Arfel took the knife out his pocket and stabbed it into the ground. "With my knife, Blue Fire! With my knife! Cough … cough … cough …" And Arfel stabbed the ground with the knife again; its handle stuck straight up out the ground.

"He … he cough … cough … finally, finally caught up with me, Blue Fire. The white man finally caught up to me."

Arfel felt something coming on, hammering his head, his brain, his heart. His hand reached to get Blue Fire from out the open guitar case but fell short, falling quietly into matted straw.

"I've sung, cough, the bluesman's cough … cough blues, Blue Fire. The … the … cough … cough bluesman's blues, B-Blue Fire. Blue …"

Arfel's blue skin glowed.

Chapter 19

The sky had cleared of snow.

The door to the farmhouse opened. The tall white man looked up at the sky.

"Storm's broke. Broke a while back. Looks that way. Me and Martha was sleeping, I guess. Ain't the last of it, though. Ain't the last we gonna see of it." His eyes were aimed toward the barn.

"Wonder if the Negro ... the colored man's gone. Told Martha he said he'd leave when the storm broke. Storm's broke: reckon he's gone."

His body turned southward toward the barn.

"Ha. Canada. Reckon he's up in Canada by now. Gone. Ha. With them Indian. Ha."

In the clear air, the empty countryside, the white man's laugh traveled far. In his big boots, he began tracking through the snow, breathing harder and harder from each heavy stride taken and breath expelled. He stopped to look back up at the sky.

"Gonna come again. The snow. Ain't seen the last of it. Smell it," he said, sniffing the morning's air. "Ain't far off. Uh-uh."

The white man was at the barn's door. He removed his gloves. He knocked the iced snow off the barn's door handle with his hands. Then he took in a deep breath, his coat adding inches to him.

Creak.

"Don't expect this!"

The white man saw Arfel's face down in the hay. He saw the empty whiskey bottles and the blood. He shook his head, unable to relieve his eyes of the barn's chaos. "He's dead. The man's dead. Thought he was supposed to leave out of here when the snowstorm broke." The white man's face looked perplexed. He walked over to Arfel's body to make sure he was dead. He put his gloves back on and then poked Arfel.

"Yeah, he'd dead all right. Seen a dead man dead when he's dead before."

The white man's eyes focused in on the liquor bottles, again. "Drank himself to death. Got drunk—and died. Uh-huh." His head shook a second time. "Me and Martha tried to help the man. And then he got to go and die on our property—in our barn. Can't help nobody these days. Goes to show …" The white man kicked snow off his boots.

"Glass …"

He walked over to where most of the glass (from the smashed liquor bottle) was on the ground. He bent his body and (his gloves were back off) picked up the bits and pieces of glass off the ground, placing them in his coat's deep pockets, carefully. Then he looked back over to Arfel.

"Ain't gonna tell Martha, though. Martha might want to pray over him. Fuss over him like he was somebody …" he said, walking back over to Arfel's body. "Like he was somebody special. I seen what he did for a living myself: don't need no formal funeral of no kind for nothing like that." Pause.

"Martha said come for the jar and spoon when the storm broke. I'll just tell Martha he left like he said—when the snowstorm broke."

The white man's eyes slid over to the rusted shovel leaning against the barn's wall.

"Reckon I'm responsible for burying him—since he died on my property, in the barn. R-reckon so. My responsibility to do." Pause. "Bury him behind the barn. Martha won't know."

He dragged Arfel's body out the hay and then lifted him up on his shoulder. He took the shovel off the wall. He looked at the barn door, taking even, penetrating steps.

Creak.

271

He looked up at the sky. "It's coming ..." he said, licking his forefinger and extending it out to the sky, measuring—almost: gauging the wind and the alignment of stars. "All right."

Arfel's body was lying on top of the snow. The white man was digging with the shovel. The shovel was pitching back snow. He was breathing in and out his nostrils like a black bull snorting in snow (oomph!). He removed his hat and wiped the ring of sweat on his forehand that was steaming up the air like it was summer air.

"That'll do it. Reckon so." He looked down at Arfel. Arfel was in front of him. "Got to get behind him, I reckon," he said, figuring out the situation.

It's when his foot began rolling Arfel forward.

"Roll him. Roll him into his grave ..." And Arfel's body rolled through the white snow and into the hole in the ground. The white man stood back to admire his work. The shovel was back in his hands, the white man shoveling dirt and snow back down into the hole.

Minutes later.

"That'll do it, I reckon," he said, pulling the hat off his large head again, sweat punching through his pores. "The colored man's packed in good and solid," he said, taking the shovel and patting down the snow one more time for good measure. Then the white man breathed in the farm's fresh, clean air.

"Aaaaah ... Aaaaaaah ..." His lungs ballooned. "When the snow melts, nobody'll know I buried the Negro, colored man, black man in the ground. Nobody knows of the Negro coming to the farm but me and Martha anyhow." Pause.

"Won't smell by spring."

Creak.

"Didn't even eat Martha's soup," the white man said as soon as he got back in the barn. He walked over to the barn's wall and leaned the shovel against it. "Martha ain't gonna like that. Uh-uh. T-take to that one bit." The white man picked up the large jar of cold soup and big spoon off the ground.

"Better pour it out—so ... so that Martha won't know."

The white man poured the soup out into the hay, into Arfel's blood. When he looked up, he looked over to the kerosene lantern. "Fire still going. Burning good." He walked over to the kerosene lantern. He blew it out. "At least he don't burn down the barn. Say that much for the black man, I reckon." Then he looked down at Blue Fire as Blue Fire was laid out open in her guitar case.

He just looked at Blue Fire intensely, with increasing strain.

"And what am I gonna do with the Negro's guitar?" The white man kicked snow off his big boots. "The colored man's guitar? Leave it here? Reckon so. Reckon that'll do." Pause. "Martha, Martha don't come down to the barn. Martha stays up in the house—summer and winter."

Again, he looked at Blue Fire.

"The colored man called himself a bluesman." The white man shook his head. "A bluesman." Again, he shook his head, more dismayed. "But they don't play that kind of music around here. Not in these parts. Uh-uh. Nobody's gonna have need for that guitar around here—no use for it." He pinched his hat smartly.

"Besides, I didn't understand a word the Negro, colored man said when he played that music of his to me before. No. Reckon that Negro's guitar better off right where it is. Right here in the barn. Laying right there."

The white man was at the barn door but turned back around, remembering something. He looked down at the knife. Cautiously he bent (he had the jar and spoon in one hand). "Might could use this, though," he said, yanking the knife out the ground (grunt!). He looked at it (the knife), examining it more sharply. "Ain't got a bad blade on it for cutting. Colored man kept it good. Can tell that much." Pause.

"Won't tell Martha," he said, putting the knife down in his back pocket. "Might ask questions." He began rising, but as he did, his eyes took one more earnest, serious turn at Blue Fire. "The black man played his guitar same as those Indians beat their drums and dance up here when they hoot and holler ... sing. Don't understand them neither, I reckon," he said as if speaking directly to Blue Fire.

Creak.

The white man shut the barn door behind him.

"Fix that creak by summer. Not spring. Uh-uh. Martha won't know." Then he looked up at the sky. It had started snowing. The white man took two more lumbering strides in the snow.

273

"Told you so," he said, looking up at the sky and then back over his shoulder to where Arfel's body was buried under snow.

"Yeah, told you so," he said, carrying the big spoon and jar in his hand, turning to head back up to where Miss Martha waited for him in the farmhouse.

Epilogue

An array of angels had converged on him when his eyes finally shut, whisking him off. It was like a magic carpet ride in the sky for Arfel the way the four angels carried him, laying his body flat in their arms, their hands linked, two of the angels on either side of him, from shoulders to midback, and his hips to calves. The four angels were beautiful apparitions to behold.

A bluesman being treated like this, Arfel had thought at the time: like a king? A bluesman!

And into the sky they flew, the four angels and him, until they had reached a huge rock where an archangel appeared. The angels called her Archangel Elizabeth. During the flight, the whole ride, as they flew through the sky, the four angels had been as quiet as grazing sheep. But when they reached the huge rock and Archangel Elizabeth appeared, they all said, "Archangel Elizabeth, this is Mr. Arfel Booker. A bluesman."

It's when Archangel Elizabeth, with a Negro face (skin as pretty as a walnut), smiled ebulliently. "Thank you, sister angels. Thank you for the delivery of Mr. Arfel Booker. Bluesman. For his soul from earth." In unison, and serenely, the four angels bowed their heads to Archangel Elizabeth, whom in turn acknowledged them. Then, as peaceably, the four angels touched Arfel as if touching a magic stone, giggled, and then took back to flight (wings and grace). Arfel had shivered at the sight.

Archangel Elizabeth sat on the huge rock, her garb white, her wings white, but her hands and face colored. Then she leaned forward, supporting her chin with her elbow that was on top of her knee. "I'm Archangel Elizabeth as if you don't already know, Mr. Booker."

"Please call me, Arfel."

"*Eventually I would have, Arfel. But formality, often, is the best approach to introducing oneself initially, upon first greeting.*"

Arfel agreed.

"*Welcome, Arfel,*" *Archangel Elizabeth said, spreading her wings wide. And suddenly Arfel was in a lush garden, which literally stole his breath away.* "*Isn't it such a magnificent sight to behold, Arfel?*" *Archangel Elizabeth said.*

"*Yes … yes …*" *Arfel replied, gulping in air.*

"*Even I am astonished by it each time I look at it. Its splendor. Such beauty as God can create. The true majesty of God's magnificence and being, Arfel.*" *Archangel Elizabeth repositioned her body. She clasped her hands together but in a loose sort of way.* "*And you're a bluesman, Arfel. A wonderful, marvelous bluesman.*"

"*Yes, yes, Archangel Elizabeth.*"

"*It is why God has assigned me to you.*"

Arfel's right eyebrow arched.

"*My father was a bluesman: Fergus 'Two-Fingers Slim' Atkins.*"

"*Picked with two fingers, then?*"

"*Yes, Arfel. The obvious.*" *Pause.* "*Would play to me every day. Every day of his beautiful life on earth. Daddy would play his blues gui-tar to me on the front porch of the house. How I remember.*" *Archangel Elizabeth's eyes watered and then turned dreamy.* "*Can't recall a day when Daddy failed to.*"

"*Your father, Archangel Elizabeth, was a bluesman, all right.*"

"*How do you say it, Arfel?*"

"*A bluesman:* true and true, *Archangel Elizabeth.* True and true."

"*Yes, Arfel, my father was a bluesman* true and true. *By the way, just for the record: my father called his gui-tar … 'Night Owl.' They would wail all night. Into the wee hours of the night, in fact. Daddy and Night Owl.*"

Part 2

That had been Archangel Elizabeth and Arfel's first meeting two days earlier. Even though it'd been only two days, the two had become fast friends since Archangel Elizabeth was God's emissary—taking Arfel (literally) under her wing.

Arfel and Archangel Elizabeth were in the garden, just the two of them. Archangel Elizabeth always sat on the huge rock, Arfel sitting directly in front of her. They'd been in the garden for possibly twenty minutes.

"Yes, Arfel," Archangel Elizabeth said joyfully. "I only see splendid things ahead for me."

"That's good, Archangel Elizabeth."

"I want to work my way up. A seraphim. You've heard the word? Seraphim?"

"Yes, Archangel Elizabeth."

"You know the Bible?"

"Some," Arfel replied. "Know a ser ... a seraphim's an angel. Uh ... uh ..."

"It's the highest order of angeldom you can attain in God's kingdom," Archangel Elizabeth said with glee.

"Don't know that."

"And three wings, Arfel, not two. Can you imagine? Just imagine—three wings!"

"Three wings for you to flap around heaven with all day, Archangel Elizabeth."

Suddenly (without provocation), Arfel sighed.

"Arfel, what's—"

"Blue Fire, Archangel Elizabeth. Blue Fire—her name was Blue Fire. My blues gui-tar. Blue Fire."

"Yes, I know about Blue Fire," Archangel Elizabeth said with deep empathy.

"Miss her. Miss Blue Fire, Archangel Elizabeth. Miss Blue Fire. Ain't the same without Blue—"

"But, Blue Fire didn't die, Arfel."

Arfel raised his saddened eyes up to Archangel Elizabeth.

"You did, Arfel."

"A-a bluesman can't carry a gui-tar to heaven, Archangel Elizabeth?"

"No, Arfel—it must stay on earth. Earthbound. It must suffer its own death. Demise. Uh, earthly fate."

It was later.

There'd been a long silence as both looked out onto what lay before them in all its radiance and dazzle and ubiquity.

Arfel was thinking: he knew the Bible all right. He knew it well enough to *know he did not belong in heaven. He was a murderer: on earth he'd killed a man, slit his throat. Why was he in heaven? Why such a rich reward? Why did those four angels transport him up to heaven and before Archangel Elizabeth when he belonged in hell, damnation, to be damned, forever damned, cursed in the precincts of hell. Why was he in God's holy garden, the beauty of which spoke volumes of his divinity and infinite, omnipotent, omniscient powers?*

This had troubled Arfel since day one, since its origin, since all of this royalty, this daily wonder began unfolding before him. Now was the time, Arfel thought, *to disturb, upset, jolt this tranquility, this gentle, false state of equilibrium. How could he, with blood on his hands, be in God's kingdom, among God's chosen children, the righteous and good, stand before God and be judged worthy of a holy place—God's home?*

"Arfel, your face …"

"Yes, my face, Archangel Elizabeth. My face. And … and my soul too."

"What's wrong, Arfel? What's … what's ever wrong? The matter?"

Arfel stood. His arms spread out before him. "Look … look, Archangel Elizabeth. Look … look where I am!"

"In heaven, Arfel. In heaven. In God's home."

"But … but …" Arfel fought the words but then blurted them out uncontrollably, "I'm a murderer! I killed a man! Slit his throat with my knife!" And those back roads were in Arfel's throat, the fear, the trains and tracks and whistles—the punishment, the pushing North, him and Blue Fire together, always pushing North to mutually find some promised freedom land.

"How can I be in heaven? Ain't no place for a murderer, Archangel Elizabeth. For someone like me!"

And in Archangel Elizabeth's brown walnut-complexioned face was kindness and wisdom and caring, a glow of eternal truth. "Thank you, Arfel."

"F-for what, Archangel Elizabeth!" Arfel asked, his eyes aflame.

"For not pretending for one day more than necessary."

"You … you …"

"I know, Arfel. God knows. He knows about the white man. About all earthly things."

"But how do I …"

Archangel Elizabeth came off the rock, and by doing so, it quieted Arfel.

"It's a long story, but one which will and must be told. He knew, eventually, you would bring it up, being the good, moral man you are. And

it will be addressed. Explained to you, Arfel. Since it's your story—yours and Blue Fire's."

"When, Archangel Elizabeth? When? When am I gonna know?"

"Tomorrow," Archangel Elizabeth said calmly. "Tomorrow, here, in God's garden all will be revealed. Just as it happened. With no exception." And Archangel Elizabeth's left wing wrapped around Arfel, comforting him.

"Y-yes, Archangel Elizabeth ..." Arfel's voice had trembled out of him. "I'll ... I'll know everything ... tomorrow. T-tomorrow."

Part 3

Archangel Elizabeth had come for Arfel (Arfel was not able to fly yet. He was without wings but was promised them soon—they were on order within the kingdom). She carried him in her arms, making him appear as light as a feather.

"I have the film, Arfel."

"Film?"

"Yes. I had to requisition it from archives. Actually, I should have requisitioned it weeks a—"

"You knew I was coming!"

"Sadly, yes, Arfel—yes. W-we, sorry, but we saw that your life was unraveling. Winding down. Deteriorating at a very rapid rate on earth."

"M-my drinking," Arfel said remorsefully.

"Yes, Arfel, that."

"And my mental state."

"And your mental state."

Arfel brightened. "A bluesman don't die easy, Archangel Elizabeth."

"Uh-uh," Archangel Elizabeth laughed back. "No way."

In short time they were there, in one of God's gardens, but what seemed to be Archangel Elizabeth and Arfel's, exclusively.

When Archangel Elizabeth landed, she put Arfel down as well.

"Thank you," Arfel said.

And then Arfel's nerves, fear returned. On earth he'd had whiskey to quell them, or long conversations with Blue Fire. But now up in heaven he couldn't find such solace, not for what was in his soul, unhinging it. "A ... a bluesman. A bluesman's life."

"Yes …" Archangel Elizabeth said, flapping her wings. A movie projector appeared out of thin air, facing out to the huge rock that was in the garden. And then the sky above grew darker and darker in rolling layers, until it was completely black.

Arfel gulped.

"You are not to be afraid, Arfel. I'm here."

And Arfel shut his eyes and felt every vein in this body pop, explode like anger.

"God does have some drama. An inclination for the dramatic. It's in all our natures, I suspect." Pause.

Arfel's eyes opened.

"I'll … the, the machine is on." The huge rock had a white beam of light cast across it. "I'll narrate for you, Arfel." Archangel Elizabeth looked at Arfel, and even in the dark, Arfel could see her charitable eyes.

"We did have to give it a title (God, again, I'm afraid!):

The Life and Times of Arfel Booker.

Arfel was in pain: deep-ridden and miserable.

Archangel Elizabeth cleared her throat. The beam of light was still cast against the rock. Archangel Elizabeth began the narration.

"The blueswoman's name, Arfel … was Miss Dorothea Dupree. She was a 'kept' woman, kept by the mayor of Gator Spring County, Arkansas. The mayor's name, Arfel, was the Honorable Percy C. White. It seems as if pretty much everyone in Gator Spring County knew Dorothea Dupree to be a kept woman for two years and the Honorable Percy C. White had a hideaway cabin in the backwoods—and that the Honorable Percy C. White beat Dorothea Dupree on occasion with his wooden cane."

It's when Archangel Elizabeth ended her narration, and the film came on.

The story, on film, began where it always began for Arfel in his dreams. The blueswoman doing her blues, that snake dance of hers. And then Arfel and Blue Fire going off to the log cabin (hideaway) and her and him taking their clothes off and them having sex in the bed. (And on the screen, that huge screen, Arfel could see the lust in his eyes, the carnal appetite in his body, and felt ashamed in front of Archangel Elizabeth. She'd sensed as much and, in some extraordinary way, sedated him.)

And so the film went on to show Arfel and the blueswoman having sex again and, afterward, the woman going over to where there was a cabinet and opening it and pulling out a whiskey bottle from all the other whiskey bottles on the shelf and her handing it to Arfel, for he could drink his fill of liquor until Arfel blacked out, totally blacked out in the bed.

But after that everything Arfel knew about his dream changed. For Arfel saw something on the screen now that his residual dream had not revealed to him.

For a short white man came bursting through the cabin's door.

(Arfel shivered.)

The white man had a wooden cane and a bad limp. He saw Arfel and the blueswoman in the bed. Immediately, the white man and the blueswoman began to scream and curse violently at each other.

Arfel saw (on the huge screen) that he was still in the bed drunk, not moving—blacked out.

The white man raised his wooden cane high above his head, and he called the blueswoman a "black whore"! Then the white man hit the blueswoman (Miss Dorothea Dupree), forcibly across the top of her shoulders and about the top of her head with the wooden cane, thrashing her repeatedly with one blow lashed after the other.

Dorothea Dupree ran hard at the white man (the Honorable Percy C. White). But Percy C. White knocked her off to the floor. Dorothea Dupree told Percy C. White she wasn't going to take any more beatings from him. He turned his back to her and took his cane and began smashing all the liquor bottles in the cabinet with it. Percy C. White turned back to Dorothea Dupree, raising the cane high above his head once again so he could thrash her once more about her head and shoulders.

But this time, Arfel saw the blueswoman kick the heel of her foot into Percy C. White's leg with the bad limp; and he fell off to the bed writhing in extreme, wrenching pain. It's then, at that point, when Dorothea Dupree's fingers dipped into Arfel's back pocket (she'd undressed him after all, Arfel thought, *she must've felt his knife, its lump in his clothing) and pulled out his knife and, slowly, deliberately opened it out.*

Percy C. White was still on the bed, at the edge of it, writhing in extreme, severe pain.

Dorothea Dupree sprang off the floor and ran and hopped on the white man's back, pulled Percy C. White's head back to her, and put the knife to his stretched white skin and shrieked out in a big ball of pain.

"You ain't never gonna beat me with your cane 'gin! N-not ever 'gin, white man. WHITE MAN!"

And Dorothea Dupree, the blueswoman, took the knife and slit Percy C. White's throat with Arfel's knife; and the Honorable Percy C. White's blood gushed out his throat. Dorothy Dupree then dropped the bloody knife on the white sheet. The Honorable Percy C. White's body lay at the bottom of Arfel's feet, Arfel lying in the bed blacked out as if dead too.

Now Dorothea Dupree turned and ran out the log cabin barefoot, without benefit of shoes—into the dusky dark, the other side of the moon.

Archangel Elizabeth then fast-forwarded the film, so Arfel didn't know how much time in real time had actually elapsed. But Arfel saw his reaction on the screen when he awakened to see the dead white man in the bed with him, at the bottom of his feet, and that that white man's throat had been slit open and that the bloodied murder weapon was his. Arfel saw the white patch of panic on his face. He saw himself hurry his clothes on and stick the bloody knife in his back pocket and grab Blue Fire's guitar case and run out the open cabin door and into that shaft of clear moon, which had now enlarged, with Blue Fire.

Archangel Elizabeth's soothing voice returned to Arfel's ears.

"Dorothea Dupree confessed to the murder of the Honorable Percy C. White when apprehended at the city line in Creek Valley County, Arkansas (a neighboring county), two days later, Arfel. Everyone in Gator Spring County realized Dorothea Dupree had revenged the Honorable Percy C. White by slitting his throat in their hideaway cabin. The murderess, Arfel, Dorothea Dupree, received a maximum life sentence in the county penitentiary by a jury of her peers three days following her apprehension. Dorothea Dupree, Arfel, had thought the Honorable Percy C. White was going to be out of town on city business for yet another day. But Honorable Percy C. White shortened his visit by one day. He did so in order to surprise Dorothea Dupree who, it was said, he'd badly missed."

And as if this wasn't enough for Arfel to know, swallow, there was more. Archangel Elizabeth cleared her throat, turned the projector off, and flapped *her wings, for light could now be seen and spread charmingly over their countenances.*

"You see, Arfel," Archangel Elizabeth continued, "the white man, the bounty hunter—John X. Smith—was sent by the town, Gator Spring County, to find you. To inform you of your innocence. That you were not guilty of any crime. That you had not killed the white man. The Honorable Percy C. White. That you were not a murderer. A killer. That Dorothea Dupree was the murderer. That she'd been apprehended. Only, as you clearly know, recognize now, he failed. Failed in his mission. The bounty hunter John X. Smith failed to communicate this to anyone in the town: Miss Millie, Lemontree Johnson, Last Round, Roadmap, and, and especially, Mr. R. J. 'Stump' McCants."

Arfel sank to his knees ...

And so the movie projector disappeared.

"I know this comes as a tremendous blow to you. A shocking blow. This sad news, Arfel.

This new reality," Archangel Elizabeth said sympathetically. "And, and that you would like to be left alone. Left to ... to yourself."

Arfel couldn't answer Archangel Elizabeth.

"You're a decent man, Arfel. A moral man. You're not a murderer. A killer. Something you thought you were. What you falsely assigned to yourself." Archangel Elizabeth's wings lifted her sylphly into the air and off the ground. She hovered over the garden and Arfel.

"I'll be back for you. Don't worry, I'll know when it's time. I'll carry you back home since you are, for the time being, without wings. Take your time with this, Arfel. Please do take your time with this for your own sake. Mental and spiritual health, Arfel."

And in a split second, Arfel was alone, by himself, in the shadow of the huge rock where Archangel Elizabeth had sat with much kindness and truth etched on her lovely countenance. He was alone and faced with the truth of his life and times, contemplation, this sad chapter in his life, this bitter wound.

"Blue Fire ... You saw it Blue Fire in the log cabin all along, Blue Fire. But couldn't tell me. You're made of wood and string. You ain't human. Can't talk, can—only can play my blues, Blue Fire. A bluesman's blues. What songs I know, not you. Me, Blue Fire. Me.

"Been running all this time from a shadow, a explosion—from the white

man what seems like for all my life for nothing. Nothing I don't do until you kill me like I thought my knife killed you. Until you slit my throat clean through with your KNIFE!"

Arfel lay prostrate in God's lush garden. Tears streamed out his eyes like a sick, diseased river.

"You pay him. S-send the white man for me. The tall white man … But he come in silence, with the South still buried deep down inside him. In his heart, not knowing how to tell a colored man he don't kill a white man. That a colored man was innocent, not guilty. A bounty hunter who don't know how. Ain't trained to do that.

"See—h-he would even die so not to save a colored man. To help him live. Stay alive. Take it that far."

The white men of Gator Spring County, Arkansas, sent the bounty hunter to tell him he hadn't killed the white man. The white men tricked him; and the horror of it was bleeding out his skin, making him feel the weight, burden and anguish of his blackness—of being black.

(MAYBE THOSE WHITE MEN WERE OUT TO PROVE IT COULDN'T BE DONE. MAYBE THOSE WHITE MEN OF GATOR SPRING COUNTY, ARKANSAS, WERE OUT TO PROVE IT COULDN'T BE DONE!)

"Sung a bluesman's blues. The white man killed me. Killed me twice. Twice …"

And in the distance Arfel heard great outbursts of laughter, hauntingly, spitefully ringing out to him and then totally engulfing him.

"White men. White men's voices. Everywhere. Sung me a bluesman's blues all along. A-a bluesman's blues."

And Arfel could hear (even in God's garden) white men's voices laughing at him.

Even in God's lush, holy garden.

Laughter.

Everywhere.

Laughter.

Everywhere.

Everywhere.

Laughter.

"Hear them B-Blue Fire … Hear them …"